JIHAD

JIHAD

H. Gerald Staub

Writer's Showcase
San Jose New York Lincoln Shanghai

JIHAD

All Rights Reserved © 2001 by H. Gerald Staub

No part of this book may be reproduced or transmitted in any form or by any means, graphic, electronic, or mechanical, including photocopying, recording, taping, or by any information storage retrieval system, without the permission in writing from the publisher.

Writer's Showcase
an imprint of iUniverse.com, Inc.

For information address:
iUniverse.com, Inc.
5220 S 16th, Ste. 200
Lincoln, NE 68512
www.iuniverse.com

ISBN: 0-595-17244-X

Printed in the United States of America

Chapter One

Alexander Petrovich Marenkov removed his spectacles and wiped his brow as he stepped outside into the midday sun. It was unusually hot, even for August in Moscow and the university building, lacking air conditioning, had offered no relief from the oppressive, muggy air.

Replacing the eyeglasses on the bridge of his nose with a tap of his forefinger, he propelled his slight frame across the empty street in his distinctive, shuffling gait. As was his custom every day at noon, he had torn himself away from his laboratory to visit the local *lafka* where he, without fail, purchased a liter of milk, the nose of a loaf of black bread and two cucumbers. After an exchange of pleasantries with the rosy-cheeked babushka who owned and managed the grocery store, Marenkov set his habitual course for the park that fronted the University of Moscow.

For the first time that day—a morning crowded with arcane calculations and irritating, mostly confused students—Alexander brightened. Here was his old friend, as always, sitting on the same bench, sprinkling sunflower seeds to an eager assemblage of pigeons and wrens.

"Ah, Professor," the old man on the bench said, doffing his trucker's cap and momentarily exposing his pink, balding scalp in the glaring sun. He was a large man, all exaggeration, from his bushy eyebrows, pudgy cheeks and fleshy jowls to his broad shoulders, thick girth, gnarled hands and hamhock thighs. At eighty—twenty years' the Professor's senior—he appeared twice as hale as Marenkov.

"*Dyadyooshka*," Alexander smiled, using the affectionate term "uncle" as a greeting for such a respected friend.

"And were you able to see any glint of hope in your *cherpakas* this morning?" the 'uncle' asked in his quiet, husky voice.

Alexander snickered at his friend's description of his students as turtles.

"No, Seryozha, they're as slow as ever," he said, sitting on the bench. "They're giving Russian nuclear physics a bad name."

"Hah! I'm more afraid they're giving turtles a bad name."

Laughing, Marenkov placed his food between Seryozha and himself. He then dug both hands into his vest pockets, producing two plastic cups. As he poured milk into each receptacle, his friend began to slice the bread and cucumbers with an old Russian army blade that he kept attached to his belt by a gold-plated chain.

"*Na zdorovya*," Alexander said, handing Seryozha a milk-filled cup.

"*Da*, and to your health as well."

They each drank slowly, savoring the cool sensation in their dry throats.

"Not quite as cool as '41, but it'll do on a hot day like this," Seryozha grinned, baring two rows of large yellow-gray teeth.

"Ah, yes, '41," the Professor said, his narrow face and black-bean eyes suddenly brightening. "Tell me about the war again."

"Again? But so many times, already, *tovarisch*...."

"I never tire of your tales."

"Hmph. Well, then...where to start...which one...? Stalingrad? Kursk?"

"No, no," Alexander replied, his teeth sinking into the soft bread. "Forty-one. You know. When the Germans attacked Moscow."

"Ah, that. Your favorite," Seryozha smiled. Biting a cucumber slice from the tip of his blade, he gazed toward the south.

"As you know, in early December of '41, those Teutonic Knights were but a stone's throw from where we sit."

Marenkov smiled at his friend's sarcastic comparison of the Nazi invasion to a similar German attack on the motherland some seven hundred years earlier.

"All the world thought Russia was lost that winter," the old soldier continued.

"And with it, all Europe," Alexander interjected. "The British would have been isolated."

"Yes, and then no base for the Americans. No D-Day," Seryozha muttered between chews. "But as I said, all the world thought we were done for—except Zhukov and his *molodyetskis*—his boys. Quite a surprise the chicks had in store for the wolf," he chuckled.

"I was with Surchenko's Rifle Brigade. We came by rail with the other brigades. Packed in freight cars. Tens of thousands of us. Day and night we rode across Siberia. We kept a little fire going at one end of our car but we might as well've just waved at the wind for all the good it did. Pah! It was the coldest winter in years. We arrived in Moscow the first day of December."

"None too soon," Alexander noted.

"Hmph. True. The very next day the Teutons approached the outskirts of our city—just over there," he said, gesturing toward the southwest.

"One division broke through the center of our lines and we were thrown into the breach. We fought them with tanks, rifles, bayonets, stones, even hammers. All was white, gray and black with tongues of flames…the white of our winter parkas, the gray of their foolish summer uniforms, the black of their congealed blood."

"That was your first wound?"

"Yes, here." Seryozha rolled up the sleeve covering his right arm to reveal a pale ribbon of flesh extending the length of his triceps.

"I was fortunate to block the bayonet thrust. My blade, however, found its mark in many Teutons that day.

"After three days, we broke them. We threw them back into the snow. It was bitter weather. Fifty, sixty degrees below zero. They had never dreamt of such conditions. The oil in their tanks turned to sludge. The crankcases burst. Their tanks died. They tried to move, to run, but their panzers refused to budge. They tried to flee on foot but they froze as surely as their tanks. I found one lost soul who had stopped to take a crap. He died where he squatted when his asshole congealed. Many of them shot themselves or held hand grenades against their stomachs to escape the cold and onslaught of our Red armies. The blowing snow swept over their twisted, frozen corpses. The Teutonic Knights would never be the same again."

Alexander removed his spectacles, carefully unfolded his white handkerchief and wiped smears of perspiration from the glasses.

"How I would have loved to have been with Surchenko's Rifle Brigade in those days," he said, patting his forehead with the handkerchief.

"Then you are madder than I imagined," Seryozha laughed uproariously. "The freezing cold, swirling snow, death all around. Pah! It was a nasty business."

"But there was meaning to it. There was still a Russia to be proud of, a socialist ideal to believe in then. Now…now…there is nothing."

Seryozha studied his friend's face, the noble forehead, the intelligent but tired eyes, the thin lips, compressed as if to seal all possibility of the soul's flight.

"Nonsense," Seryozha shrugged. "You have everything. A loving wife. Two fine sons. The Order of Lenin for your work in nuclear physics…."

"The Order of Lenin," Alexander grinned mirthlessly, "will not buy you a head of cabbage today. In fact, I would much rather have a head of cabbage."

"It's not the cheap piece of metal or the pretty ribbon that's important," Seryozha said, flicking some seeds to his feathery disciples. "It's what they stand for. The work you did. All Russia still thanks you."

"All Russia," the Professor said, before falling silent, his thoughts drifting. Oh yes, Russia thanks him. He, one of the foremost nuclear physicists of the Cold War. Once the darling of the Soviet government, dinner guest of premiers and presidents—Khrushchev, Brezhnev, Gorbachev. A *dacha*—a country house—on the Black Sea. The best schools for his sons. Strings pulled. Doors opened. The most modern laboratory, the best equipment money could buy. The brightest students flocking to it...to him. And, of course, his generous salary.

Then it was all gone like the blue wisps vanishing from a Cuban cigar. Overnight. The first changes started with Gorbachev. Then, with Yeltsin, they became rampant, out of control—but not for the better. The *dacha*—gone. The salary—gone. The laboratory run down. The equipment in disrepair. The socialist ideal—gone. In its place, the brave new democracy, with its mercenaries and mafias. The almost overnight explosion of honky-tonks, strip-joints, drug-addiction, and AIDS. Widescale unemployment. Currency devaluation. Bankruptcies. The bizarre, virtual reality state of the Russian economy with a destroyed banking structure, nearly one hundred percent annual inflation, and a government and financial system that existed on bartering. Salary payments in the form of *veksels*—IOU's—that were traded at half face-value for groceries, clothing, heating oil, and other necessities of life. Disrespect for all things academic, particularly his profession. The upheaval of all the old Russian traditions; the inability to readily adapt to those of the West.

It was as if the once proud country was a ship cast adrift on a wind-ravaged sea and the doomed passengers were having their last big fling. It was no wonder that so many of his colleagues had considered the offers that were quietly tendered in dark, out-of-the-way places. Some had even succumbed to the temptations. And why not? Great sums of money—any sum of money—was extremely enticing in these uncertain times. It represented a chance to lift one's family from a mere animal existence. And why not take it? Look at what this new government has taken from us. Our livelihood. Our dignity. Our very souls. Yes, who could blame those who went over. And yet, and yet. There were those stories. Those who went over were never heard from again. Some said that the Israelis, or the Americans, with their long reach, found them, eliminated them. Yet they were just stories. No one knew for sure.

Alexander suddenly became aware that he was being questioned.

"Are you all right, my friend?" Seryozha asked again.

"Yes, yes, of course, but I'm afraid I must be going."

"So soon today?"

"Yes. I must catch the two o'clock train for Peredelkino to…uh…meet a colleague." Alexander had no idea why he blurted that information, other than he was not skilled at deception and Seryozha was the last person he wished to deceive.

"Well then, 'til tomorrow."

"Tomorrow? Oh, yes. By all means."

Alexander stood, shifting his weight from one foot to the other, confusedly.

"Would you mind cleaning the cups. I don't have time to return them to the lab."

"My pleasure, Professor," Seryozha replied, making a kissing sound toward the pigeons.

"Well, then, *proshai*, Seryozha Ivanovitch."

The old soldier looked up at his friend. Alexander was a creature of very fixed habits, and had always before said *a zaftra*—'til tomorrow'— when leaving. A simple *docvidanya*, or good-bye may have gone unnoticed, but 'farewell', and with such formality?

He clasped Alexander's outstretched hand and firmly shook it.

Alexander turned, again wiping the perspiration from his forehead as well as dabbing other trickles of water that had formed from the corners of his eyes.

As he exited the park, he glanced over his shoulder for one last look at his friend flicking seeds to his beloved birds.

*   *   *

Peredelkino had changed little since the days of Boris Pasternak. The great author and poet was buried in a copse of pine, birch and alder trees just outside of the small country village. Wooden, brightly painted blue, yellow, and white *izbas*—peasant cottages—lined unpaved streets that ended in black-earth fields. A one-room shanty sitting on a wooden platform that extended only a few dozen yards to either side served as the train station. Professor Alexander Marenkov stood on this platform, as the train from Moscow, having deposited its lone Peredelkino fare, began rolling and picking up speed.

Marenkov was initially pleased that he disembarked alone—a sign that he had not been followed. This euphoria quickly waned, however as he watched the train rumble toward the horizon, its plaintive whistle dying in the distance, beckoning him, chiding him. How he wished he had never gotten off. When the train shrank to a dot and then disappeared, squelching all hope of rescue, he wiped his glasses and ambled down the steps leading toward the quiet huts.

As he shuffled along the dusty road, his mind was a jumble of confused thoughts. What had seemed like a good idea a week ago when he was first contacted suddenly struck him as horribly wrong. As bitter as he was toward his government for their shoddy treatment of him, he could not betray Russia. He realized that now and regretted that he had been unable to come to so clear a resolution earlier. And, too, he could not deny that his new resolve had been spurred somewhat by thoughts of the mysterious disappearances of his colleagues who had "gone over."

So, be that as it may, he thought, fortifying himself. I'm here. I've made my decision. I'll simply tell them I've considered their offer, I'm flattered, but I cannot accept. That will be the end of it. Just like last time.

Movement in a field to his left diverted his attention and he turned to see the first signs of life since he detrained—a farmer plodding behind a plowshare pulled by a dilapidated brown nag.

"*Zydravctvootya!*" Marenkov shouted, waving a hand at the peasant.

The farmer acknowledged the greeting, and setting his plow aside, trudged across the black soil to meet the stranger. The Professor, who spent virtually every waking hour cloistered with pale-complected, soft-handed intellectuals was taken aback at the farmer's appearance.

He was swarthy, although it was difficult to discern where the dirt left off and the swarthiness began. The deeply-etched lines in his face bore a startling resemblance to the furrows in the field he was plowing, and the black soil itself seemed permanently embedded in his fingernails. The farmer smiled, revealing a mixture of brown and black teeth in those few places where they existed.

"My friend," the Professor said, mopping his forehead, "my name is Marenkov. I'm a university professor, writing a work on Boris Pasternak. I'd like to visit the great man's gravesite, but I'm not from these parts. Perhaps you can direct me."

"But of course, *soodar*," the peasant grinned. "Follow me. I'm Yura. Like in Zhivago, you know?"

"Yes, the doctor. But follow you? Your horse...?"

"My sweet Sonya? Don't worry, sir. She'll welcome the break. In fact, she loves nothing more than standing still...except her oats of course. Come!"

Marenkov stepped into the field, his newly purchased shoes sinking into the mixture of soil and manure fertilizer. He was amazed at how nimbly and swiftly the bent wire of a man hopped through the thick concoction, chattering as he went.

"Ah, Pasternak," he sighed. Let me think. What would be appropriate. Why, the one called 'August', certainly."

And to Alexander's complete astonishment, this black-nailed, weather-furrowed, sun-dried prune of a peasant began to recite Pasternak's "August":

The sun splashed with sultry ocher the woods nearby, the hamlet's houses, my bed, my dampened pillow and the wall's angle near the brook's hill.

"Hmm. I forget a few stanzas, but it's not important. It's the words you see. Yes, yes. Let me think—ah—

Death stood like a state surveyor within God's acre in this forest, scanning my lifeless face, as if it thought how best to dig my grave to proper measure."

As he listened, Marenkov began to gaze at the poet-spouting peasant with much greater scrutiny. For half an hour they walked across the fields, with Yura rattling off his repertoire of Pasternak poems. Finally they approached the little grove of trees. Only two pines now remained among the birches and alders.

"So, we have arrived," Yura grinned with that note of pride and pleasure which a host might welcome a friend to his house. "And here lies the poet himself." He pointed to a simple white tombstone with the engraving "B. Pasternak." A cross had been etched above the name.

"Years ago," Yura said with a twinkle in his eye, "the officials would sand off the cross. We'd wait until they left, and then re-carve it. So it would go, year after year. Now of course, no one comes any more to scrape it off. It's almost a pity that we can no longer have our fun. But change is the nature of things, is it not, sir? And the hare that does not change its path is the hare that gets devoured, true?"

"Indeed," Alexander replied, eyeing the bandy-legged farmer with yet more intense curiosity.

The sun had dipped below the treetops, but at this time of the year in this northern latitude, twilight would last for well over an hour.

"Drink, sir?" Yura asked, producing a silver flask from his hip pocket and twisting off the cap. "Mineral water."

Marenkov thanked him, grasped the container and raised it to his parched lips. He gagged on the first swallow, quickly separating the flask from his mouth.

"Oh, yes, and a touch of the devil's sweat—vodka," Yura chuckled.

"Well, Citizen Marenkov, I must be on my way. It will be dark by the time I get my Sonya to her oats. And she'll be quite testy."

"Thank you," Alexander said, shaking the peasant's hand. "Let me give you something."

"Oh, no sir. You already have—an hour or two to ramble over the land unfettered to a plow, and with a learned man. That's enough. *Proshai!*"

With a wave of his hand, Yura turned and began to retrace his steps across the open field.

That word again, thought Marenkov. "Farewell." He had used it for a very real purpose that morning with Seryozha. Now, how odd that this peasant, too, should use such a formal word of parting. But he felt too sleepy to dwell on the matter any further. In fact, he felt too sleepy to stand. He lay down, his body resting on a cool bed of grass and leaves, his head against Pasternak's white-washed tombstone. His brain swirled. He could barely keep his eyes open, although he knew he must. Why was his mind, his strong will letting him down at such a critical moment? His contact was to be here at sunset and the sun had already disappeared behind the trees, leaving an orange glow that seemed to color, then to smear his thoughts. All was a tangerine blur. Yura. The mineral water. No…no. The copper smudge became darker, deeper, turning brown, then black as he passed out.

*   *   *

The freshly painted blue cottage glowed softly in the waning sunset as Yura approached his home.

"Katya," he shouted as he led Sonya to her stable and bag of oats. "I met the Muscovite and took him to the gravesite. We'll now have enough money to buy that water pump and a new dress for you."

He stopped to listen. Ordinarily his wife would have come spilling out the door by now, carrying on about this or that chicken or some other momentous event of the day. However, now he was greeted only by silence. In fact, Katya could not come chattering to her beloved Yura now, or ever again, as her throat was slit from ear to ear.

Cursing his wife's inattention, Yura ambled to the back of the stable to retrieve a bale of hay. The sound of a footstep behind him, at the stable's entrance, caused him to turn.

"Ah, it's you," Yura said recognizing the silhouetted figure in the fading light.

"I've done as you asked, so I hope you've come to pay me."

Without replying, the silhouette's right hand raised, pointing a black stick-like object toward Yura.

He never heard a sound. The bullet smacked into his left cheek, exiting the back of the neck a half-inch to the left of his spinal cord. Yura fell heavily into the bale of hay, then slumped to the stable floor. He was still conscious however, when he saw the torch flying toward the hay. As the flames licked around him, he worried about Sonya and hoped that Katya would come to let this beloved mare out of the barn. For, try as he might, he couldn't move. And now he was inhaling smoke and could feel the searing heat of the flames next to his flesh.

* * *

When Marenkov awoke, the full moon had already risen and was peering at him through puffy brightly-illuminated white clouds. He still felt groggy, but not so incapacitated that he could not sense the presence of someone near. Perhaps it was Yura, but no, something deep inside his partially functioning brain convinced him that it was a being of quite a different nature than a black-earth peasant.

He heard the distinctive strike of a match, smelled the powder, glimpsed the tiny yellow flame through half-closed eyes. Then a rustling. The being was moving toward him. The Professor felt cold beads of perspiration break out from the pores on his forehead, neck and back. A hand touched his shoulder and he struck out with his fists as he sprang to his feet. A strong hand grabbed his throat. He clutched at his antagonist, ripping some flesh, some material. A thud against the back of his neck sent bolts of lightning through his brain. He fell unconscious to the ground. The next time he would wake up, the world would be a different and far more dangerous place.

Chapter Two

James Slater was extremely pleased with himself. Still a few months shy of his fortieth birthday, he was president and CEO of a multi-million dollar high technology corporation. On top of that, he was handsome, single—thanks to two messy divorces—and quite a charmer, at least by his own account. This charisma was greatly enhanced in the eyes of some by his recent acquisition of a bright new blood-red Ferrari 550 Maranello. He looked forward to showing off his new toy later that afternoon at *Clyde's*, a popular watering hole in northern Virginia, just outside of the Washington Beltway. Now, however, he had an important luncheon engagement in D.C.

"Jennie," he said, keying the intercom that rested on a marble desktop alongside a gold Mont Blanc pen and pencil set. "I'll be at *Mr. K's* for lunch, and then at *Clyde's*. If absolutely necessary—and the operative word here is 'absolutely'—you can reach me on the cellular."

"I doubt that mere sound waves will be able to catch up with you in that rocket ship," a laughing female voice responded.

"Fine with me. I really don't want anyone to reach out and touch me. That is, until I get lucky at happy hour."

Jim Slater laughed, feeling even better about himself, which, considering his already ebullient condition, was a magnificent feat. *This is going to be a fantastic evening,* he predicted, as he stood before the full-length mirror and straightened his tie. There was one minor annoyance—a thin, purple scab that threaded across his right cheek, near the ear. At one week old, it was now barely visible. He ran his fingers across it pensively, then smiled. A most profitable blemish, he thought.

Half an hour later he roared to a stop at the stylish Chinese Restaurant on K Street in the Nation's capital. Mr. K's was his favorite place to do business, with its elegant oriental decor, its quiet, tucked away niches that permitted discreet discussions and assignations, and the best Peking duck this side of Shanghai. Then too, some of its appeal could be attributed to the management's overwhelming desire to please its biggest spending client, including allowing his thoroughbred machine to be parked directly in front of the restaurant's door.

His luncheon partner was already at the table when he entered.

"Falcon, good to see you again," he said exuberantly as he extended his right hand.

The man who greeted him stood just over six feet, with a frame that hinted of a keen athleticism beneath his light beige-colored suit. His face, tanned and finely weathered, was topped by a sandy tousle of hair and accentuated by aquamarine eyes.

"We'll both have the Peking duck," Slater said as the waiter seated him. "And your best Merlot. That O.K. with you, Mike?" he said as an afterthought.

"Fine—except for the wine…the office will still be there after lunch, you know."

"Oh yeah, I forgot about the strict regimen you bureaucrats have to observe. Guess the committee's pretty busy reviewing the new agreement with Rurik."

"We're almost finished. Looks like we'll approve it," he said affably, hoping he had masked his disdain for Slater.

"All quantities, prices and delivery times for enriched uranium?"

"Yes, for the next twenty years."

"Truly magnificent. Pound those commie warheads into capitalist electricity," Slater laughed, thinking what a pack of dolts, that Uranium Oversight Committee. Though, for someone on the UOC, Mike Falcon was O.K. Hell, like himself, he was even ex-Navy—some sort of fighter jock. What else had he ferreted out about Falcon—now he remembered—a degree in Russian studies and masters in cosmophysics or astrophysics or some such shit. He certainly wasn't stupid, but like the others who served with the committee, he didn't have a clue. If they only had an inkling of his activities during his recent trip to Moscow...the very thought made him feel even more effervescent and oddly magnanimous.

"Of course, your company would still have the problem of competing for that business," Falcon said, not reluctant to splash cold water on this remarkable boor.

"Money in the bank," Slater snickered, with a dismissive wave of his hand. "Say, since things are going so well, why don't we celebrate this afternoon at *Clyde's*? Ever been for a spin in a quarter million dollar sportscar? I've got 480 of Mr. Ferrari's finest horses out there that'll take us to sixty in just four point three seconds. Whaddya say?"

Falcon hesitated, not wanting to seem over anxious. Here was the moment toward which he had been working for several months, the reason he was on loan from the National Security Agency as an advisor to the committee. In its task as monitor of worldwide enriched uranium trade, the committee had been very curious as to why Slater continued to grow wealthier and spend more lavishly in spite of the fact that his company, Micratom Inc. continued to lose contracts to its chief rival. Then there were the other interesting entries in the Slater file: his cashiering from the Navy Seals after a sexual entanglement with an Admiral's wife; the two hotly contested, nasty divorces, leading to settlements costing hundreds of thousands of dollars; the many trips to the mid-east and Russia, including the most recent to the International Conference on Slow Neutron Fission Theory in Moscow.

"Well, it's usually pretty quiet on Friday afternoon. I suppose the place won't fall apart without me."

"Terrific," Slater said, as a waiter poured the wine. "In the words of the immortal Richard Blain, I think this might be the beginning of a beautiful friendship."

The last thing Slater actually wanted was a friendship with Falcon. Lasting relationships were not his strong suit. His first marriage had lasted a full six months, the second one, a couple of weeks. He had no use for intimate, long-term involvements—which was not to say that he had no use for people. In fact, his extravagant taste for sleek, fast, well-constructed automobiles was a mere extension of his gargantuan appetite for women of the same caliber. It was a compulsion that was exceeded only by his need for access to people in well-positioned places. People such as Mike Falcon, who as adviser to the UOC, was the best-positioned person on the planet to help him further his ambitions. Cultivation of this relationship would be very useful. The Peking duck seemed especially moist, tender and succulent that afternoon.

*   *   *

What a magnificent day so far, he thought, as he steered the Ferrari north onto the George Washington Parkway. His taste buds were slaked, he had the UOC Special Advisor sitting in the passenger seat and he was anticipating an evening with an as yet unmet female. He pressed lightly on the accelerator and the hand-crafted engine responded with a throaty growl, effortlessly and quickly propelling them to one hundred miles per hour.

They sped up the Parkway in less than fifteen minutes, not slowing until they reached the traffic lights on Dolley Madison Highway, just beyond the entrance to the CIA—a landmark that both men studiously ignored.

"How was that for a ride?" Slater grinned toward Falcon, before turning and flipping the keys to the valet as he stepped out of the car at *Clyde's*. "Park it right in front—here's a twenty for your trouble."

Happy hour was already in full swing when they entered the lounge. It was becoming increasingly crowded every month as the number of high-tech companies continued to burgeon in the Dulles Airport access corridor.

Slater wasted no time in pressing his way through the throng of lawyers, secretaries, software engineers, salesmen, doctors, stockbrokers, and business entrepreneurs. Like a heat-seeking missile, he locked onto his target, a particularly curvaceous redhead that had attracted a squadron of male admirers at the bar.

His newfound friend, Mike Falcon, a tumbler of scotch and water in hand, backed against a post in the hope that by such unobtrusiveness his suit might not be splattered by the already happy crowd. His modest wish was immediately dashed however, when a particularly effusive group of celebrants crushed blindly into him, knocking his drink against his suit coat.

"I'm so sorry," a woman said, turning toward him.

Having been focused on Slater and the business that had led him here, Falcon found himself totally unprepared for the sight that met his eyes: a vision of golden hair tumbling about a clear, flawlessly complected face, cat-green eyes, slightly turned up at the outer corners, fleshy, strawberry-red, inviting lips. Her classic figure was highlighted by a form-clinging black minidress. A string of black pearls accentuating a fair-skinned neck and deep cleavage was her only concession to jewelry.

"Please, here's a napkin," she said, dabbing the spill on Falcon's lapel.

He noticed a slight accent when she spoke again, "I believe I saw you drive up. Your Ferrari?"

"No, his," he said, nodding toward the laughing, gesticulating president of Micratom. At that instant, Slater's eyes happened to fall absently in Falcon's direction, stopping cold as they locked onto the woman at the side of his new best friend. The redhead was in mid-sentence when Slater launched away from her. Weaving through the human chaff, he honed in on the objective that now completely dominated his scope.

"There you are, Mike! I thought you went home to your wife and three kids," he blustered, throwing his arm around Falcon, knowing full well that no such familial ties existed. Then, turning to the focal point of his interest, "I'm Jim Slater, and you are...."

"*Tres ennui.*"

"Terry..., he boomed confidently, "So nice to meet you." Then, glancing at her empty glass, "I'll freshen your drink. What's your brand of poison?"

He had seized her glass and was already pressing through the revelers when she responded, "Merlot."

"Terrific! What a coincidence. Don't go away!"

"Forceful fellow, isn't he," she noted with some amusement, as she watched Slater bowling through the crowd. "Do you know him well?"

"Not really...Ms. 'Ennui'," he grinned.

"I'm sorry," she laughed. "I'm afraid he brought out the claws in me. It's actually Tigere, Cherisse Tigere." She extended her hand.

"Mike Falcon," he said, clasping her hand. "I couldn't help noticing your accent."

"Oh, I thought I had lost it. It's been fifteen years since I left Lyon."

Falcon searched her eyes. Lyon—in the south of France—stirred a recollection of verdant hills, neatly rolled bundles of yellow hay, a vivid azure sky soaring above the Maritime Alps. He tried to picture this elegant woman in such a rustic setting. The fact that he couldn't was mildly disconcerting.

"You must know the little town of Romanieu, then?" Mike asked, his eyes fixed on her.

"Oh, yes. Very quaint. How do you know it?"

"I lived there for a year—a long time ago. Perhaps we can share our experiences some time."

"I would enjoy that very, very much," she said touching his arm.

"Might I have your number?" he asked.

"Of course."

She rummaged through a small black purse that hung from her shoulder, unable to locate the desired bit of writing paper.

"Use this," Falcon said, handing her one of his business cards. "This and my stained suit will remind me to call you."

Laughing, she quickly jotted the number and pressed it into his hand.

"Oh, Falcon, you're still here," Slater bellowed above the din as he pushed his way forward, gripping a splashing wine flute in each hand. "Listen, I'm going to take Terry for a spin, and…" in a winking aside to Falcon, whispered, "maybe a road test, too. You don't mind taking a cab home, do you? I didn't think so. Thanks. I'll call you Monday and we'll discuss that Rurik business over lunch. See you."

Falcon glanced at Cherisse, whose face bore a beguiling expression, as though dawdling with Slater might prove amusing.

"Some other time, then, Ms.…'Ennui,'" Falcon said.

She smiled, squeezing his hand.

Working his way to the bar, Falcon ordered a double scotch—forget the water. He had barely been handed his glass when he noticed Slater and the woman depart together. Very beautiful, he thought as he watched her disappear. And very un-French. His time spent in Romanieu had trained his ear to the lilting language of that area. No, her accent was of a quite different region, belonging to a completely separate nationality, somewhat further to the east. He wondered why she had lied.

*   *   *

"How about a sip of the god's nectar?" Slater asked airily, dropping his keys in a Waterford glass tray that sat on a waist-high Corinthian pedestal in the foyer of his Great Falls mansion. He felt flushed, strong, like the predator who had successfully cornered his prey.

"I suppose one more wouldn't be fatal—to me," she laughed coyly.

"Excellent! Make yourself comfortable."

He sauntered across the marble hallway to a brass-railed mahogany bar, shedding his suit jacket and necktie in his wake. From the bar, the foyer led down several steps to a spacious living room, the large bay window of which presented a panoramic view of the Potomac River, flowing quietly a few hundred feet below. The other sides of the room were adorned with post-impressionistic and modern oil paintings, all originals. Bronze and marble statues, mostly of female nudes stood in mute testimony to the owner's wealth and taste.

"Quite a place," Cherisse said, kicking off her high heels and settling into a large, u-shaped sectional couch. Ferrari. Mansion. What kind of business did you say you're in?"

"Nuclear energy. Import, export. But let's not talk about that now," he said, crossing the foyer and descending into the living room. "Would you like to see the rest of the dump?"

"Please."

Taking the glass of wine proffered to her, she clasped his hand and followed him down a thickly carpeted hallway. They passed six guestrooms, three baths, a den and a library before he led her up a spiral staircase to the second floor.

"And here we have the *piece de resistance*," he grinned. "The master bedroom."

As she stepped in the doorway to obtain a better look, her breasts brushed against his arm. Having contained himself for far longer than any normal male, let alone James Slater, could be deemed reasonable under the circumstances, he seized her and pulled her against him. His hands slid eagerly over her firm shapely rump, running under her short flimsy dress to the warm smooth skin underneath. His fingers pressed against the supple flesh, finding no obstacle to their probing search around her thighs, over her rounded cheeks, tracing the arch of her back, then slipping to her taut abdomen and moving higher to cup her full resilient breasts. Holding her by the buttocks, he lifted her so that her now exposed right breast, its nipple stiff and protruding, rose to his eager lips.

"Wait, wait," she panted, pushing him away. "Strip!" she commanded.

"What?"

"You heard me. Strip!"

"So it's going to be like that," Slater grinned, revealing two neatly capped rows of chiclet-sized teeth.

Discarding a fleeting thought to milk the moment with a slow striptease, he opted for a more rapid consumption of his urge. In a few seconds, his clothes were in a heap at his ankles, and he stood before her in the disappointing pudginess of his lost prime.

"Oh baby," she affected a moan. "Now get into bed."

James Slater prided himself in not being stupid. Instantly, he was lying naked on his king-sized bed, staring at his own reflection in the overhead mirror. Slowly, she slid the remaining strap from her shoulder, letting her dress drift noiselessly to the floor.

Slater groaned as he eyed her body, the shapeliness of which put to shame his man-made statues. Her breasts were lush and uplifted, the nipples pointing directly at him like two delectable cherries. Her narrow, sculpted waist gave way to slender, curving hips, then long, lissome, gracefully muscled legs. In concert with her lynx-green eyes and flaxen, leonine hair, the full impact was evocative of a slinky stalking savanna feline.

"I brought a few toys," she whispered, as she drew some objects from her purse that had fallen to the floor.

She strolled to the foot of the bed, then slowly straddled him. Her scent, not artificially masked, was clean and fresh, like a summer peach.

He painfully awaited her touch, reaching toward her, but she batted his hand away.

"My, aren't we anxious," she laughed, in a mischievous, reprimanding tone. "First, we must learn who is really in control here."

She leaned forward, her right nipple hovering tantalizingly above his mouth as she seized his right wrist and tied it to the bed post.

"Whoa," he chortled. "Is this going to hurt?"

"Absolutely. You, that is."

She leaned across in the other direction, binding his left wrist.

He raised his head so that he was able to encircle her left nipple with his mouth. She pulled back, clutched a handful of his hair and slapped his head against the pillow.

"As I said, you're much too anxious. You must learn to savor the pleasurable moments. They don't last forever you know."

"O.K. O.K. I just wanted you to know that I'm ready for the pleasurable moments."

She slipped down to the bottom of the bed, where she strapped each ankle to a post, making certain to draw the nylon restraints tightly so that he actually winced.

"Pain is good for you," she intoned, as she crawled over his spread-eagled body. Kneeling above him, a leg on each side, she leaned over so that her string of black pearls fell lightly onto his chest.

The sensation of her warm thighs against his legs and the hard, cool gems tickling his skin swelled his enthusiasm.

"Do you like that?" she purred.

"Yes," he moaned.

"Good. Don't go away," she said, easing from the bed. "I have one more surprise for you."

She glided across the room to retrieve another object from her purse.

Slater, his body and mind tingling in joyous expectation, tugged playfully at his restraints.

Returning to the bed, she again straddled him, holding the new object behind her back.

"Now is it time?" he pleaded.

"Yes, *lyoobeemets*. Close your eyes."

Eagerly obeying, Slater squeezed his eyelids shut, grinning happily.

The sensation that followed was of a quite different nature than that which he had expected, however. His eyelids popped open and his head jerked upwards as he felt a jabbing pain in his left forearm.

"What the hell…" he uttered as he glimpsed a hypodermic needle sinking deeply into his flesh.

"I said yes, it is time…time to bear your secrets to me and to your god, if you have one."

"Wha…what are you talking about," he spluttered, writhing to free himself. Each twist and turn only served to secure him further. She knew her business well.

"Soon you'll tire of that," she said disinterestedly, as she pressed the plunger of the hypodermic. "And this little touch of the henbane plant…scopolamine…will help you to be less inhibited. Then, after you have fulfilled my simple request, I have another treat. Designer crack."

James Slater emitted a piercing shriek as he pounded his head over and over into the pillow. He begged, he sobbed, and then he could hear or feel nothing.

When she left a few hours later, he lay very still on the bed, his red-veined, watery eyes staring blankly at the overhead mirror.

Chapter Three

Sergei Medved felt drained of all his energy. He could not remember Moscow ever having been this sweltering before. El Nino, he mused, turning the fan on his desk so that his face could enjoy the full impact of its breeze. He chuckled softly to himself. It used to be we'd blame everything on the Americans. Now it's El Nino.

Taking a drag from the cigarette that played constantly at his lips, he lifted the last stack of papers from his in box. Sighing at the thought of slogging through the documents, he glanced at the clock on the faded yellow, paint-peeled wall to his left. Five p.m. He had only a few minutes remaining to sort through this batch if he were to keep his promise to Galena. His eight year old daughter would be performing in a ballet recital this evening. For the past three years, by foregoing as much as a thread of new clothing for himself, he had managed to scrape together just enough spare *veksels* to pay for her ballet lessons. *What is that she is dancing tonight?* he mused. *Ah yes…the Nutcracker, and she is dancing the role of Clara. How incongruous. A Christmas ballet in August. In this heat wave. Yet, these days, everything in Russia is topsy-turvy.*

He wearily began scanning the papers, all of which were marked 'Confidential' in bold red letters. The same boring lists of passport applicants and conference attendees. Shuffling papers in the "Travel Section" of the *Federal'naia Sluzhba Bezopasnosti*, the Federal Security

Service, the FSB. How had it come to this, to one who had commanded the admiration of his colleagues in the KGB and the grudging respect of his enemies. At age fifty, he knew that he was at the peak of his powers. Physically he was as strong as he had been fifteen years earlier when his troops had reverently dubbed him the Bear of the Hindu Kush. His face showed some of the wear of those days: the deeply etched lines at the corners of his eyes and mouth, the crease on his right cheek where it had been kissed by a Mujaheddin bullet. Mentally, he was as sharp as ever and now added to that keen intelligence a wealth of experience from fighting both hot and cold wars.

But much had changed after Afghanistan. He, and the other so-called "Chekists"—the nickname having derived from Lenin's secret police organization, the Cheka—who were once the backbone of the Bureau, were now a problem, an embarrassment. When the Committee for State Security—the KGB—was "abolished," they were trotted off into lower level desk jobs in several newly created security services, where their vast storehouse of knowledge and peculiar expertise could be tapped until they were finally turned out to pasture.

In the FSB, Medved followed the movements of important scientists, academicians, and industrialists into and out of Russia, searching for patterns. What foreign engineer visited Novgorod? Why? Who did he really represent? Who was his local contact? Which biochemist from St. Petersburg attended an overseas conference? With whom did he meet? Patterns. Searching for patterns. It was tedious, sedentary work, emphatically distasteful to one possessing Medved's action-oriented temperament. The Chekists called it the "dry" world. The real action was in the "wet" world.

Frowning, he gazed to his right through the tightly sealed window that provided a view of Red Square and the fairy-tale like domes of St. Basil's Cathedral. Tourists were milling around the landmark, snapping pictures of the buildings and each other. A short distance across the

Square a long line of humanity snaked toward Lenin's Tomb. Not nearly as long as it used to be before Perestroika.

He remembered the time when Russian folk would stand for hours, even days, for the honor of passing before the old man's wax—mummified body. They would even gladly let foreigners into line ahead of themselves. The foreigners mistook this gesture for politeness. They didn't know that a longer wait at the tomb meant greater prestige to a simple peasant in his home town. Of course, that had all changed with the overthrow of Communism.

Some of the long queues now snaked into banks where desperate and wildly overoptimistic Muscovites hoped to retrieve some of their rapidly devaluating currency. All too often, their wait would be in vain, as the bank would quickly exhaust its supply of rubles. More successful were those who waited in lines winding into the numerous neon-lit nightclubs, strip joints, and brothels that blighted the historic old neighborhood surrounding the Kremlin. Red Square was now red light.

The smoke of his cigarette curled upward before his eyes, mixing with the scene of desperate Muscovites below to evoke another image: Napoleon's *Grande Armeé* retreating, leaving Moscow in flames. He wondered what the scene must have been like: the city ablaze, soot and ashes swirling in the air, Muscovites scurrying about in panic, unlucky ones being lined up and shot, children lost in the shuffle, women raped and bayoneted; the French and other foreign soldiers—many in distinctly unmilitary dress as discipline eroded—carrying off mantle clocks, silverware, curtains, the nearest contraband at hand in their headlong flight to the west, into the snow.

Soon the invaders would adopt into their language the Russian word for quick—*bistro*—as they broke into and demanded food in every inn and house in their path. *Bistro! Bistro!* they would shout in panic as the Cossack horsemen, sabers flashing, bore down upon them. Only a fraction of those poor souls—a handful of the original half-million man army—would live to inject this word into the vocabulary of the western world. Mother Russia had a way of reducing to dust the most arrogant of dreamers, he mused.

Inhaling a puff from the cigarette, he instantly felt a pang of guilt. His daughter hated his smoking and had tearfully begged him to quit. "Are you so anxious to leave me too, Papa?" she would sob, referring to the death of his wife, Irina, taken by cancer two years earlier.

I could finish this one, then not have any in front of her tonight, he rationalized, staring at the half-smoked cigarette, its remaining length of tobacco balanced by an equal length of ash. Sighing, he stubbed the butt into an empty McDonald's styrofoam coffee cup that bore a picture of the Littlest Mermaid and turned to the papers. As he read, he leaned against the back of his metal-framed chair, tilting it onto its rear two legs.

That was the moment he noticed it. Tucked at the bottom of the interminable columns of applicants and conferees was a short list entitled "*Nichevo*."

This "Nothing" section contained the names of significant persons who, for one reason or another, had disappeared momentarily from the FSB's tracking radar. The appellation of "Nothing" for this list was quite appropriate, for invariably the missing person would be accounted for within a day or two and the hiatus would be found to be completely innocuous.

Now, however, in spite of the stifling heat, he felt as if a cold breeze wafted across the back of his neck and down his spine as he read the fifth name on this list:

Alexander Marenkov.

He quickly leaned forward, the front two legs of the chair thudding to the linoleum floor, and began typing the name Marenkov into his IBM computer. As he waited for the information to flow, he cursed the Service for not upgrading to the latest, much faster model. After ten or fifteen seconds, however, characters began to fill the screen.

There were numerous pages of information concerning Dr. Alexander Marenkov, Department Head, Nuclear Physics, University of Moscow...degrees, accomplishments, honors, books, lectures...official acquaintances, finances, personal data...more pages than on anyone else he had ever seen in the FSB's vast bank of files. But he quickly scrolled through it all with the purpose of one searching for a gem among coals.

Finally, he came to it: *Ribnaya Loflya*—the Service's quaint application of the word "fishing" to denote interesting contacts of prominent Russian citizens with foreign elements. There was only one entry: 1992, a French physicist supposedly representing a nuclear power company in Toulouse. He was better known to Russian intelligence as an *osyol*—a donkey—for the Iraqi government. The situation had been closely monitored until it became clear that Marenkov had firmly rejected the offer. Additionally, although not contained in the Service's files, Medved knew that the French *osyol* had been killed shortly thereafter in an unusual single-car accident on a country road outside of Toulouse, snuffing out a budding career. But not in physics, Medved smiled.

Now he was at a dead end. Marenkov's record was impeccable. Perhaps the Professor's disappearance was "nothing" after all, an innocent trip to a Black Sea resort or north to St. Petersburg to escape the heat. Perhaps. All of Medved's years of training and his gut instincts led him to a different conclusion, however. He scrolled back through Marenkov's dossier, searching for the key that he knew was there. If he could only gather his wits enough to recognize it.

Undoing his earlier resolve, he lit another cigarette, opened the electronic file entitled "Conferences" and began scanning. To his amazement, he noted that the Professor had attended eleven conferences already that year, all within Russia. When does the man have time to work, teach and write so many books, he wondered. Eight of the conferences were attended only by Russians and citizens of the former Soviet Republics. The other three, being international in flavor, seemed a more profitable area of investigation. He scanned the names of each foreign attendee, correlating the names with information contained in the computer's storehouse.

He had worked his way through the first two international conferences with no meaningful connections and was halfway through the third, "The International Conference on Slow Neutron Fission Theory," when he landed on the name:

Slater, James A., President & CEO, Micratom Inc., USA.

He typed the name on the keyboard and tapped "retrieve." Lighting another cigarette, he awaited the response. Nearly twenty seconds later, two letters appeared on the screen:

НИ

It was the computer code for *Nyet Informatsiya*.

Medved stared in disbelief at the screen. He retyped the name and again tapped retrieve.

НИ

He knew that the Federal Security Service was not nearly as sophisticated or thorough as its predecessor the KGB, but this was beyond incompetence. A simple name on a list of conferees. He could've gotten more information out of an American telephone book than he was now getting from a Russian intelligence computer.

Determining to approach the problem from another angle, he dragged the computer mouse across its pad. Now, however, the screen remained frozen. He tried pressing different keys, turning the machine on and off, even unplugging it and rebooting. The screen refused to change. He lit another cigarette and inhaled while tapping the fingers of his free hand on the desk, and staring intently at the immobile image.

Absent-mindedly he glanced at the clock. Seven p.m. Medved sat bolt upright. *Bozha moy*! My god! Galena—the ballet. He quickly turned off the computer, locked his papers in the safe behind his chair, doused his cigarette in the cup and sped to the door.

✶ ✶ ✶

"Thank you for being there tonight, papa. I love you," Galena said, tightly hugging her father. In her white night gown, with her long black hair framing her youthful radiant face and flowing over her delicate shoulders, she was the living embodiment of the Nutcracker's Clara.

"And you are my fairy princess, my Galyooshka," he said, sitting on the edge of the bed. "I'm so proud of you."

"Papa, do you think mama saw my performance tonight?"

"I'm sure. And she was most pleased."

Galena fell silent, gazing through her bedroom window to the full moon hovering just above the neighboring rooftops.

"Yes. Oh, papa, I know she's watching. I'll make her proud. Some day I'll be in the Bolshoi or the Kirov, and we'll travel to Paris and then America. I want so much to see those sky scraping buildings in New York and to dance at President Kennedy's Center, and to see the Great Canyon and to ride those little trams in San Francisco. They call it 'Frisco', you know. And we'll be together…in America."

"Yes, yes, but now you must get some sleep," he said, gently tucking a patchwork quilt under her chin.

"I'll try," she tittered, hugging her father. "Papa…."

"Yes, Galyooshka." It was obvious that the excitement of the evening was easily overpowering any inclination his daughter might have toward slumber.

"Papa, tell me the story of the Tsar Ivan and Maria Morevna."

"But you have heard this story a hundred times—"

"Please. Then I promise I shall sleep. Pleeeze."

Medved smiled resignedly and for the hundred and first time began to recount Galena's favorite fairy tale. He told how Tsar Ivan and the ravishing Maria Morevna fell in love and how Koschchei, the Deathless Giant, stole Maria from the Tsar. Although he strove mightily not to miss a word or a nuance of the tale, he occasionally lapsed. Galena was always quick to correct his fumble.

"Then one evening Ivan slipped into the giant's palace," he spoke softly, "embraced Maria Morevna and escaped with her on his charger. Learning of this outrage, Koschchei leaped on his magic horse, crying, 'Beast, can you catch them?'"

Galena joined her father in reciting the horse's reply, which was her favorite part of the tale:

"If we sow barley, wait till it grows quite tall,
harvest it, thresh it, make it into beer,
drink the beer until we are quite drunk,
sleep off our drunkenness, then go after them,
we shall still catch them!"

They broke into laughter, at both the silliness of the words and their happiness at having once again successfully recited the lines together.

"And of course, Ivan slew the wicked giant and he and Maria lived happily ever after," Medved said.

"Oh, papa, that was too fast," Galena giggled, trying to feign a pout.

"Perhaps, young lady, but you must go to sleep." He kissed her forehead and began to stand when she grasped his arm.

"Papa...what is a prostitute?"

Medved sighed, wishing Irina were here to answer this one...always these questions out of the blue, and always just at bed time. Summoning his courage, he asked, "Where did you hear such a word?"

"At ballet school. Some of the older girls were talking about how they were starving and how they could make a month's salary in one day by being a prostitute. The older boys laughed and said they planned to quit and become hooligans with the mob."

He brushed a lock of hair from her face. "The girls who say such things do not believe in themselves. Because of that, they will never become prima ballerinas in the Kirov and they will never go on tour to America. But my little *goloobcheek* believes in herself and all her dreams will come true. So you have no cause to even listen to the prattle of those girls. Enough, now. Sleep!"

Not giving her a chance to protest, he quickly kissed her cheek and rose from the bed.

"Sweet dreams, Galya," he said, crossing the room. Shutting the door behind him, he whispered a little prayer. It was not so much that he actually believed in a god but he was prepared to pay homage to a deity if that would ensure his daughter's welfare and happiness in these troubled times.

Striding to the kitchen, past the sink filled with unwashed dishes, he reached to the overhead cupboard and selected a clean white and blue porcelain cup. He placed the cup under the spigot of a brightly enameled red, gold and green samovar that sat on the sink countertop. This teakettle was his prized possession and one of the few things of any value that he still owned. Made by the renowned Tula artisans nearly two hundred years earlier and passed down through his family ever since, its enameling depicted a scene from the fairy tale that he had just related to his daughter.

While the cup filled, he ran his free hand gently over the warm kettle, as if the touch with such an antique might connect him with the Russia of old, a Russia that was like the samovar—robust, enduring, its ungainly mass redeemed by an appropriate graceful line or masterful artistic expression. But now, like the depiction of Tsar Ivan and Maria Morevna fleeing from the Deathless Giant, his poor country was running from its own nightmare. *And we shall sow barley, harvest it, make it into beer...* the words of the fairy tale recurred to him. *And we shall get drunk, fall asleep, wake up...and still catch them.*

When his cup filled, he entered his "office," which was simply a lesser portion of the already modest-sized living room. A six-foot tall Chinese silk screen that depicted the four seasons represented the official line between his private work area and the rest of the apartment. Galena graciously respected this delicate boundary, always knocking on the screen before disturbing her father at his work.

Within the "office" were a card table that supported a telephone, a laptop computer, a gleaming little black lacquer box handmade by a Palekh master, and a metal lamp that swiveled. A wastebasket, a three-drawer metal file cabinet and a folding chair completed the furnishings.

Yawning, he plopped himself into this chair, placed the cup of tea on the table and switched on the computer and its modem. The earlier outage had been nagging him all evening and had distracted his attention from his daughter's performance. Fortunately, she had not noticed his late arrival or he would still be explaining that away.

At the computer's prompting, he entered the appropriate encrypted command and awaited the response. With some pride, he successfully resisted the temptation to light up while enduring the excruciating, time-consuming encryption process. It was bad enough that the FSB's computer hardware was five years old. But it was outrageous, Medved fumed, that the cryptography system was the even more aged IBM Data Encryption Standard.

True, the use of random binary digits virtually nullified code-breaking. He even recalled reading somewhere that the Americans had calculated it would take several years to perform the billions of steps necessary to crack an average message. It was because of these safe probabilities that the Service permitted its agents to log in from remote sites—for unclassified information only. But *Bozha Moy*! It was cumbersome and slow. And the Americans had long ago moved on to quantum cryptography using lasers and a photon protocol. "Light years ahead," he smiled, enjoying his pun.

As he waited for the FSB's central computer to digest and decode his inputs, he glanced at the paintings and framed photographs that hung on the walls around him. A colorful batik—a hand-painted fabric—captured the stately white, blue and gold cathedral of Novgorod. All the photographs were black and white: Medved and a group of a dozen smiling young men in *Spetsnaz*—Special Forces—uniforms, posing confidently before an Mi-24 assault helicopter; his wife and Galena, hand-in-hand on a beach, laughing about something—had he cracked a joke or mugged at them—he couldn't remember; Irina alone, brushing her hand through her long, auburn hair, her full, sensuous lips curved in a half-smile, her dark sienna eyes turned toward him with that wry, pensive expression that he had so loved…and still loved.

A muffled "ting" from the computer alerted him that he was into the FSB's mainframe. He quickly keyed in the name, Alexander Marenkov.

Fifteen seconds later, the screen blinked.

НИ

Medved froze. He reentered the name. Marenkov's file had been erased. Of no little consequence was the realization that the party responsible for this action would be quite aware that he had accessed the file earlier that evening. That party, who had taken the extraordinary step of destroying information contained in the Service's computer banks, could not take the chance that he had already connected the dots. The earlier disappearance of the file of the American, Slater. The crash of the computer system. Medved knew that it had to be the work of someone extremely powerful and clever. Someone who had the ability to compromise the computer mainframe of Russian intelligence. He also knew that such a party could not permit him to transmit any knowledge gleaned from these files. Ever. Whoever had erased Marenkov's file would come for him tonight.

He lifted the phone receiver. It was dead, as he had expected. He began to think through his options. He could stay in the apartment and perhaps pluck the feathers of his antagonist. If he could take him alive, he would learn much. But that would be problematic as his opponent would certainly assure himself of a firepower and probably numerical advantage. More importantly, concern for Galena completely negated that course. No, he must get both of them out. But how? Perhaps positions have already been taken outside his door, in eager anticipation of his attempted flight.

One of Medved's greatest qualities, the one to which he owed most of his success—first as an infantry commander in the Afghan war, then as a Bureau Chekist—was his ability to relax, to actually lower his heartbeat and breathing rhythm and to gain a much more lucid conception of his environment when faced with a life and death situation.

He walked to Galena's bedroom, stooped beside her bed, and gently lifted his daughter.

"Quiet, Galyooshka," he whispered as he carried her toward the front door.

"Wha...?" she said, rubbing her eyes and trying to make sense of the situation.

"Shh...you must be like a little mouse in your ballet. Trust me."

He set her down against the wall a few feet from the living room window that looked out over the street, then crossed back to the front entrance. There he turned the locks on the two mechanisms that secured the door. These locks, the favorite of the old KGB, each consisted of three finger-sized stainless steel bolts that could withstand nearly two tons of force. He then returned to his office where he clicked off the computer and modem.

Unlocking the metal file cabinet, he reached inside the top drawer with his right hand. He felt his fingers close around a cold, hard object—the handle of a *Gurza* 9mm. He removed the gun, satisfied himself that it was loaded, seized two additional clips, closed the drawer and locked the cabinet. Shoving the clips into his pockets and the *Gurza* into his belt behind his back, he turned off the desk lamp. The apartment was now cloaked in black, with only a sliver of soft white moonlight seeping through the slightly jarred door leading to Galena's bedroom. In the darkness, Medved groped toward the kitchen, wondering if his long shot plan would actually work.

Chapter Four

Abdul bin Wahhab stepped carefully across the rubble-strewn ground, gathering his ankle-length white robe in his hand. He was followed by three more men, whose sun-browned faces and hands contrasted sharply against their red and white checkered burnooses and bleached robes. A Nikonov AN-94 assault rifle, the Russian army's new replacement for the revered Kalashnikov AK-47, was strapped to each of their backs. As much as possible, the small group clung to the shadows cast by the jagged shale-encrusted mountains that surrounded them on all sides. Their caution was not so much to avoid the blistering late afternoon sun as it was to evade a probing eye of another sort that orbited unseen many miles above them.

"The missile struck here," one of the followers said, pointing to a crater filled with powdered bricks and stones, splintered wood, and shards of glass.

"My bedroom," he nodded. To the surprise of the others, he stepped into the sunlight, picked his way across the debris and paused. His followers remained in the shadows, intently watching as their leader—the "Servant of the Beloved"—stooped, grasped an object, then slowly straightened.

Turning slowly to the others, he raised the object in his right hand.

"It is a sign from Allah," he said firmly, joyfully. "Only the Koran has survived."

"Allah be praised," whispered his companions.

"Come, we have nothing to fear in the daylight," bin Wahhab exclaimed. "There is probably no safer place in the world right now than this valley. We will pray in the light of day, as befitting the servants of the one true God."

The three men emerged from the shadows and knelt with bin Wahhab amid the ruins of their former stronghold. Facing southwest, toward Mecca, they touched their foreheads to the ground and prayed.

"In the name of Allah, the Compassionate, the Merciful," bin Wahhab cried.

"There is no god but Allah, the living the eternal! Veils have been thrown over the hearts of the unbelievers, the infidels, and into their ears a heaviness. Surely, Allah will fill hell with demons and unbelievers together and prepare a place for his chosen in Paradise.

"Give us, thine servants, the strength, oh Lord, to destroy the infidels and the wisdom to receive your blessings and beneficence.

"In the name of He who rules the heaven and the earth, the sublime and the all-knowing Allah, Amen."

"Amen," the others repeated before rocking back onto their haunches.

"Now bring me the prisoner," bin Wahhab said barely audibly, but in a voice of one accustomed to commanding respect and deference.

The three other men leaped to their feet and trotted back across the rubble. They returned momentarily, dragging a semi-conscious, bloodied, battered man who appeared more dead than alive. The hapless creature was thrown roughly at the feet of bin Wahhab. From his supine position, he gazed up through swollen eyes at the imposing Arab. A rifle butt slammed into his head as a reminder not to look upon 'The Chosen One'.

"Be careful," bin Wahhab admonished his eager follower, "I do not wish to kill him just yet. Soon the sun will sink behind the mountains. We will eat on this spot and spend the rest of the night here, under the moonlight, on this hard and broken ground so that the evil of our enemies will be impressed upon our minds and bodies for all our days."

The full moon had risen well above the saw-toothed mountain ridges by the time they finished eating. Its soft white glow snaked through the crags and crevices, filling the valley with twisted spectral shapes. Over an open fire, a battered coffeepot hung by its handle from a jury-rigged scaffolding of charred, splintered wood.

Bin Wahhab, slowly sipping from a cup of coffee, sat several feet away from his disciples.

"I say we strike again at one of their Muslim lackeys," said one of them, an unusually burly man for a son of the desert.

"Yes, Talil, you are right," responded the man to his left, more diminutive in frame, but every bit as impressive in facial attributes, the main feature of which was a prominent aquiline nose. "We must reclaim the blessed lands of Islam. Those of the faith who defend the Great Satan are not true believers and deserve to feel the sword of Allah."

"The cowards. They hide behind the skirts of the Americans." He glanced with contempt at the crumpled figure of the prisoner. "And the Americans send cruise missiles to do their fighting. They are not men. At least the Russians sent men," Talil growled.

"That is why the Americans send the missiles," blurted the third man, Fawaz bin Sufya, the wiriest and darkest of the group, sitting cross-legged to Talil's right, "because Talil, they saw how you annihilated the Russians."

All three men laughed, their eyes searching bin Wahhab for a sign of approval. Receiving no reaction from their leader, they fell silent, staring pensively into the crackling fire.

Finally, Talil, his resounding bass voice bouncing off the looming mountain-sides, spoke.

"What say you, Mahdi? Shall we strike our daggers deeper into the hearts of the traitorous Muslim puppets? Shall we attack the House of Saud?"

Again they were met with silence, as dark as the shadows that very nearly concealed bin Wahhab.

The diminutive hawk-nosed one, known as Abu Yusuf, stirred the waning fire with a twig. The other two stared unblinking at the renewed leaping of the flames.

"No," bin Wahhab replied quietly.

All three faces, contorted by the illumination of the fire, spun to face their leader.

"No?" Talil gasped. "You do not want to carry the struggle forward? I—we—do not understand."

"Ah, Talil, my faithful servant. No one is braver in battle," bin Wahhab continued in his soft tone. "But there are forces at work in this world that are greater than perhaps you can imagine. Forces that began with the prophet Muhammed fourteen hundred years ago and are culminating in our lifetime. Forces that, through no wish of my own, have devolved upon me to fulfill. But I am a Muslimin, a 'surrender' to the true faith of Islam and thus I must surrender myself to these forces.

"The *Sharia*, the path, that the Blessed One used to bring me personally to his service began one hundred years ago. It is a tale that I have carried with me all my life but have never spoken of. Would you wish to hear it?"

"By all means," Talil responded eagerly. "And perhaps our friend here from the CIA would also enjoy it."

"Yes, bring him closer, and make sure he is still awake."

Using the strength of just one arm, Talil seized the captive by his blood-matted shirt and dragged him across the fire, scattering sparks and ashes, before depositing him in front of bin Wahhab. In spite of the searing, the CIA agent did not cry out.

"Perhaps he is dead?" Talil sighed, disappointedly.

"This should rouse him," bin Sufya said, splashing a cup of hot coffee on the prone man's face. A cry of pain reassured them that their victim was still in this world.

"Good. Then I will proceed," bin Wahhab said softly, sonorously. "You well know the story of the Prophet Muhammed's flight from Mecca to Yathrib."

"Yes, the Hajj," Talil said, his eyes glowing, reflecting the dancing flames of the campfire." The Quraish clan in the holy city of Mecca was plotting his assassination."

"Of course, we all know this story," blurted Abu. "How the Jews in Yathrib also turned against the Prophet, so that our people no longer bow to Jerusalem in prayer."

"But rather to Mecca—" Fawaz interjected.

"To Mecca—that is the key," bin Wahhab said, his voice becoming stronger, more commanding.

"After dealing with the Jews in Yathrib, Muhammed marched upon Mecca, where he put his foes to flight, destroyed their idols around the sacred mosque of the Kaaba and proclaimed Mecca the Holy City of Islam. And of course Yathrib, from whence he began his glorious march, was honored with the name of Medina al Nabi—the City of the Prophet.

"Allah be praised," his three disciples muttered, almost simultaneously.

"Now I must bring you forward in time, to the turn of this century when a similar event occurred—an event that was predestined by Allah to use me as his instrument in bringing about the final triumph of Islam."

The others fell silent, becoming mute reflections of the pale moonlight.

"And now I wish our CIA friend to pay especially close attention," bin Wahhab said, seizing the prisoner by the scalp hair and raising, then dropping his head. "One hundred years ago, my ancestors lived in their ancient and rightful home of Riyadh. However, their rivals, the Rashid clan, forced them from their houses, threatening to kill them. My great-grandfather, like the Prophet Muhammed, was forced to flee. Then ten years of age, he traveled in a Damask bag slung from the side of his father's camel. His elder sister balanced his weight in a bag on the opposite side of the beast, bouncing and rocking to the swaying gait.

"For two years my ancestors roamed, homeless and impoverished on the fringes of the endless desert the southerners call the Rub al Khali—the 'Empty Quarter.'

"Finally, they were taken under the wing of the Al Sabah family in Kuwait Town. There my great-grandfather grew into manhood, honing his skills, becoming strong in body, mind and faith. Often he would venture outside of the gates of the town to sit on a little hillock in the desert where he would gaze toward Riyadh while scraping plans in the sand with his camel stick.

"Then, in his twenty-first year, his sand drawings hardened and became real. He conceived of the impossible. With a band of only two dozen faithfuls, he attacked Riyadh. It was at night, but not such as this, for it was the end of Ramadan and the moon was but a sliver of a crescent. They threw an old palm tree against the wall of the town, scrambled to the top and dropped noiselessly inside the town. There they waited until the muezzin's call from the minaret of a nearby mosque signaled the first rays of dawn.

"When their enemies appeared in the streets, they charged, shouting 'God is Great!' The Rashid clan was shocked, befuddled. The fight was furious but brief. Many Rashids descended into Hell that morning, including their leader, whom my great grandfather beheaded. With this very sword."

Bin Wahhab reached behind his back and produced a long, broad, curving scimitar. "At age twenty-one," he said, running his thumb along the blade's cutting edge," by his daring and faith, my ancestor had struck the enemy and slain him where he lived, restoring his people's rightful place in Allah's eyes.

"Perhaps, Talil, you may now better understand my answer to your question, and the answer to a much greater question posed to us."

Talil stared blankly at bin Wahhab. The big man had enjoyed listening to the story and learning something of the sheikh's ancestors, but was blissfully unaware of any further meaning to be gained from the tale.

Abu Yusuf, however, nodded and leaned toward his leader.

"If I am to understand you, sheikh, you mean to follow in the footsteps of the Prophet and your great-grandfather—to take the war not to the Saudis or the other Muslim lackeys but directly to our greatest of enemies—in the place where he lives!"

Bin Wahhab did not reply. The moon had arced to its zenith so that its light now suffused him in an opalescent glow. He sat still, the sword lying across his lap.

"Can you tell us of the plans that you have drawn in the sand, like those of your great-grandfather?" Abu asked after a momentary silence.

Bin Wahhab straightened the folds of his robe that lay over his crossed legs.

"I cannot tell you the details at this time. Only know that the hand of Allah is already writing, and once written, Allah's will cannot be undone. As we speak, a man is being brought into our fold, one who is 'Death, the Destroyer of Worlds.' I will fashion him into my instrument so that, in one stroke, our most hated enemy will perish by the hundreds of thousands, even millions. Countless more will be maimed, burned, and broken in body and spirit. On their lips as they descend into their graves will be the name of Abdul bin Wahhab."

As he spoke, he raised the scimitar high over his head.

"My faithfuls, the long-awaited Holy War, the Jihad, has now begun and I am the Mahdi, the Chosen One who will wield the terrible sword of death and destruction."

With a swift arm motion, the scimitar whirled downward, bringing the CIA agent's misery to an end.

Chapter Five

The ringing in Mike Falcon's head was becoming louder and more insistent. Wishing he had never drunk that second double scotch, he rolled to his side and covered his head with his pillow. For a brief moment the irritating clang ceased, only to abruptly restart, jolting him from his dream world. Coming to his senses but without opening his eyes, he groped for a book, shoe, or other handy object to fling at the irritating noise. Before he succeded in finding a projectile, however, the ringing was replaced by the sound of a man's voice.

"Mike, get the hell out of your rack and pick up the damned phone. This is Jensen. We've got a situation here."

Falcon swung his feet onto the teak deck, barely missing the hindquarters of his black Labrador retriever, who always slept at the foot of the aft cabin berth.

"Situation" was a word that was used very rarely in the business, as it denoted the highest level of importance or peril. Rick Jensen, his colleague at the NSA would not have employed the term indiscriminately. Falcon stumbled through the galley of his forty-seven foot ketch, splashing his face with cold water from the sink, on his way to the phone that hung above the navigation table. He grasped the receiver just as Jensen was about to hang up.

"Rick, I'm here...what time is it?"

"After ten already. Are you alone?"

"Yeah...unless you're willing to count Jocko," Falcon replied, glancing at his Lab, who had resumed sleeping.

"Oh, I can see you got lucky again last night," Rick laughed. "Listen you need to come in right now. Meet me at Twelve-0-Seven Old Chain Bridge Road in Great Falls. Do you need directions?"

"No...I can find it, but it'll take about an hour from Annapolis."

"The sooner the better. Bring your NSA badge. And Mike...it's not pretty."

The receiver clicked, followed by the hum of a disconnect tone.

Falcon mulled over the address as he hung up the receiver. Turning, he whistled softly to the Lab, who responded by leaping to its feet.

"No time for games this morning, buddy. You're on your own. Go!"

The dog, bony paw-nails clicking on the hardwood deck, scampered through the galley and clambered up the ladder leading topside.

A few minutes later, having hastily donned jeans and a blue workshirt, Falcon followed the same route, emerging into the sunlight and a neatly arranged cockpit. He paused momentarily, scanning the length of the whitewashed teak-trimmed deck, even now not losing an opportunity to appreciate the aesthetics of his ship as well as its seaworthiness. *Stardust* had borne him through many tests of wind and sea, not the least of which was a China Sea typhoon. He was himself rather a human incarnation of his ship—slightly weathered now in his late forties, and sturdily, yet trimly constructed.

He hopped the two feet from the deck—it was high tide in the Chesapeake Bay—onto the pier. Jocko was sitting patiently on the dock, hoping that perhaps he would not be left behind. His ears dropped, however, at Falcon's words "Jock, you guard." He lay down and watched despondently as his master jumped into the jeep and sped off.

The trees had just begun their annual metamorphoses in northern Virginia, donning their regal scarlet, purple and gold cloaks. With the

Potomac River as a backdrop, Old Georgetown Pike leading into Great Falls had become a showcase for autumn's majestic transformation. Now however, the show was somewhat gaudier, as blue and red twirling lights sitting atop several Fairfax County police cars reflected off the shimmering leaves.

Falcon downshifted, letting the jeep roll slowly to a stop across the street from his destination. He had barely alighted from the vehicle when he was confronted by a frowning black-uniformed policeman, lightly tapping a baton in his palm. The officer was about to command Falcon to move along when a civilian intervened.

"It's all right," the mustachioed, slightly corpulent man said, motioning Mike to step over the yellow police crime-scene tape. "He's with me."

Falcon displayed his NSA badge to the disgruntled officer and followed his colleague, Rick Jensen, through a clutch of police officers milling around the grounds and up to a massive, white columned, Italian brick mansion.

"We picked up the Fairfax County police call-in on the scanner. I almost beat the little buggers here," Jensen said circumspectly as they entered the marble foyer. Falcon noticed a set of keys in a glass container sitting atop a Corinthian pedestal. There were yet more police officers inside the mansion than on the grounds, prompting Falcon to wonder if the whole Fairfax County Police Department were here. Beyond the foyer, the interior of the house was in a shambles. Furniture was overturned, cushion padding was ripped open, foam rubber was scattered in hacked fragments, bronze statues were smashed, lying in disfigured shards.

"The domestic called it in. That's her over there," Jensen said, nodding in the direction of a sobbing middle-aged Hispanic woman who was being comforted by two female officers. "Unless she's told otherwise, she comes in every Saturday morning at eight to make breakfast and clean up the prior night's mess."

"No wonder she's crying," Falcon said surveying the ruin.

With Falcon in tow, Jensen chugged across the foyer, past the sunken living room and mahogany bar and down a long corridor.

"Who's the big shot?" Falcon quipped.

Jensen paused at the foot of a spiral staircase.

"Damn, Mike, I thought you knew when you arrived. It's Slater."

Falcon whistled softly. "I was just with him last evening."

"Yeah, we know. And it won't be long before the Fairfax cops and the FBI do too. Which reminds me—the Bureau agents are already here. Now, I know how you feel—"

"The Fucking Bureau of Idiots," Falcon blurted.

"—but we need these guys right now. Try to be civil. Also, I wouldn't volunteer any information just yet about your whereabouts last night. By the way, you do have an alibi, right?"

Falcon pushed Jensen's back and they continued winding upwards on the spiral staircase. At the head of the stairs, and all along the corridor leading into the master bedroom, business-like FBI agents were dusting white powder on handrails, doorknobs and walls. More agents were performing similar tasks inside the bedroom, leaving no ashtray, drawer handle, brass tissue holder, or other conceivable fingerprint candidate unsprinkled.

"Make sure you get every side of the frame of that painting," a brown-suited man, shorter in stature, but clearly higher in command, barked. "And for crissakes, be careful. It's original."

Falcon nudged Jensen. "A Dali. What do you think that's worth?"

Jensen shrugged, then noted that a wall safe had been found behind the painting. Its lock had been blown open by a small plastique charge and the contents, if any, had been pilfered.

"Ah, Mr. Jensen, you're back," the diminutive agent-in-charge said, with ill-disguised lack of enthusiasm. "And I see you've brought reinforcements."

"Agent Burke here is honcho-ing the investigation," Jensen informed his 'reinforcement.'

Falcon extended his hand to the FBI man, who took it with studied reluctance.

"We've got things under control," he growled. "No need for you boys to hang around. It's a beautiful fall day. Why don't you get up a game of tag football or take the families for a picnic?"

"Why don't you kiss—," Falcon began.

"Mike, you need to see this," Jensen interrupted, pulling his colleague away from the glowering agent.

Falcon followed Jensen's lead deeper into the room. The area was as thoroughly violated as the rest of the house, but was distinguishable in one very important aspect. There, spread eagle on a king-size circular bed, with his swollen, blackened tongue dangling to one side and his protruding eyes staring vacantly into space, lay the purple-white corpse of the master of the house.

A burst of light from just over his left shoulder startled Falcon. He stepped back as the Bureau photographer circled toward the head of the bed and flashed another photograph.

"Take a look for yourself," Jensen said. "It's really quite interesting."

Falcon moved toward the bed, scrutinizing the lifeless shell of the now permanently terminated president of Micratom Inc. At one point, absorbed in thought, his gaze followed that of the vacant eyes upward, until he caught his reflection in the overhead mirror. Falcon then stood and crossed the room to a large bay window overlooking the smoothly flowing Potomac some two hundred feet below. Jensen joined him.

"The river's pretty low," Falcon said.

"Yeah, not much rain this past August."

Jensen glanced back toward the bed, the purposeful FBI investigators, and Agent Burke, who was issuing an order to a subordinate in the hallway.

"They can't hear us, Mike. So, what do you make of it?"

"Clear cut," Falcon replied. "Sex, murder, and robbery. I bet that's their take on it."

"Yep."

"Except you and I know differently."

"Yep."

Falcon continued to gaze at the slowly coursing Potomac below. Occasionally the smooth flow, encountering partly submerged gray boulders or the finger-like projections of a drowned tree, would erupt into little white ripples.

Then, surprising Jensen by a sudden movement away from the window he said, "You stick around here and keep an eye on these guys. I need to follow up on a couple of things."

As Falcon walked swiftly toward the doorway, Jensen called after him, "Where can I reach you?"

"I'll be at the Worm's office," Falcon shouted back just before he disappeared from sight.

*   *   *

The day of the week, the hour of the day was a triviality to the Worm. He was invariably ensconced in his ten-by-twelve cubicle at NSA Headquarters in Fort Meade, Maryland, making love to his computers. There, collecting the most insignificant bits of data and, churning the information through the NSA's classified electronic files—the largest such depository in the world, including that of the CIA's—he would solve the most arcane and seemingly insoluble puzzles. It provided him a thrill that nothing else could match, but then he had never had a woman.

Known affectionately, in fact, reverently, for his uncanny ability to burrow anywhere into cyberspace, this twenty-five year old MIT dropout was the recognized master of the computer blackworld. Surrounded by drooping and fallen stacks of software manuals, computer magazines, physics books, dirty laundry, cereal boxes, empty Coke cans, and a few unwashed cups, he was bent intently before his computer screen. In the last square foot of clear space, hovering over the Worm's shoulder, stood Mike Falcon.

"Try brown hair," Falcon said, staring at the screen's color image of a female face.

The Worm pressed a button on the keyboard and the blonde gradually transformed to a brunette. He then prompted another computer sitting to his left, causing innumerable lines of data to flash dizzily across the screen.

"One hundred, ninety-six hits," the Worm said, after the flickering ceased.

Falcon whistled softly. "Download just the eastern Europeans."

"Fifty-two," the Worm shortly repeated.

"O.K., let me have that print-out along with the earlier info. Now for the hard part."

"Micratom?" the Worm tittered, "Piece of cake. The system hasn't been built that I can't hack."

In preciously few instances could such an utterance be anything other than bravado. Here, it was a simple statement of truth. While the computer to his left had been processing the information that Falcon wanted concerning 'Cherisse Tigere,' the Worm had been preparing a third computer on his right to invade the archives of Micratom Inc.

"Just as I figured. We're already at the firewall," he snickered, gazing at the screen. "Could be a packet-type. That examines both the source and destination addresses of every bit of data going through the company's network. It uses a cryptographic identifier to block unauthorized packets from entering. Well, good for them. They're not completely tech-illiterate over at Micratom. They've gone beyond the packet technology and have a set up more sophisticated application-level type wall."

"Is that a problem?"

The Worm tossed Falcon a quizzical look.

"Sorry," Mike said.

"Problems do not exist in my vocabulary. Instead I recognize entertainment levels. And this will be extremely entertaining. The application firewall raises the bar by scanning the incoming data so that even if you beat the cryptographic ID, it reads the substance of your message. It spots abnormalities, like detecting a fox in the chicken coop. It then shunts the fox into an empty coop. But that's not the end of it for the poor fox. Now the inquisition begins, and the fox is forced to give up its secrets—like where it came from. That's why we need to set up a root kit."

"A what?"

"Think of it as a Trojan Horse. It hides us when we get inside the wall. I wrote my own kit, just to be certain. I've been inside, let me think, one thousand two-hundred and some walls so far and have never been detected. And, in the one chance in a billion that we get sniffed out, my program will destroy our identity and all evidence of our break-in. It's one hell of a rush being inside, you know."

Falcon was slightly disconcerted by the rhapsodic expression on the boy wonder's face.

"Just a few more minutes and we'll be ready to go," the Worm continued, becoming more effusive as his excitement grew. "Some people like to slide up and over, others like to try to jam it right in. How Neanderthal in this day and age! They almost never get in. We're going to finesse our way in."

His fingertips fluttered over the keyboard as his face moved closer to the computer. It seemed to Falcon that the Worm was actually attempting to peer through the screen, into the virtual world of electrons and photons that lay beyond.

"O.K.!" the Worm exclaimed, stiffening, "the kit's up and we're going in. First we transmit a premature FIN flag. For your info, Falcon, that means finish flag. Every transmission is completed with a FIN flag. By sending a premature flag, we might get a stray modem to send a reset response. Because the flag was sent out of sequence, our hacking is not recorded in their computer log. Are you with me?"

"Just do it", Falcon responded, shaking his head.

"Right. Waiting for the reset package...bingo! Getting the RST response...now for the receiver protocol...good...good...excellent! Activating the war dialer...that calls each of the extensions in Micratom's phone system, looking for a negligently left open modem... scanning...scanning...got a stray modem here...we're probing it...go...go...bang! Gotcha!"

The Worm, perspiring and breathing heavily, pushed back from the computer.

"We're in?" Falcon asked.

The Worm simply nodded.

"Need a cigarette after that?"

"What?"

"Nothing. Now, please get me into Slater's private files."

Wiping his brow with his sleeve, the Worm bent toward the machine again.

"Slater...Slater, James A.," he intoned as he pressed the down arrow and scrolled through the Micratom personnel roster. "Got it."

Falcon, too, now leaned forward.

"Clever man," the Worm said. "He's got his own separate fire wall. Looks like a byte-code verifier. Oh, this is going to be fun. But we must stroke this one very gently or she'll...damn!"

"What?"

The Worm sunk back in his chair.

"She's good," he smiled, his eyes sparkling. "Bounced me right out of there on the first try. This one will require a little more thought."

The Worm reset his program and tried again, only to be rebuffed a second, third, and fourth time.

"This is harder because there's no stray modem to tap into. She's locked up tight as a drum."

"Can we use a different approach?"

"Yeah, give me his password, and I'll get us in. Other than that, it's going to take some time."

"Do what you can," Falcon said, just as the pager on his belt beeped. "Where's your phone?" he asked, noting the indicated number on the pager.

"On the floor, under one of those stacks, over there somewhere," the Worm waved his arm, his eyes remaining fixed on the computer screen.

Falcon rooted through several piles of magazines before finally uncovering a promising cord. It led, as hoped, to the telephone and he punched in the number for the Annapolis City Docks Marina.

"Chester," the gravelly voice of the marina manager answered.

"Chet, this is Mike…you called me?"

"Yeah, Mike. Just wanted to let you know that some gorgeous blonde gal was poking around your vessel. Thought maybe yuh screwed up agin and forgot yuh had a date," Chester said in his heavy Eastern Shore twang.

"Chet, have you seen Jocko?" Mike asked in a fearful tone.

"Oh, yeah, that ol' scamp is beggin' at our door as usual."

"Good. Do me a favor and keep him at your place. And don't go near my boat. I'm on my way."

He hung up, placing the phone on the nearest stable stack of books.

"I'll get back to you," he said hurriedly to the Worm as he turned to leave. "Almost forgot…." He reached into his wallet, extracting a smudged business card. "See if you can find any prints besides mine on this. Ignore the phone number. It doesn't exist."

The number didn't, but Cherisse Tigere did, whatever her real name is, Falcon thought motoring east on Route 50. He opened the glove compartment, removed a fully loaded Glock M34 and laid the weapon on the passenger seat.

Chapter Six

Sirens pierced the still night air as fire engines sped down Smolensky Prospect, careened around the tight corner that marked Gorky Street and screeched to a halt at the foot of Medved's apartment building.

The first part of his plan had worked better than expected. Maybe some things had improved since the demise of the Worker's Paradise, he mused. It had taken only eight minutes for Fire Engine Brigade Number Seventeen to respond to his triggering of the building's alarm system. Holding a smoldering rag against the smoke detector in his kitchen was the easy part. Now came the much more difficult element—the one that would determine whether he would escape with his daughter or appear in *Izvestya's* obituaries as another tireless servant of the Motherland struck down in the prime of life.

The hall beyond his door was already filled with the sounds of bewildered, scurrying people. He knew that they would not all be streaming down the staircase, seeking refuge outdoors from an unseen conflagration. No. A certain few would be flowing upstream, pressing against the human tide, heading directly for his door. There, these unwanted visitors would be confronted by a barricade consisting of a wooden table, a sofa, and four chairs; that is, every stick of furniture that he owned. He knew that it would present only a temporary hindrance, but it might buy him just the few precious moments he needed.

Peering from his living room window, three floors above the street, he glimpsed the sight of the discombobulated tenants—a jumble of robes and pajamas—intermingled with rushing, purposeful black-slickered firemen.

To his delight, he noted that one of the fire engines was parked almost directly below his window.

"*Ey, droog!*" he shouted to a tall fireman who was alighting from the rear of the truck. "Friend," he repeated, "can you send that ladder up here—we're trapped!"

"Can you not get through the hallway?" the heavy-set firefighter responded, gazing up towards Medved.

"No, too much smoke—and I have a young daughter—you must hurry if we are to save her!"

"*Harasho*, sir—o.k.!"

The lanky man seized two of his colleagues who happened to be scampering by at the moment and turned them to the business of the ladder.

Medved retreated from the window and strode stealthily past the furniture piled at the door. As yet, there was no sound, no ominous click or scrape from that direction that would have announced the presence of the uninvited guest.

"Come, Galena," he said, reaching down to his daughter. She clasped his strong, rough hand, using his strength to pull herself upright.

It was then that the doorknob turned, clicking once. Twice.

"Go to the window," he whispered. "As soon as the ladder appears, climb down. Do not look back!"

"But, papa, I'm afraid…."

"Of course. So am I. That's why I'm sending you first—to see if you make it. If you don't break your bones, then I'll go too."

"Oh, papa," she smirked, rolling her eyes upward, her fear dissipating.

"Now go!" he commanded, pushing her away.

She obediently hurried through the darkened apartment to the moon-bathed window.

Another click of the doorknob was followed by a scraping noise in the doorjamb. Medved, reaching behind his back for the *Gurza*, moved slowly away from the door. Several seconds of silence ensued in which he was not even conscious of the cacophony of voices, sirens, and engines in the street below. All his senses were focused on the barely discernible objects that barricaded his door.

Suddenly, with a muffled thud, the stack of furniture trembled. Another blow—much louder and more forceful—was followed by a cracking sound as the door buckled.

He glanced quickly over his shoulder toward the window. Galena was on the sill, grasping the top rung of the ladder.

His head snapped around at the sound of metal clattering to the floor. The doorknob had been shot away, the report of the gun quashed by a silencer.

Safe to say that you're not with the fire brigade, he thought as he directed his pistol toward the door and squeezed the trigger. Three times, in rapid succession, the *Gurza* jerked in his clenched hands. A cry, more of surprise than pain, followed by a dull crash, emanated from the hallway.

He glanced toward the window. It was empty. In the next moment, he was on the sill, gazing at the milling crowed below. A noiseless hail of bullets now shattered the door, table, sofa and chairs, spewing splinters of wood throughout the room. By the time the intruders burst in, he had slid down the rungs, jumping the last several meters to the ground.

Swooping up Galena, who had been anxiously awaiting him at the base of the ladder, he greeted the firefighter responsible for their rescue.

"Thanks, friend," he said dashing by, his daughter held in one arm. Without pausing, he ran to a car parked a few paces away. The Zhiguli 4-door sedan was topped by two rotating red lights and the door

Medved yanked open read *Pozharnaya Komanda—Marshal*. Plopping Galena in the passenger seat, he raced around the front of the auto and slipped into the driver's side. To his considerable relief, the Fire Brigade Marshal had left the keys in the ignition.

Ignoring the startled yells directed at him from some nearby firefighters, he turned the key and the engine popped to life. The Zhiguli lurched forward as he pressed the accelerator, its tires screeching in free spin before biting onto the hard macadam surface of the street. As they sped away, Medved adjusted the rear view mirror, which now reflected the emergence from the apartment building of three black-clad, obviously distraught men. He flicked off the rotating beacons, swung the wheel to the right at the intersection of Gorky Street and Smolensky Prospect and stomped the accelerator to the floor.

* * *

The house on Pushkin Hill, in sharp contrast to his own dilapidated tenement complex, stood majestically, quietly, in the soft moonlight. A hundred meters away, Medved cut the engine and headlights, letting the Zhiguli drift almost noiselessly to a stop. For several minutes, he sat motionless, listening and observing.

"*Harasho, goloobcheek*," he said to Galena, who had curled her knees to her chin and dozed off, exhausted by the evening's fast-paced events. "We get out here."

A few minutes later, Medved, cradling his daughter in his arms, was standing before the double door of the imposing house. First one, then two, then three lights illuminated windows above him and on the ground floor as he pressed the doorbell button. Voices in the vestibule were soon accompanied by the shuffling of shoes approaching. A short pause was followed by the click of the door latch releasing.

"General Aksanov," Medved said, greeting the bespectacled, white-haired somewhat portly man who opened the door. Although he was the civilian Director of the FSB, the officers who had served under him in Afghanistan still affectionately accorded Aksanov the respect of his former rank.

"Medved, what is...? Come in, come in."

Aksanov's wife, Ludmilla, emerged from behind her husband, her wrinkled, kindly face expressing agitation and concern at the sight of Galena.

"She's o.k.," Medved said. "Just a bit sleepy. It's been quite a night."

"I'll take her," the elderly lady smiled. "I'm sure you have business to discuss with my husband." She led Galena by the hand into the kitchen.

"So what would drive my Travel Section Director to such a profession-terminating move of waking his boss up in the middle of the night?" Aksanov said as he and Medved deposited themselves in two large leather-covered chairs in the General's den. The room was twice the size of Sergei's "home office", yet still intimate. An Afghan tapestry on one wall, a brick fireplace in another. Over the fireplace mantle hung a late 19th century Martini-Henry rifle, the weapon of choice of the Afghans in their war against British colonialism. The weapon of choice for the late 20th century bureaucrat—the computer—was nowhere in evidence, however. Instead, the Director's working habits were evident in the presence of several books, a pad of writing paper, and two pens that all resided neatly in their assigned places on a cherrywood desk.

"Something very important is happening, General," Medved began in a low, grave tone. "Something significant enough to cause an attempt on my life tonight—simply because I had accessed a file."

He paused, then added, "Alexander Marenkov is missing."

The FSB Director turned noticeably ashen.

"Go on," he said dryly.

Medved recounted the events of the day and evening, trying to include every detail that he could remember. In the event that he met with a sudden 'cardiac failure' in the near future, at least the highest levels of Russian intelligence would have the information that the assassins wished to suppress.

When he had completed his tale, Aksanov rose and stepped to his desk where he seized two glass tumblers and a brandy snifter that were hidden behind the books.

"Ludmilla doesn't approve," he winked, grinning mischievously. He poured the clear peach-hued liquid into the tumblers, one of which he passed to Medved.

Settling again into his chair, he permitted himself an extended draught of the brandy.

"An unsettling train of events," he finally spoke. "What do you make of it, Major?"

Medved slowly shook his head.

"As far as the Professor's disappearance, I have little to go on. It's there, in his file. I just don't see it yet."

"Yes, It is peculiar. And the assassins?"

"God knows. Perhaps the GRU, maybe the FIS. It could even be our own people in the FSB. That's why we have computers now. With the loss of centralized control, all the splinter groups need them just to track each other."

"We must never slide back to the KGB," Aksanov spoke firmly. "Never."

"I fully agree. It's just that, in matters such as this, it is exceedingly more difficult to understand objectives and to know who are the Tatars and who are the Tsar's soldiers."

"I understand. Tell me. Do you think it might be the work of the Feliks?"

Medved hoped that he had masked his surprise at the Director's utterance of that word. The Feliks, a rumored shadow organization of disgruntled KGB and Defense Ministry—GRU—officers, was never discussed openly. Surely this was not a casual slip. He contemplated Aksanov's motive.

"Ah, the Feliks," Medved laughed. "Our favorite punching bag when we have no real answers."

"Quite," Aksanov smiled, his eyes mirthless. "All right then. We must address ourselves to the present situation. You'll stay here until morning. Then you'll ride with me to the Lubianka headquarters. Once your would-be assassins realize that you have made contact with me, they will assume that your information concerning Marenkov has been successfully transferred to the upper echelons of the Service. I should think that would greatly reduce their fascination for you. However, as a precaution, I will assign one of my best people to look after you and to work with you on this case."

Medved brightened. "You mean I am to lead the investigation?"

"Yes, I'm sending you back into the wet world, as you old Chekists so quaintly phrase it. After all, it falls within your department, you stumbled on it, and you've come this far already."

Medved felt his pulse racing. At last—escape from that mundane desk job and that loathsome stinking computer screen. Back to the front line. Almost simultaneously with this elation, his thoughts were tempered by another consideration.

"My daughter…Galena…."

"Don't worry. We'll put her in a *Byezo*," Aksanov said, using the cryptic FSB term for a *Dome Byezopasnee*, or 'Safe House'. "She'll be tutored, she'll still have ballet and a whole troupe of new friends—and, of course, round the clock protection of the Service. Now, I'll show you to a bedroom. You can still get a few hours sleep before we head for the Lubianka."

Medved, his head swimming in the events of the past evening, then floating in the possibilities of the future, gulped the last swallow of his brandy and, sensing the onslaught of sleep, followed his old commanding officer from the den.

* * *

Viktor Buzhkin was a concrete block of a man, whose gravelly voice aptly suited his chiseled face. Before embarking on his career, first with the commando unit—*Spetsnaz*—and then the Federal Security Service, he had been a legendary Russian athlete. In the international circles of Greco-Roman wrestling, where only the toughest of the tough need apply, he was known as the "Siberian Nightmare". The sobriquet was somewhat due to his record of having never been defeated throughout his career, and partially based on the seven consecutive world heavyweight championships and three Olympiads which he had won. But for the most part, the nickname was a recognition of the fact that resisting his throws and holds often resulted in his adversary's broken limbs or torn muscles. In the final defense of his Olympic Gold Medal, his victories had come laughably easy as every one of his opponents, including the highly regarded Silver Medalist from Turkey, had opted to be quickly pinned rather than risk permanent injury.

"*Bozha moy*," Medved had winced upon first meeting this 'one of my best people' that the General had foisted on him. Buzhkin had barely stitched together two sentences since their introduction at the Lubianka earlier in the morning, through their review of intelligence concerning the missing Professor, and the questioning of Marenkov's wife, Marianna, that ended a few hours later.

Now, in the early afternoon, they had begun the tedious task of interviewing students and faculty at Moscow University. Even with the window fully open, the interviewing room was sweltering and rank as nervous academics sought to find the answers that would most quickly obtain their exit from the FSB agents.

After the departure of the tenth interviewee, Medved proposed that they break for some fresh air.

"*Harasho*," Buzhkin nodded. "I noticed a *lafka* across the street. I'll get us a bite to eat and meet you in the park."

Medved agreed, marveling at his colleague's loquacity.

Exiting the university, Buzhkin ambled across the street to the grocery store and Medved settled on a park bench. Seated across from him, a burly old man was flicking sunflower seeds to a busily pecking flock of pigeons and wrens.

"Some heat wave, eh, *starozheel,*" Medved said.

Seryozha sprinkled another handful of the birdfeed to the ground before looking up.

"Who are you calling old-timer," he said gruffly. "You *malcheeskas* don't know anything. You haven't lived. I was with Surchenko's Rifle Brigade when you were still only a wet dream."

"I meant no offense."

"Pah. I know. I've been out of sorts lately."

"The heat will do that."

"Hmph. If it were only that simple."

The old soldier ceased distributing seeds and let his hands droop on his thighs.

"Are you all right, uncle?" Medved asked.

Seryozha perked up. "Ah, my friend used to call me uncle. But now he's gone."

Medved straightened, scrutinizing this robust *starozheel* as he leaned towards him.

"Your friend?"

"Yes...Professor Marenkov. I believe I may have been his only friend. We used to meet here everyday for lunch—weather permitting of course. Let me think it's been—pah—my memory fails me—maybe twenty years now. But lately, he seemed very occupied. Not himself."

"When did you last see him?"

"Perhaps three, no, four days ago. Monday, yes, I'm sure it was Monday."

Only two days before the FSB report of Marenkov's disappearance had landed on his desk, Medved reflected.

"Do you recall anything out of the ordinary, anything he might have said to you?"

"Well, as I said, he was preoccupied. Even agitated. We talked about the battle of Moscow. He always enjoyed hearing my tales of the War to Save the Motherland. That was it."

In his peripheral view, Medved noted that Buzhkin was approaching, carrying a cardboard box filled with food and drinks.

"Nothing else?" he said, his gazed fixed unwaveringly on the old man.

"No. Nothing. I liked him very much. He was not like all the others who have forgotten the sacrifices made by their fathers and grandfathers."

To Medved's dismay, the old-timer lapsed into a pensive silence. He had hoped to elicit information—a clue of any sort—before Buzhkin arrived. Now his partner was crossing the street and would join them momentarily.

"There was one thing," Seryozha said, obviously wrestling with his memory. Buzhkin had entered the park and was now only a few dozen paces away.

"He was to meet a colleague somewhere…in the country…I can't remember…wait now…It's that place where the writer is buried."

"The writer? Which one?"

"Pah! The name escapes me. He wrote about that doctor in the Revolution…I was a young lad then in St. Petersburg, you know…."

"Pasternak!" Medved interjected. "He's buried in Peredelkino."

"Hm? Peredelkino! That's it," Seryozha said, beaming at his ability to recall Medved's parting words.

"Thank you, my friend. Now I want you to promise me that you will not mention this to anyone else. If you are questioned by other officials, I want you to call me immediately. Ask for Sergei Medved—at the FSB."

At that moment, Buzhkin arrived with his box of refreshments.

"It's too hot here in the open sun," Medved said. "Let's move to that bench under the oak tree."

Buzhkin nodded in agreement, glancing briefly at the old man before walking to the oak. The old soldier ignored him as he resumed feeding his patiently waiting birds.

"You know, Viktor, I think we have done all we can today. After we eat, we'll return to the Lubianka and make our report to Aksanov."

"Fine," Buzhkin said, biting into a slice of black bread piled high with salmon, tomatoes and black peas.

"And, oh, yes. We'll have to postpone further investigation for one day. I'm moving my daughter from one school to another tomorrow, and if you're a parent, you know what a bureaucratic nightmare that is."

"I'm not a parent," Buzhkin said, without interrupting his chewing.

Medved wondered if the fiction had done more harm than good. Aksanov may very well have revealed to one of his 'best people' that Galena was being placed in a safe house. Yet, there was no sense in blurting such information to a near perfect stranger.

The two men ate in silence, never once even looking at each other.

Chapter Seven

"He's up. He's waking up."

Alexander Marenkov, hearing the voices, struggled to open his eyes. He knew that he was lying on his back, but had no concept of whether it was day or night, or how long he had lain there. His thoughts raced, trying frantically to reestablish coherency, to reconstruct the recent events of his life that were frustratingly shrouded in mist. Yes. Now he began to recall. Peredelkino. The black-earth farmer. The mineral water, followed by unconsciousness; the poet-spouting peasant was more than he seemed, after all.

Then what was it—the moon. Bright—as radiant as the light that now glared in his eyes. And then, his assailant. The man was known to him, but try as he might, he could not make the connection. And there were others, speaking strange words, not Russian. The sound of an engine. He had been moving then, over a dusty, bumpy road. The sharp odor of diesel fuel had filled his nostrils, the chugging drone of a truck motor had resonated in his ears. After some time, he had no idea how long, its steady hum was replaced by a much larger roar. Even in his semi-conscious state, he was certain it had been an airplane. But now, this glaring overhead light was burning his eyes and he was aware of people standing, breathing, talking around him. He turned his head to the left, where his gaze fell on four white-cloaked figures. He strained to focus the blurred images, but his mind was still muddled and his spectacles were nowhere to be found.

"*Zdravctvootya, Professor, kok vwee pozheevaiyetya,*" one of them said.

Marenkov was not about to be fooled by the fact that one of the creatures spoke Russian. He knew exactly who they were. His mind was not so clouded that he did not recognize the devil's minions. No time could be lost, if he were to escape. Quickly, he rolled to his right, barely gathering his hands and knees under him before crashing from his cot to the floor.

Instantly, he was on his feet, amid shouts and flailing limbs, darting for a door a few paces away. He had just burst through the doorway, when he was tackled and wrestled to the ground.

"He's not ready yet. Tranquilize him again," a voice rang out. As his captors pinned him to the floor, he glanced into the room that lay beyond the doorway. It was spacious, blinding white, with gleaming machinery, silvery pipes and tubing and populated by more of the devil's disciples. With every ounce of strength that his slight frame could muster, he clung to the doorjamb, as might someone who was resisting being dragged into hell. Which, in fact, was precisely what was happening to Alexander Marenkov.

*   *   *

"Papa, I don't want to go," Galena sobbed, her arms clasped tightly about her father's neck.

He held her head close to the side of his face, not wanting her to see the disconsolate expression in his own eyes.

"Ah, my little *goloobcheek*," he said, making certain that he first cleared his throat. "It will all be fine." He didn't believe a word of that.

"But my friends, my ballet…I was to be Odette in Swan Lake…."

"You'll have wonderful new friends—and the best ballet instructors in all of Russia."

While she made no verbal response, her muffled sobs and tears moistening his cheek provided more of an answer than he had wished.

"Is Odette the good swan?" he said, groping for a thought that might serve as a distraction.

"Yes, she is actually a princess."

"And the one in black...."

"Odile."

"She was the princess' mischievous look-alike?"

"Yes."

"Well, that's much more suitable to your personality."

"Oh, papa, stop it." He felt her smile against his cheek.

"No, seriously. I can arrange this for you at your new school."

At that moment a black Mercedes sedan rolled into the circular driveway that fronted the apartment complex. He knew that it had to be the transportation promised by General Aksanov. Either that, or the toy of one of Russia's new, twenty-something, capitalist millionaires. All doubt of ownership was erased, however, when both front doors opened and two broad-shouldered, cheerless men clad in long black overcoats stepped out.

"Now, *goloob*...." he swallowed the word, then recomposed himself. "It's time."

He felt her body begin to shake in his arms as she, too, fought back tears. She knew how important it was to her father that she appear as strong as possible.

A few seconds later, the Mercedes was speeding down Gorky Street, carrying the vision of Galena's dispirited, questioning gaze toward him from the back window. He was even more undone by the uncanny similarities—the pouting lips, the entreating, doe-like eyes—that she bore to her mother. Then she and the automobile were gone.

Medved, again clearing his throat, dragged the sleeve of his right arm across his eyes. Feeling ashamed and cursing himself, he swiftly turned his thoughts to the mission he had set for himself this day.

This operation would not take him to the FSB headquarters in the Lubianka, nor, hopefully, anywhere near Viktor Buzhkin. Instead, he would begin his search at Kievsky Railroad Station where, he believed, could be found the beginning of the thread that would lead to the tapestry that was Alexander Marenkov. He did not proceed directly to the station, however. First, he took a trolleybus to Red Square. Then he ambled casually along Nikolskaya Street, occasionally crossing and recrossing before ducking into GUM, Moscow's largest department store. There, he began weaving his way through the crowd that consisted almost entirely of scarf-shrouded, tightly buttoned, heavy-booted *babushkas*. This was a somewhat delicate operation, as these elderly Russian ladies were inclined to wield their *avocee*—fishnet totebags—into the kneecaps of those senseless enough to blunder into their paths.

Successfully negotiating this gauntlet, he scurried through a rear entrance and then doubled back to Red Square. There, fifty meters from the imposing cupolas and silent, austere watchfulness of St. Basil's Cathedral, he descended an escalator to the nearby Metro platform. The train was just appearing in the clean, chandeliered station. Glancing in both directions, he waited until all the passengers had boarded, then darted into the car just as the doors were closing. It was a short ride to the Kievsky Voksal, where he bought a round-trip ticket and entrained for his next destination.

Less than one hour later, he was standing on the Peredelkino train station platform, in front of its one-room shanty, watching the green and red train recede into the distance. Lighting a cigarette, he surveyed the length of the platform. Just as Alexander Marenkov had been a week earlier, he was the sole Peredelkino fare from Moscow. He didn't know exactly what he was seeking, or even where to start, other than in this town—the clue transmitted by the old soldier at the university.

He descended the same steps, plodded along the same dusty road, inhaled the same sweet scent of plowed soil, and gazed at the same spacious black-earth fields. One sight in particular, however, arrested his attention. In contrast to the gaily painted red, blue, and yellow huts, a charred ruin scarred the ground near the edge of the town. Instinctively, he strode toward the anomalous dark blotch, scrutinizing the mangled, burned timbers that once had been a house and the detritus that once had been a home.

A metal object, glinting in the noonday sun from beneath a pile of rubble, captured his notice. Stepping over a timber that had been reduced to charcoal, he bent over and resurrected a battered, brass samovar from its sooty grave. As he dusted the ashes from the urn, he was startled by the dull thud of wood knocking against wood. He turned toward the sound, seeming to emanate from behind a brick chimney—the lone remaining standing structure of the destroyed building. With a reassuring pat on the *Gurza* tucked in his belt behind his back, he stepped cautiously forward. Unexpectedly, a slight figure bolted from the security of its hiding place behind the chimney and darted across the debris, moving more like a jack-rabbit than the adolescent boy that he actually was.

"Halt!" shouted Medved, to no avail as the lad continued his headlong flight.

"*Pobachnaya rebyawnok!*" he cursed between his teeth, defaming the youth's parental legitimacy. Dropping the samovar, he quickly gave chase.

Although he was much faster, his quarry was nimbler and blessed with greater stamina, causing Medved to once again rue his nicotine habit. The two-legged hare would have eluded his grasp but for a rubble-concealed hole. His foot trapped, the lad tumbled tow-head over bare heels.

"Gotchya," Medved wheezed, clamping a vice-like hand on the youth's scrawny shoulders.

"Please, *soodar*, kind sir, don't hurt me. I wouldn't have stolen anything."

He hoisted the boy by the scruff of his neck and shook him, touching off a small tornado of ash and dirt.

"What were you doing then, if you were not stealing?"

"I...I...was looking for the harness for Yura's old mare, *soodar*."

"Explain yourself."

"Yura's horse, don't you know, sir? She is all that is left after the fire. All the rest—the old man, his old wife, his chickens and pig are all gone. Burned to death."

"Tell me your name, boy."

"Ivan, *soodar*."

"All right, Ivan the Terrible, tell me all about this Yura and the fire."

The youth related how the disaster had occurred a week earlier, just after sunset, and how both Yura and his wife, Katya, perished in the flames before the townspeople arrived to help. As Ivan spoke, Medved guided him back to the charred ruins.

"...and his body was burned most awfully, *soodar*. I saw it with my very own eyes...there."

Medved, maintaining his tight grip against his captive's inclination toward flight, advanced in the direction indicated.

"All right, Ivan the Terrible, I'll make a deal with you. Here's an American dollar. Start sifting through this rubble, and I'll give you another dollar for everything you find that's of interest to me."

The urchin's eyes widened.

"Yes, sir!" he cried joyfully, needing no further prodding to seize the tendered bill. Then, after further reflection, "But...what sort of thing would be of interest to you?"

"Anything that seems out of place for poor old Yura and his home."

Ivan, a perplexed expression on his face, but with dollars on his mind, eagerly applied himself to his task.

"Ah, if I may say so, sir, you're very much like the stranger who was here last week...asking crazy questions and not knowing as much as an ignorant *shkolnick*."

Medved wheeled around, roughly seizing Ivan. "What stranger," he demanded harshly.

"A...a man with an accent. He too gave me an American dollar—just to show him to Pasternak's grave," he said, clearly alarmed at Medved's tone. Ivan was beginning to lose his enthusiasm for more of the bills with George Washington's picture.

"He was about your size, *soodar*, but younger, and his hair was lighter. He was also much nicer."

What else, my little *tsarevich*," Medved said in a gentler tone, hoping that he had not frightened the youth into a memory paralysis.

"Nothing. I showed the stranger the way to the gravesite, collected my dollar and never saw him again."

Deep in thought and forgetting his recent promise to himself, Medved flipped a cigarette into his mouth and struck a match.

"I'll be back in an hour or two," he said, inhaling the smoke and striding away.

"I can lead you to the gravesite, sir."

"Not necessary. I know the way," Medved responded without looking back. "Keep working—and think American dollars."

Half an hour later, Medved was standing before the tombstone marked 'B. Pasternak'. He walked around the marker twice, feeling as much as hearing the rustling of the birch tree leaves as they trembled in the soft caress of a welcome breeze.

Wearily, he plopped to the ground, wondering what images may have flitted before Professor Alexander Marenkov's eyes in this very place. As he lay back on the resilient bed of grass and leaves, his head recoiled, having bumped against a hard object. Working his hands through the tightly clumped green blades, he uncovered the culprit: a pair of horn-rimmed glasses that were skewed on the left side and smashed on the right. He placed the broken spectacles in his shirt pocket and began to scour the area more thoroughly. His efforts were rewarded with the discovery of an elegant brass button, a square centimeter of bloodstained silk material—apparently the elderly Professor had not succumbed without a struggle—and a gold pen marked 'Mont Blanc' and engraved with the initials 'J.A.S.'

Elated with his finds and insensible to his usual lung incapacities, he trotted nonstop back to the scorched dirt that had once been the peasant Yura's cottage.

"Ey! Sir! I thought Pasternak's ghost had swallowed you," Ivan chirped, dropping a stick with which he had been churning a mound of ashes. "Come see my treasures."

Medved began sorting through the gathered flotsam, surprised at either the thoroughness of the inferno or the sparseness of the peasant's worldly goods. Then he came upon it.

"Ah, and where did you find this?" he said triumphantly raising a spent bullet.

"Just there, sir, where the blackened corpse of Yura himself lay."

"You've done well, Ivan the Terrible. Is your mother still alive?"

"Yes, *soodar*."

"Good, buy her a gift."

Medved handed him twenty American dollars, more money than Ivan had ever seen in one instant.

Speechless, the boy took the money, holding it in his hands as if it were a newborn baby. Then he leaped into the air and fairly flew over the blackened rubble. It was only upon reaching the dirt road that he collected himself, paused, turned and shouted, "Thank you, *soodar*! *Spaseeba*!" With that, he disappeared down the road, leaving a plume of dust in his wake.

Medved, too, had what he wanted, not the least of which was the gold pen containing the initials, 'J.A.S.' He knew that he had found the link to the name and information that had appeared on his computer screen just before it froze: Slater, James A., President & CEO, Micratom Inc., USA.

Chapter Eight

It was dark when Mike Falcon pulled into the parking lot of the Annapolis City Docks. The bright three-quarter moon had just emerged above the town's low-profile buildings.

Falcon shut down the engine and switched off the lights. Stepping out of the jeep, he grasped the Glock from the passenger seat and tucked the weapon in the small of his back behind his belt, under his shirt. He stood motionless, surveying his environment. Across the Severn River, he could see and hear the bustling excitement of a September Saturday night in the Maryland capital's downtown waterfront area. Naval Academy midshipmen, tourists, hucksters, lovers, sailors—genuine and pretenders—were all taking advantage of the best weather of the year. In another month, Indian summer and its worshippers would be gone and the city would be as empty and still as this side of the river, where the buildings and docks were cloaked in shadowed silence.

Shifting his gaze toward these docks, muted white reflections of the soft moonglow, he sorted through the naked forest of masts and rigging. Finally, he recognized the distinct lines of *Stardust*, which rested placidly in her slip. The only motion was the noiseless spinning of the small generator blades set high on the mizzen mast. Moonlight shimmered off the alabaster hull and poked through glass-covered portholes, leaving gray and black phantoms in its wake. One shadow, in particular, captured his attention. It was in the forward cabin and unlike the other shades, immobilized by the glassy sea, it stirred.

His muscles tensed as he concentrated on quelling their very smallest motion, all his focus now directed to the starboard porthole in the forward cabin. Again, the phantom moved and this time he was able to discern the vague outline of a face. *Quite brazen, Ms. Ennui, or Tigere, or whatever the hell your name is.*

Boarding the ship undetected would be problematic. The natural motion of the vessel with the rhythm of the wind and sea would be disturbed. Any old salt would notice it. Would Cherisse Tigere? He decided to find out.

He crept along the pier to the stern of the ketch, then cautiously legged over the knee-high taffrail. Ducking under the mizzen boom, he alighted softly into the open cockpit. At the helm, he paused, crouching, listening for any tell-tale sound from below decks that he had been discovered. His patience was rewarded when his ears detected a faint rustling, followed by a sound of metal grating on metal. Suddenly, thirty feet away, the forward hatch opened, a hand, an arm, then the back of a head appeared.

There was no shimmer, no opalescent glow that might be expected of blonde hair in this brilliant moonlight. Perhaps he had guessed right when he had instructed the Worm to input her as a brunette. Now the torso emerged, then legs swung up and onto the foredeck. It was obvious that he had not been detected. But there was something else that was becoming equally as evident. Falcon stowed his weapon into a cockpit bin and smiled. He never would have imagined this particular turn of events.

Slowly rising, he worked his way forward. The unsuspecting woman was completely startled when he flung his arms around her waist, hoisting her into the air. Emitting a frightened cry, she wriggled around in his arms. Her hair, thick and long and black as the night flung around his head. She was so slight of frame that his arms easily engulfed her.

"Mike, you almost gave me a heart attack," she laughed, throwing her slender arms around his neck.

"Likewise," he said, kissing her lips and pressing her tightly against him. "It's been a long time, Suzie."

Yang Lin Su rejoiced in once again being enveloped in his strong arms, a sensation which rekindled embers of a warmth that had once blanketed and filled her. His voice, soft but confident, had a soothing effect, particularly when it carried his pet name for her.

"I miss you," she said, cupping the back of his head with her petite hand and drawing his cheek to hers.

"And whose fault is that? It didn't have to be this way," Falcon said, not smoothing a sharp edge in the tone of his voice.

She pushed away.

"Why are you so blind? I acted only to protect your honor. Why can't you see this?" she exclaimed crossly. "Perhaps I shouldn't have come. I just wanted to see…."

She turned and walked to the bow, grasping the forestay for support.

Silence descended upon them.

As she was about to step onto the dock, she felt a hand on her shoulder. She turned to face him, touching his hand.

"I love you," he said.

"You're so stupid," she replied, peering up at him with shining, gracefully upswept almond-shaped eyes. "These past three months have been every bit as hard on me. You don't know how I feel…I—"

His lips flush against hers clipped the thought. The kiss was returned softly and hesitantly at first, then with complete surrender.

"I guess that means I'm to shut up," she whispered, running her fingers through his hair.

He nodded, turning to kiss her fingertips. "Will you spend the night?"

"I don't know…perhaps that's not such a good idea…after all that's happened."

Her real answer, however, came in the form of her breasts, thighs and hips pressing against him.

"I'll take the body language as a yes," he smiled. "Only we can't stay here."

"We're leaving *Stardust*?" she asked, stepping back.

"No, we're taking her with us. Call Chet—his number's on the chart table—and tell him to send Jocko over. I need to get into open water, to clear my thoughts."

This seemingly impulsive decision was taken completely in stride by Lin Su, who well knew Mike's affinity for the cleansing, renewing effect of fresh salt air. What she could not know was that a much more immediate, pragmatic, and ominous cause was driving him.

Less than fifteen minutes later, docking lines had been cast off and *Stardust* eased out of her slip. Donning Falcon's leather, fur-collared old Navy flight jacket, Suzie bundled herself in a blanket on the foredeck, holding Jocko against her for additional warmth. It seemed like old times. She began to feel an overwhelming sense of calm and repose—a sensation that she had not experienced since she had broken off their relationship three months earlier, after the FBI incident. The soporific lap of the waves against the bow, the drone of the steady breeze in the rigging, the gentle heel of the ship to port, the lazy clouds floating before the moon, the body heat and cadenced breathing of the great black Lab next to her all conspired to lull her to sleep.

At the helm, Mike Falcon, too, reminisced about how it used to be. How all his prior romantic relationships had ended in blameless, bittersweet partings. How he had immersed himself in his work, the demands of which afforded easy rationalization of a companionless life. Then one day she appeared, sitting demurely, intensely focused, in the audience during public hearings of the Uranium Oversight Committee. She had introduced herself afterwards as a technology advisor to the

Chinese-American Trade Association. Barely five feet and one hundred pounds, she had swept him from his snug moorings with the force of a China Sea typhoon.

He taught her how to tack a sailboat, spin an airplane, and ride the winds in a hot-air balloon. She taught him how to appreciate the finer points of art, ballet, and the opera—-*Madame Butterfly* would always hold a special meaning for them, for it was to those arias that they first made love. But most of all they taught and learned from each other about those places in their souls where no one else had ever reached. Their chemistry was immediate; the humor—that saving grace of relationships—was a bit eccentric, ever near the surface; the sex was gentle, rough, uninhibited, fresh, unpredictable, constant; the relationship was complete. "I am your karma," she would laugh. "Here to punish you for transgressions in your past lives." She had a way of making him wish he had transgressed more.

He should have known it was too good to last. It ended that day the two FBI agents casually dropped by his office. "No big deal, just an annual file update," they had lied. Two hours later, he was still answering questions about his relationship with Lin Su. They didn't believe his answers and their references to her became peppered with terms such as 'undercover agent' and 'espionage.' They were unable to give him any specifics about their allegations against her. "Perhaps you can enlighten us," they had said, "if you have nothing to hide. Tell us in detail about the nature of your personal relationship with her."

He remembered well his feelings at that moment, of the little hairs rising at the base of his neck, of his lips compressing, and of the control he exerted to prevent his hand from coiling into a fist and smashing the arrogant Fed into the wall. It seemed by the tack they next pursued that they sensed his inner rage and wished to expose it.

"We'd like you to come down and take a polygraph test. If you pass, we have a little job for you," was the way they put it, the way they began to ask him to spy on her. "Of course, if you don't want to cooperate, we'll pursue this case to its 'logical conclusion'"—which was FBI thinkspeak for blackmail.

He knew they would see to it that his Top Secret clearance would be suspended—along with his career—until he knuckled under to their offensive demand. That was when the agents succeeded. Succeeded in triggering the simmering fury. One of the agents actually reached for his shoulder holster as Falcon lunged toward him, seized him by his polyester lapels and hurled him into the hallway. The other G-man, popping awkwardly to his feet, stumbled backwards against his chair, and tripped to the floor. All motion, all keyboard typing, all talking in the office spaces of the Uranium Oversight Committee ceased. Both agents were immediately on their feet.

The one in the hallway straightened his tie and angrily grinned, "You've just screwed the pooch. We'll be workin' this from the top down now. Have a nice day." The two FBI men left. Glancing down the silent hallway, Falcon was greeted by blank faces that peered above cubicle dividers and from open doorways.

Lin Su never called him after that day, never returned his calls, and—until now—had refused to see him. Although he had no proof, he was certain that Jensen had apprised her of the incident, probably before the FBI agents had departed the building.

He knew that, by terminating their relationship, she was merely trying to protect his Top Secret clearance, his career, his reputation. *Now there's a goddamn admirable objective,* he chuckled softly. Thoughts rose of Slater's purple-white meat slab of a body, only the latest in a long line of hollow-eyed, contorted, maimed, or scorched former human beings that had adorned his 'career.'

God, he was sick of it. If only he could just keep sailing south with Suzie and Jocko in this gorgeous night and in this perfect fifteen knot breeze hard off the starboard beam. Maybe the timing was right. Perhaps he should just chuck it all, head for the Caribbean and set up the charter business that he had been dreaming about. They could put into St. Michael's before sunrise, spend a day wandering through that picturesque Eastern Shore town, pack down some hard-shell crabs, and have a serious discussion about their future together. Jensen could take over his cases and....

His thoughts were interrupted by a barely audible beep emanating from just inside the main hatchway. Trimming the port jib sheet, so that *Stardust* would remain steadily on course, he swung through the cabin opening and lifted the cellular phone from its pocket above the navigation table.

"Falcon—hope I didn't wake you," the voice said. "This is—"

"I know who it is, Worm. Jeezus, it's two a.m. Are you still at work?"

"Always. I never know what time it is. You know Einstein showed that time is only relative to the speed with which you travel through the universe and—"

"Skip the part where the earth cooled, Worm. Just tell me what's so damned urgent that can't wait for a normal person's hours."

"Right. I busted your blonde friend's cover. And I gotta tell ya, nothing ever shocks me anymore, but this one...this is...You better see for yourself. And there's other stuff...about the dead guy...it's all a little spooky. Can you get here right away?"

"I'm on a sailboat, in the middle of the goddamn Chesapeake Bay," Falcon said, feeling the weight of his lost chance tomorrow with Suzie. "If the wind holds, I can be back in Annapolis by sunrise. That would put me in the office by around seven or eight. I trust you'll still be there?"

"Always."

Mike shoved the phone back into its pocket and returned topside. During the conversation, the ketch had plowed steadily ahead, not losing one degree of her course. Lin Su, still fast asleep, had scarcely moved since they left the dock. Falcon knelt next to her, gently brushing a long strand of hair from her cheek. He leaned over and kissed her lips. Instinctively, she smiled, reached up and wrapped her arms around him. Her eyes opened.

"Ah, so it's not just a dream," she smiled.

"Perhaps it is," he said. "Close your eyes."

As she complied and once again began to drift off, he rose and returned to the helm. Loosening both jib sheets, he twirled the wheel to port. The ship slowly responded, her stern swinging through the westerly breeze and her hull tilting gently toward starboard.

Neither of his passengers moved. Falcon winched down and cleated the starboard jib sheet, then attended to the mizzen sail. The mainsail took care of itself. Settling back into the cockpit, he gazed toward the east. Before long, it would turn gray, then pale blue, then the sun would break above the Eastern Shore, bringing with it stark, glaring reality.

Chapter Nine

For the first moment in what had seemed like endless time in fathomless space, Alexander Marenkov had begun to sense a clarity of mind. Without opening his eyes, he realized that he was once again lying on some sort of hard cot, but now he was completely immobilized. His arms were wrapped tightly across his chest, held fast in a strait-jacket, and his legs were strapped together, chained to the floor.

Cautiously, he peered from beneath one tentatively raised eyelid. Directly overhead, the same glaring light eyed him. He became more confident in his mental acuity when he noted that he was able to distinguish fine detail in the light: a central bright yellow bulb surrounded by eight concentric circles of dimmer, greenish radiation.

Rolling his half-closed eyeballs to the left, he hoped that the minute aperture by which he surveyed his surroundings would be imperceptible to an observer. A lone man, clad in a white smock, sat in a metal chair, hunched over an open book. Involuntarily, Marenkov's eyelids fully retracted, his eyes opening wide.

"Valentin!" he exclaimed, recognizing an old colleague and friend from their days together at the Moscow Polytechnic Institute.

"Ah, Alexander Petrovich, you have decided not to leave us after all," Valentin Tschernin responded, his florid complexion turning pinker after being startled by Alexander's outburst. He closed his book and set it on the floor.

"Where are we?" Marenkov said, his struggle to sit up frustrated by the restraints.

"That's not important." The significant consideration is that you're here. Everyone will be pleased that you've finally regained consciousness and, I trust, lucidity."

"Why am I here? And you...why are you...Can you first untie me?"

Valentin crossed his legs and placed his folded hands on his knee.

"You are here simply because, like the rest of us, you wanted to be."

"What are you saying? I have been kidnapped."

"It must be admitted that you did cause somewhat of a ruckus. However, you would not be in this situation if you had not voluntarily met with the American."

"But I went to Peredelkino to reject his offer. As miserable as my life may have become, I cannot sell myself like a common *schlyooka*—a whore. It was too ignoble."

"Ignoble!" Valentin sneered, the ruddy hue of his face deepening to scarlet. "And what was so noble about your—our—existence! Some of the greatest minds in the world groveling for potatoes and cucumbers. A once powerful and proud people—feared and respected throughout the world—reduced to a joke! Cast adrift by incompetent, drunken leaders...sucked dry by the money leeches! You tell me, Professor Marenkov—where is the nobility?" His agitation stirred to a fine level, Valentin removed his wire-rimmed spectacles and, with trembling hands, wiped the glasses with the sleeve of his smock.

"But surely you cannot approve of the purpose for which we were being recruited," Alexander replied. "And please untie me."

"How is that different than the purpose to which we devoted our careers—ourselves—over the past three decades?" Tschernin said, ignoring Marenkov's plea. "You, yourself, Alexander, were fond of telling me that our work would ultimately lead to a world free of war—to an unprecedented era of peace and prosperity for Russia. And look what your predictions—our work and our dreams—have come to. But there is still a chance that your prophecy could come true—and that our efforts could bear fruit."

"How? By causing the deaths of millions of innocent people?"

"Come now, Alexander. You must have a greater perspective. Some lives are always lost in the peoples' struggle for freedom and equality."

Marenkov was stupefied. It had been nearly a decade since he had heard such words. And to hear them from Valentin Tschernin, an eminent physicist, a rationalist, a card-carrying elitist. But even this neo-Marxist diatribe would pale in comparison with the words that next escaped Tschernin's lips.

"It is explained in the Koran, if you would only take the time to read it—and you will. 'There is not one whose place is not already written by Allah whether in fire or paradise.' Our lives have been predestined since the beginning of time for this moment—to serve Allah, the magnificent, the divine, the one true god."

The Professor felt short of breath, as if clammy cold hands were gripping his chest. He was unsure if this man, this seeming impostor of his once logical friend and compatriot, Valentin Tschernin, was speaking from conviction or abject fear. Never before had he heard—or even imagined—such a muddle of communist ideology and Moslem theocracy—two faiths historically so diametrically opposed.

"It seems that the wrong person is strait-jacketed here, Valentin. I'm afraid you've become a raving lunatic."

"You know so little, Alexander Petrovich. I was like you once. Then the words of the Prophet Muhammed opened my eyes. Your eyes will be opened as well. But we shall have more time later in which to discuss the purpose of our lives. Now it is time for you to meet someone else. Someone very special."

Tschernin leaned forward, reaching near Marenkov's head to press a buzzer that was fixed to the frame of the cot.

Several minutes later, the door behind the Professor swung open and Tschernin sprang from his chair. Yes, the man was frightened, Alexander thought. He craned his neck around but was unable to turn all the way toward the doorway.

"Release him," a soft, yet authoritative voice spoke in English. Tschernin immediately obeyed, undoing the ties, buckles, and snaps that constrained Marenkov.

Having done as ordered, Tschernin stepped back from the cot, staring expectantly at the unseen source of the voice.

"Leave us," it commanded.

Tschernin bent down, seized the book that he had earlier placed on the floor, and with a troubled glance flung toward Marenkov, fled the room.

Alexander slowly sat upright and, facing directly forward, shed the loosened strait-jacket. Behind him to his left, footsteps drew nearer. The Russian turned, raising his eyes to meet those of the being who now hovered over him.

He was tall, nearly two full meters Marenkov estimated, cloaked in a vertically black-and-white striped floor length robe. A camel-colored headdress crowned the narrow, elongated head. The face was the hue and smoothness of creamy coffee, a mustache hid the upper lip and a full black beard extended from his thick lower lip to the middle of his chest. The nose was prominent and angled outward at its middle, the cheeks were high and bony, the dark protruding eyes were intense, riveting.

"Welcome, Professor Marenkov," he said, with a slight bow of his head. "I understand you speak English."

The Professor nodded.

"Good. We shall communicate in that language. I am Abdul bin Wahhab—the Servant of the Beloved. You are my guest here and will be accorded the dignity, respect, and material rewards deserving of one of your eminent stature. In return, you will perform an important service for me and the people of the true faith. Are you familiar with the meaning of the word Islam?"

Marenkov, experiencing a flash of dizziness and nausea, shook his head.

"Islam means submission—submission to the will of Allah," bin Wahhab said, his eyes brightening. "You will learn to submit. That I can assure you. Now, rest. I will have someone sent to show you to your quarters."

With the graceful swirl of his robes, the Arab strode to the door.

"Think well upon what I have told you," he said, pausing as he opened the door. Then he was gone.

Marenkov rested his elbows on his knees and his head in his hands, his mouth and throat parched and dusty, his stomach in turmoil.

*   *   *

"It's not as though I'm dealing with a first-form *shkolnick*," Viktor Buzhkin said into the telephone transmitter. He did not tolerate being upbraided, no matter how senior or respected his critic. "He is an old, experienced Chekist, and he is not stupid."

"Perhaps I can find someone who is not so awed and who won't get lost so easily in the ladies' underwear section of GUM," came the voice at the other end of the phone.

His blood now boiling, Buzhkin wrestled with the driving urge to smash the phone through the glass of the booth in which he was standing. His years of training, however, gained ascendance and he collected himself. He knew he must choose his next words carefully.

"You know I am the best man for this job. I assure you it won't happen again."

"I certainly hope not, Buzhkin. You realize the consequences of another failure."

"Of course."

The phone clicked in Buzhkin's ear followed by the hum of a dial tone.

"*Sookee Seen*," he cursed, kicking open the door of the phone booth and stepping onto the sidewalk.

* * *

Across town, the very same 'old Chekist' of Buzhkin's invectives had also been standing in a phone booth.

"Dmitri, I remind you again that I can trust no one at the FSB. These articles must not leave your possession," Medved said into the phone's mouthpiece, as he glanced uneasily through the glass panes.

"Don't worry, *moy droog*. I shall be present during all the tests. If there is anything to be gleaned, I shall find it."

"I am indebted to you, old friend."

"Shut up. Your sentimentality is making me sick."

"Well then," Medved laughed. "I'll call you in a week. Under no circumstances should you call me. It is too dangerous for you, understand?"

"Don't worry about me. I've got the entire Moscow militia to protect me. Those FSB wolves will be sorry if they try to gnaw this moose."

"I believe that Dmitri, but for once in your bull-headed life please just do as I say. I will call you exactly at this time one week from today. *Docvidanya*."

Returning the receiver to its hook, Medved lit a cigarette and reflected on his conversation with Dmitri Kirilovich, the precinct chief of the local Moscow *Militsiya*. Kirilovich was one of a handful of men with whom Medved could trust his life. In fact, it was precisely such a bond that linked them, stemming from their tour of duty in Afghanistan when he had dragged the wounded Kirilovich from a burning tank. Now, some fifteen years later, Dmitri had risen to a position where he could help, if not repay, his old comrade. Unquestionably, the *Militsiya's* resources and laboratories were not nearly as extensive as those of the FSB's. But if anyone could wring a tale from the trinkets uncovered at Peredelkino, it would be Dmitri. Certainly, turning these items over to the Service was not an option. After the attempt on his life, no one there could be trusted. That begged another disturbing question.

He inhaled slowly, savoring the aroma, before allowing the cigarette smoke to escape from his mouth.

Buzhkin. How much could he be allowed to know? That sullen hulk may very well have been one of the uninvited guests at his apartment two evenings ago. And if that were so…there would then be the issue of the man who had assigned Buzhkin to "protect" him. Tomorrow he must make his report to General Aksanov. He didn't relish deceiving his old commander concerning the Peredelkino clues. Perhaps he was just letting his imagination run away…yet…in his business, only fools were not suspicious, and no fools made it to old age.

He had still one more call to make. Lifting the receiver and dropping several kopecks into the coin slot, he punched in the number for his broker. Money managers were an endangered species in Russia. A bare handful had survived personal bankruptcy, total loss of clientele, physical thrashings, and even murder in the crash of '98. While his broker had been one of the few who had not been wiped out, the same could not be said, unfortunately, for Medved. Nearly every ruble, every kopeck, that he had managed to scrape into savings from his thirty years of service to the Motherland had melted into Moscow's hot August air in less than two weeks. No longer burdened with the cares of a financial portfolio, it was not for personal monetary matters that he placed this call, but to play a hunch in his investigation.

The broker was more than happy to provide assistance to a rare potential client, promising Medved that the information he requested would be immediately posted to him. Rejecting further appeals for investment advice, i.e., offers to separate him from his last kopeck, Medved hung up and pushed open the phone booth door.

The sun had just dipped below the taller buildings of the city when he stepped onto the sidewalk. The heat wave had finally broken and there was a distinct nip in the air. Soon, snow geese would be overhead, winging toward Ukraine, the Black Sea, and points further south. Turning up his collar, he fastened the top button of his light jacket and began walking west on Borodino Street. Mulling the events of the past forty-eight hours, he thought it would be good to be a snow goose. He flicked his cigarette into a street gutter and jumped on a passing trolley-bus. How to phrase his report for tomorrow's meeting with the General was now his chief concern.

*   *   *

"Sergei, so good to see you," Aksanov said, motioning Medved toward an ample-sized leather chair that fronted his great oak desk. The Lubianka office of the FSB Director was unpretentious, even spartan, but its furniture lent it an unmistakable aura of solidity and strength.

"Do you have a report for me?"

"Yes," Medved responded, handing his boss the thin sheaf of papers that he had drafted the previous evening. "I'm afraid we don't have much to go on at present. Just a number of interviews with Marenkov's family and some colleagues and students at the university."

"I see," the Director responded as he scanned the report. "Nothing else?"

"No, sir," the agent said, suppressing his distaste for his deceit and wondering if Aksanov was doing the same.

"Well, we can't expect to crack this case in one day. Tell me. How are you and Buzhkin getting along?"

"Famously. He's quite personable, you must know."

Both men eyed each other guardedly.

"Oh, I have a message from your daughter," Aksanov smiled suddenly, producing a white envelope from his inside coat pocket. "She's very well settled in, I can assure you."

Medved took the letter, thanked the Director, and departed. Once within the confines of his own office, he lit a cigarette, gently broke the seal on the envelope, and unfolded the paper. The sight of her handwriting alone brought a smile as he read:

> *Dearest Papa,*
> *I thought about telling you how much I hate it here but I knew it would upset you. So I will do as you wish and tell you that I love it. Can you really arrange for me to get the part of Odette? I know you were jut teasing, but you make me happy when you do. I love you and miss you and hope you come soon to take me away from this wonderful place.*
>
> *Love,*
> *Galyooshka*

He carefully folded the letter and slid it back into the envelope. That "wonderful place"...was it in fact the 'safe house' that it was purported to be by General Aksanov, or something terribly different? And, by handing him Galena's letter, was Aksanov merely emphasizing the trump card that he held? Medved had barely begun to dwell on these thoughts when he became aware of the presence of another being looming behind him. He turned to meet the gloomy visage of Viktor Buzhkin.

Chapter Ten

"Highly enriched uranium? U-235? That's preposterous!" Alexander Marenkov sputtered. "It is too tightly controlled. How can it possibly be in the possession of this madman?!"

"Believe it, for it is true," Valentin Tschernin retorted, grimacing. "As to what magic caused it to be here, I cannot tell you. But I do suggest that, for both our sakes, you keep your voice down."

Half an hour had elapsed since the two Russians had been alone together in a spartan white-tiled room. During that time, Marenkov had been receiving his indoctrination from Tschernin into his strange new environment.

Now the Professor slumped back in his chair, not wanting to believe his ears, much less dwell on the implications of this distressing news. U-235. Incredible. The Russian Federation's foremost atomic physicist well knew that the U-235 isotope was found in less than one percent of all natural uranium ore. Extremists might buy or steal the more abundant U-238, but that relatively stable isotope would frustrate attempts at a chain reaction. No, they would have to squeeze the chain reactive U-235 out of the ore and that technology—gaseous diffusion or laser separation—was well beyond the capability of even the most sophisticated terrorist operations. How, then, could they possess this highly enriched uranium? Marenkov kept turning the paradox over in his mind, until a more important thought occurred to him.

"What are their plans? Why have they kidnapped me?" he demanded, acknowledging Valentin's admonition to speak softly. Tschernin, appearing ruddier than usual in the fluorescent lighting that glared harshly in the all white room, removed his spectacles and began cleaning them.

"They want us to construct a device...a physically small one...but still quite powerful."

"A device. How small...how powerful?"

"That's where you come in, Alexander. You see, we're having some trouble...computations weren't working...we don't have our usual equipment, understand."

"What size and yield?" Marenkov persisted, becoming more agitated.

"Physically as small as possible...while still able to take out a large city," Tschernin said, replacing his spectacles on the bridge of his nose, but not allowing his eyes to meet those of his compatriot.

Involuntarily, the physicist in the Professor's mind began tumbling through calculations.

"I see.... With U-235, the minimum size necessary to sustain a chain reaction would be a sphere around twenty centimeters in diameter—smaller than a basketball. Critical mass would be around fifteen kilos. Of course that could be reduced by compressing the uranium, wrapping it with a suitable neutron reflector, and installing a neutron generator in its core—but I venture that you've already thought of that."

"Indeed, but we have been unable to compute the desirable neutron speed for a device that small. If the neutrons are too fast, they'll escape before the chain reaction can take place. If they're too slow, the partial detonation will blow the device apart before the chain reaction can release its full energy—the explosion will fizzle."

"I appreciate your dilemma. I should think you wouldn't want to get those numbers wrong. You should've come to my last lecture,"

Marenkov quipped. *When was it,* he ruminated—*only a week or so ago that I lectured at the International Conference on Slow Neutron Fission Theory. It was there, too, that I met the American, James Slater, and that my life began to unravel.*

"I'm afraid that I was already incapacitated," Tschernin replied, somewhat sheepishly.

"Now tell me, Valentin," Alexander spoke solemnly, "What does this madman plan to do with such a device?"

"Just as I do not know the origin of the U-235, I do not know its destination. But I am convinced that it is meant only to be a negotiating tool. It would be insanity to actually trigger the device."

"Insanity! How dare you speak of insanity," Marenkov fumed, desperately trying to control his rising voice. "Are you not the same Valentin Tschernin who yesterday assured me that the loss of millions of lives may be necessary for the sake of the liberation of the masses?"

"You don't understand anything yet, Alexander. You are still a victim of your bourgeois, atheistic upbringing. But you shall be re-educated while you are here. You will find the true *Sharia*, and all will become clear to you—as it has to me."

"That, I would not count upon, Valentin."

Tschernin had barely opened his mouth to reply when the door behind him swung upon. A slight figure, clad in a black and white, vertically striped burnoose and wearing a small white, brimless cap swept into the room.

"I must be leaving you now, Alexander," Tschernin whispered. "Know this—I bear you only good will, in spite of your attacks on me. But know also, that you may want to subdue your arrogance if you wish to survive here."

*   *   *

Sergei Medved eagerly tore open the large manila envelope containing the package he had just received. It had been over a week since he had placed the order with his broker, a week of pseudo-investigations with Buzhkin, interviewing clueless minds and pursuing mindless clues.

Now he finally had it before him, in the privacy of his apartment. He read the black print on the glossy red, white and blue cover:

MICRATOM, INC.
1998 Annual Report

Quickly, he scanned the first page:

> *...Micratom Inc. and the United States Enrichment Corporation (USEC) were established in 1992 as the first step in transferring the government's uranium enrichment activities to the private sector. One year later, Russia's commercial nuclear energy organization, the Russian Uranium Korporatsiya (RURIK) signed an agreement for the conversion of its nuclear warhead uranium for sale to these two American companies.*
>
> *To date, the equivalent of 3160 Russian nuclear warheads (sixty-three metric tons of highly enriched uranium, U-235) has been converted and sold to Micratom and USEC. The two American companies have since processed the uranium and provided it to the nuclear power industry both domestically and abroad. The conversion of nuclear warheads to the peaceful uses of electricity—Megatons to Megawatts—has been the quintessential example of pounding swords into plowshares."*

The next page in the report contained a pair of black-and-white photographs of two distinctly different men. The first, peering directly at the reader above a caption that read 'John E. Lawrence, Chairman', was elderly, gray-haired and decidedly somber. The other, radiating a youthful confidence in his broad smile, sat atop a caption that read 'James A. Slater, President and Chief Executive Officer.'

Medved carefully read each sentence of the forty-page report, paying particular attention to the financial statement towards the end. When he was finished, he replaced the report in its envelope and glanced at the clock on his desk. Five p.m. Dmitri would be expecting his call in an hour. Rising from behind his desk, he donned his jacket, tucked the report inside, and left the apartment.

*   *   *

The entire red disk of the sun had cleared the horizon by the time *Stardust* was once again in Annapolis waters. Falcon opted to tie the ketch to a mooring buoy in the Severn River, opposite the U.S. Naval Academy. This increased isolation, while not an absolute protection, would complicate the schemes of a potential intruder.

Once secured to the buoy, and with the sails having been furled, he lowered the launch from the davits on the stern. With Lin Su and the black Lab on board the dinghy with him, he motored toward the City Docks.

"But I don't understand," Lin Su said, "how you can part with Jocko."

"As I said, it's just for a little while," he answered.

"What on earth is more important to you than this guy?" she laughed, hugging the big dog. She had hoped her casual air would relax his guard, but was disappointed when he again ignored her probing.

"I want to see you again—soon," he said. "We need to talk…about us. But you must promise me that you won't come back out to the boat. Do you understand?"

She gazed at the nearing harbor, with its moored herd of colorful dinghies.

"There's someone else, isn't there? That's understandable. I just wish you'd be honest with me."

"Now who's being stupid," he replied, slowing the dinghy as they approached the sea wall. They were still a few feet away when Jocko leaped onto the concrete landing.

"You're acting so strange, Mike…so secretive," she said, rising and stepping ashore. "I had very mixed emotions about coming here last night. I had hoped that…but it doesn't matter."

She turned and began ascending the foot path that led to the gravel parking lot.

"I'll take good care of Jocko. You needn't worry about that."

She never once looked back as she strode resolutely away."

"I'll call you," Mike yelled.

Still not turning, she reached her vehicle, where she collected the Lab, started the engine, and sped away.

*   *   *

It was mid-morning when Falcon arrived at NSA Headquarters in Fort Meade. Upon entering the Worm's office, he found the computer whiz at his desk, slumped over, face down in his keyboard.

Suppressing an unpleasant welling of anxiety, he stepped over a collapsed pile of magazines and approached the still figure. He laid a hand on the Worm's shoulder.

The thin figure remained motionless. Then, sensing the weight and heat of Falcon's hand, the Worm stirred, opened his eyes, and sat up.

"Ah, Mike. What took you so damned long?" he said, glancing sleepy-eyed at the clock.

Falcon received even these words of chastisement with welcome relief.

"Haven't quite figured out how to get the winds to do my bidding," he said. "Now show me why I've given up my Sunday afternoon with a beautiful woman to be stuck here with you and your computers.

"You're going to love this," the Worm said, becoming more animated as he swung into action, switching on all three computers. I was able to scan in one barely usable print from your business card and correlate it with the other data we had…See if this looks familiar."

Falcon stared at the middle screen, which was gradually being filled with the image of a woman's face.

Full, sultry lips appeared, set against a background of creamy white skin; above them emerged a small, slightly upturned nose, which was shortly offset by a pair of green, feline eyes. The elegant face was framed by shoulder-length light chestnut hair.

"So that's the color that's between her legs," Falcon mused aloud.

"Hmm? Oh yes, I suppose. Want me to give her a blonde make-over?" the Worm asked, tweaking the image so that it became even clearer.

"That won't be necessary," Falcon responded, feeling once again the intense, seductive gaze of 'Cherisse Tigere' upon him. "What's her real name?"

"Ahhh—now comes the good part," the Worm said, swiveling in his chair to the computer on his left. "I picked this up through Echelon," he noted, referring to the NSA's massive, worldwide electronic eavesdropping infrastructure. The Worm keyed in several commands and the screen began to flicker with information.

Falcon scanned it, then carefully reread.

"Unbelievable," he breathed, stepping back and almost stumbling over a tall stack of computer manuals.

"Yeah, I've never seen anything quite like it either," the Worm shook his head. "Ms. Svetlana Popova…Institute of Oriental Studies—better known as 'Spies are Us'; then School 101—alias, the Red Banner Institute, training ground of the old KGB; finally, post-graduate work with Military Intelligence—the infamous GRU—with a Triple Q level, no less…."

"Carte blanche for assassinations."

"Precisely."

"Does she have a Legend?" Falcon asked, referring to the Intelligence Community term for a complete makeover of one's personal history…the fabrication of an entirely new being.

"No, we would've picked that up on Echelon. She occasionally uses a temporary cover like Cherisse Tigere, but essentially what you see is the whole ugly—or beautiful, depending on your perspective—truth."

"Then it gets even better," the Worm continued, his eyes gleaming. "The Muslim terrorist activity, the bin Wahhab connection, and finally—the best of all—the Feliks."

"We all know there is no such organization," Falcon smiled wryly.

"Tell that to Gorbachev and Yeltsin. Neither of them would be where they are today, if it weren't for this non-existent organization."

Falcon folded his arms across his chest, gazing at the deceptively unimposing strange little computer mole, and wondered what momentous secrets of the world…the CIA's involvement with JFK's assassination…Reagan's Iraqi arms deal…the Roswell cover-up…were known only to him.

"Say, you wouldn't happen to know where Jimmy Hoffa is buried," Falcon quipped.

"Hm?"

"Never mind. Suppose you tell me what you do know about the Feliks," Falcon said, sitting on the computer manual pile.

The Worm pushed away from the computer table.

"Ah, yes…interesting phenomenon, the Feliks," he said, propping his feet on the table. "About eight years ago, a number of disaffected GRU and ex-KGB officers joined together in a sworn effort to re-establish the Soviet state in all its former glory. For their name, they took that of one who represented the essence of the old police state."

"Feliks Dzerzhinsky."

"Yeah, the first chief of police of the 'Worker's Paradise' and one of the great murderers of history. No one knows how big the 'Feliks' is, who's in it, what activities can be ascribed to it. Or even if, in fact, it exists."

"You seem convinced that it's real," Falcon interjected.

"Sure, I've seen enough information in my cyberspace wanderings that leave no doubt. But you'll never hear anyone else admit it in public. It's a very sore subject. It's embarrassing to the Russians to have such a reactionary shadow organization pulling the strings of their government. And it's just as embarrassing to the Western world's intelligence communities to be so woefully ignorant about such a powerful, nasty organization.

"For example, your friend Svetlana, here…if indeed, she is with the Feliks…her links to Muslim terrorist activity and to bin Wahhab are cause for pause, wouldn't you agree?"

"It is somewhat disconcerting," Falcon replied, "but there's another connection that's just as unsettling." The image of James Slater's purple-white body and glassy-eyed stare flitted through his mind.

"The Micratom affair," the Worm said, sliding his chair forward to the table.

"Were you able to slip through Slater's firewall?"

"Does your President have a spring-loaded dick? Which reminds me—I recently got into a Secret Service file that confirms his tryst with that Hollywood starlet…but, never mind. Of course, I got in. I will admit that the byte-code verifier bruised me a bit, but I was able to construct a root kit that…."

"Just cut to the bottom line, Worm."

"Sure, all right. It's coming up now. I don't know if you can make any sense of this gibberish."

Falcon scanned the information which consisted of business strategies, financial data, and explicit commentary on public officials, competitors, his own employees, and women he had bedded. Other than the romantic escapades, nothing appeared out of the ordinary.

"Quite the colossal egotist, this Slater," the Worm said as Falcon scrolled through the pages. "Looks like he was in training for the sexual Olympics."

Falcon was hardly conscious of the Worm's chatter as he scanned the steady stream of information.

"Here's something...what's this?" he said, depressing a key and freezing the display. Squinting, the Worm leaned toward the screen.

"Oh yeah, that...'Salvador.' It seems to be peppered throughout. 'Met Salvador...Received payment from Salvador'...Salvador this. Salvador that. I tried to correlate the name with Micratom official files—no luck. Whoever Salvador is, he's personal to your man."

Falcon scrutinized the name, rolled it around on his lips, massaged it in his mind. There was an odd sense of familiarity to it, as though he had somehow already encountered it in connection with Slater.

He rose from the mound of computer manuals, staring straight ahead, seeing neither the computers nor his mystified onlooker.

"Salvador!", he exclaimed suddenly. "Thanks, Worm...for all your work. Print the Slater file for me. I'll see you tomorrow. Why don't you go home and get some sleep."

"I am home."

"Oh...right. See you tomorrow, then."

Falcon weaved his way through the clutter of the Worm's office, already turning over in his mind his plan to play his Salvador hunch.

Chapter Eleven

Yang Lin Su ran her fingers through her hair, brushing it from her eyes as she scanned the information just handed to her by the Director of the Chinese-American Trade Association. She wanted to be perfectly sure that she did not misread a word in the report that was now before her. The Director, a short thin middle-aged man, was content to give her all the time she needed. After all, she would play the key role in the next stage of intelligence gathering. He turned away from her and watched the rain drizzling on the window pane of his office.

When she finished reading, she replaced the report in a folder that was marked "Top Secret" in Chinese characters. She continued to sit rigidly in her chair, knowing, but not wishing to hear the words that must come next.

"I need hardly tell you, MsYang," theDirector said, approaching her, "of the importance to the Peoples Republic to obtain as much information as possible about this disturbing development."

She made no answer.

He lifted the report from her hands, turned, and walked back to his desk. Sitting, he took a cigarette from a small silver case.

"It is rare that we are in possession of such intelligence before the Americans," he said, tapping the filter end of the cigarette against the case. "And in this instance, extremely dangerous. The partnership between Abdul bin Wahhab and the Feliks and this uranium business pose a grave destabilizing threat to our region of the world. To have these two most powerful terrorist organizations acting in conjunction…and right on our doorstep…well, it's simply unthinkable. You do understand?"

Not replying, she turned her eyes to the streaks of water running down the window. There was no need to answer. Not one word from her could change her fate.

The Director continued nervously tapping the cigarette. "It is imperative that we find out what the Americans know and what their course of action is. Naturally, you will have to intensify your relationship with your friend, Mr. Falcon."

Finally, she spoke. "Will that be all?"

Her boss ceased punishing the cigarette butt and looked directly into her eyes. "No. There is one more thing. I want you to be honest with me Lin Su. I know that something more than we expected happened between you two. If you feel that you can no longer do what we ask of you…."

She stood and crossed the room to the window. Between the raindrops chasing each other on the pane, she gazed at the pedestrians scurrying through puddles to flag down passing taxicabs. How nice it must be to be so blissfully ignorant of all that now weighed her down, she thought.

"It's my karma," she said softly, without turning to face the Director.

"Yes, it is," he replied.

*   *   *

For days, perhaps weeks—he could not know for certain—Alexander Marenkov feared that he was about to die. Then a curious transformation occurred. He began fearing that he was going to live. For living only meant more torture to the brink of death.

He had ample time to dwell upon these thoughts as he lay in the dark, upon a cold, hard, damp floor. His ankles were tightly bound, his wrists were tied behind his back and his elbows were drawn together by a thick, abrasive cord. Every few hours, the heavy metal door to his cell would clang open, a jabbing white light would flood his eyes, and several indistinguishable figures would tramp in. Rough hands would seize his arms, shove an iron bar through the crook of his elbows, knot a thick rope to the bar, and the agony would begin anew.

He would feel the now familiar first sign—the triceps pulled up and forward, the elbows pinched together. Next, the shoulders would roll outward, threatening to burst from their sockets. They sometimes succeeded. Then he would be face down, the blood rushing to his head as the rope drew on the bar, hoisting him by the elbows. Although he would be swaying in the air, he would be anything but weightless, for his entire frame would now sag heavily from his wrenched shoulders.

The unnatural twisting of the joints, the splay of the bones, and the tearing of muscle and tendon would send waves of electric shocks through his entire body. He remembered having read somewhere that the Afghan Mujaheddins had learned this particular amusement from the Soviet Army, which had borrowed it from their North Vietnamese allies. "The Parrot" was the Asians' avian euphemism for this treatment of American POW's.

He wished, for just once, he would die swaying there in the air, to be lowered down as a corpse to the dismay of his tormentors. But though he would invariably descend into unconsciousness from the excruciating pain, he could never quite achieve this ultimate goal. Always he was lowered alive to the floor, where a splash from a bucket of water ensured that he did not miss a moment of this special sensation. Then he would be jerked to his knees, shoulders would be re-socketed as necessary, and he would be pelted alternately with taunts and offers of relief.

But the price for relief, an end to this withering torture, was unthinkable. Nearly delirious, he was still in sufficient control of his faculties to reason that the lives of millions far outweighed his miserable existence. No, he must never, never give in. Let them break his shoulders, his arms, every bone in his body, but he must somehow summon the strength to resist.

He would be vaguely aware of their admonitions that they would accomplish their objectives with or without his aid; that without him, their work would take a short while longer, but that would be insignificant from the perspective of history. Sometimes, they would appeal to him in a sympathetic manner, providing him bits of food, which his broken and ravaged body could barely assimilate. It was in these gentler moments that they would lecture him, construct a logical base for his capitulation, identify their enemy as his. More often, they would threaten him with interminable days, weeks, and months in the Parrot's maw. Recently, they had even raised the spectre of reuniting him with his wife and two sons, not in the friendly confines of his Moscow apartment, but here, in hell. Then they would tramp out, the iron door would ring shut, and he would again be plunged into darkness and into a mental, as well as physical, torment.

Occasionally, still bound as he lay on his side in his own excrement, he could detect the faint patter of a rodent's paw or even the scratching of a scurrying insect. If he still had some strength, he would push himself across the cell, dreaming that he might capture one of the creatures with his teeth. He never succeeded.

In addition to his gnawing hunger and abiding physical and mental agony, he was subjected to another, more subtle, but equally devastating travail. The visits to his cell occurred at irregular hours, depriving him of blessed sleep, enervating his body and soul, and reducing him to tremorous exhaustion. As time went on, he helplessly felt his strength of mind collapsing, his reason disintegrating, until he finally slipped into delirium.

He was floating over a freshly plowed field, the redolent loamy scent of tilled earth mixed with hay was strong in his nostrils, the boundless sweep of blue sky was lifting his gait. Now he was standing on a wooden train platform and a red and green locomotive was approaching him. Soon he would be onboard heading back to Moscow, to home and to his plump, loving wife. Marianna would give him a good boxing on the ears for being late, he smiled. The locomotive now chugged to a stop, hissing and groaning, the door opened with a slam, and a blinding white light emanated from the car. Merciless hands grasped him, he felt his elbows being pulled taut, his shoulders popping. His eyes squinted in the piercing light, his lips trembled, and his ears heard a feeble voice, curiously like his own, say, "Please no more. I'll do as you say."

*   *   *

"Dmitri, do you have something for me?" Medved said, glancing through the glass of the *Taksophon* booth in all directions.

"Ah, Sergei, your friend has expensive tastes," the voice crackled in the receiver. "His suit cost more than your monthly pay."

"There's very little that costs less, Dmitri, so don't think that's such a clever remark."

"Ha, my friend, I can't one-up you on that point. But as to the other point—the matter of…shall we say…the matter? It's a very fine weave—Italian. Armani to be precise. The button also confirms this conclusion. We are preparing the blood sample from the material for a DNA analysis. Of course, we will need a sample from the principle if we are to attempt a match. We have run fingerprints from the pen, but have not yet correlated them."

"And the bullet?"

"Shit. I'm afraid I can't help you much there. It's a 9mm caliber—possibly fired from a Stechkin automatic pistol. Since that's quite popular among Spetsnaz and you old Chekists, that narrows the field to several thousand, unless of course it was bought or stolen by any one of a million other hooligans in our peaceful country. However, I'm not totally convinced. I need to run a few more tests still. I'll match it with the right weapon if you can ever find it."

"Thanks, Dmitri. I hope to get you the items you need. Now if I could ask you for yet another favor."

"Are you endangering my life, Sergei?"

"That's very possible."

"Harasho! I was getting bored with having to deal only with the Russian Mafia."

"Listen. There is a company in Moscow known as Rurik. Here's what I'd like you to do...."

An absolute *molodyets*—a brick!, Medved marveled as he hung up, having given Dmitri the necessary instructions. He hated putting his great friend in danger, but all his experience and every fiber of his being convinced him that the Marenkov case was worth the complete toss of the dice. Hopefully, his conversations with his former sergeant were not being intercepted. Dmitri was shrewd enough and had the equipment in place to foil a tap on his end, so a breach there was highly unlikely. A greater danger was the use of directed beacon sound amplification equipment from hundreds of meters away. He felt reasonably certain that he had negated this option by his careful selection of the phone booth: it was tucked against an embankment at the entrance to an underpass. The absence of straight line approaches to the telephone would thwart such equipment, which required direct line of sight for a successful intercept.

Stepping from the booth into the cool, early September evening, he lit a cigarette and surveyed his surroundings. Summer was definitely gone, the days were now obviously shorter. Very possibly, the crisp air played a part in the bounce that now powered his step. But the real cause for this new-found spring lay elsewhere. For the first time since he had been aware of the Professor's disappearance, he felt that he was getting a handle on the case. All the trails led back to the American. If he could just have a few moments alone with him...but how? Going after

Slater in the States would be extremely problematical, if not prohibitive. Perhaps he could be lured back to Russia, where he would be on Medved's turf, and would be playing by Chekist rules. This would require some more thought. Meanwhile, the other loose end—Rurik—could be tied up, with Dmitri's help. He looked forward to reading tomorrow morning's *Izvestiya*....

* * *

It was on the second page of the next day's *Izvestiya*, below an article concerning a meeting of the WTO Economic Council in Geneva. Medved poured himself a cup of coffee and began to read:

FIRE DAMAGES RURIK BUILDING

Moscow. A serious fire erupted late last night in the headquarters of the Russian Uranium Korporatsiya (Rurik). No injuries were reported; however, many Rurik offices were scorched and gutted by flames and water from fire hoses. The extent of the damage as well as the cause of the blaze have not yet been determined.

Two days later, a shipment of three bankers boxes was delivered to *Gospodeen* Sasha Borzov at the Gorky Street Apartment Complex. The day manager had received a note from a 'Mister Borzov' to hold the packages for him at the front desk. A short while later, the manager took an urgent call that a water main had sprung a leak on the north side of the building. He returned to his desk fifteen minutes later, frustrated and angry that kids—hooligans—had made a prank call. There he found a note and ten American dollars from '*Gospodeen* Borzov', thanking him for holding his shipment. The packages were gone.

Medved set the boxes in the middle of his living room floor and bolted the door behind him. He doubted if any connection had been made between him and the Rurik files, but one must never be complacent in this business. Sitting on the floor, he laid his *Gurza* next to him and began opening the first box.

A whole new world was now spread before him. A world of destroyed nuclear warheads, of megatons and isotopes, of international trafficking in uranium, of billions of rubles—hell, he corrected himself—billions of American dollars changing hands in such trade.

It was no secret that, in a desperate attempt to salvage its ailing economy, the Russian Federation had decided to cash in its most valuable commodity—its nuclear arsenal. Not until now, however, had Medved appreciated the extent of this business.

Sitting on the floor of his apartment, surrounded by Rurik files, notebooks, binders, and reports, he scoured a thick, soft-covered sheaf of papers that detailed the operations of the Russian uranium conglomerate. Each time he encountered a mention of Micratom Inc., he uncapped a yellow felt-tip marker and made a notation. After several hours the notebooks, binders, reports and sheaf of papers were peppered through with yellow marks. A picture was beginning to take shape.

The documents revealed how the Russian Federation had set about converting the uranium of 20,000 nuclear warheads into hard foreign currency. To facilitate this effort, it had established Rurik as its agent to garner buyers, negotiate contracts, collect payment, and then deliver the goods. How quaint, Medved noted, that the Russian uranium conglomerate had taken the name of the destructive Viking prince who became the first true ruler of Russia. He was further amused by the audacity of his own government. There it was selling the only leverage it had in the world arena, yet at the same time demanding advance payment. It was as if the wolf had miraculously persuaded the hunter to free it from a trap; then, once free, allowed the hunter to pry out its fangs.

Medved also noted with interest that 'the goods' to be delivered was not the fissionable U-235 isotope. Instead, the deadly warhead uranium was to be diluted to a benign level which, of itself, could not be used in weaponry. It would be left to the purchaser to process the downgraded uranium so that it would become chain-reactive. Only a handful of countries possessed the necessary technology to effect such a transformation. Of these countries, the most avid purchasers of Rurik uranium resided in the United States.

Only a small percentage of the total business in America, however, went to James Slater's company. Medved lifted the Micratom annual report that he had kept at his side, its pages dog-eared and creased from constant referencing. Again he thumbed through it, by now so familiar with its contents that he went almost directly to the page he needed. He compared the Micratom numbers with those he had found in the Rurik report. They were identical. Some 3.4 metric tons of low enriched uranium delivered thus far to Micratom, for the price of $55.1 million, American.

Medved settled back on his haunches, staring at the two reports. They had both been constructed very professionally. The business overviews were thorough, logical, precise. Facts and financial data were impressive. Their numbers agreed.

Something stunk.

Circumstantial evidence be damned. His own eyes, his soul be damned for all that mattered. But of one thing he was certain—this American, this president of Micratom was responsible for the disappearance of Russia's foremost atomic physicist. Now there was this business of uranium shipments to Slater's company. Non-fissionable, as clearly represented in both documents. How exquisitely interesting it would be to have a chat with Mr. Slater in the basement of the Lubianka. But then, of course, the FSB has rejected the practices of its disfavored predecessor, the KGB. He permitted himself a wry smile.

But now where to start? Where to start? The question had just begun to repeat when his gaze fell on the last line in the Rurik report:

All deliveries of low enriched uranium to be made F.O.B. St. Petersburg, Russian Federation, for use in commercial nuclear reactors.

He closed both reports and pushed himself up from the floor. His legs were cramped and his knees were stiff from the hours of sitting, kneeling, and squatting. Standing in place, he alternately raised and flexed his semi-century legs. Then he crossed to the window overlooking Gorky Street, leaned against the sill, and stretched. Feeling somewhat healthier, he lit a cigarette.

So…St. Petersburg, he mused. Images of the majestic city flowed into his mind. He and Irina had often visited "Pete", as the city was affectionately termed by Russians, even when it was officially Leningrad. It had been his wife's favorite place. He shoved away from the sill, driving away the thought of her. But his carefully raised wall had been cracked opened.… He wished Galena were here.

Now, however, he must make his plans to visit the city of Peter the Great. It would be impossible to euchre the General on this one. But how wise would it be to tell him? Revealing this information to Aksanov could be sealing his own death certificate. If it weren't for Galena, such a fate in this country and in his circumstances was not to be feared.

But perhaps his imagination was overactive. He was suspicious of his old commander only because of the General's assignment of Buzhkin to him as his "assistant." And for what reason did he suspect that granite column of a man?

For several minutes, he paced around his room, stretching his legs, puffing his cigarette, and sifting his options. The sun had begun to set and the unlit room was succumbing to shadows.

He stopped again at the window sill, admiring the multi-colored pastel hues of dusk. His plan and his resolve were now clear.

Chapter Twelve

Viktor Buzhkin's head was flung back, his mouth was wide open. He had been that way for several hours. A fat fly buzzed perilously close to the snoring orifice, providing Medved with a welcome diversion. It had been nearly six hours since they had departed on the Aurora Express from the Leningradsky train station in Moscow and now the trek had grown beyond wearisome. As much as he was fascinated by his native land, he had stared at enough endless miles of monotonous flat terrain stretching to the horizon, and had had his fill of the identical weed-encrusted ramshackle cottages and dark apparitions of hunched-over peasants laboring alongside sway-backed horses and chugging farm machinery.

Of late, as they approached more northern latitudes—a scant few hundred miles from the Arctic Circle—the scene had become a somewhat more interesting blend of birch trees and pine forests. In spite of the improved vista, Medved was much more focused on the drama of the buzzing insect and Buzhkin's gaping mouth. Gradually, the fly became irrelevant and he found that he was concentrating solely on the slate-chiseled, whisker-stubbled face of his 'assistant.' What lay behind the eyelids of this particular old ex-KGB Chekist, he wondered.

He knew that Buzhkin had not swallowed his contrived rationale for this expedition. For that matter, neither had General Aksanov. They had both observed him and listened in stony silence when he suggested that Marenkov's trail could best be rediscovered in St. Petersburg. After all, he had argued, the Professor spent nearly as much time in that city as in Moscow, he had strong ties with colleagues there, and St. Petersburg University had been heavily involved in the seminar from which he had disappeared.

Aksanov had asked several perfunctory questions, reflected quietly for a few moments, and then approved the proposal. Buzhkin had not uttered a single word during the meeting. He had improved upon that effort by a full two or three sentences before nodding off in the first hour of the trip.

It was now only a matter of minutes before they would arrive in the Moskovsky Station in downtown St. Petersburg. The plan that Medved had advanced, and that the General had now accepted, called for him and Buzhkin to proceed along separate paths. Buzhkin would visit the University and begin interviewing Marenkov's academia acquaintances and colleagues. Medved was to plow through a list of hotels, restaurants and other establishments frequented by the Professor. In reality, once ridding himself of Buzhkin, Medved planned to head directly for the Morskoy Slavy Seaport, at the mouth of the Neva River. It was there, according to the Rurik report, that Russian nuclear warhead uranium was transferred to James Slater's Micratom company. It seemed a promising spot to search for some truth.

The outlines of the metropolis—the northernmost of all the great cities of the world—were beginning to appear. Medved never failed to be enchanted by this "Venice of the North," so-named because of her criss-crossing canals and rivers and her beautiful Italian architecture of pastel buildings and golden spires and cupolas. How often he had made this trip with Irina—especially in the White Nights of early summer, when the northern sun virtually never set.

The Aurora Express jerked suddenly as it slowed nearing its destination. The uneven movement caused Buzhkin's head to roll forward and his mouth to snap shut. To Medved's disappointment, the fly escaped.

"Ey, I must have dozed off. Have we much farther to go?"

"We've arrived. Do me a favor, Viktor, and check us in at the hotel. Take the yellow line from Dostoevsky Metro Station—it'll take you right there. I'll meet you at the hotel for dinner at eight."

Medved hoped that sending Buzhkin in the opposite direction of his own intended path would permit him the freedom of movement that he needed.

Buzhkin, his nail-head eyes screwed distrustfully on his partner, nodded assent.

Several jolts later the Aurora came to rest amidst a long metallic screech and a bursting hiss of steam. With no more than a *docvidanya*, the two men separated, Buzhkin heading toward the Dostoevsky Metro stop and Medved proceeding to the Morskoy Slavy Seaport. As Buzhkin toted both of their bags, Medved's only luggage was the *Gurza* in the holster beneath his left armpit.

The air in St. Petersburg, already nippier than that in Moscow, was given yet more bite by the wind that was blustering in from the Gulf of Finland. Emerging from the Metro stop, Medved zipped up his jacket, lit a cigarette, and hailed a cab on Bolshoi Prospekt. Viktor Buzhkin, having stuffed their bags in a Moskovsky Station locker, flagged the very next taxi on the same thoroughfare.

*   *   *

Several freighters were tied at the Morskoy Slavy piers and dozens more were anchored in the Nevskaya Inlet, waiting their turn to transfer cargo. Their skippers were anxious to conduct their business before the winter freeze set in—only a few weeks away. Icebreaking ships would be employed to maintain an open lane to the seaport throughout the winter, but commerce in this northern latitude would become much more problematic. The teams of dock workers had been increased and many men had even gone to double shifts, but they were still hard-pressed to satisfy the demands of the sea captains.

Alighting from the cab, Medved settled with the driver and began ambling along the docks. Occasionally, he pulled aside a longshoreman or a supervisor, telling the same story to each, asking the same questions. He had nearly reached the end of the waterfront, with nothing to show for his efforts, when he spotted another promising candidate. The man, pot-bellied, gruff, rosy-cheeked, was barking orders to a group of men struggling with a swaying cargo net.

"Ey, *gospodeen*," Medved said approaching. "A moment of your time, please." Receiving no reply, Medved stepped between his quarry and the dock workers. "Ey, *gospodeen*, I need to register a complaint."

The rotund man jutted his belly forward, set his knuckles on his hips and eyed the annoying intruder.

"You're in the way," he growled. "Move!"

"Your name, please," Medved said, reaching inside his jacket for a notepad and pen.

"Who the hell are you?" the man replied, nervously eyeing the pad.

Good, thought Medved. *This one's old enough to remember the days when interrogations from authoritative strangers carried a bit more weight.*

"That's not entirely important. However, since you have asked, I am with a company that sent a shipment to your dock last May. Some of the cargo was missing when the ship arrived at its destination. Again, your name?"

His interviewee shifted his weight from one foot to the other, then back again. It was obvious that the salt-water pipes in his brain were creaking as he tried to assess the situation.

"Gudenko," he muttered.

"Gudenko," Medved repeated, making a notation in his notepad.

"Now, *Gospodeen* Gudenko, can you tell me if you were overseeing loading operations on this dock last May?"

"Ey, be careful with that donkey-line!" Gudenko shouted at his crew of longshoremen. Then, turning back to Medved, "A fine mess of it they'd make, if you didn't stay on top of them all the time. Last May, you say?"

He rubbed a meaty hand against his double-folded chin. "That was a while back. Maybe if you was to tell me your company, *soodar*...."

"Rurik *Korporatsia*." Medved's eyes, which had been dancing indiscriminately among the ships and docks, suddenly froze on those of the longshoreman supervisor.

Gudenko blinked twice, glanced at this troublesome visitor, then looked away from the icy gaze.

"Rurik," he mused. "Can't say I recall it. No...maybe you should ask the other foremen up the docks."

"Certainly. Sorry to have troubled you. Thanks for your time."

Medved tucked the pen and notepad inside his jacket and stamped out his cigarette. He could feel the foreman's glower on his back as he strode away. Stepping between two old shacks on the street side of the docks, he paused, peering through a cracked window frame. *Yes*, he whispered to himself as he spied Gudenko scuttling toward a low-set red brick building approximately thirty meters away. He moved toward the same building from the backside. Working his way around some rusted lading equipment, frayed and greasy old coils of rope and piles of trash, he edged toward a slightly opened window at the far side of the building.

Peering through the smoky pane of the window, he saw that Gudenko was standing and gesticulating before a man who sat at a large paper-cluttered desk. Only the back of the bald head and one arm of the seated man was visible. By the movements of both of their heads, it was obvious that a third person—completely hidden from Medved's view—was being consulted.

"Rurik...he knows something...." could be heard in snatches of Gudenko's nervous chatter.

"You should not have spoken to him," the hidden man growled.

"I had no choice...he was insistent." Gudenko's voice and demeanor betrayed an anxiety bordering on terror. "But I told him absolutely nothing. In fact, it was only by my talking to him that we know he represents a danger." He glanced hopefully from one of his interrogators to the other.

Several moments passed where no one spoke. Finally, the man at the desk lifted a phone receiver and leaned back in his large padded armchair, disappearing from Medved's line of sight. Two minutes later, he swiveled forward and hung up.

"End it," he said, turning to the one still unseen.

Gudenko stepped back, allowing a hulking figure to precede him through the doorway. Medved had hoped for a better glimpse so that he might confirm or allay an uneasy suspicion. The footsteps of Gudenko and his companion grew fainter as the pair worked their way further down the docks.

Medved peered back through the smoky window. The man at the desk was standing now, unlocking a metal file cabinet drawer. *To be in those files, to be in that man's head, would be to solve many mysteries,* Medved mused. He knew that, in thirty seconds he could have this one selling his grandmother to him, let alone spilling his guts about the Rurik business. But the timing was not favorable. There were still too many people milling about and the companion of Gudenko must be reckoned with. No, better to wait until sunset, which was only an hour away. It would most likely mean that he would be late for his dinner appointment with Buzhkin. But then, he had a strong suspicion that his 'assistant' also would be detained.

Selecting an auspicious moment, he turned into a back street. There, he hoped to be beyond the search of Gudenko and his friend, while still being capable of watching the activity around the low-set brick building on the docks. As the sun dipped lower, the wind from the Gulf chased gray clouds inland. The fresh scent of rain was in the air.

✶ ✶ ✶

Just after sunset, the rain began to fall in earnest. Even the dock workers, in a rarity, were driven from their labors in a dash for cover. Although the visibility was greatly reduced in the darkness and the pounding storm, Medved did not fail to see the auto that splashed to a stop behind the brick building. Two men got out—one had the rotund plug-like appearance of Gudenko; the other was not so nearly discernible. Fifteen minutes later, one man splattered back, leaped into the car and sped away.

Watching the vehicle disappear down Bolshoi Prospekt in the rain and gloom, Medved darted toward the brick building. The window at the side of the structure was still slightly open. He peered in but was unable to distinguish anything in the grease-black darkness. Cautiously, he raised the window higher. No sound or motion came from within. Drawing the *Gurza* from its holster, he pulled himself onto the windowsill and slipped into the room.

He took one step forward, his foot landed unexpectedly on a soft and mobile surface, and he tumbled forward. His head landed alongside that of Gudenko's. The longshoreman supervisor, lying face up, was unperturbed at being landed upon. At this close proximity, even the almost total lack of light could not conceal the thumb-size hole in his neck. It was then that Medved felt the sticky substance matted in Gudenko's hair and spreading under his head.

Medved pulled himself across the still body, which had already become perceptibly cool. He had crawled only a few more feet when he knocked against another object lying on the floor. It was smooth, round, hard. Pulling himself closer, Medved realized that he was cupping a bald head, one eye of which was no more than a blood-filled socket. He cursed softly, realizing that some crucial information had perished with these two. There was still one remaining hope. Rising, he stepped over the second corpse and moved toward the metal file cabinet. His optimism was immediately dashed, however. The drawers were all fully open and their contents were scattered over the desk and floor. It was doubtful that he would find anything of use in these discarded papers.

A kopeck-size red glow suddenly was reflected from the top metal drawer. As the dot moved quickly toward him, Medved spun and dove for the floor. The smoky windowpane shattered as a high-caliber bullet streaked into the room.

Chapter Thirteen

The conditions could not have been more favorable. The moon was hidden by a thick layer of clouds, providing no light to ferret out the activities of one who wished to remain covert. Mike Falcon was now such a person. When he departed NSA Headquarters earlier that day, he had returned to Annapolis to gather the equipment he would need this evening. Now he sat on an isolated spot on the east bank of the Potomac, carefully reflecting on his plans. A passerby would have stumbled into him before seeing him as he was—clothed completely in black, including black gloves and black knit pullover cap. His face, too, was grease-blackened. Beside him rested the Zodiac dinghy that he had just finished inflating and inside it lay two oars, a grappling hook connected to a large coil of rope, and a small bag containing some tape, a glass-cutter, a screw-driver, and a penlight.

Satisfied that all was in readiness, he rose and pushed the dinghy into the quietly flowing river. Locking the oars into place, he settled on the bench and began rowing toward his destination, some hundred yards away. Although the Potomac was somewhat subdued, due to the lack of rain at the end of summer, its current was still a force to be reckoned with. Falcon bent his back to the oars, steering his craft diagonally across the water to compensate for the southerly flow. Occasionally he would crane his head around toward the bow, anxiously searching for any telltale ripple that would signify a sharp hidden boulder or a snagging projection of tree limbs. Fortunately avoiding such mishap, he arrived at the opposite bank in less than ten minutes.

Securing the dinghy to a tree trunk, he gazed upwards. The embankment, consisting of large granite boulders and the occasional shrub poking through crevices in the slippery rocks, rose two hundred feet almost vertically from the river's edge. He slung the bag over his right shoulder and ducked his head and left arm through the heavy coil of rope. Slowly, he began edging his way along the bank, toward the base of the imposing gray structure that jutted out over the river.

Slater's house seemed much higher now that he had to scale a cliff to get to it. Unfortunately, there was no getting around it. If his hunch was correct, the information he needed was within those walls. There was only one way to snatch it from under the noses of his associates at the FBI, who were keeping the mansion under twenty-four-hour surveillance. The Feds recognized a murder/robbery red herring when they saw one. Given the scope of destruction of the household goods, it appeared that a desperate search had been conducted for a specific item or items. Very possibly, the effort had failed and the perpetrator may be driven to revisit the scene. In that event, the Federal Bureau of Investigation would be there, waiting.... Waiting out front Falcon hoped, for they shouldn't reasonably suspect that anyone would attempt to enter the house from the cliff side.

Readjusting the coiled rope and bag to a more satisfactory position, Falcon inhaled deeply, then began his ascent. His fingers groped above, clearing dirt and loose pebbles from cracks, fumbling for a secure grip, then clamped tightly down. Cautiously, he trusted increasing amounts of his own weight to the tenuous handhold. Next, his feet followed the same procedure, scratching the face of the rock, fervently seeking a stable toehold. Upward his hands pulled and his feet pushed, his mouth, nose and eyes sprinkled with tumbling dirt, his arm and leg muscles taut and trembling from the strain. Whenever possible, he clung to a well-rooted bush where he partially recovered his strength and breath.

After fifteen minutes, he finally reached his destination—one of a pair of steel beams that jutted diagonally from the rock into the base of the house. Swinging onto the crook of the girder, he leaned against a giant boulder and allowed himself a moment's respite. For the first time since he had begun the ascent, he gazed down. Over a hundred feet beneath him, little white ripples at the base of the cliff were the only evidence that a mighty river lay below. The thought of whether this was all worth it was fleetingly considered, then discarded.

Slipping his head and arm from the coil of rope, he leaned outward and peered up. Above him lay the balustraded porch that led to the master bedroom. He slowly let the rope unravel, pulled down by the weight of the grappling hook at the free end. When he was satisfied with the length of line, he began a slow pendulum-like swinging of the hook. Then, with a sudden jerk, he flung the apparatus in an arc toward the balustrade. The iron knocked against one of the supporting columns, rebounded and plunged down past him. On the second try, with two more feet of line let out, it soared over the railing and wedged between two of the columns. Falcon tugged hard and while still clinging to the safety of the girder, let his full weight settle onto the line. Then, taking a deep breath, he pushed clear of the beam and swung into black space.

With his legs tightly entwined around the rope, he shinnied up to the balcony, pulled himself over the rail, and plopped down onto the cold marble tiles. Removing the bag that had been hanging from his shoulder, he extracted the roll of tape and glass cutter. Re-slinging the pouch, he rose and moved to a pair of French doors at the back of the house. Just above the brass latch of one of the doors, he etched, then taped a fist-sized patch of window. With one slight tap, the small area noiselessly broke away. He reached through the opening, unhitched the lock and swung the door open.

The master bedroom had changed little since his last visit, except for the absence of the owner's rigid corpse.

Falcon drew his penlight from his bag, moved around the now empty bed, and proceeded toward the far wall. The probing ray of light revealed the wall-safe and its still open door. On the floor, exactly where it had been left propped against the wall by the FBI agents, was the original oil by Salvador Dali.

Falcon briefly studied the melted clocks and the exaggerated limbs of the figures in the painting before flipping it face down on the floor. The back of the frame was covered with a thin sheet of wood which was easily unscrewed. Lifting the backing, Falcon slowly dragged the pencil-thin light across the reverse canvas and around its sides.

Then he saw it, in the lower right hand corner, taped to the canvas back.

He grasped the thin rectangular object, dropped it in his bag, and began rescrewing the wooden backing to the frame. As he put the final twist to the last screw, he heard a muffled creak from below. He paused and listened. The barely audible sound coming from the direction of the spiral staircase was repeated. Quietly, he rose and slipped across the room, through the French doors, and out onto the patio. As he stepped over the hand-guard of the balustrade, he glanced back into the house. Two shadows were moving through the bedroom.

Grasping the rope, he swung over the side and began rappelling along the side of the cliff. He was halfway down when he heard alarmed voices from the balcony. Increasing his efforts, he quickly descended the remaining twenty yards, falling the final few into a heap on the muddy embankment. Scrambling to his feet, he yanked the trip line and the grappling iron hurtled down in front of him. Hastily gathering it and its long tether, he worked his way along the river bank to the Zodiac. As he had planned, his escape route would be much faster now that he would be paddling south with the current. Still, he knew he would be fortunate to evade the dragnet that the FBI must now be mounting.

Only five minutes elapsed in his re-crossing of the river. Reaching the east bank, he drove his screwdriver repeatedly into the inflatable pontoons of the dinghy. When it had sufficiently collapsed, he collected it and weaved his way through dark, grasping trees and bushes to his waiting jeep. There, he flung the tattered dinghy into the back of the vehicle, hopped into the driver's seat, and turned the key.

Across the river, lights could be seen snaking in and out of the shrubbery along the bank. The lights of his jeep, however, remained off as it moved slowly over a dirt trail leading to a two-lane road. Soon Falcon was speeding down John Hansen Highway, wondering what gems lay hidden in the CD-ROM that lay at his side.

* * *

Medved lay huddled on the floor for several dozen seconds before he became aware of a burning sensation in his right cheek. Lightly running his fingers over the painful area, he encountered a warm trickle of blood. He was relieved that it was no more than a flesh wound.

It was a short-lived reassurance, however, as another ping resounding from the metal cabinet underscored the precariousness of his position. A shrill whine was audible as the bullet ricocheted near his head. The red dot moved from the cabinet, danced across the far wall, then swung toward his position. Realizing that he had little chance against a high-powered telescopically-sighted rifle, he decided upon a temporary defensive measure.

Rolling to his left, his hands fumbled for, then grasped the shield he needed. The red dot traveled slowly across the desk directly behind him as he tugged the object. With the second heave, he was able to pull Gudenko's heavy corpse over him.

Another windowpane shattered, the sound of its splintering glass followed almost instantaneously by a dull thud emanating from the dead longshoreman's frame. The lack of a rifle report confirmed Medved's suspicion that the would-be assassin was using a silencer. The entry of the next bullet into the room was quieter yet, as it streaked through the void of the now missing pane. Its arrival was announced by the explosion of Gudenko's head just above his own. Instinctively, Medved recoiled from the blast, wiping chunks of brain and skull from his hair and face.

He felt that his position had become untenable. But he also knew that attempting to escape through the door or a window was not an option. Even that hazard, though, might be better than lying here, where in a few more minutes his head would surely resemble Gudenko's.

The red dot snaked toward the back wall, briefly reflecting off a shiny round metal object. Medved hoped that his eyes had not deceived him. Waiting until the light moved to the far side wall, he pushed Gudenko's mutilated body aside, then dove behind the large desk.

His movement was greeted by flying shards of glass and splintering wood as the desk began to fly apart. Wasting no time, he reached toward the spot on the back wall where he had seen the reflection of the shiny round object. His hand closed around a doorknob and with a quick twist and forward thrust, he tumbled into a one-toilet bathroom. Several bricks on the back wall of the lavatory disintegrated in powdery eruptions, indicating that his movement had not gone undetected.

The faint glare of a street light entered a small window above the toilet. The red dot moved toward him, then stopped and dropped to the floor. Again, it circled back, halting in the same place, before moving away. *He doesn't have the angle,* Medved thought.

Quickly stepping on the toilet seat lid, he reached up and threw the window open. Barely squeezing through the narrow passage, he emerged into the driving rain and dropped onto a pile of wet trash. He rolled to the ground and rose.

"Now, you son-of-a-bitch, you're mine," he spoke through tightly clenched teeth. Circling around the neighboring building, he peered from under a sheltering eave through the tempest to the water-swept docks. He did not have to wait long.

A large, shadowy form carrying a long instrument emerged from behind a mooring piling and lumbered in the opposite direction. Medved darted from his cover, slogging after the retreating figure. His quarry, sensing the pursuit, wheeled and raised his device.

Medved belly-flopped onto the rain-slicked planks as a bullet whizzed by his ear. Lying in a cold rivulet, he held the *Gurza* with both hands and squeezed the trigger three times. The *Gurza*, known affectionately among Chekists as the Viper, could penetrate thirty layers of Kevlar at fifty meters, rendering flak jackets useless. It was their favorite weapon. The dark, barely visible figure spun around, collapsed to one knee, then struggled up and limped away. Splashing to his feet, Medved took aim again, then lowered his pistol. Better to take this one alive, he thought. He sloshed across the dock, following the trail of his wounded prey around a tumbledown shack. Holding the *Gurza* upright with both hands next to his grazed cheek, he slowly edged along the wall of the building. Cautiously, he peered around the corner.

A street light provided some dim illumination of rusted dock machinery and gnarled old lines. Taking aim, he squeezed the trigger once and the light exploded in sparks and a white puff of smoke. He then stepped around the building, keeping his back planted firmly against the wall.

A car engine suddenly roared to life near the low-set brick building from which he had just escaped.

Medved began racing toward the sound of the running motor. With its lights still off, the vehicle lurched onto Bolshoi Prospekt and spewing a watery rooster-tail in its wake, disappeared in the pelting rain.

Chapter Fourteen

It was just after midnight when Medved arrived at the Ladoga Hotel on Alexander Nevsky Square. He was tired, sticky, matted with grime, and soaked clear through to the bone. In his arms however, he still carried hope that the night had not been a complete loss. For, after his assailant had fled, he had returned to the brick building to collect all of the documents that had been strewn about the office.

He now lugged himself and these files into the hotel lobby. At the front desk, the night clerk, trying valiantly to mask his distress at the sight of this spectre, presented Medved with his room key and a small paper. It was a telephone note from Buzhkin, stamped at 6:00 p.m., sending dinner regrets—he had been unavoidably detained.

Medved rode the lift to the third floor, then trudged to his room. Peeling off his soggy and filthy clothes, he lit a cigarette and sank blissfully into a hot-water tub.

∗   ∗   ∗

The room in which Alexander Marenkov stood was brilliant white from its acoustic-absorbent paneled ceiling to its thoroughly scrubbed tile floor. The Professor, himself, was clad in a clean white smock and worked at a white greaseboard that, crammed with equations, took up half of one wall. Behind him were two dozen opened metal folding chairs arranged in four neat rows of six chairs each. However, only two seats, both in the very front row and directly behind Marenkov, were occupied. One of the occupants was his old colleague, Valentin Tschernin; the other was a Tatar-featured, gray-haired *starozheel* named Stephan Vasilyich Perov, also an ex-patriot Russian physicist.

"Your liquid-drop model of the fission process is basically correct," Alexander Marenkov said, twirling a felt-tipped pen between his fingers as he paced before the whiteboard. His reference was to the breakthrough understanding of the atomic nucleus to be similar to a droplet of water. "Two opposing, yet balanced, forces hold a water drop together—the attraction between their molecules versus the repulsion of their 'hard' molecular cores. In a similar manner, an atomic nucleus is squeezed together by a strong nuclear attraction that is offset by a repulsive electrical charge."

Valentin Tschernin, who for the past hour had been sitting with rapt attention as he took copious notes, looked up at the Professor. "If the model is correct, then why can we not properly derive our equations?"

"Your problem is you failed to properly consider quantum effects, specifically the Pauli Exclusion Principle," Alexander said, removing the felt-tip marker's cap and rapidly scribbling a lengthy equation on the whiteboard. He winced from pain as he wrote, the residual effect of having his shoulders repeatedly wrenched and even separated. Lowering his arm, he waited for the stabbing sensation to pass, then again attacked the board.

The equations that he scrawled were, he knew, irrelevant to the construction of the device. He would convey nothing useful. They were so elegant, however, that his audience could not help but be mesmerized. As he wrote, he maintained a discourse that, while descriptive of his equations, would be of no value to the work of the terrorists.

"Pauli showed that no two particles in a given atom can possess the same quantum numbers," he muttered. "It is because of this remarkable property that our world can exist. Otherwise, every atom in the cosmos would look the same—a boring round little ball—and we would not be here having this interesting discussion. For we would not be here at all. But because of the physics of the Exclusion Principle, subatomic particles are forced to take up interesting combinations that we know as the elements of the universe. Now, as we delve ever deeper into these elements, as in the construction of a miniature atomic device, this principle becomes increasingly more significant."

Finishing the equations with a forceful exclamation mark, he dropped the blue marker on the whiteboard tray, wiped his hands on his smock, and stepped back to admire his work.

"Brilliant!" exclaimed Tschernin. He had marveled once again at the genius of his former mentor—how Marenkov had instantly recognized quantum physics problems that had stumped his own team for months, how he had swiftly attacked them, wielding his felt-tip marker like a Cossack slashing with his saber. How in only a matter of minutes he had vanquished them, and how he had made it all look so simple. Yet, at this moment of triumph, the Professor appeared anything but a conquering hero. His face was gaunt and ashen, his black-bean eyes were sunk in deep gray sockets, and his thin lips often trembled as he spoke. He moved slowly, deliberately, painfully, slightly hunched over, his left arm hanging uselessly at his side. Tschernin was overwhelmed with a sense of horror, outrage, and shame.

Turning to Perov, he said, "Stephan Vasilyich, would you be so good as to allow me a few moments with my old friend?"

Perov hesitated, somewhat affronted by the implication that his status with Marenkov was inferior to that of Tschernin's. Nevertheless, he departed, consoling himself with the remarkable mathematical and physical insights that had been revealed by the Professor during the past hour. When the door closed after Perov, Tschernin summoned his courage to address Marenkov in a more personal manner.

"I…we…wish you had agreed to join us earlier. It would have…that is…so much…could have been avoided."

"Don't get the wrong idea, Valentin. I have not joined with you," Alexander replied hoarsely. "I have agreed to provide these fiends certain information"—all of which was useless, he failed to add. "This was based on the condition that the device we are building can never be put to its ultimate use. It will be used as a negotiation tool only."

"Yes, yes, Alexander. You are so right! And I believe they are being truthful on this point. To actually use such a weapon would be inhuman, in fact counterproductive to the cause. We would lose that very support of the public which we so value. And we'd also lose the moral high ground. Only one country—the object of our Jihad—has ever used such a weapon against humanity. We must never forget that!"

Feeling faint and still weak from his trips to the Parrot's maw, Marenkov stumbled to an empty chair and fell, rather than sat, down.

"Can I get you something, Alexander—water, perhaps?"

"Please," the Professor responded, wiping his cold, perspiring forehead with a sleeve of his smock.

Tschernin hurried to the back of the room where a pitcher of water and two glasses sat on a plain tile countertop.

"This will all be worth it," he said filling both glasses and returning to the front of the room.

He handed one of the tumblers to Marenkov saying, "Even if you don't accept our faith, our philosophy, you must admit that knocking America from its elevated pedestal will restore some dignity to our beleaguered country."

Marenkov swallowed a long draught of the lukewarm water, then lowered the glass.

"Tell me, Valentin," he said, staring blankly at the floor. "Do you know where we are?"

Tschernin glanced nervously about the room as though ensuring that no phantoms had entered during their conversation.

He bent closer to Marenkov and whispered," I'm not absolutely positive…but occasionally one hears a word here…another there…I would say that we're somewhere in eastern Afghanistan, near a town they refer to as Khowst."

The Professor nodded, rubbed his hollow eye sockets, then with an effort, spoke again. "That means we are only just across the border from...."

"Don't even think of it!" Tschernin exclaimed, alarmed.

"Escape," Marenkov said quietly.

"No!" Tschernin said, quickly rising and striding to the whiteboard. "Don't be stupid!"

Embarrassed by his own outburst, Tschernin collected himself and returned to his chair. He turned to Marenkov with a softer tone of voice.

"Alexander, I'm afraid it's impossible. Even if you were physically sound which we must both sadly confess you are now not, it would be madness to think you could survive. Trekking to the east or south, you'd only manage to wind up in Pakistan; that is, if you lived. Of course, the Pakistanis would return you. And it would be beyond madness to think you could cross the Hindu Kush to the north, let alone the Pamirs beyond that.

"Besides, the whole Afghan army would be looking for you, not to mention the Israeli Mossad, the CIA, and the FSB; the Afghans would usher you right back here and the others would be happy to kill you. If by some miracle you made it to Tadzhikistan, you would only face capture by the Muslims there. Remember, it is no longer a republic of the Soviet Union. Those days are gone. Face it, Alexander, your life is not worth one plug kopeck outside of these walls."

Marenkov listened in stony silence to the weight and logic of Tschernin's words.

"Very convincing," he responded, thinking that somehow he would prove his colleague wrong. For he well knew that the conditions of his participation in this project would not be honored, and that the crushing weight of a nuclear holocaust was bearing down on his fragile, maimed shoulders. The world must be alerted...a way must be found...but it seemed so impossible. He suddenly felt very weak and hopeless.

Chapter Fifteen

Medved sat alone at a white-clothed table for two in a corner of the Hotel Ladoga. One hand clutched the morning *Izvestiya*, which he scanned somewhat disinterestedly, while the other slowly raised a cup of lukewarm coffee to his lips. A half-smoked ash-laden cigarette lay smoldering in a ceramic ashtray to the right of the paper.

Viktor Buzhkin, who was to meet him for breakfast, had just emerged on the staircase next to the front desk. The ramrod stiff man now appeared even more stilted as he picked his way down the stairs. Although there was no evidence of pain in his face, it was obvious by the way he leaned against the railing and cautiously set down his right foot, as though a nail was driven into its sole, that he was in discomfort.

Descending the final step, he gathered himself, turned and spied his breakfast partner. Without flinching, he allowed his full weight to settle on his right leg and lumbered forward.

"Viktor, you seem to have met with some misfortune," Medved said, lowering the newspaper.

"Me? I'm fine," Buzhkin scowled, renewing his effort to conceal his hobble.

As he reached the table, however, his awkward negotiation of the chair could not be masked. Under Medved's silent intent gaze, he fidgeted briefly before feeling compelled to say, "Ah, this old Mujaheddin souvenir acts up when it rains. Never did get all the shrapnel out."

Medved sipped his coffee pensively, then lowered the cup. "I didn't know you served in Afghanistan," he said.

Buzhkin grunted, which Medved interpreted as an affirmative response.

"Which unit?"

"Ey, *droog*, some coffee here," he growled at a passing waiter. "They act as if you don't exist," he shook his head.

"Which unit," Medved persisted.

"Hmm? Unit?"

"Yes, in which outfit did you serve in the war?"

The etched lines in the corners of Buzhkin's eyes screwed down tightly as he riveted his gaze on Medved.

"Vaznetsov's 32nd Rifle Brigade," he spoke dryly.

Medved downed another swallow of coffee, then held the cup casually in both hands.

"Vaznetsov's 32nd…I remember that unit…it was on our left flank just northwest of Kabul in '81. That was some fighting. Surely you must have known Major Pavel…."

"Listen, Medved," Buzhkin interrupted. "I'd love to reminisce with you some day. Maybe when we're in the Old Soldiers' Home. Right now, we have more important things to discuss."

"Of course," Medved said as he moved back to allow the waiter to freshen his cup. "Would you like to eat something?"

"*Da*." Buzhkin turned to the waiter. "Bring me three boiled eggs, a loaf of black bread, some sausages, a couple slices of herring, shredded cabbage, and a potato…and, oh yeah, a bowl of *kvass*. And you, Medved?"

"Nothing for me…got here a little early and I've already eaten."

"I see. What time did you finally get in last night?"

"Late. I got your note that you also were detained."

"So I was. Did you have any luck?"

In between long draws on his cigarette, Medved spun a mythical tale of restaurants and hotels that he had "visited" and people that he had "interviewed." Regrettably, he informed his assistant, no significant information had resulted. By the time he concluded, the waiter reappeared with Buzhkin's meal.

"And you, Viktor, perhaps you had better luck?"

Medved observed with no small measure of astonishment as Buzhkin poured the *kvass*—a sour brew of fermented rye bread—over the cabbage, herring, and sausages. The hulking man stuffed a heaping forkful of the mixture in his mouth, which was immediately joined with a *kvass*-sopped chunk of black bread.

"Nothing to speak of," he mumbled between chews. Then, washing the concoction down with a swallow of coffee, "Just a lot of academics pissing in their pants at the thought of talking to me."

"I can't imagine," Medved smiled sardonically.

"Mmph," Buzhkin muttered, before shoveling in another small mountain of food. "Personally, I think this whole trip is a colossal waste of time. We'll find nothing here."

"You know what, Viktor. I couldn't agree with you more. The Aurora Express heads back to Moscow at noon. Let's plan to be on it."

Buzhkin tore off another fist-sized knuckle of bread with his teeth and dipped it into the *kvass*. His face betrayed no emotion as he bit into it and replied simply, "*Harasho*."

"Well, then, I'm off to my room to pack. We have a couple of hours, so perhaps I'll take a walk afterwards. Would you like to join me? Oh, sorry…I forgot…your old wound…."

Buzhkin temporarily abandoned his assault on his food to glower at Medved. "You go along. I'll meet you in the lobby at ten, ready to depart."

Medved rose, fluttered several ruble notes to the table, and left. Returning to his room, he placed a chair next to a window that overlooked the graceful granite statues, sculptured shrubs, and tombstones of Lazarus Cemetery. Gathering the files that he had salvaged from the Moskoy Slavy Seaport, he plopped in the chair and lit a cigarette.

For nearly two hours he pored through the scores of papers, which contained thousands of bits of data concerning ships, bills of lading, and dock handling. He had limited expectations, as the seaport office had been thoroughly scoured by his assailant. But one page, with an invoice stapled to it, had slipped through his enemy's hands. He scanned avidly—*Vendor: Rurik Korporatsiya, Russian Federation… Purchaser: Micratom, Inc., USA…Carrier: Murmansk…Cargo: Low Enriched Uranium…Weight: .565 Metric Ton.…*

The dockside Bill of Lading acceptance was signed by A.A. Gudenko.

The Stapled sheet, impressed with the light blue logo of the merchant ship Murmansk, contained the same information, with a noteworthy exception—*Received On Board: .545 Metric Tons.…*

Medved stood, cradling the two papers gently in his hands, as if the slightest motion might cause this remarkable find to disintegrate. "Twenty kilograms of warhead uranium," he spoke softly, "gone…vanished into the thin St. Petersburg air."

He slowly sank back into his chair, his mind rapidly sorting through facts and possibilities related to his discovery. The American, Slater, had never received the uranium, yet he had somehow been involved in its diversion. Diversion…to where…and to whom? The answer lay here in St. Petersburg and with the Russian company, Rurik. Yet he could proceed in this city no longer, not when his every move was being dogged. His suspicions about Buzhkin had been confirmed the moment he had spotted his 'war-wounded' associate limping down the hotel staircase. As painful as it might be to admit, he must now also paint his old commanding officer, General Aksanov, with the same brush. The betrayal of loyalty…the untrustworthiness of his own organization, the FSB…the rising specter of the Feliks.…

Medved felt an oppressive sense of isolation as he turned to gaze through the window. The downpour of the previous evening had ceased, but the sky was still thick with melancholy gray and black clouds. Across the street, puddles of water were dammed among the wet mausoleums and tombstones. Somewhere down there, he knew, were the remains of some of Russia's greatest composers...Glinka, Mussorgsky, Rimsky-Korsakov. One, however, weighed particularly heavily on his mind. The thought of Tchaikovsky...of Swan Lake...of the princess Odette...evoked not beauty, but anxiety within his soul. The danger to Galena in the *Byezo* was no longer hypothetical. Getting her out of there, and out of Russia was now his sole focus. It might require his ultimate sacrifice.

*   *   *

The steady cadence of hup, two, three, four, emanating from the throats of dozens of young men, roused Mike Falcon from his sleep. Throwing aside his quilt and peering through the starboard porthole, he glimpsed a company of Midshipmen pumping through their morning calisthenics on a Naval Academy drill field approximately thirty yards away. He shivered momentarily, a response to the cold front that had swept in from the northwest just before sunrise. Donning sweat pants and a heavy pullover, he swung from the stern berth and padded out of the aft cabin.

Reaching the galley, he switched on a propane gas burner and started a pot of coffee. *Stardust* seemed quite empty and lifeless without the routine antics of his big black Lab. But with the possibility that the very lovely, and very murderous, Svetlana Popova might revisit the ketch, he couldn't risk leaving Jocko on board. The old gentle dog would be safe with Lin Su. Suzie...the thought of her rekindled a tangle of emotions he had been attempting to suppress for three months...love... desire...hurt...regret...anger...The love and desire that existed between them then, and now, was pure, uncomplicated, readily fathomable. Coming to terms with the hurt and regret was like wrestling with a phantom that remained elusively beyond his grasp. And then there was the anger. Some of it was directed at her for leaving him. More was directed at himself for letting her slip out of his life. But the lion's share was reserved for the FBI, for causing the rift between them.

He wondered if the Agency had made any connection between him and last evening's business. Barring the possible DNA traceable strand of hair, he felt reasonably confident that he had left behind no incriminating evidence. Even if he did come under suspicion, the Slater mansion break-in had been worth the risk. Damned if he would allow the Hooverettes control of this case. They'd freeze him out, sure as hell. And that would never be acceptable, not where this strange convergence of Russian nuclear warhead uranium, the Slater assassination, and the mysterious Feliks organization was concerned. Then there was the CD-ROM....

He had debated whether to run it himself or let the Worm handle it. There was a very real danger that the disk was protected with a virus. Downloading it could wipe out his hard drive and all the information that the disk contained. He was not entirely unprepared to deal with such a threat, however. The Worm had provided him with a program which he had written to defeat viruses at their onset. The Enfant Terrible had dubbed it Battle Vax, short for Battle Vaccine.

Pouring the now hot coffee into a mug, Falcon entered the main cabin and sat at the navigation table. He set the mug to one side, opened the doors beneath the table, fumbled through some charts, and withdrew his laptop computer and the disk.

Falcon turned the thin CD-ROM several times between his fingers, debating his decision. Then, blocking out his anxiety, he inserted it into his drive and entered "Start".

A flashing red light in the upper right hand corner confirmed his suspicion. Slater had wisely taken the precaution of infecting the disk with a bug. He had not reckoned on the Worm, or Battle Vax, however. Falcon eased back against the navigation seat bulkhead, his gaze anxiously glued to the rapidly flitting numbers on the screen. A battle truly was raging before his eyes, in which the terrain was algorithms, the troops were photons, the movement was at light speed, and the outcome was impossible for a mere human to predict. After several fretful minutes the data flow finally ceased. The red light clicked off. Then one word appeared:

SALVADOR

"God bless you, Worm," Falcon spoke softly. The Battle Vax had performed as advertised, attacking the virus and devouring it. He could picture the whiz kid's face—screwed in perplexity at Falcon's incredulity.

With a few taps on the keyboard, the Salvador story began to unfold.

Chapter Sixteen

Alexander Marenkov knelt on a rectangular carpet that was barely large enough to accommodate his legs from knee to toe. His feet were bare, his shoes having been left near the entrance of the mosque, at the pool where he had performed the ritual ablutions—cleansing of the face, nostrils, mouth, forearms, hands, and feet. Kneeling to his left was Valentin Tschernin and to his right, Stephan Vasilyich Perov. Several other former countrymen flanked those two and behind them were a dozen ranks of darker skinned, mustached, raw-boned worshipers.

A door swung open to the right and an Imam, wearing a pure white robe and brimless cap and with the Koran tucked under one arm, swept in.

"*Praise be to Allah, the Lord of the Worlds*," he began reciting the *Fatihah*:

the compassionate, the merciful…Guide thou us on the straight path, the path of those to whom thou has been gracious, with whom thou art not angry, and who go not astray.

Marenkov and the others pressed their foreheads to their prayer mats, then sat upright to receive the sermon. Thirty minutes later, his message having been conveyed, the Imam ended the midday prayer meeting, the second of five such daily sessions. The Professor rose with the others and was about to return to work when he heard his name called.

"You are to come with me," the Imam said sternly.

Tschernin grasped Marenkov's arm and, with a worried expression, sputtered, "Alexander, be care—"

"Don't worry," the Professor interrupted. "I'm sure at this point they will do me no further harm. They need me."

He turned and followed the Imam through the side door of the mosque. The chamber they entered was much more elegantly appointed than any other he had seen in the compound. Richly decorated Persian tapestries hung from the walls and a majestic, multi-hued, room-sized Afghan carpet adorned the floor. A low circular wooden table, surrounded by dozens of large brightly colored pillows, dominated the middle of the room. Silver trays containing bread, fruit, lamb, pastries and other delicacies crowded against sweating glass pitchers of juices, tea, and water on the table top.

"Sit there," Harun barked, pointing to one of the over-sized pillows.

Marenkov proceeded to the designated spot, sunk down and folded his bare feet under him. Satisfied that all was in order, Harun quickly exited.

For several minutes, he sat alone in the silent room, neither moving nor looking about. Finally, another door, directly opposite him, opened. Immediately recognizing the tall imposing dark figure, he began to rise.

"That is not necessary," bin Wahhab spoke in English, raising his hand to stem Marenkov's obeisance. In three great strides, the Arab crossed to the table and, with surprising grace for a man of his lanky proportions, settled cross-legged into the pillows. "Please…indulge yourself," he said, motioning to the food. "I'm afraid you'll have to humor my Bedouin idiosyncrasies, as I allow no utensils in this room."

The Professor nodded, reached forward and broke off a nub of pita bread, wishing that a fork were available. For, if it were, he would most surely plunge it into the neck of his host. He made a mental note to always carry a sharp instrument with him in anticipation of another such opportunity.

"And are you being treated well? If you have any complaints, I wish to know," bin Wahhab said as he buried a slab of pita bread into a bowl of hummus.

"I would like some more blankets," Marenkov spoke softly. "It is very damp and cold in this place and my circulation is not as good as it was before my interesting treatment here."

"It shall be done," bin Wahhab replied, ignoring his prisoner's sarcastic tone. "What else?"

"Spectacles. The ones provided me are not focused properly."

"That, too, shall be rectified. Small requests. Is there nothing more?"

"Yes. I do have one last request."

"By all means…."

"I would like to return to my home in Moscow."

Bin Wahhab licked his fingers, then dipped them into a silver water bowl that contained slices of lemon. "I'm afraid that's not possible for the present. Your work here is much too important. Which brings me to the point of our meeting. Tell me, how is our project faring?"

Alexander slowly, methodically, nibbled a small bit of his bread before responding.

"My lifelong study of physics has taught me to be a humble man, so I hope I do not seem arrogant when I say that you are fortunate to have me here. Your people had assembled a stack of highly-enriched uranium very near its critical mass. If I had not made the necessary changes, a runaway reaction could have been caused just by someone leaning too close and allowing hydrogen from the sweat in his body to interact with the stack. They were well on their way to blowing you and themselves into the next world and vaporizing everything within ten miles. And what a pity that would have been."

The Professor's statement produced the effect he had desired. The Arab's smug expression vanished, replaced by an unguarded blend of inquisitiveness and anxiety. Perhaps this angst could be exploited.

"For your expertise, I thank you. However, your perpetual tone of sarcasm is vexing", Bin Wahhab said.

"And why should the manner of one so insignificant as myself be so troubling to one as exalted as you?" Marenkov replied, scooping his bread into the hummus.

"It is precisely because you are not insignificant. Your mind is among the world's finest. Yet, I am continually disappointed in your inability to see the righteousness of our cause."

"I have no quarrel with your cause. In fact, I don't even think about it. My objection is to your means. I cannot ever countenance the cold-blooded murder of innocent people in the name of any objective, no matter how beautifully rationalized."

"Ah, bravely spoken for one of your profession, country, and faith. Tell me, just exactly how many nuclear warheads were you responsible for designing—?"

"—A last resort to defend my country—"

"Yes, of course. A fine rationale. And let us speak of your country...your whole society was born, raised and maintained on terrorism. And as for your faith...surely you have not forgotten that it was the Jews who introduced political terrorism to the world two thousand years ago. I still study the tactics they used against the Roman invaders. Quite remarkable."

"I am well aware of that history and of the fate that befell those particular ancestors of mine."

"I assume you speak of their last stand at Masada and their mass suicide. They are to be envied. Nine hundred men holding off the Roman legions for over half a year before making the ultimate sacrifice. To die for one's faith is the most glorious of fates. Surely, even with your atheistic attitude, there still burns within you a spark of belief in something more magnificent than the dust and clay of which we are made…something worth dying for."

Swallowing the last portion of his bread, Marenkov avoided the Arab's eyes, fearful that if he looked upon the intense beatific gleam he might lose his self-control and do something foolish.

"I do believe in something greater…the unity and harmony of the cosmos, as revealed in the eternal laws of physics…the power of reason…our ability to understand this cosmos."

"Then you are doomed to failure, for reason alone will never reveal the mind of God. Eventually reason fails, even for one of your genius, and faith must be relied upon."

"I would fully agree with you, sheikh," Marenkov nodded as he selected a handful of figs from another of the silver trays, "if you would stop there. However, you go beyond mere reliance on faith. You believe faith is something to fight for, to die for, to kill for."

"And what is the worth of life if one has no such convictions?" bin Wahhab shrugged. "Sometimes a purifying Jihad is necessary."

"Jihad…a Holy War," the Professor mused. "Perhaps it would be wiser to turn to faith only when one has fought a Holy War in support of reason. One's reason must never be surrendered to cowardice or laziness."

"I am not sure I follow your meaning. Cowardice…Laziness of reason? Please explain." Bin Wahhab poured himself a cup of tea.

"I refer to those who, out of fear of retribution or of being ostracized, surrender their reason. Or those who are all too willing to place their brains in someone else's hands…say, for example, a religious fanatic…simply because they lack the energy to think for themselves. To me, it's a great sadness…a crime, even…to surrender one's reason to anyone without a gallant battle."

Bin Wahhab smiled. "But always the brain will fail. And, as I have said, "Some things, indeed, those that are the most important in the universe cannot be understood through the mind. Eventually reason *will* fail. In the end, perhaps, we shall find that your religion of physics is compatible with Islam. Take the project you are working on, for example. Your physics can describe the elements of matter involved and the material forces at work, but it does not explain the fury released by the *jinn* that dwells within the atom."

"I can assure you that there is no genie at work here. As to whether or not there is a god—your Allah or any other, for that matter—I will leave to you. But the processes, in my mind, are quite simple and logical functions of nature—the splitting and fusion of atomic nuclei."

Bin Wahhab stroked his beard, never dropping the gaze that he had fixed upon the Russian.

"Tell me then, Professor, if this awesome force is not the work of a supernatural being, what is the secret of its power?"

Marenkov reflected a moment before responding, then smiled, patting his stomach, "Weight reduction."

The Arab's brows knitted, stitching together the weathered seams of his forehead.

"Do not jest with me," he said.

"I would never joke about such a serious matter. Perhaps if you'll permit me to explain...."

A nod from Bin Wahhab urged him on.

"You see, sheikh, it is one of nature's mischievous ironies that one of the major ingredients she has used to brew the cosmos—and to create uranium—becomes lighter when it is paired with others of its kind. This ingredient—an infinitesimally small particle—is squeezed together with countless trillions of its duplicate in the interior of massive clouds of gas and dust floating through our galaxy. Under this great pressure, they are trapped and held together by nature's strongest force."

As he spoke, Marenkov selected two apples from a silver tray and moved them together.

"When they fuse, they shed some of their excess weight, converting their own matter into pure energy." He pulled the stem from each fruit and held them before bin Wahhab. "These may appear inconsequential in relation to the apples...and the amount of matter lost in atomic fusion is even relatively more insignificant. Yet, the results at the atomic level are quite astounding. I'm sure you are well aware of Einstein's principle that conversion of a miniscule amount of matter results in a tremendous amount of energy. In this way, the intergalactic clouds become colossal thermonuclear bombs, held together by the weight of their gravity...what we call stars. By such means, all of the elements of the cosmos, including uranium, are created and all inanimate objects, and every living being is made possible."

Bin Wahhab dabbed the corners of his mouth with a white linen napkin. "But you say that uranium was formed in the stars. Tell me then, how did it come to be here on earth?"

"As I noted, the stars are gigantic nuclear bombs held together by their own gravity. This is a precarious balance, however, for they are burning away their fuel and their gravitational force eventually overwhelms their weakened outward nuclear explosion. Over five billion years ago, one of these stars collapsed under its own weight. The compression resulted in the heating of its interior to a hundred million degrees. A cataclysmic blast was triggered—a super star that lit up the galaxy—ripping the star apart and spewing its contents into space in a multi-trillion mile wide cloud of cosmic debris.

"This cloud, containing all the elements cooked in the star's interior, including uranium, floated through the Milky Way Galaxy for many millennia. Eventually, its gravity again began to dominate and it began to fall in upon itself. The core of the cloud reheated and ignited another atomic reaction. But this time, insufficient material was involved to allow gravity to crush the star. Our sun was born and out of the remaining debris, the planets of our solar system came into being. All the elements that had been baked in the supernova, including uranium, were deposited on the earth."

"But if uranium, itself, is so volatile, why does it not then explode all around us?"

"Because almost all uranium is relatively stable. Thus, in its most abundant condition, uranium would remain quietly tucked away in the dark earth, a purely scientific curiosity. However, locked inside this ore, in almost negligible quantities is a type of uranium that is of much greater interest. It is slightly lighter but vastly more unstable. Man's boundless imagination has turned this scarcer substance—U-235 we call it—into devices that can meet all the world's energy needs—or totally destroy…well, I believe you know.

"And how is that this U-235 contains such powers?"

"Precisely because it is unstable. Its particles interact at an ever-increasing rate…a chain reaction. Now the key in sustaining this chain reaction is to ensure that particles are smashing nuclei and not flying off harmlessly into space. This is done by having a sufficient amount of U-235 packed together very tightly—critical mass, as we say."

"But, is there not a danger," bin Wahhab said, his intensity reflected in the shine of his eyes and forward tilt of his body, "when you obtain this critical mass? Why does it not ignite and send a True Believer to Paradise?"

"As I noted earlier," Marenkov replied, raising one of the apples to his mouth, "One must perform this process correctly. The mass of the U-235 in your device is subcritical. However, it is surrounded by a sphere of high explosives. When these chemical explosives detonate, the U-235 implodes. The uranium then goes 'supercritical', the nuclei split, or fission, and their energy is released. But that is only the first step.

In the second step, the heavy sphere of U-235 is surrounded by a layer of much lighter material. The great heat and energy of the splitting uranium causes the nuclei of the lighter material to fuse. This is similar to the fusion that powers the stars, which I have described to you, but is actually much more violent. The thermonuclear device does not enjoy the massive gravity of a star upon which it can rely to hold itself together. Thus, it must force a more rapid fusion before it blows itself apart. In fact, while the temperature of the sun's core is fifteen million degrees, the inside of a thermonuclear device can reach one hundred million degrees."

"And so the bomb goes from fission to fusion…?"

"Yes, but it is still not done. There is yet a third layer. The sphere is encased in U-238. The tremendous energy of the fusion causes this layer to fission, tripling the yield of the device. So, with its several concentric spheres of explosives, it is designed much like a layer cake. In fact, Andrei Sakharov, who developed the Russian version, dubbed it the 'Sloika'…after a layered Russian pastry."

Bin Wahhab sat rigidly at attention as he dwelled on the Professor's every word. Clearing his throat he said, "So, if our device performs as expected…."

Marenkov gnawed his apple, reflecting on his answer. The physics of the bomb and its exact destructive power were not the issue, as these had already been easily derived by him. He was now solely concerned with his relationship with bin Wahhab and what approach, what words, could best be applied that would allow him to destroy this madman. He sensed that he was slowly ingratiating himself and that opportunity lay along continuation of this path.

"As of necessity, *your* device is quite small physically," he said, swallowing a juicy chunk of the apple. "Nevertheless, it will still have the explosive energy of one half million tons of TNT. To put that in perspective, that is over ten times the *combined* power of the bombs that destroyed Nagasaki and Hiroshima, killing hundreds of thousands of people."

Marenkov noted that bin Wahhab was not completely successful in suppressing a fleeting expression of delight.

"Of course, as you indicated to me earlier," he continued, "this device will never be used against humanity."

"That is correct. We will explode it in the great Rub al Khali desert—the 'Empty Quarter.' Then our enemies will know that they can no longer bully us, but respect as equals."

"Of course," Marenkov responded, finishing his apple.

Chapter Seventeen

"Morning, Mr. Falcon. Mr. Jensen," a round-faced, stocky Secret Service agent greeted the two visitors to his booth at the Fourteenth Street entrance to the Old Executive Office Building. "Mr. Higby and the others are already here. I assume you'll both be going down to the Dewar as well."

"Yeah, hell of a way to spend such a beautiful autumn day," Falcon said, presenting his badge.

"Yessir," the guard responded, running the badge through a scanner and making an entry in his computer. "Go on in."

Falcon and Jensen passed through the black wrought iron gateway and into the old, garishly designed building that stood next door to the White House. Having once served as the Admiralty, the multi-columned gray structure now housed the offices of the Vice President of the United States and a number of federal government organizations, including the Uranium Oversight Committee. Inside the entrance, Falcon handed his aluminum alloy briefcase to another Treasury agent and strode through a metal detector. Retrieving the case he and Jensen turned left and proceeded down a dimly lit corridor. At the end of the passageway, they displayed their credentials to another sentry, who also greeted them by name and then inserted a key into an elevator keyslot.

The doors parted, the two NSA agents stepped in, and Jensen touched the sensory pad marked 'basement'.

When the doors reopened a few seconds later they were met by another Treasury agent. He commented, "They're expecting you," as he made the proper computer log entry. Falcon walked to a door behind the sentry's desk and slid his badge through a magnetic slot. A buzzer sounded and the heavy metal barrier unlocked and swung open. He stepped into a large, brightly-lit room. The barely audible sonorous refrains of a muzak recording met his ear—the tunes meant not for listening pleasure but to mask the hum of the electronic countermeasures concealed within the wall. The center of the room was dominated by an oval glass-covered, cherrywood table that was flanked by twelve armchairs, one for each member of the Uranium Oversight Committee. Five of the chairs at the far end of the table were now occupied by gray and pinstripe-suited members of the committee.

"Mike, good to see you again," said an elderly man at the head of the table looking up. The Presidential Security Advisor, Preston Higby, was nearly seventy and had conceded his white hair and care-worn facial lines to age, but none of the spark in his gray eyes nor keenness of his intelligence.

"Have a seat. Do you need any audiovisual equipment?"

"No, sir," Falcon responded, setting his valise at the foot of the table and flicking the locks open. Jensen took a seat to his immediate right.

"I want to thank everyone for coming on such short notice," Higby said. "Mr. Falcon has asked me to convene this emergency session of the Uranium Oversight's Intelligence Subcommittee based on some disturbing news that has come to his attention.

"Mike, I believe you know everyone here—Colonel Frank Pittard from the Pentagon. Larry Dahlgren of the CIA, Hal Pettigrew over from State, and Warren Fredericks of the FBI." Each man nodded in turn to Falcon.

"Yes, sir, thank you," Falcon replied. "Gentlemen, you are all aware of the recent murder of James Slater, the CEO of Micratom Inc. Information has surfaced that his slaying is related to the illegal trafficking of uranium with certain terrorist organizations."

Amid the subdued whispers and murmurings of his audience, Falcon extracted five individually stapled thin sheaves of paper from his case and slid them along the glass covered table top.

"Please note on page one of my report that Slater was assassinated by an agent of the clandestine Russian organization known as the Feliks."

"Preposterous...here in the U.S.?" Dahlgren, the florid, bespectacled CIA representative sputtered, removing a pipe from his thick lips. His bushy eyebrows knitted as he fixed his gaze on Falcon. "The Feliks are barely a Communist hypothesis in Russia and it would certainly be a stretch to claim that this conjectural Red organization would be operating within the U.S."

"Mr. Dahlgren, I'm afraid we're woefullyly ignorant of the extent and operations of that 'Red organization,' as you term it," Falcon replied. "But would you be willing to bet your reputation and that of the CIA on its non-existence?"

Dahlgren tamped his pipe, not responding.

"I am not only certain that Slater was assassinated by a Feliks agent, but I also believe we have the name of his assassin. On page two, you will see a biography of Ms. Svetlana Popova. Please note her alleged connection to the U.S. embassy bombings in Tanzania and Kenya and to the terrorist financier, Abdul bin Wahhab.

"You all are well aware of the reputation of bin Wahhab. He not only financed those bombings in Nairobi and Dar Es Salaam, but he also was behind the explosions of the Khobar Towers and the World Trade Center. He has declared a Jihad—a Holy War—against the U.S. and has reputedly offered his terrorists $10,000 for each American man, woman, or child killed. Although he may seem insane, believe me, he's lucid enough to know that he can't go toe-to-toe with our armed forces.

Therefore, he's embarking on a non-conventional military strategy of biological, chemical, and nuclear weapons."

"Hmph," the CIA representative grunted. "We've had a glimmer of this. We finally managed to penetrate bin Wahhab's organization with one of our best operatives just a few months ago. We were starting to get valuable information when the message stream stopped. Unfortunately, we have received nothing from him for weeks now."

"Are we to assume..." Higby began to ask.

"I'm afraid so, Preston," Dahlgren replied. "He's been cancelled."

"Which makes it all the more urgent," Falcon said, "that we find out why a Feliks agent, who is linked to bin Wahhab, would take the extraordinary measure of assassinating the CEO of a multi-million dollar corporation. And not just any multi-million dollar corporation, but one that is involved in the trade of highly enriched Russian nuclear warhead uranium. Which brings us to page three. I've learned that Slater conducted a number of highly unusual transactions with a group he referred to as the *Salvadorans*."

"He dealt in uranium with El Salvador? We would've known about that at State," Pettigrew shook his fleshy-jowled, bull-sized head.

"No, it's some sort of code he used," Falcon answered. "This is only one aspect of the great lengths he went to in order to conceal his clandestine operations. You'll see on the next few pages that he lists a number of communications and transactions with the *Salvadorans*. Of particular interest are references to the transfer of a total of 75 kilograms of an unspecified commodity to the *Salvadorans*. This correlates with payments to Slater totaling over two million dollars. We were able to trace the deposit of this sum in Slater's name to a Zurich bank account. He had already withdrawn nearly all of it in order to maintain his somewhat lavish lifestyle."

"I assume you're implying that he diverted 75 kilograms of uranium to the Salvadorans, or Hondurans, or whoever they may be," the bald-headed Army Colonel said. "But that's impossible. Every micro ounce of uranium is accounted for, from the time it's pried from Russian nuclear warheads until this very moment. There's no way that Slater would have been able to obtain the warhead uranium and divert it without our knowledge. And even if he could get his hands on a nuclear weapon, the PAL system would render it harmless."

"Unfortunately, the Permissible Action Link, which we, Russia, and all nuclear powers rely upon, is irrelevant in this case," Falcon retorted. "The PAL ensures that all nuclear devices built by these nations are inoperable unless the proper access code is entered. We are facing a situation, however, where it's not the bomb, but rather the element critical to its assembly, that has been hi-jacked. Toss in the secret payments of two million to Slater and the bin Wahhab terrorist connection and, well, I think you get the picture."

"Yes, that does raise some interesting issues," said the crew-cut, square-shouldered man to Higby's left. "I, and I'm sure my colleagues at the FBI, would like to know just how you obtained all this information."

Jensen stared straight ahead, hoping that his gradual slide down in his chair would go unnoticed as Falcon spoke.

"This is precisely the reason the committee asked the NSA for my help, Mr. Fredericks," Falcon replied. "My job is to ferret out such information and report it to you. Fortunately, I have the resources of the NSA computer data bank and the world's best cryptographers and analysts."

It was obvious that Fredericks wasn't buying it. "A patented response—but not an answer. I want to know exactly how you were able to derive this information."

"Warren, that's not the important issue now," Higby interrupted. "Of much greater significance is ascertaining whether Slater did in fact divert uranium illegally, and if so, to whom. There is enough evidence here to support the notion that it may, indeed, have gone in a very unacceptable direction. I must also add another piece of information which came to my attention just last evening and which may have some bearing on this issue. I received a call from Yevgeny Aksanov, director of Russia's Federal

Security Service. He reported, per our nations' joint uranium agreement, that Professor Alexander Marenkov was placed on their list of missing persons. I believe you knew him, Mike."

Falcon nodded. "It was quite a few years ago...I was a student, doing graduate work in astrophysics at the University of Moscow...he was one of my professors."

"Other than the fact that he teaches courses about the stars, what's so damned significant about his being on the list?" the Colonel grumbled.

"I can answer that," Dahlgren said. "In the critical stages of the Cold War, Marenkov was the brains behind the Soviet nuclear warhead effort. More importantly for us now is that he is perhaps the world's ablest designer of physically small, high-yield nuclear bombs. We often thought of 'deleting' him from the equation in order to negate this very type of problem."

"Deleting? Is that the Company's euphemism for assassination?" Pettigrew huffed.

"Don't start getting sanctimonious on me, Hal. You don't like the rough part; then one day like today, you wake up and find a big boil on your butt. Then you have yourself a much more delicate and painful problem."

"Which is?" the Colonel interrupted.

"That's what I intend to find out," Higby said. "Obviously, the Russians are a lot further down the road on the Marenkov problem. But I'm certain that the information you've unearthed, Mike, would be quite useful to them. And working together, I believe, will provide our best chance to successfully resolve the issues related to Slater's murder, Marenkov's disappearance, the Feliks, and the missing uranium. That's why I'm sending Mike to Moscow."

"Me?" Falcon said, raising his head and gazing into Higby's eyes.

"Now just hold on," Dahlgren groused. "I've got plenty of well-qualified people in Langley...."

"And we've got no shortage at Quantico," Fredericks hastily interjected. "After all, this is an international murder investigation suited for the expertise of the FBI."

"Both of you go back to your headquarters, then, and find me someone who has a physics background, speaks Russian, and has spent over half a year advising this committee," Higby replied.

"Dammit, Preston!" Fredericks blurted as he stood. "Don't push my button! I refuse to approve sending Falcon on this mission and you know damned well why!"

Before Higby could answer, Falcon said quietly but firmly, "Suppose, Mr. Fredericks, you say it to my face."

Jensen slipped further down in his seat.

"Since you ask, I will," the FBI official retorted. "You're a security risk, Mr. Falcon. A goddamn loose cannon. We have an inch-thick dossier on you and your Chinese pillow lady. You won't be the first person who's been turned by a good lay."

Falcon smiled.

"What's so goddamn amusing?" Fredericks sputtered.

"I was just thinking," Falcon said, "Being turned by a good lay is one thing you'll never have to worry about."

"You son of a—"

"That's enough!" Higby exclaimed. "Warren, sit down and keep your mouth shut. The President has already approved this plan. Unless you want to file a formal protest with the chief, we're going forward. Mike, you've got until nine a.m. tomorrow."

"Tomorrow!?"

"Yes," Higby said, reaching inside his coat jacket and removing a white envelope. "Here's your plane ticket."

He slid the envelope across the table to Falcon.

"Your flight leaves from Dulles in the morning."

*　　　　　*　　　　　*

It was just after 6:00 p.m. when the Aurora Express jolted to a halt at the Leningradsky Vokzal in Moscow. During the six hours of the return trip from St. Petersburg, Medved had been weaving his plans to locate and free Galena from the *Byezo* and ultimately to engineer her escape from Russia. One of the major contingencies of the plan revolved around the possibility that achieving his objective would require the sacrifice of his own life. It was a contingency that had presented itself to him the moment he set his eyes on his newborn baby girl. He had a brother in London, a dissident who had incurred the wrath of the KGB in the late 80's. That brother, Sasha, was still alive and prospering, thanks to a timely phone call from Sergei. The Bureau agents arrived at Sasha's apartment only five minutes after their quarry had vanished. Sasha owed him. He and his British wife would look after Galena.

"Moscow…end of the line…Leningradsky Vokzal…." a conductor wailed as he passed through the car.

Medved and Buzhkin retrieved their bags from the overhead rack and proceeded to the exit. Having descended to the platform where he was about to say his parting words to his assistant, Medved pulled to an abrupt halt. Approaching them from the street-side of the platform were two burly, solemn-faced men. Medved immediately recognized them as fixtures in the anteroom that adjoined Aksanov's office. He quickly suppressed his compulsion to take defensive measures.

"Come with us," the foremost one said, his hands plunged into the pockets of his nylon jacket. "The General wishes to see you both immediately."

The four men piled into a black Mercedes four-door sedan and fifteen minutes later they arrived at the Lubianka.

"May I offer you something to drink?" General Aksanov said affably as Buzhkin and Medved took their seats before the massive oak desk. "As the temperature dips, a little brandy can heat up the stove."

Buzhkin began to decline when Aksanov interrupted, "Or perhaps something a little stronger? Stolichnaya? Nothing for you, Major

Medved?" he said pouring the vodka into a glass and handing it to Buzhkin.

The Major respectfully refused, wishing to retain complete use of his faculties for any eventuality.

"Tell me," Aksanov said, replacing the cap on the vodka bottle, "how was the great northern trek? Did you find Professor Marenkov in a brothel up there?"

"We found nothing," Buzhkin growled.

"Worse than that," Medved said. "I'm afraid Viktor's old war wound started acting up. The one he received serving with Vaznetsov's 32nd outside of Kabul. You remember that action, General…in the fall of '81."

"Hmmph," Aksanov grunted. For a moment, he gazed beyond them both, seemingly beyond even the walls of the office, to a distant place. Then, returning to once again fix his intense gaze upon them, he said, "There has been an important development in your absence."

"This morning, I had a very interesting conversation with Preston Higby, the National Security Advisor to the President of the United States. *Gospodeen* Higby conveyed some startling news to me. It appears that an American businessman, the Chief Executive Officer of Micratom, and one of the major players in our uranium trade with America, has been murdered. Higby indicated that this American… James Slater…had been in Moscow just over a month ago, attending a seminar in which the keynote speaker was Alexander Marenkov. Were either of you aware of such a connection?"

Buzhkin threw back another shot of Stolichnaya and shrugged.

Medved made no reply.

"Hmm, I see," Aksanov continued. "We—*Gospodeen* Higby and I—decided it would be in everyone's best interest if our governments worked together on this case. An American agent will be arriving here the day after tomorrow. Major Medved, I want you to meet him at Sheremetyevo and put him up at the Metropol."

"Ey, these Americans do go first class," Buzhkin said.

"Then Sergei, I want you and Viktor to work with him like a troika pulling a sled. How long has it been since you've used your English?"

"Ten…twelve years."

"Well, I understand he speaks passable Russian. The American security advisor and I both have a very uneasy feeling about the connecting links in this case. It's urgent that we get our arms around this matter. My secretary will give you a package containing specifics about the American. Are there any questions?"

Neither of the agents spoke.

"Thank you, then. That will be all."

On the way out of the Director's office, Medved collected the Falcon dossier from Aksanov's secretary.

"Ey, Medved, that's a sad fate," Buzhkin said as they descended the staircase to exit the Lubianka.

"What's that?" Medved responded, tucking the package inside his overnight bag.

"Going from the father of a young daughter to babysitting a grown man. Well, I'm off."

Buzhkin zipped up his jacket, stepped into the chilly Moscow night and lumbered away.

Medved's eyes followed the retreating form of his fellow agent until it disappeared in the street shadows. Then he too fastened his jacket, turned up his collar, and lighting a cigarette, ventured across Lubianka Square. An empty stone pedestal arrested his attention as he passed by. Memories of a day eight years ago flooded his mind; the unsuccessful coup against Gorbachev, the subsequent demolition of the statue that had stood for so long on this pedestal—the statue of the infamous KGB founder, Felix Dzerzhinksy. Where in the Russian soul was he now?

Just a few paces further, he passed *Dyetsky Mir,* the country's largest children's store. Only in Russia would there be such a juxtaposition of ruthlessness and innocence, he thought. It was no wonder that this land of contradictions seemed so enigmatic to foreigners. How can we even explain it to ourselves? He descended the steps of the Lubianka metro stop, reflecting upon the meeting with Aksanov and this latest twist of fate. For now, the plans he had concocted during the train ride from St. Petersburg would be temporarily suspended. He was curious about what the American knew and where this information might lead. Then, too, perhaps this American might prove useful in furthering his plans. He opened the dossier and began reading.

Chapter Eighteen

It was seven a.m. when the taxicab bearing Mike Falcon pulled to a stop in front of the stone-fronted town house in Georgetown, just beyond downtown Washington. Telling the driver to wait, Falcon bounded up the flight of half a dozen steps and pressed the doorbell button. After waiting several moments with no response, he tried the doorbell once more. He began pacing along the stoop in front of the door. Perhaps he had miscalculated? Perhaps she had already left for work? The thought that he might now leave without saying good-bye to her left him with a hollow, empty feeling. He turned to go.

"Mike, what are you doing here at this hour?"

At the sound of the familiar voice, he looked up to see Lin Su jogging toward him. Jocko, who had been running at her side, spotted his master and leaped up the steps.

"Did you two have a good run?" Falcon smiled as he knelt to hug the Lab.

"Yes, five miles, and fall is in the air," she said, inserting a key in the door lock. "Perfect for running. The Rock Creek path is beautiful…the leaves are turning color. You should run with me some morning. But you didn't answer my question. Is something wrong?"

"No…. I just wanted to see you…before I left."

"Before you leave? What do you mean?"

As she spoke, she swung the door open and they entered the apartment.

"How's this guy been?" Falcon laughed, affectionately stroking Jocko who continued to nuzzle his hand.

"Very loving. Very sweet. You could learn much from him."

"O.K. I can't argue about that."

"Can I get you a cup of coffee before I shower and change?" she asked as she tugged her sweatshirt over her head and headed to the bedroom.

"No time. I have to catch a flight at Dulles…The cab is waiting for me. I just wanted to see you before I left."

"You've already said that." The awkwardness between them was so alien to her, especially after the free and easy rapport they had once enjoyed. That had all changed after the FBI incident. Perhaps their worlds were too different. She had put his honor and reputation above all else, even the future she had cherished with him. And yet he had not understood her sacrifice…had even resented it. She sadly recalled that day when Jensen had taken her to lunch and had told her that Falcon was about to lose his clearance and probably his career because of his relationship with her. "Hell, the really wonderful thing is that Mike is willing to give it all up for you," Jensen had said with calculated innocence. He knew that she would never allow that. If only he had also known the depth of my love for Mike, she thought. Would he have then been so eager to dash my dreams? But they both knew then what she had to do.

In order to effect a clean break, she had asked the Director for a temporary assignment back to the home office in Shanghai. For the three months that she was gone, she had no contact with Falcon. When she finally returned to the States, she found it impossible not to see him that night on the boat, to know by her own eyes and feel with her own body and soul that he was well and happy. Yet, at the same time, she was frightened that she had killed something very special between them. She tried to disguise her sorrow through humor and nonchalance. She wondered if they could ever recover what they once had.

"How long will you be gone?" she asked, emerging from the bedroom in a red silk knee-length kimono.

"It's impossible to say…weeks…perhaps months."

Falcon wanted to sweep her up, to hug her, to lavish kisses on her face and neck…but he was unsure if she wanted that…if she still felt the same way.

"Can you stay in touch?" she asked. Gazing into his eyes she felt a sense of warmth and despair. She longed for him to throw his arms around her and tell her how much he still loved her.

"Only sporadically. I can't tell you where I'll be but Jensen will always know how to reach me. You can leave messages for me through him."

"Oh, how romantic."

"Yeah. Romance is my life. I'm afraid that's the best we can do for a while. But when I get back…if you still want to see me…."

"I have no choice since I'm taking care of your most valued possession."

"Jocko? I suppose that's where that saying 'lucky dog' comes from…he gets to sleep with you every night."

"He has great karma."

"Damned sight better than mine, that's for sure."

"Perhaps it's because he lives a better life."

He started to answer, then stopped and glanced at his watch.

"God, I have to get going."

He opened the door, paused, and then turned toward her. Embracing her tightly, he lifted her from the floor and kissed her.

"Mike, you're going to Russia, aren't you?" she said, surprising herself by uttering the thought.

He released her and stepped back.

"Russia? Why would you say such a…?"

He suddenly felt as though his blood had turned to ice. "You *are* a spook, aren't you," he stated in a manner that precluded contradiction.

"Mike, I…if I denied it, would you believe me?"

He gazed in her eyes, seeing the truth that he had hoped against.

"So, that's what happened. That explains everything...it was all just...a pack of lies. All for the Peoples Republic."

"No, Mike, it's not like that. There are things I want to tell you...I know what danger you now face. I want to help you."

"No, Lin Su. Save your breath for your next dopey target."

"Mike—"

He turned and quickly departed.

*   *   *

Fourteen hours later, after a brief stop in London, British Airways Flight #390 touched down at Sheremetyevo Airport in Moscow. It had been twenty years since Mike Falcon had been in Russia—then a Republic of the Soviet Union—and even before the plane landed he began experiencing the change. The last time he arrived, it had been on Aeroflot, where the accommodations had been just fractionally above that offered in the gulags.

Before deplaning, he set his watch ahead eight hours to adjust for Moscow time, then stole another glance at the photo of Sergei Medved in the dossier provided by Higby. The picture was seven years old, raising the question of how much its subject—particularly one in this profession—had changed in this tumultuous decade in Russia. Tucking the photo and dossier into his briefcase, he rose and proceeded to the gangway.

Inside the airport, he was greeted by another change, one that he should have expected but nevertheless took him by surprise. The red, white, and azure banner of the Russian Federation now hung in lieu of the red and yellow hammer and sickle. For a moment he relived that nervous excitement he experienced two decades earlier when he first saw the symbol of the Soviet Union in its homeland and faced the unsettling fact that he was then subject to the whims of the Communist authorities. He wondered what other surprises were in store for him in the new Russia.

Sergei Medved glanced at the photo in his hand, then again at the man gazing at the Russian flag in the airport concourse. It was a perfect match, in spite of the age disparity between the image and the reality. Medved was amazed that his counterpart betrayed no signs that ten years had elapsed since the taking of the photo that he had been studying. Life must be good in America, he thought.

"Michael Falcon?" he said, approaching the man.

"Yes...Sergei Medved?"

The two men smiled and shook hands as they began making rapid calculations of each other.

"*Da, awchen priyatna....*"

"Pleased to meet you, too," Falcon responded, easing into his host's language. "I apologize for being responsible for inconveniencing you."

"*Ah, nichevo.* It's nothing! Come. We'll get your luggage and I'll take you to your hotel."

Falcon was relieved that Medved had recognized him, for he would not have been able to return the favor. The past seven years had obviously been quite punishing for the old warhorse.

"You must be exhausted," Medved said as he steered the Mercedes provided by Aksanov along the Teatralny Thoroughfare. "Get some sleep. Freshen up. You have no obligations until our meeting tomorrow morning."

Falcon had been gazing at the changed scenery—the commercial stores, McDonalds, Coke machines, street vendors, German and Italian cars, western-style clothing. He was particularly struck by the numerous seedy establishments that were a curious Russian blend of off-strip Vegas titty-bars and Bourbon Street bordellos.

"Hmm? Oh, yes, tomorrow morning," he said. "Who will be there?"

"Besides me, General Aksanov of course. And one other."

Medved inhaled deeply on his cigarette, then spoke as he exhaled, "My assistant. A man named Viktor Buzhkin."

A stolen glance detected no obvious change in Falcon's expression. Perhaps he truly is unaware, Medved thought. Perhaps he may be the one who could be trusted. It was an issue that needed to be resolved decisively and soon.

"Well, we have arrived," the Russian said wheeling the Mercedes into the entrance drive of the Metropol Hotel. "It's Moscow's finest so I would think all your needs will be met," he said as he unloaded Falcon's suitcase from the trunk. "If not, or if you have any problems whatsoever, call me at this number." He handed the American his business card.

"Well, *ah zaftra*—until tomorrow morning, then," he said extending his hand. I'll pick you up at seven—thirty." Falcon shook the proffered hand, thanked the Russian and entered the hotel.

The Metropol was in a different galaxy from the living quarters of his last visit—Moscow University, where the walls were bare, access to the rooms was controlled by a battle-axed *dezhurnaya*, the rooms were bugged and the toilet tissue was a coarse grain sandpaper. The Metropol, in contrast, offered all the amenities of a luxury hotel—the abrasive bathroom paper excepted.

Once in his room, he set the suitcase on the stand at the foot of the bed. He unlocked the bag and removed the box containing his Glock and its ammunition. To his relief and mild amazement, the customs authorities hadn't flipped into a tailspin when he presented his Interpol license permitting his international transport of firearms. Satisfied that the weapon had successfully survived the trip, he loaded the weapon and placed it on the stand next to the suitcase. Entering the bathroom, he inserted the bathtub drain stopper and turned on the hot water. As the tub filled, he returned to the bedroom, unpacked, and called room service. A hot meal would be delivered in an hour, no sooner, as he instructed. He then returned to the bathroom, settled into the hot, soothing water and closed his eyes.

Thoughts of the rapid developments of the past few weeks—his relationship with Lin Su, the Slater assassination, his unexpected return to

Russia after two decades, the changes he had already witnessed in this roiling land—spilled through his mind.

He had been luxuriating in this manner for a number of minutes when he became aware of the flitting of a shadow across his closed eyelids, the barely perceptible scent of peach, the subtle energy of a living being hovering near him. *Room service was distinctly told not to come for an hour and they surely would have knocked first.* He slowly opened his eyes to see the curvaceous naked body and beautiful smiling face of Svetlana Popova. She stood confidently with her palms resting on her hips, her well-toned long legs spread apart. She was even more gorgeous without the slip of a dress she wore when they first met.

As he surveyed her lissome, voluptuous form, he noted that the Worm had once again been correct—her natural hair color was chestnut. Glancing beyond her, he saw that the Glock remained exactly as he had left it on the suitcase stand, but now was accompanied by what appeared to be a black dress. A pair of spike-heeled black shoes lay at the foot of the stand.

"*Zdravctvootya, lyoobeemets.* Hello, darling. Welcome to my country," she said. "I thought you might like some company."

She began to step into the tub.

"The service certainly has improved since my last visit," Falcon said, "but I was just getting out."

As he began to stand, she pressed her hands against his shoulders.

"But I thought you wanted to see me again," she said, leaning forward so that all her weight came to bear on his shoulders, preventing him from easily rising. He relaxed, leaning back against the tub. "I've wanted to see you…just like this."

"How did you get in?"

"That's rather insulting, Michael. It was hardly a challenge."

"Hardly a challenge for one trained by the Feliks, you mean."

"Do you want to keep talking or do you want to have some fun," she laughed, sliding a bar of soap along his inner thighs.

"The kind of fun you had with Slater?" He grasped her wrist and took the soap.

"Oh, he was such a boor."

"True. But that's not why you canceled him. And now you've come here to dispose of me." He rubbed the soap around the curve of her breasts, feeling the nipples hardening.

"Why do you say such things? You're so distrustful," she pouted. "Why would I want to hurt James or you, *lyoobeemets*?"

Falcon knew that she could have easily killed him earlier. The fact that she hadn't led him to believe that she hoped to glean information from him. After all, it was for a similar reason that he wanted to keep her alive. He would first need to play her little game of cat and mouse in order to obtain an edge.

"Poor Slater," he said. "Died so young. Such a loss to the world of international trade, haute cuisine restaurateurs, and Italian car salesmen. Did you know that he was also quite the art connoisseur? Odd, though, that he kept his most precious information concealed in an art treasure."

"An art treasure?" she smiled demurely as she wriggled her toes in his crotch. "Tell me more."

"Apparently, he was fearful for his life—if you can possibly imagine that—concerning his black market uranium dealings", he responded cupping the playful toes and rubbing them with soap. "As a form of security, perhaps blackmail, he kept a compact disc containing data—places, dates, names—of those transactions hidden in one of his expensive oil paintings."

"Oh, how clever", she purred, slowly removing her foot from his grasp. "Which artist?"

"That's the real irony. He hid his most valuable possession inside a Dali painting that hung in front of a bedroom wall safe. I wonder if there was anything at all of value in the safe."

There was no longer any doubt in her mind that the American agent possessed the information she sought. Which was why she had eased her foot from his palm. Bracing her back against the porcelain tub, she drove her heel toward Falcon's solar plexus.

In anticipation of this action, he blocked the blow with his forearm, seized her ankle and shoved her down so that her head submerged. From beneath the water, she thrust her right hand upward, fingers pressed together in a rigid plane, straight into his trachea, jamming the tube shut and denying the flow of oxygen into his lungs. causing him to tumble backward as he gasped for air. She hoped he would not struggle too much as she didn't want to kill him right away. There was important information to be pried loose and some hard sex with the finely-sculpted American—provided he were safely bound—was quite enticing.

Falcon rolled out of the tub onto his hands and knees, struggling for oxygen. She rose and stood behind him. Partially recovered, he pushed himself up from the floor and scrambled toward the suitcase stand. His hand was within inches of the Glock when he felt her full weight slam against his shoulders and her thighs clamp around his neck. The momentum spun him around so that he was on top of her, the back of his head against her abdomen, the vise-like grip of her thighs expertly controlling the flow of air through his trachea. Each time he struggled, her thighs tightened, curtailing the transfer of oxygen to his brain and debilitating his motor functions.

Falcon went limp. The woman smiled.

"I love my work. Especially with you. And the best is yet to come." she whispered, running her sharp fingernails over the firm contours of his strong shoulders and chest.

Gradually, she relaxed her quadriceps muscles. It was the moment Falcon had anticipated. Summoning his strength, he thrust an elbow into her midsection, causing her to cry out and release her hold. Again he bolted to his feet, but she was equally swift, springing between him and the Glock.

"You're fun, *lyoobeemets*," she laughed. "And quite fit for someone your age. I like that." She surveyed his body from head to toe and winked.

He made a movement toward the weapon. She crouched, her blonde hair spilling wildly over her shoulders, her supple body shimmering wet, a feral gleam in her green eyes.

With a slight cry, she snapped her right foot at Falcon's head. The air whooshed by his ear as he avoided the blow and seized the extended leg. Sweeping the limb upward, he spilled her to the floor, then crashed his knee into her chest. The air expelled from her lungs with a wheeze and she wilted. He rolled from her, crawled to the suitcase stand and grasped the Glock. His throat burned and each swallow, each breath, triggered electric currents of pain in his head and neck. He placed his head between his knees, battling against his nausea and dizziness.

A metal clicking sound coming from the doorway stirred him. He glanced around the bed to where he had left the Amazon bitch. She was gone, along with her dress and shoes, and the door was wide open. Ignoring the stinging jabs of pain, he pulled himself to his feet and stumbled to the doorway. He peered along the hall in both directions. There was no sign of life. Closing the door, he sat on the bed, next to the telephone. He placed the pistol alongside him and pressed the button for the concierge.

"Hello, Mr. Falcon," a Russian-accented voice sounded in his ear. "May I help you?"

"Yes," Falcon responded. "I'd like to register a complaint."

Chapter Nineteen

"I must confess, sheikh, I like it not. I feel totally naked without my AN-94", a stocky Arab, clad in a white full-length seamless burnoose, said brusquely. He was one of tens of thousands similarly dressed pilgrims trudging along the dusty road from the Red Sea to Mecca. The True Believers were making their way to the Holiest of Cities to commemorate the Muslim New Year, as dated from the Prophet's flight from Mecca exactly one-thousand, four hundred and twenty years ago. Billboards on either side of the tamarisk-lined thoroughfare warned in seven languages that non-Muslims were forbidden to proceed further. A roadblock manned by armed troops was positioned to enforce this injunction and to keep a watchful eye for enemies of the faith and the state, which in Saudi Arabia were considered one and the same.

Enemies such as the unusually tall, coffee-hued, bearded figure who responded to his companion, "The Merciful One looks down upon us and will protect us, Talil. If it is His desire that we pass unscathed through the hands of our enemies, so be it. If, however, in His wisdom, He determines that we are to be discovered and are sent to Paradise on this very day, then Allah be praised."

"But, sheikh—" Talil said, becoming increasingly fidgety as they neared the guardpost.

"Allah would also be most pleased," bin Wahhab interrupted, "if you would remember my admonition and do not refer to me either by my title or proper name. For now, I am simply Abdullah." Bin Wahhab had chosen this pseudonym for himself surmising that its similarity to his actual name would be easier for the very brave—but very slow—Talil to remember. "Open your Holy Book and act as if you are reading," he said to his illiterate companion. "I shall do likewise."

Talil did as he was instructed, wishing that the Koran was his assault rifle, instead. Bin Wahhab also bent his head over his open book, peering from beneath his lowered brows at the looming Saudi troops. In spite of the casually brave demeanor he had assumed for Talil's sake, he knew he was taking an enormous risk. He was one of the most hunted men in all of Saudi Arabia—in all of the world, for that matter. The Americans had even put a million dollar price on his head. There would be many a True Believer who would be happy to sell him to the infidel for that amount. And yet the risk was well worth taking for it was a rare opportunity to meet together with all his lieutenants who were scattered throughout many nations.

But there was a much more profound reason for this seemingly injudicious escapade. It was the same reason that, after his fortress in Khowst had been demolished by a cruise missile, he had sauntered out into the open, in full view of the American spy satellites. He had to confirm, before the eyes of those disciples who still harbored some doubt, that he was invincible—indeed the *Mahdi*, the Chosen One. Only when they truly believed this would they rise and follow him in the Jihad.

They were now abreast of the troops. The combination of thousands of pilgrims, the confusion of many languages, and the woeful inattention of the guards—no highly visible state enemy would dare run their gauntlet—worked to the advantage of bin Wahhab. One of the soldiers, however—a shavetail officer—carefully scrutinized the visage of the stately pilgrim who approached his station. He had seen this face before, but could not quite place it. It would be discourteous to stare at one who exceeded his own social position—one could never be quite sure owing to the monotonously uniform garb of the *hajj*—but the haughty gaze of the man upon him proved too disconcerting and the officer turned his attention to more promising rabble. In that moment, the world's most-wanted international terrorist and his Koran scanning companion passed the roadblock and entered the sacred city.

Other than its holy status among Muslims, there is little by which Mecca can commend itself. It nestles in a hot dry valley of a mountain range that was formed a few hundred million years ago when the continent of Africa slammed into the Eurasian landmass. The earth on both sides of the collision crumbled, piling rocks over two miles high. The plates continued to grind away at each other until further stress ripped the stitching between Asia and Africa. In a curious twist to the Exodus tale of the Israelis' flight from Egypt, the land, rather than the water, split and the Red Sea flooded the rift. And while they were now separated by this relatively narrow finger of water, the previously adjoining lands still shared their primary feature—endless tracts of windblown sand.

For nearly ten thousand years, since the retreat of the glaciers of the last ice age, the sun pounded relentlessly down upon these regions. Hot air currents rose, flowed north and south into cooler latitudes where their moisture condensed and fell as rain, forming the great expanses of northern wooded lands and the southern tropical rain forests. The consequent absence of rain clouds over the Sahara and its neighboring deserts of Saudi Arabia not only deprived these lands of life-giving water but also denied life-saving shade to their sun-baked inhabitants. The denizens of the two-legged variety had a word for it: *arab*. It meant arid.

Mecca aptly fit the description. Enclosed by the mountains of bare rock that had been tumbled up by the collision of Africa and Eurasia and trapped in the rainless belt of the earth's wind currents, its location ensured that it would be subjected to intolerable heat and such dryness that hardly a garden grew. Nevertheless, a quarter of a million people from all over the world were pressing toward it this day for it was the time of the New Year *hajj* and Mecca was still the holiest city in Islam.

Its sacredness actually predated the Prophet and the Muslim religion by a number of centuries. At least two thousand years ago, a football size black stone fell from the sky into Mecca's sandy glen. Perhaps, bin Wahhab mused as he tramped along to the Grand Mosque, this object was no more than a left-over building block of the solar system, as described to him by the Russian Professor. But he, and the other worshippers, believed it was much more. For was it not the stone which was described in the Koran as falling in the days of Adam? And was this not the rock of the Book of Psalms which was the corner of the House of the Lord? He was angry with himself for allowing Marenkov's secular explanation muddy his righteous thinking.

He and Talil, almost carried along by the vast multitude, jostled into the courtyard of the Grand Mosque where they performed the ritual ablutions. They then bumped their way toward the *Kaaba*, the cubic three-story structure that housed the sacred Black Stone, a sight denied to all but Muslims. Tradition held that the *Kaaba* had been resurrected on ten occasions, the first time by angels from heaven at the dawn of history. Tradition also demanded that the faithful make seven circuits around the imposing shrine, each time touching or kissing the *kiswa*— the Egyptian tapestry—that hid the holy relic from view. When all had completed the ritual, the great mass of humanity halted in front of the mosque. There an Imam in a minaret approached a microphone and led the silent multitude in prayer.

How reminiscent the scene was to another that had occurred exactly twenty years earlier in this very same spot and that had changed the life of bin Wahhab forever. As the worshippers pressed their heads to their mats, he glanced up at the Imam, almost expecting history to repeat itself. For, two decades ago, as he knelt and lifted his eyes toward the minaret, he was startled by the sound of gunfire and the vision of an acolyte spilling over in a pool of blood. Other shots had followed and more victims fell bleeding to the ground. The unthinkable had occurred. Gunfire, bloodshed, mayhem at the sacred shrine. Pandemonium had ensued as the tens of thousands of worshippers trampled each other in their race to the gates or areas of shelter within the courtyard.

Security forces, completely unprepared to deal with such an unimaginable desecration of the holy *Kaaba*, mounted ineffective counterattacks in the direction of the gunfire and were themselves cut to pieces.

It was with exhilaration that bin Wahhab recalled these events. Unlike the panic-stricken, he had not moved from his mat, nor even bent down to avoid the hail of bullets. Yet, men on either side of him who had leaped to their feet in a wild-eyed hope of escape had been immediately gunned down. The acolyte himself lay sprawled directly before him, his lifeless hand touching the sheikh's mat. Soon, miraculously, bin Wahhab was the only being that remained alive in the courtyard. He did not know it at the time, but the Saudi government had been paralyzed. The shock of the attack was compounded by confusion over the nature of the insurgents. Rumors abounded that a foreign hand must be at work, Zionists or perhaps communists. The truth would be more chilling, bin Wahhab reflected.

The insurgents were true sons of the desert—simple but fierce Bedouin—who were disgusted with the 'avaricious' western ways and 'corrupted faith' of the Saudi family. They had resurrected the half-century old radical evangelistic movement known as the Brotherhood—the *Ikhwan*—to cleanse Islam of this abomination. Bin Wahhab had known of the existence of the Brotherhood and, in spite of the fact that he was a wealthy Saudi family member, had passingly sympathized with them. It was not their puritanical ideals as much as their fervent opposition to the government that had attracted him. Because of the rigid family structure, he could never realize his limitless ambition and would always remain an insignificant figure in the Saudi scheme of things. His only hope to achieve his rightful position above these lesser lights was to scale the wall from the outside, much as his great-grandfather had vaulted over the parapets of Riyadh nearly a century ago.

Now he recalled how, at noon on that fateful day, a soft-featured, scholarly looking young man stepped to the microphone at the minaret and began speaking the most amazing words that had ever descended upon his ears. This baby-faced, unimposing creature announced that he was the Rightly-Guided One—the *Mahdi*. He spoke of how the House of Saud had consorted with unbelievers and atheists, how they did not follow the Koran and the Muslim traditions, how they no longer deserved respect or obedience, but must be opposed and overthrown. The words caused the heart of bin Wahhab to race. He felt that he was not looking at this inconsequential impostor of the Mahdi, but rather into the depths of his own soul and into his future. This charlatan was merely leading his faithful *Ikhwan* disciples to a senseless death. They began dying that evening.

Saudi troops, automatic rifles blazing, had charged into the courtyard just after sunset. In an attempt to avoid the murderous crossfire, bin Wahhab raced across the Rukn courtyard of the Grand Mosque and hid behind the *Makam*, a small building holding a stone with the purported imprint of Abraham's foot. The meaning of this chance retreat was not lost upon him, for he was well aware of the *Ikhwan* prophecy that the true Mahdi would arise from between the House of God and the foot of Abraham and that he would come at a time of disorder. He also knew the Brotherhood foretold that the Chosen One would bear the patronymic of the Prophet—Abdullah. Close enough, bin Wahhab had determined in his then ecstatic state. When this reckless false *Mahdi* was destroyed, he would accept the role that Allah was clearly presenting to him.

As the Saudi military advanced, he had ducked into a *khalawi*—one of three hundred hermitages that had been carved out of the gray stone of Mecca. There he survived for two weeks on water, figs, and dates as the battle raged before his eyes. Finally, the remaining *Ikhwan*, who had repelled one attack after another, littering the courtyard of the Grand Mosque with dead and wounded, surrendered. They were then summarily decapitated.

Bin Wahhab had learned much in those fourteen days. This small band of religious zealots, though woefully misled, had withstood an army for a fortnight. His mind reeled at the thought of what a similarly dedicated force that was one hundred...one thousand...one million times greater, that was directed against the proper enemy, and that was under the inspiration and intelligence of the true Mahdi, could accomplish.

"Ah, shei...I mean Abdul...lah," Talil said, gently nudging his leader. "The Imam has finished. Are you all right?"

"Yes, of course, Talil," bin Wahhab replied, returning to the present. "Come, we have important people to meet."

The two men rose and walked across the Rukn courtyard, past the *Makam* containing the stone with the imprint of Abraham's foot, to the hermitage that had served as bin Wahhab's hideaway twenty years ago. There they were greeted by two dozen others, all of different languages and customs but each sharing the common zeal and militancy of the *Ikhwan* Brotherhood, the fire of the Jihad, and the devout belief in the true *Mahdi* that now appeared in their midst.

Chapter Twenty

"Ah, Major Medved…Mr. Falcon…*awchen priyatna*. Welcome," General Aksanov said as he rose from behind his massive oak desk to greet the NSA agent. He clasped the American's proffered hand with both of his own and shook it warmly.

"Thank you for coming half way around the world to work with us on our common problem. Please meet my assistant, Viktor Buzhkin."

No wonder, Falcon thought, that Medved had cast that sidelong glance at him at the mention of Buzhkin's name during the ride from the airport to the hotel. The physical appearance alone of the larger-than-life, cinder block man was disconcerting enough. But there was something more, something in the eyes and bearing that induced a sense of caution.

"*Zdravctvootya*", Falcon said, extending his hand.

Nodding, Buzhkin enclosed his bearpaw around the offering, nearly squeezing the blood out of it.

"Ah, now I remember," Falcon smiled. "Buzhkin…you're the Greco-Roman champ…the one they call the Siberian Nightmare."

"*Pravo*. Correct," Buzhkin nodded. "Are you familiar with the sport?"

"Enough to know that I don't ever want to subject my body to that. Freestyle for fifteen years was enough punishment for me."

Medved thought he actually saw the traces of a slight smile cross Buzhkin's face.

"*Sadeetya*...Sit...please," Aksanov motioned the three men to large leather-covered chairs that surrounded a low mahogany table. A brass samovar, a coffee pot, and a tray of *pirozhki*—assorted pastries—sat on the tabletop alongside four white porcelain cups and saucers and a matching set of hors d'oeuvre plates.

"*Pervee*...first, I must be asking you...if you are O.K. with speaking Russian...my English is not being so good."

"Certainly", Falcon nodded.

"*Harasho*. Perhaps I can interest you in some samovar-brewed Georgian tea", the FSB Director said, relieved to be speaking in his own language as he settled into his chair. "I promise you that you have not tasted tea if you have never taken it from a well-worn Russian samovar."

"Thank you," Falcon said. And I do agree. I was fortunate to have that experience a few years ago. "

"Of course...when you were studying here at Moscow University. I understand that Alexander Marenkov was one of your professors. "Nuclear physics, I believe?"

"Actually, it was astrophysics——specializing in the study of quasars and black holes," Falcon said, before sinking his teeth into a cream-filled torte. He knew he would have to sample the *pirozhki* so as not to commit a social blunder; however, he would have to carefully pace himself, for in this land the generosity of a host was exceeded only by the amount of calories in the Russian cuisine.

"Black holes? In this case, it would be fair to say that the teacher was properly preparing the student, for it appears that Professor Marenkov has indeed disappeared into a black hole."

"Yes, it is rather curious. Can you tell me what you know so far?"

"Sergei, perhaps it would be best if you update Mr. Falcon," Aksanov said as he poured a cup of tea for the American.

Swallowing the last bite of a *pirozhki*, Medved wiped his mouth with a linen napkin and sat back in his chair. He hoped that he could remember exactly what he had related to Aksanov and Buzhkin and what he had held back.

"Yes, of course," he said. He explained how Marenkov had appeared on the 'Nichevo' list, how his file had been erased from the Russian Intelligence computer system, and how an attempt had been made on his own life by unknown parties in Moscow...he omitted St. Petersburg. Unfortunately, they yet had no leads in the case.

"And I am sure I do not need to explain to you the significance of these events," Aksanov said, sipping the burning tea from his cup. "The thought of Marenkov working for certain groups or states is quite troubling."

"Do you think that he voluntarily went over?" Falcon asked.

"No...I would say no," Medved caught himself, as he reflected upon his discoveries at Peredelkino. Discoveries which, hopefully, were still unknown to Aksanov and Buzhkin.

"And why do you seem so sure, Sergei?" Aksanov smiled affably, as he lowered his cup.

"Well, we know he declined an offer six or seven years ago. His record of service to Russia...the conduct of his life...his age...it's just my opinion."

"I see," the Director said, glancing at Buzhkin. "And you, Mr. Falcon, what are your thoughts on this point?"

Falcon momentarily followed Aksanov's eyes. Buzhkin was spreading sour cream on a salted mushroom, with a demeanor that convincingly suggested that nothing else in the world was more important to him at the moment.

"I must say I agree with Sergei," Falcon said. "Certain events in America, plus our investigation at the NSA reveal a pattern of activity...and linkages related to a Mid-East terrorist organization and a subversive group within your own country, sir."

"Mid-East terrorists and Russian subversives joining forces?" Aksanov said, his eyebrows rising.

Medved wished he could send a warning signal with his eyes to the American, so that he would say no more. That being impossible, he poured himself a cup of the Georgian brew and settled back to observe the reception of the information about to be conveyed.

"Yes," Falcon continued, "an American businessman, James Slater, was cancelled by an operative of the Russian group. He was the Chief Executive Officer of a corporation that was buying nuclear warhead uranium from a Russian company known as Rurik. We also know that he was involved in the illicit trade of this uranium…probably with some very unfriendly Muslims. Find the people responsible for negating him and I think you will also find Professor Marenkov's kidnappers as well as Sergei's would-be assassins."

Falcon paused and a heavy silence descended upon the room. Finally Aksanov spoke.

"This is rather startling information. And a good deal to assimilate. At present I am most interested in knowing more about this Russian subversive organization that you believe is involved. Does it have a name?"

"Yes, sir. It's virtually never spoken of between officials of our countries, but you—and we—both know it as the Feliks."

Aksanov topped off his American guest's cup and then his own. "Tell me," he said slowly stirring the steaming tea, "Does American Intelligence seriously acknowledge the existence of such an entity?"

"I cannot speak for the CIA or Military Intelligence. My own agency, the NSA, would never admit it publicly, although privately, it is quite a different matter. Personally, having survived at least one attempt on my life by the very Feliks agent who neutralized Slater, I have zero doubts as to its existence." Falcon was fully aware that the Director of Russian Intelligence—at least of the service that succeeded the KGB—was quite aware of the reality of Russia's most dangerous underground operation. But if Aksanov chose to play it this way, he would follow his lead—for now.

"Is this not remarkable, Viktor?" the General said, turning to his special assistant.

Buzhkin shrugged his shoulders and mumbled something imperceptible.

The Director turned again to the American. "And, if we might assume, for the sake of argument, that such an organization exists, what is its connection to Mid-Eastern extremist operations?"

"We have strong reason to believe that there is a link between the Feliks and the Ikhwan Brotherhood of the terrorist financier, Abdul bin Wahhab. "

"And somehow this is all related to the disappearance of Professor Marenkov, the cancellation, as you say, of your American businessman, and vanishing warhead uranium?"

"Yes, but we have not yet been able to stitch it all together. Which brings us here today. My side believes that our best chance of solving these mysteries lies in pooling our resources. "

Aksanov lowered his cup and saucer to the table, then turned to Medved. "Well, Major," he said, tapping his napkin to the corners of his mouth," the Russian world truly has turned upside-down, now that an old Chekist such as yourself is working with the once mortal enemy."

"I see no enemy,"Medved replied, looking directly at Falcon.

"*Harasho!*", the Director chuckled. "Well spoken! How would you like to begin, Mr. Falcon?"

"I would like to know more about this Rurik operation…their methodology for dismantling your warheads…their transportation logistics…their delivery protocol, and much, much more."

"It shall be done. Our resources will be made available to you, and Sergei and Viktor will assist you every step of the way. Well, then. Enough goose cackling. Time to get to work."

Aksanov rose to signal the end of the meeting, and as the others followed his lead, he once again extended his hand to the American. They shook hands affably although Falcon was somewhat taken aback by the Director's parting words: "You are one of us."

*   *   *

The rest of the morning and most of the afternoon was spent in processing the American's official pass into the Lubianka and setting up his office in the "V.I.P." wing. Medved assisted him throughout and was especially helpful with the clearance ordeal.

"No worse than the NSA's red tape," Falcon said in response to the Russian's apologies. "It's the nature of the beast."

"I suppose," the Russian sighed, flopping wearily into one of the two metal folding chairs that he was able to scrounge for Falcon's office. "I wish I could offer you better accomodations, but our budget—"

"Forget it. This is fine. I was hoping for the ocean view, though."

"Sorry, it's not as nice as the Metropol," Medved laughed.

"Oh, the Metropol has its problems. My room was pest-infested. I had to change it. Which reminds me—can you get me a couple of those great KGB three-prong steel door locks?"

"Sure." Medved decided not to pry, thinking that they would come into each other's confidence when, and if, they merited it. He reached for the stash of cigarettes that he habitually kept tucked in his shirt pocket, coughed as he opened the pack and offered one to his counterpart.

"There's a rumor that those things'll kill you," Falcon said, declining the courtesy.

"*Bozha Moy*, you sound like my...." Medved paused, deciding against letting the American into this corner of his life. "So, I believe you made some points with Viktor with your wrestling background."

"Oh, that," Falcon laughed. "Ancient history."

"Hmm. Not exactly ancient, but it was twenty-some years ago that you were invited to the U.S. Olympic camp. You missed that opportunity because the Navy needed every one of its fighter pilots for Vietnam."

"Well, duty called...you know how that is, Sergei," Falcon said as he began to work on the connections to the IBM desktop computer that had been supplied by the FSB.

"You flew two hundred and ten missions in the F-8 Crusader—the MiG Master as you Navy pilots fondly called it," Medved continued.

Falcon smiled, momentarily ceasing his work. "Yeah, and they were almost all up north." He referred to North Vietnam, where the anti-aircraft threat was thousands of times greater than that faced in the South. "But then, you know all about that, too."

The Russian grinned as he lit his cigarette. "I suppose we have fewer secrets than we wish to imagine. I also know that you fired a couple of Sidewinder heat-seeking missiles into the tailpipes of two of our MiG-21's, sending them down into flames over Kep Airfield in North Vietnam. "For which you received a Distinguished Flying Cross."

"I guess you're right, Sergei, we do have precious few secrets."

"Ah, but there is one thing I do not know concerning that matter—a footnote to Russian history which has always been of great interest to me."

"Ok, let's see if I'm not a complete plumber," Falcon said, finishing with the last computer connection and sitting before the terminal. "So what is it that's so interesting about my combat record?"

"The MiGs that you...bagged...I believe is the correct terminology...what nationality were the pilots?"

Falcon ceased his fiddling with the computer and stared incredulously at the Russian. "You're serious. You really don't know."

"We Russians also have many secrets from each other."

"Well, I tell you what," Falcon smiled. "I'll give you this Top Secret tidbit, but I'll want a return in kind some day."

"Deal."

"O.K. They were either North Viets who spoke totally unaccented Russian...or maybe Chinese who spoke your language flawlessly. But the Russian was damned perfect, considering how excited they were at the particular moment."

"Thank you," Medved said, drawing a long puff.

"And you, Major Medved…the Bear of the Hindu Kush. If memory serves me correctly, you were in that first commando raid on Kabul in 1979. You attacked the Dar-ol-Aman Palace with sixty men. Half were dead or injured by the time you reached the ground floor. Your friend, Anatoly Danchenkov, had his right hand nearly blown off by an Afghan grenade. In the heat of battle, you fashioned a tourniquet from your own shirt, which kept the hand attached. You and one other Spetsnaz soldier made it upstairs to the communications center in the Palace. You were the one who didn't get his face shot off. You lobbed a grenade into the center, putting it out of commission, then returned downstairs, hoisted Danchenkov on your shoulder and escaped in a captured Afghan armored car. You received the award of Hero of the Soviet Union. Did I miss anything?"

Medved stared at the floor, slowly exhaling the blue-gray smoke. "The other man's name…who I left on the second floor."

"Tyucha. He was a seventeen year old private."

The Russian's eyes began to mist.

"You couldn't have gotten him out. There's nothing more you could've done."

"Did you also know that the bodies of our brave boys—the soldiers of our Motherland—were not even given a proper burial. We brought them home but the funerals were held in secret. There were no bands, no ceremonies, nothing. And it was only the beginning of ten years of the same. Just as it was for you in Vietnam. For what?"

"Perhaps we are too prone to seek purpose where there is none, particularly when it comes to war."

"Yes, perhaps," Medved muttered, crushing his cigarette in a glass ashtray on the desk.

"Say, I need to get to a bank to exchange my dollars for rubles," Falcon said, glancing at his watch. Is it too late?"

"No. The Metropol has an exchange office that's still open for another half-hour. I could drop you off."

"Nonsense. I'll take the metro."

"You had better hurry, then. The Liubanka stop is right outside the front entrance. Take the Red Line toward Yugo Zapadnaya and get off at the first stop—Teatralnaya."

"Thanks. See you back here in the morning."

"Eight a.m.—"Medved shouted after him. "And don't forget your pass. Some of the old Chekists at the gates occasionally forget themselves and shoot those who show up without their proper ID."

"Nice try," Falcon shouted back, but that doesn't square us for the MiG info. You still owe me."

Medved smiled. Working with the American would be interesting.

* * *

Falcon arrived at the Metropol exchange counter just as the bank clerk was closing his window. Two decades ago, waving a stick of dynamite would not have cowed an indifferent Soviet official into remaining open for a mere one minute longer to conduct a quick and simple monetary transaction. But the Soviets—for the most part—were gone and the capitalist philosophy pervaded, meaning that a quick profit was worth a few moments of overtime. With the wholesale deflation of the ruble, dollars were eagerly gobbled up. The Russian government estimated that there were as many dollars as rubles circulating in the Russian economy but no one knew the exact amount, as the greenbacks were only traded on the black market or hoarded in savings.

The clerk rolled his window back open, re-keyed his register, and happily exchanged the daily devaluing rubles for the stable dollars. Unfortunately, Mike Falcon had no choice in the matter, for it was illegal to use foreign currency in the new Russia.

He counted the stack of rubles—which was almost ten times as thick as the wad of dollars he had swapped—and proceeded to the elevators. As might be expected in a large luxury hotel, a number of people were milling about the lobby. Only one, however, had been following Falcon's every move. Dressed in an expensive Italian suit that hung loosely on his thin frame, he sat on one of the many couches in the lobby and feigned reading the latest edition of *Izvestiya*. When the American passed him, he rose, folded the newspaper, stuck it in the crook of his arm and ambled toward the same elevator.

* * *

A short distance away, in the Old Arbat District, Viktor Buzhkin stood in a phone booth.

"We must have a complete rundown and then we will decide how to deal with him," a voice at the other end of the line said. "But we cannot conduct this discussion by such means. You must come in immediately."

A click was followed by a dial tone. Buzhkin replaced the phone on its hook and stepped from the booth. Zipping his jacket, he walked west for several blocks on Old Arbat Street which, beginning with glasnost, had become Moscow's answer to Paris' Montmarte. Once the home of Russia's nobility and the setting for its most famous poems and novels, the pedestrian-only thoroughfare was now the domain of sculptors, painters, and souvenir sellers who hawked their wares on sidewalks before fashionable cafes and boutiques.

Weaving his way through the tourists—a much easier task now that the chill of winter was nigh—Buzhkin made his way toward the Moskva River until, just before reaching the waterfront, he made a quick left turn into a quiet alley. Navigating around three wrinkled, portly, rag-layered *babushkas* who sat mutely on a bench, he entered the hallway of a dilapidated tenement.

A knock on a paint-peeled door resulted in the sound of metal bolts clicking. The door swung open and Buzhkin entered a dimly lit room.

"Wait at the table," a man's voice said from behind him. Buzhkin squinted, straining to adapt his eyes from the sunlight to the blackness. He was barely able to discern the shadow of a table and chair situated a few feet away.

Groping forward, he reached the chair and carefully lowered his massive frame into it. His right hand slid inside his jacket for a reassuring touch of the *Gurza*, although he doubted that it would be of any use if a decision from on high had gone against him. He waited for ten, fifteen, twenty minutes. The indistinguishable murmurings of voices, some seemingly angry, could be heard emanating from the next room. Gradually, furnishings emerged from the shadows and took on their shapes—a cupboard with several plates…a three-tiered bookshelf overflowing with volumes…a bottle of Stolichnaya on the table.

He had not heard a sound, yet now a hand touched his shoulder. He turned and gazed into a pair of sparkling green eyes.

"Hello, Svetlana," he said.

Chapter Twenty-One

The dwelling which bin Wahhab and Talil entered was dank and dark, little more than a cave. It had been carved out of that very same millennia-old gray rock that constituted the surrounding mountains flung up by the African-Eurasian landmass collision. Several dozen candles mounted a feeble counterattack against the gloom, but the inhabitants actually preferred the lack of light and the inconspicuousness it afforded.

"*Sallam al laikum*" bin Wahhab said, bowing to the standing assemblage of two dozen white-robed men.

"*Al laikum al sallam,*" They replied in unison.

The 'Mahdi' then sank into a cross-legged position on the cold, moist, rock floor. The others followed suit.

Bin Wahhab waited until they had settled and there was no further rustling or whispering. And then he waited yet a few moments longer, his face tilted down, his eyes closed. His disciples gazed upon him in hushed expectation. Finally, he raised his head, opened his eyes and began to speak—at first, very slowly and softly, almost inaudibly.

"A thousand years ago, when the infidels of Europe were living in mud huts and in the squalor of their own ignorance, the greatest civilizations of the world followed the Muslim banners. Our armies defeated the Greeks, conquered the Spaniards, destroyed the Crusaders of Christendom, and drove like the withering wind of the desert into Africa, India, and all the way to China. Every nation trembled before the sword of Islam." His voice rose ever so slightly as he emphasized this last point.

"Yet, it was not only our military might that demanded respect and awe. For we could boast of the world's greatest science academies, astronomical observatories, libraries, schools of medicine, and centers of learning. Our cities were rich with fountains, canals and lush gardens. We gave the world much of its mathematics and science, timeless poetry and philosophy, and supplied its peoples with writing paper, fine clothing of silk, gold thread and silver lame, and beautifully crafted copper ornaments, and exquisitely woven carpets! *Allahu Akhbar!*"

"Allah be praised!" the rejoinder exploded from two dozen throats.

Bin Wahhab waited until the buzzing had ceased. And then, in the deathly silence, he waited a few minutes more. When he began again, he returned to his subdued, sonorous delivery. His disciples strained to hear every word, eager to ride the crescendo and burst at the climactic moment. It was not an accidental technique that he employed nor one that he had invented. It came from his exhaustive study of the speech style of the world's champion demagogue, Adolph Hitler. Drown them in silent anticipation, titillate them with barely audible, cadenced words. Slowly build. Raise their heartbeats. Pull back, then build some more. Increase the beat, add some thunder, control their rising frenzy, then excitedly gush the denouement. The words were secondary. The delivery was paramount.

It took only a few minutes for one of his skill to bring his audience to the frenzied stage. Having reminded them of their historic greatness, he launched into a diatribe against those who were responsible for their downfall: the Mongol barbarians of Jengiz Khan who, in a period of only forty years, turned the once magnificent cities of Islam to dust and ashes, cut their population in half, and shattered the souls of the survivors; their even more ancient foes, the Jews, who 'stole' their lands and fought their faith; the Zionists' mercenary and materialistic partner in crime, the Americans; and the most unforgivable of all, the cowardly, corrupted, irreligious Muslim leadership, as most blatantly exemplified by the American lackeys—the House of Saud.

The listeners could contain themselves no longer, shouting approval as they pounded the ground with their fists. "Truly you are the Mahdi!" one cried. "You will lead Islam back to its former greatness!" blurted another.

Bin Wahhab permitted himself the luxury of basking in their adoration for a few moments. After all, he reasoned, it was equally as important to them to heap their praise upon him. But there was also important business to conduct; therefore, though it was with some reluctance, he cut short their effusiveness.

"Soon the Jihad will be visited upon the false believers and the infidels," he said. "Before the crescent moon of Islam has appeared a fourth time, the Ikhwan Brotherhood will be called to battle. Will you be ready to answer this call?"

"Aiyee!" they cried in unison. *"Allahu Akhbar! La ilaha il-Allah!* There is no god but Allah! Allah bless the Ikhwan! Bin Wahhab is the Mahdi! The Chosen One!"

Smiling, bin Wahhab raised his hand to still them. They were his now, more surely than ever. The vista of the Jihad, the rewriting of history—and his own, magnificent place in it—stretched before him like a beckoning odalisque, a harem seductress.

"Tell me, then," he said turning to one of the excited disciples, "How will Hamas answer the call?"

"The Islamic Resistance Movement stands ready to die for you, Mahdi," answered a man, whose only visible features were his shining onyx eyes and leathery brown hands. "As proof of my words, this past year we have conducted three suicide missions, blowing up two fully loaded passenger buses in Jerusalem and a shopping mall in Tel Aviv. Our forces are gathering in Syria, Iran, and Sudan. We only await your call."

"Allah be with you, brother," bin Wahhab said, prayerfully folding his hands and slightly nodding his head.

"May He be with you eternally, Mahdi," his disciple replied as he returned the gesture, his eyes glowing with the pride that came from being the subject of the Chosen One's attention.

"And you, Hussein," bin Wahhab said, transferring his gaze, "what may we expect of Hizballah?"

"The Party of God will be at the forefront, even ahead of its Hamas brothers," Hussein answered. "Our suicide missions against the Americans in Lebanon prove our resolve. We are ready to rise up in Kuwait and Lebanon to overthrow the false believers that rule those countries."

"Allah be with you."

"And you, Mahdi."

Bin Wahhab turned his gaze toward a smallish, pockmarked face man sitting opposite him. "And may we expect the same from our Egyptian brothers?" he asked.

"Al Gama will overthrow the unlawful and sacrilegious Egyptian government," the man replied. "We only await your command."

Around the room, bin Wahhab put the question to each of his twenty-four disciples, and all pledged undying devotion to the Mahdi and the Jihad. Finally he came to the Iraqi representative.

"No nation has endured more at the hands of the Great Satan," the Iraqi said, trembling with emotion. "Our land has been bombed by the cowardly use of cruise missiles. Our people have been denied the basic human rights of obtaining food and medicine. Our children have suffered and died. Iraq calls upon all of its Muslim brothers to join with it in the Jihad and to cleanse the world of these non-believing devils!" The room erupted with excited cries and more thumping of fists on the stony floor.

"Praise God," bin Wahhab said, upon receiving this final report. "You are all to be commended. Our immediate numbers are not yet great and much work still remains to be done. But only remember that the Prophet, with far less strength than our own, took by force this sacred city in which we sit and brought to Allah the submission—the Islam—of the Arab people. We, the Ikhwan, shall pick up his sword and bring to Allah the submission of the world. *Allahu Akhbar!*"

"*Allahu Akhbar!*" the room reverberated.

*   *   *

Viktor Buzhkin poured himself a glass of vodka and shoved the bottle across the table.

"You know I never touch that," Popova laughed. "One never knows when one might need full command of one's mental and physical faculties."

"That's precisely why I drink it," he answered gruffly.

"I'll join you," said the third person at the table, a stocky, coarse-shaven man to his left. In normal society, he would have been considered large and muscular, but sitting near Buzhkin, he appeared rather inconsequential.

"Well, Viktor, what do you make of the American?" the woman asked.

Buzhkin raised the tumbler to his lips and, throwing his head back, downed the drink in one quaff.

"He knows a great deal. He has linked you, the uranium, our organization, and bin Wahhab. Working with Medved, it will only be a matter of time before they know everything."

"*Tfoo! Proklatiya!* Damnation!" the other man said, slamming his fist on the table. "I told you that you should have killed him when you had the chance, Svetlana!

Now everything has become much more complicated!"

"Either you control yourself, Gregori, or I will do it for you," Popova said matter-of-factly but firmly. "And let us not forget how you and Slater botched the handling of the Professor at Peredelkino."

Gregori Yusopov glanced at her, his eyes burning and his lips moving as if to reply. He thought better of it, however, and consoled himself with pouring a shot of the Stolichnaya instead.

"Our friend from the east has demanded that we find out exactly what the American knows before we dispose of him," she continued. "I need hardly add that such intelligence is critical to our own organization if we hope to proceed with our plans to take control of the government."

"You could have easily extracted such information already," Yusopov retorted. "It is obvious that you simply wish to toy with him for your own perverted sexual amusement. I doubt if either bin Wahhab or our superiors would be pleased with your handling of this matter."

Buzhkin leaned slightly back so as to be clear of Gregori's head in the event that Popova, the Feliks' most lethal agent, chose this moment to send it flying from Gregori's body. He almost felt sorry for the other man as he sensed his tension and smelled his fear.

Svetlana studied Yusopov for a long moment, then turned away, as one might ignore a fly. Ordinarily, she would have thoroughly punished the perpetrator of such an outburst. In this case, however, the fool had spoken the truth and the very accuracy of his words had amused her.

"Viktor, I want you to stay as close as possible to both the American and Medved," she said. "I want you to know everything they know about our project. You will report back to me every day. I will have further instructions for you later."

"As for the American," she said, fixing her bright green eyes on Gregori, "I will take care of him in my own time and my own way. Unless of course you have something further to say on the matter, *Gospodeen* Yusopov."

Buzhkin wondered if the man would be stupid enough to display some machismo. Yusopov wasn't.

"Good. In that case, you may both go, now. Viktor, you leave first."

With a scrape of his chair, Buzhkin pushed away from the table and stood. He tossed a glance at the other man, wondering disinterestedly if he would see him in one piece next time. He knew that her intolerance for insolence was matched only by her joy of inflicting pain. Poor, dumb bastard, that Gregori Yusopov.

The sun had set and the temperature had dipped to below freezing when Buzhkin emerged from the tenement. It was the sort of weather that he loved best, although a good snowfall was still to be desired. The thought stirred memories of his home and his childhood in Irkutsk, Siberia—*Sibi*, the "sleeping land" of endless forests…pristine, soot-free snow…the dark blue waters of Lake Baikal…the mink, sable, fox, and bear which he loved to track…chopping wood on a zero-below day when the activity warmed one's blood enough to melt the ice from one's bones. Someday, when this was all over, he would return there for good, he mused. But he knew deep inside, they would never allow this.

Chapter Twenty-Two

It was nearly midnight when Vasily Kuzmitch stumbled out of the cold, blustery Moscow night into his apartment. He was drunk. His wife of one year, Yelena Pavlovna, lay in bed, terrified. She had prepared his meal six hours ago, re-warming it several times, then leaving it on the table and scurrying to bed when she heard his clumsy approach to the door. She harbored the slim hope—fantasy, more appropriately—that he would be distracted by the food and thinking her asleep, would leave her in peace.

For a moment, Kuzmitch actually was sidetracked by the aroma of the beefsteak, potatoes, and cabbage. He collapsed into a chair at the table, thrust a fork into the beef and tore off a chunk that was almost too large to shove into his elfish mouth. As he worked the unwieldy chaw with his teeth, he glanced around the table for some vodka to wash down this damned mouthful of dried-up dishrag. *Why can't this foolish woman cook? She thinks she can get by on her looks alone. And once again she has set nothing here for me to drink, except watered-down tea. Schlyooka! Slut!* In an awkward but rapid motion, he swept his arm across the table, knocking the brass teakettle to the floor.

Hearing the clatter, Yelena pulled the quilt over her head and sobbed as her body convulsed with fear. Even beneath the heavy blanket, she could still hear him rummaging through the cupboards, slamming their little wooden doors as he searched for a bottle of vodka. She wondered if she had done the right thing in hiding the alcohol, for it was bound to exacerbate his anger. On the other hand, the more he drank, the more severely he thrashed her.

She could not report him to the police. She could not even run away. Those options were not available to the wife of a member of the *Chornaya Rooka*—the 'Black Hand'—Moscow's most notorious mafia. She had been unaware of his criminal connection when he was courting her and, as an impoverished young dancer, she had been dazzled by his flashy world of Mercedes automobiles, Italian clothes, and expensive jewelry. Now she wished she were dead.

Searching for the vodka had made Kuzmitch's head spin. He slumped back into his chair, hoping to steady himself. The beefsteak sitting on the table had not changed, but for some reason now looked completely repulsive to him. Again, he swung his arm forward, sending the meat and its silver platter crashing to the floor. The splat of the lump of food struck him as ridiculous and he began to laugh. "And why have I let her put me in such a black mood," he marveled aloud. "It was a good evening. Shramlik loved my idea. We'll kidnap that rich American at the Metropol and get a few hundred thousand—not worthless rubles, but real dollars—for our troubles. Maybe a few million…who knows?"

He began reflecting upon his good fortune in having seen the American exchange that wad of dollars at the Metropol cashier's. *It'll be easy money no matter how you cut it. Then they'll take me seriously and I'll get promoted to lieutenant. I'll finally get out of this stinking rat hole and move into one of those palaces on Pushkin Hill. And I'll parade women through there…dancers, actresses, each one more gorgeous than the last. Of course, in spite of her stupidity, it would be difficult to find even one as beautiful as my Yelena.* He knew that she was not unintelligent but had begun belittling her on that score in order to assuage his own insecurity. "*Yelena….*" The vision of her long auburn hair, her clear, smooth skin, and her enticing curves appeared in his burned-out brain.

Perhaps she is still awake and would like a little taste of Vasily.

He shoved away from the table, knocking the chair over as he stumbled to his feet. Cursing, he kicked the interfering piece of furniture across the room and lumbered to the bedroom. "Yelen-ooshka, my little dove," he slurred, pushing open the door. "Are you awake?"

He clumsily shed his Versace suit, catching his right foot in the pants leg and tumbling onto his butt. Lying on his back, he squirmed out of his underwear and wrestled free of his shoes. In his stupor, the socks were overlooked. In the next moment, she felt his weight on the bed and his hand on her shoulder. She squeezed her eyelids down tightly, as though that action might make her invisible.

"Yelen-ooshka, wake up," he grumbled, pulling the quilt down. He shook her but got no response. "Vasily has a little surprise for you…more than a little," he snickered. He pushed her nightgown above her hips and began grasping at her panties. It was more than she could bear. Without thinking, she rolled from under his bony body and slid to the floor. No matter what the ultimate consequences, she would not endure this humiliation one more time. He gazed at her, stupefied, his brain unable to analyze such an unprecedented action.

As he hesitated, she bolted for the door. Unfortunately, Kuzmitch was in her path. Besotted though he was, he was still able to launch himself from the bed and grasp her ankles as she flew by. Kicking and struggling, she managed to scramble to her feet. Draped around her, he pulled himself up and, as she turned to pass through the doorway, he seized her by the hair and spun her around. In the same motion, he swung his other arm with all the might his spindly frame could muster. His clenched fist smashed into her face, knocking her into the hallway.

"Now you'll get what's what…. Run from Vasily, will you?" he sneered at the moaning figure.

He turned to look for the pants that he had kicked off on his way to the bed. Finding them in a heap behind the door, he picked them up and pulled off the belt. He slapped the buckle in his hand. "You'll beg to fuck Vasily next time," he said as he lurched to the hallway.

The words had barely escaped his lips when a searing pain shot through his head, electrical sparks exploded in his brain, and a loud clang reverberated in his ears.

He slumped to his knees, then pitched forward landing on his face and breaking his nose.

Gingerly touching the rising welt on her cheek, Yelena Pavlovna tossed aside the now-dented brass tea kettle. She stepped over the motionless body, not knowing if the bastard were dead or alive and certainly not caring. It took only several minutes to gather a few clothes into her overnight bag. Even long after she had gone, Vasily Kuzmitch had not so much as moved an eyelash.

*   *   *

Every day for the past three weeks, ever since his conversation with bin Wahhab concerning the physics of a nuclear "device," Professor Marenkov had been making his preparations. From each meal, he would secrete away any food that had a reasonably long shelf life. He had built a cache of preserved figs and dates as well as raisins, nuts and bread that, by his conservative estimates, would sustain him for at least fifteen days. All of the food had then been carefully wrapped in strips of a pillow-case that he had cut for this purpose and then stitched shut. He had also put his cigarette allotment to advantage, using the tobacco to lower the barriers between himself and a nicotine-addicted guard. The acquaintance led to casual discussions, ranging from describing their families, homes, and friends to more scientific subjects such as the weather and geography of their respective lands. It was only a short time before he was able to construct a rudimentary map of his location.

He calculated that they were less than thirty kilometers from the Pakistani border to the east. Most importantly, the relations between

Pakistan and Afghanistan were not happy. In spite of Valentin's pessimism, perhaps the Pakistanis would take him in. At any rate, it was worth the chance, for to stay here was unthinkable. And if his flight were successful, he would be able to alert the world concerning the mad sheikh's intentions.

He had also worked out the means of his escape. The Ikhwan guard change occurred three times daily, the last shift taking place at 11:30 p.m. Every Friday, the departing soldiers would be accompanied by a large bin containing the week's laundry. The changing of the guard, insofar as the 'lab rats' such as Marenkov were concerned, was quite lax. After all, with the sole exception of himself, all the inhabitants were here voluntarily. The laundry receptacle was always rolled directly into a large truck which then proceeded to the town of Khowst. The trick would be slipping unnoticed from the vehicle.

He glanced at the clock. It was 11:00 p.m. It was also Friday. Around his waist he wrapped the bags containing his contraband food, then donned three layers of clothes, and lastly tucked his lab garment over all. Shifting the paraphernalia until it seemed reasonably passable, he seated his spectacles on the bridge of his nose, grasped his clipboard, and switched off the remaining light in his room. Opening the door, he glanced along both directions of the dimly lit hallway. No sign of life could be detected.

Drawing a deep breath, he walked quietly down the passageway toward the laboratory. If detected, he could make a plausible argument that he was working late on some intractable physics problem, describing it in such arcane detail that any guard would be happy to flee his presence.

All the way to the lab, he encountered not one soul. The scientists and engineers were in their quarters, where they were sleeping or bending their brains attempting to fathom Marenkov's abstruse quantum mechanic equations. The Ikhwan were several floors above, changing shifts at the entrance to the underground hideaway. Soon, if all went well, he would be in the same area.

He glanced through the thick, tempered glass window of the lab. In the middle of the work area, on a concrete-reinforced bench that stretched for several meters, sat three rather unimposing black cubicles. The trunk-sized boxes were constructed of steel walls that were fifteen centimeters thick. He did not need x-ray vision to picture the contents of the containers—one held the whitish-gray lump of basically inert U-238; the middle case held lithium—submersed in naphtha, as contact with air would cause it to ignite; and finally, the box containing the plum-colored sphere of highly-enriched uranium. Although the U-235 was subcritical, boron rods had been inserted into the box to capture stray neutrons and prevent a spontaneous chain reaction. Shiny robotic machines, their steel and wire arms hanging at their sides, stood ready to handle the lethal material when called upon.

Another concrete support structure, on the near wall, held two hat-sized boxes. One housed beryllium and the other contained blue-glowing polonium. These two elements, mixed together at the triggering of the device, would initiate the nuclear explosion by producing a hundred million neutrons per second.

A third bench on the far wall supported a container of the world's fastest-acting chemical high explosive, HMX octogen…'His Majesty's eXplosives' as British soldiers had dubbed it in WWII. Lead-azide primaries, argon-filled spark gaps, and fast-reacting krytron switches were in various stages of assembly. It would not be much longer before the ignition mechanism was complete and the contents of all the boxes were arranged together. The thought instilled yet a greater sense of urgency within him.

He passed beyond the laboratory, slipped into another barely lit corridor to his left and opened a heavy metal door leading to a staircase. The stairs led down one flight, to the basement of the complex. There, he pushed through another steel door and emerged into a room that was lit by only a single low-wattage bulb. His eyes had barely fallen upon the laundry bin when he heard the whirring sound of a motor starting. It was a noise he had become familiar with during his stay in the compound. The elevator had started and was probably now heading toward the basement with soldiers who were to collect the laundry. Of all the nights for them to be prompt, he mused. He had only a few moments to act.

Quickly moving to the receptacle, he pulled several layers of the rumpled clothes to one side. He then dove into the bin and began frantically covering himself. The elevator door was opening before he had satisfactorily completed his camouflage—his right foot remained partially exposed—but to improve upon it would be to attract attention. He lay completely still as he heard the guards, laughing and talking boisterously, approach the bin. A bump and then he was moving, being wheeled into the elevator. The doors closed and once again he heard the distinctive whirring sound of the elevator motor.

When the doors opened a few seconds later, he was jostled once more as the bin was rolled through the entrance of the compound. Many more voices were evident and, even beneath the covering laundry and his own three layers of clothing, he was aware of the chill air of the wintry Afghan mountains. The movement stopped and the voices faded, leading him to believe that he had been left alone. It seemed an opportune moment to drag that last bit of laundry over his still exposed foot. No sooner had he begun to cautiously rearrange a few of the rags, however, when a cough just above his head startled him.

His heart stuttered as a voice suddenly cried out. Several others responded to this call and he could hear their boots crunching gravel as they drew near. Thinking that he had been discovered, he almost leaped from his hiding place when their hands thudded against the bin. He felt himself pitch on an incline and heard the clatter of the wheels on wooden planks. It was then that he realized that the soldier had simply been calling for assistance to push the heavy load up a ramp and into the waiting truck. Several of the Ikhwan clattered on board with it, slamming the iron tailgate shut behind them. A grinding sound was followed by the pungent odor and staccato puttering of a diesel engine until finally the vehicle lurched off and began winding its way through the mountain passes of the Hindu Kush.

By Marenkov's reckoning, half an hour had elapsed by the time they came to a halt. Shuffling of feet within the truck was followed by the clang of the tailgate swinging open. The laundry bin was jockeyed around and he once again experienced a steep forward pitch as the Ikhwan rolled their cargo down the ramp. A brief discussion ensued, an order was barked, and he was on the move again, twisting and turning, passing across a grating and eventually coming to a stop inside some sort of building. That he was indoors was evident by the stillness of the air and the perceptible—albeit slight—increase in temperature. The voices and footsteps then receded until a door slammed shut and they disappeared altogether.

He waited ten minutes in the total silence, then waited ten minutes more. Finally, he poked through the rags over his face. He found himself in complete darkness. Cautiously, he pushed aside the covering laundry and sat up. Satisfied that he was indeed alone, he grasped the rail of the bin and swung his legs over the side. Landing in a crouched position, he somehow felt much younger than his sixty years. A most curious thought then flashed through his mind, causing him to smile as he shed his laboratory smock. He was thinking of his friend, Seryozha Ivanovitch, their many years of conversations in the park at Moscow University, and in particular, their last discussion before his kidnapping at Peredelkino. He remembered listening with envy to Seryozha's heroic exploits in defense of Mother Russia against the Nazis in the Great Patriotic War. And how Seryozha had politely scolded him for this envy. If only his great friend could see him at this moment. He, too, was now risking all for *Mat' Rossia*. He had never felt more alive.

It took only a few minutes to carefully work his way across the darkened enclosure to the door through which he had recently been wheeled. His right hand encircled the doorknob and twisted. The latch clicked and the door swung open. Peering outside, he was surprised to see a light dusting of snow on the ground. The building from which he now stepped appeared to be well on the outskirts of the town. Khowst, itself, was fast asleep. Gazing in the opposite direction, he could see the silhouetted peaks of the Sulaiman Range bordering Afghanistan and Pakistan. The mountains were about thirty kilometers away. With luck, he would be across the border by this time tomorrow evening. He set off with a fairly nimble trot.

Chapter Twenty-Three

"As I am sure you are aware, Michael, World War Two cost the lives of twenty million Russian people—more than all of the other allies combined," Medved said as he paused for a drag on his cigarette. Unlike the Federal buildings of the U.S., it was still permissible to smoke within the confines of a Russian government complex. He and Falcon were now ensconced in one of the FSB's "study rooms", a windowless cubicle on the third floor of the Lubianka that was used for research and briefings. They had arrived early that morning and were waiting for Buzhkin.

"For a couple of years," he continued, "we withstood the onslaught of the Nazi war machine virtually alone. In addition to military losses and 'unavoidable' civilian casualties, we also suffered a holocaust. Although it's not well known in your country, Hitler was exterminating Slavs in the death camps at a rate comparable to that of his murder of the Jews. And it is this suffering that our nation experienced, not the Communist dogma, that led to the Cold War and the nuclear missile race. Ninety-five percent of the Russian people couldn't have cared less about spreading Marxism throughout the world. But we all vowed that never again would we allow such a calamity to befall our country. That meant we could not be militarily inferior to any other nation."

"Yes, I understand," Falcon said. "When I was here twenty years ago, I had an interesting conversation with a young Red Army enlistee. He told me that Russians greatly admired Americans and looked upon them as kindred spirits. He also said, however, that his land had been invaded over the centuries by Swedes, Poles, Mongols, Frenchmen, and Germans and that they had all been eventually defeated by the Russian people. He hoped that the U.S. would not make the same mistake, for if it did, he assured me quite matter-of-factly, it would meet the same fate."

"Ah, the confidence of youth," Medved laughed. "But of course, he was only speaking that which was in the minds of almost all Russians. "This is why we built thousands of nuclear missiles—"

"To maintain parity with us—which we could not accept."

"Yes, your side kept railing about a missile gap—which didn't exist—so you built more and more…."

"And the madness literally continued. 'Mutually Assured Destruction'…MAD…we aptly termed it in the U.S. Each side could wipe out the other several times over."

"Perhaps mutually *absurd* destruction would have been yet more apt," the Russian said. "For neither side could prevent the catastrophe. We had thousands of SS-18 Intercontinental Ballistic Missiles hidden in the forests of Siberia and all the way into the deserts of Kazakhstan. Some were on trains, others on trucks that moved daily so that it was impossible to target them. You would have had about ten or fifteen minutes of warning thanks to your North American Aerospace Defense Command in Cheyenne Mountain. But no way of stopping them."

"You had the same problem with our triad of missiles, bombers, and subs—particularly the subs, the boomers—which were essentially invisible to you. It's a miracle that we didn't annihilate the planet in those days," Falcon said, shaking his head. "I'm also amazed, considering your resolve after World War Two, that you were willing to take the first steps toward reducing the nuclear arsenals."

"We had no choice, Michael. We are a rich country in many ways—literature, art, music—but we are a poor country, financially speaking.

We could not keep pace when you raised the ante with your Strategic Defense Initiative. Particle beams, lasers, kinetic energy weapons. We just didn't have the rubles to keep up. And if you had been able to implement that particular system, where would we have been? You could have launched a nuclear attack against us without fear of counterattack. No, we had to come up with a radical strategy...like cutting our warhead numbers in half if you would agree to curtail the SDI."

"And the rest was history...the thawing of the Cold War."

"Right. In truth, the Soviet Union had been quite feeble for many years, but the bear still had all its teeth. When we reached a real arms reduction agreement, however, the bear started losing its fangs and then even rabbits began kicking it. It was a simple decision for a poor country to at least try to make some money in exchange for giving up its superpower status."

"And some sort of capitalist company is needed to act as the broker with the West for this purpose. Thus, *Rurik Korporatsiya* is born."

"Ah, yes...Rurik. Licensed by our Ministry of Atomic Energy to convert our nuclear warhead uranium to your American dollars."

"Some of those dollars came from Mr. Slater's company. But I'll wager that Micratom did not always receive full value for its investment."

"Correct on both points. They did not receive all the uranium they paid for. Ah, but here's Viktor," Medved nodded, acknowledging Buzhkin's entrance.

"Sorry I'm a little late," Buzhkin said gruffly, taking a seat.

"You're not late at all, Viktor," Medved replied, puffing a ring of smoke. "We were here a little early. It gave me an opportunity to bend Mr. Falcon's ear with a bit of Russian history. But now that we're all here, we can get started on today's business. Michael, I believe you were going to speak to the connection between the Ikhwan and the Feliks."

"Yes, I also have a few pictures," Falcon said, rising and approaching a slide carousel at the end of the table. Medved clicked off the room lights and the first image appeared on the screen at the front of the darkened room.

"I'm sure you know this character," Falcon said, as the others focused their eyes on a lanky, Rasputin-eyed, white-robed Arab.

"Of course," Medved said. "Abdul bin Wahhab."

"Correct. He is a member of the Saudi family and is believed to be worth close to one billion U.S. dollars. According to the CIA's Counter Terrorism Center, he has used his wealth to finance numerous terrorist operations, including the World Trade Center bombing in New York, the Khobar Towers bombing in Saudi Arabia, attacks against tourists in Egypt, and the recent bombings in Tanzania and Kenya." As Falcon spoke, he clicked a picture of each of these events onto the screen.

"For some years, bin Wahhab has fancied himself as the Expected Mahdi—the Chosen or Rightly Guided One. The Mahdi is a muddling of Jewish and Christian concepts of the Messiah. It is believed by some Muslims that the Mahdi, a direct descendant of the Prophet Muhammad, will appear one day and sound the triumphant call of Islam and the Resurrection of Jesus to defeat the forces of the Anti-Christ. He is at least the third person to lay claim to the Mahdi title. The first claimant appeared over a hundred years ago in the Sudan and wiped out the British forces in Khartoum. He died, however, without fulfilling the prophecy, and was thus considered a false Mahdi.

"The next claimant, as far as we know, arose much more recently. Twenty years ago, he and his band of zealots—the Ikhwan—stormed the Sacred Mosque of Mecca and announced the dawn of a new world order. Within two weeks, they were all dead or captured. And, of course, for his failure, he too was declared a false Mahdi. That brings us to bin Wahhab...."

"One moment, Michael," Medved interrupted. "This Ikhwan that you speak of...who are they? What is their nationality?"

"They are many nationalities. The Ikhwan—the Brotherhood—first appeared among the Bedouin over three-quarters of a century ago.

They believed they were the true interpreters of the Koran and declared a *jihad* upon those who believed otherwise. They were utterly fearless in battle and totally merciless. They were even known to execute those who believed as they did, but failed to read the Koran properly.

"In those early days, a British-trained Arab force set out into the desert to bring them under control. The Ikhwan, outnumbered five-to-one, fell upon their enemy's camp at night. Screaming that the sinners should prepare themselves for Hell, they annihilated the 'False Believers'. The bones of the dead can still be found in the desert to this day. They were finally defeated on the battlefield several years later by the overwhelming armies of the House of Saud. The Ikhwan survivors melted back into the desert where they continued to nurture their fanatical beliefs, waiting for the true Mahdi to lead them forward again."

"Enter bin Wahhab," Medved interjected. "But where is the Feliks connection?"

"Ah, yes. That brings us to this fascinating person," Falcon responded, clicking the carousal control button.

Beyond the blue haze of Medved's cigarette smoke, the image of an attractive green-eyed, blonde woman appeared on the screen.

"Her name is Svetlana Nikolayevna Popova—alias Cherisse Tigere. We know that she is a graduate of your alma mater, Sergei—*Shkola* 101. Perhaps you know of her?"

"Ah, the Red Banner Institute," Medved responded noncommittally. "Then she must be very well trained."

"Yes, the KGB excelled in certain aspects of education. She further honed her skills at the Military Intelligence Directorate—the GRU—and now she's a full-fledged assassin for the Feliks. Perhaps you are well aware of that as well. At any rate, I'm afraid you'll have to trust me on this, as my source for this info is classified. We have long suspected her—and the Feliks—of involvement with bin Wahhab. Now we're positive. She is the agent who neutralized James Slater. She did it in an attempt to recover incriminating evidence he possessed concerning his illicit trafficking of Russian nuclear warhead uranium with bin Wahhab."

"Russian missiles?" Buzhkin spoke. "And how is such a thing possible? And what is the connection to the disappearance of the Professor?"

"If I may…." Medved interrupted. He decided that this was an auspicious moment to put his burly assistant to the test. "I would like to speak to that issue."

He rose and stepped to the end of the table, next to the slide carousel.

"Professor Marenkov had met with Slater here in Moscow only days before his disappearance. I believe that he was kidnapped. I have evidence of a struggle. And he was then delivered to the forces of bin Wahhab…this so-called Ikhwan Brotherhood. They obviously needed his expertise in order to transform their stolen uranium into a nuclear bomb. The uranium itself came from the Russian company known as Rurik. It was supposed to be shipped to Micratom in the U.S., but somewhere between the Urals and St. Petersburg, it disappeared."

"Into the hands of this bin Wahhab character," Buzhkin ventured.

"Precisely."

"But where would that be?"

"Perhaps I can answer that," Falcon said. "Last year, after the Tanzanian and Kenyan atrocities, the CIA managed to infiltrate his hideout in eastern Afghanistan, near the town of Khowst. There he enjoyed the protection of Taliban, the Islamic extremist Afghan government. Perhaps I should say partial protection, for we pretty much demolished his buildings with a couple of well-placed Tomahawk cruise missiles. However, we now have reason to believe that there may be a significant hidden complex that escaped unscathed."

"This is all very interesting, but there seems to be a good deal of conjecture," Buzhkin said.

"You're quite right, Viktor," Medved answered. "This is a very grave situation, demanding decisive action. But first we must confirm our premises. "One who may be able to answer our questions is this man...."

Medved clicked the carousel control button and on the screen appeared an image of a stocky, stubble-chinned middle-aged man. "Until recently, this *doo-rok* was the Director of Transportation for the Rurik Company. He was responsible for the shipment of warhead uranium from the Urals to St. Petersburg. Unfortunately, he seems to have grown weary of his job, for he has been AWOL from work for over a week now. His name is Gregori Yusapov."

Buzhkin stared intently and silently at the smoke-clouded image as he recalled the recent sight he had of the 'nudnik' cowering before the green-eyed killer.

*   *   *

The *Borzoi*, in spite of its canine cognomen, was a favorite restaurant of upscale Moscow. The Georgian food was excellent, the prices guaranteed exclusivity, and celebrities from movie stars to Mafiosi provided excitement for wealthy merchants and their spouses. With good connections and some 'grease', it was possible to obtain a private dining salon that looked out upon the main dining room floor and yet provided intimacy. In the case of the members of the *Chornaya Rooka*, 'grease' was not required. A half dozen of such patrons now sat around a thick wooden table in one of these salons. The table itself was barely visible beneath the collection of glasses and bottles of vodka and bowls of beet soup that were in various stages of depletion. All but one of the men were laughing uproariously.

"Ey, Vasily, don't lean forward," one of them said. "You'll bleed into my *borscht*."

They howled in delight, stomping their feet and pounding their fists so that the glasses, bowls, and bottles jumped.

"Perhaps you *should* fall forward," another one chimed in. "Maybe you can smash your nose back into place." Again they thundered in laughter until some were almost in tears.

Vasily Kuzmitch was not participating in the hilarity. It was bad enough that he had a broken nose and a lump that was the size of a large Ukrainian potato on the right side of his head. It was even worse that his pain had been inflicted by that *schlyooka*, that slut, that whore. But worst of all was having to endure this ridicule from those whom he had longed to impress—his superiors in the *Rooka*. They had gathered to consider Vasily's plan for kidnapping and ransoming the wealthy American at the Metropol. It was to be his moment of glory and instead, because of her, he was subjected to this humiliation. Oh, when he would get his hands again on Yelena, she would die an exquisite death.

"Well, enough, enough," a heavy-set, well-coiffured man in a hand-tailored suit blurted. The others fell to snickering, but ceased their comments.

"Vasily, you have to stop falling down the stairs when you get drunk," he said, alluding to the fiction that Vasily had invented to explain his injuries. Of course, that tale had only added to the glee, as they had all guessed that Vasily's demure little wife had knocked him silly. "If you're not careful, you're going to look like me."

"Oh no, Shramlik, that won't happen...." As soon as the words had left his mouth, Vasily realized his blunder.

"What, am I so hideous?" Shramlik scowled. All joviality stopped and a pall settled over the salon. They each knew how touchy their boss was about his facial scars.

"N—No, that's not how I meant it.... I mean I'd be honored to look like you, boss. I just meant I'll be more careful...about falling down and all...."

Shramlik held the thoroughly uncomfortable Kuzmitch in his gaze for several long seconds, then smiled broadly.

"Ah, c'mere you little hooligan," he laughed, throwing his arm around Vasily. "Did you hear that? He said, 'I want to look like you, boss.'" The others, although still unsure, began joining in the mirth. They were hesitant because of Shramlik's reputation for his mercurial mood swings that often ended in fatalities.

"We've all had our fun," Shramlik continued, his arm wrapped tightly around Kuzmitch's pencil-like neck. "But, Vasily has a good plan for snatching this American. I like it." The others, particularly Vasily Kuzmitch, began breathing a bit more easily. "Tell us more about it, Vasily." He released his grip.

"Sure, boss," Kuzmitch said, coughing as air once again began flowing into his throat. "I figure a couple of us can wait outside the Metropol tonight and nab him when he walks in. We toss him in the auto and take off before anybody knows what's what."

The others glanced in silence at Shramlik. "The Metropol's no good," their boss said. "Too many *militsiya*."

"Yeah, that damned, Dmitri Kirilovich!" they began to mutter. "He's bad for our business. Ever since he became Chief of Police, the Metropol has been locked up tighter than a nun's thighs. If you sneeze, you'll spray six of his *militsiya* men. We must deep six him in the Moskva River, Shramlik."

"All in due time," Shramlik said, ending their grumbling. "First, we take care of this business. Vasily, I want you to get the name of the American from the hotel concierge. Grease him with fifty American dollars. If he still refuses, let him know who you work for. Klopi, once we have the name, I want you to contact our friend at the American Embassy. Have him call his countryman at the Metropol to tell him that there's a problem with his passport. They're to meet at the Bistro Diner tomorrow night at 7:00 to take care of it."

Kuzmitch was too far down in the ranks of the *Rooka* to appreciate the extent of its reach. He hadn't known until just now that even the American Embassy was not immune. "Good. Then it's set," Vasily said, in an effort to appear intelligent. "Klopi and I will snatch the American at the Bistro. It shouldn't take more than the two of us with a little bit of persuasion." He smiled and tapped the little *Malysh* 9mm semiautomatic in his shoulder holster.

"We'll all go," Shramlik said, ignoring Kuzmitch. "Nogi, you will drive the first auto. Klopi and I will make the snatch and we'll depart with you. Zaponki, you'll drive the second auto, with Vasily and Sootba. "And we're not going to rely on those peashooters like that so-called 'Fly' in your holster, Vasily. "We're taking the AN-94 assault rifles and the *Kashtan* submachine guns. It's always good to have more firepower than anybody else on the block. Any questions?"

There was no response.

"Wonderful!" Shramlik laughed. He then bear hugged Kuzmitch and kissed him on both cheeks. "I love your plan, Vasily!"

*　　　　*　　　　*

Dmitri Kirilovich could not believe his good fortune. Neither could his detectives and lieutenants who crowded around the one-way mirror so they could get a better look at this remarkable woman. She had wandered from the street into their *militsiya* precinct headquarters, mumbling the most extraordinary story. If it were true, it would be the first instance of a *Chornaya Rooka* wife turning against the Russian Mafia.

"Are you feeling better?" Dmitri asked. He had gotten her an ice pack for her swollen cheek and some mild sedatives.

Yelena Kuzmitch thanked him and smiled as much as her puffy face would allow.

"You know, you're safe here now," Dmitri continued in his most tender manner. He felt that a wrong word or a loud noise would cause this frightened deer to bolt. "You won't ever have to worry about that worm hitting you again. We will put you in a nice, comfortable place tonight."

"Safe?" she asked again for confirmation.

"I'll put my own saint of a mother in there with you, if you'd like."

"No...I believe you."

"Good. Now please tell me one more time what you know about this Metropol business. Then you'll be off to that nice warm bath."

"I'm sorry. I wish I knew more, but I've already told you everything. He was bragging about kidnapping a wealthy American at the Metropol. And he said something about Shramlik loving his idea and that they would make hundreds of thousands of American dollars. And then he flung the dinner on the floor and came to the bedroom. I tried to escape but he knocked me into the hallway. He turned back into the bedroom. I could hear him getting the belt. I know the sound. He has done this to me before."

Dmitri was amazed at her demeanor as she calmly related the tale, as if she were a detached observer.

"I was stunned but still conscious. The tea kettle lay at my fingertips as if God had placed it there...and to think I had almost lost my faith.... I seized it, rose, and when he stepped into the hallway I swung with all my might. I hit him quite hard...on the head...just above his left eye. It was an awful sound. I think he may be dead."

"All right. Thank you, *Gospozha* Kuzmitch," Dmitri smiled, patting her hand softly. "I'll have one of my female officers escort you to your accommodations."

When Yelena Kuzmitch had departed, Dmitri's lieutenants gathered around him. They were anxious to arrest Vasily Kuzmitch, that is, if he were still alive. This was a grand opportunity to take down one of the *Chornaya Rooka*. Dmitri saw it differently, however. They could pick up Kuzmitch any time. But to do it now would be to tip their hand about their knowledge of the Metropol scheme. No, better to leave that little minnow for now in favor of frying bigger fish. He ordered an immediate tripling of his plain-clothes force at the Metropol. Uniformed *militsiya* in the vicinity also were to be increased and all personnel were to wear Kevlar jackets and carry assault rifles. With any luck, he would finally be able to filet Shramlik, one of the boss sharks of the *Chornaya Rooka*.

Chapter Twenty-Four

Although its source was only at half phase, the moonlight reflecting from the snow amply illuminated Marenkov's path. For six hours, he had been picking his way along deserted foothill roads, as much as possible keeping the North Star over his left shoulder. By his calculations, Pakistan lay only another five kilometers to the east. Although his weary old bones were rebelling against his youthful enthusiasm, he could not rest. In another hour the sun would rise and his absence would be noticed at the compound. Then, the Ikhwan surely would send a patrol in search of him in this direction. Steeling himself, he continued trudging through the light snow, munching on a handful of dates and washing them down with snow.

After another half-hour he heard the burbling of a stream in the forest to his left. He knew by his crude map that this small rivulet, ignorant of the man-made border, flowed directly into the mighty Indus River in Pakistan. Realizing that he must be nearing the border sentries, he decided to leave the open road and follow the stream through the woods. Almost immediately, his decision proved to be fortuitous. A pair of headlights snaked in and out of the hills on the road he had just exited. Momentarily, a canvas-topped, heavy troop truck rumbled past, whirling snow in its track as it headed east. *Too soon for the Ikhwan to know of my disappearance. Most likely it is the Afghan Army, changing shifts at the border.*

He proceeded cautiously along the stream bank, nervously peering through the silent black trees, the branches of which seemed to claw eerily into the inky night while they tore at his face and snagged his clothes. Abruptly, the forest ended and a broad field opened between two looming mountains. The road he had earlier trod ran through the middle of the clearing, past two small buildings that were separated from each other by approximately fifty meters. One stood in Afghanistan, the other in Pakistan. The troop transport which Marenkov had just managed to avoid was now parked next to the structure on the Afghan side. Several soldiers were taking gear from the vehicle. Others, rifles slung over their backs, were lighting cigarettes and talking and laughing.

There was no going forward through that field, even in darkness. He would have to slip over one of the two flanking mountains. The one on the right was ruled out as it would require crossing the road and thereby exposing himself. The one on the left would necessitate doubling back through the woods, but he had no alternative. Already a faint glimmer of pink was appearing beyond the ridges to the east. *If I can push this rusty bucket of bones just a little bit further, I can be on that mountain before daylight. Perhaps then I can rest.* He set off again, but the nimble trot had deserted him.

*   *   *

Gregori Yusapov was almost certain that the green-eyed bitch couldn't touch him. He was too well connected with the upper echelons of the Feliks—her superiors—and even she would not act without their approval. Yet, the way she had fixed those eyes on him had been disconcerting. It was because of that image and the nagging doubt it invoked that he was now standing in the cold before an empty artificial pond and its collection of lifeless water fountains.

The feeble warmth of the early winter sun had succumbed to night over an hour ago and the fountain's statues had lost their golden luster. An icy breeze scurried leaves about his ankles and sliced around his neck. He stamped his feet and blew his hot breath into his freezing fingertips. He would ordinarily not have agreed to such a meeting—he didn't care to be outside where he might be spotted by FSB agents—but the voice on the phone had been so chillingly compelling. *Your life is rapidly becoming worth less than a snail's head*, the caller had muttered with an indistinct voice. *The green-eyed one has requested permission to deal with you. There are many in our organization who feel as you do and believe that she must, shall we say, be retired. All now hangs in the balance. If you want to live and if you want to dance at her 'retirement', meet me at the International Friendship Fountain tonight, six p.m.*

Yusopov checked his watch for the third time in the last five minutes. *Proklyatiya! Damn! The caller, whoever he was, would have to be late!* He turned toward the fish statuary that adorned the circumference of the pond, their water-spouting tasks terminated until spring. It was as he was gazing at these muted images that he saw the large, dark, blocky form standing on the far side of the pond. The figure beckoned to him and then began to walk away, disappearing in the night. Yusopov glanced nervously around and then set off in pursuit.

Proklyatiya! I've lost him! he cursed as he circled the pond. Finally he caught a glimpse of the phantom again, tucking into a narrow alley between two large buildings. Yusopov quickly crossed the street and entered the alley.

"Hello. Are you there," he asked tentatively, as he drew his *Groza* silent pistol.

"Yes. Back here." The voice was hoarse, muffled.

Yusopov walked cautiously through the shadows toward the voice. "Where—"

It was the last word he uttered before his world went black.

*   *   *

"It's a simple matter, but it must be rectified if you wish to remain in the Russian Federation," Sam Boresman spoke into the phone. "I thought I'd save you a trip to the embassy by meeting you at the Bistro Diner. It'll be nice for me, too, as it'll give me a chance to talk to somebody that's only recently come from the States. Dinner will be on me."

He listened to the response, then said, "Good. I'll see you tonight at seven. I'll make the reservations."

Boresman didn't question why his Russian friend, Klopi, had asked him to make these arrangements. He only knew that he had been well rewarded in the past for performing such small favors. As a low-level American Embassy passport administrator with a king-size impression of his self-worth, he felt entitled to the money. Of course, he never knew, nor did he care to know, the ultimate consequences of his deeds.

*   *   *

When Medved poked his head into Falcon's office, the American was still on the telephone.

"Sorry, I'll come back later," the Russian apologized, turning to leave. He was halted by Falcon's motioning him to stay.

"All right, seven o'clock then, the Bistro," Falcon said into the phone receiver just before hanging up.

"The most amazing thing has happened," Medved beamed excitedly, reentering the room. "You remember that Rurik official…the one we were speaking of yesterday and who had disappeared?"

"Yes…Yusopov…I believe his name was Yusopov."

"Exactly. Well, miracle of miracles, he has reappeared," Medved laughed. "In fact, he was discovered this morning, handcuffed to a rear door of the Lubianka, with his balls nearly frozen off. Some of our people are trying to thaw him out now."

"Wonderful. Is he going to live?"

"Certainly. But some of his favorite appendages may never again be functional. We might even be able to interrogate him later this afternoon."

"In that case, I better call the American Embassy back. One of their staffers wanted to meet me tonight concerning a problem with my passport...I can reschedule."

"Oh?" Medved blurted, with a studied expression of interest. "Perhaps I know this official. What is his name?"

"Boresman. Sam Boresman."

"Hmm, yes, that does ring a bell."

"As I said, I can reschedule."

"No, don't change your plans. It's probably best that we give our Rurik friend a full day to recover. We'll start him off fresh tomorrow, when he can more fully appreciate his situation." He turned again to leave. "By the way, if you are looking for a restaurant tonight to entertain Mister Boresman—"

"He's already suggested one—the Bistro."

"Oh, yes...how appropriate. "Bistro—'Quick'." He paused, reflecting upon something. Then turning to leave once again, he said, "Try their *zhulien*—their mushroom casserole. It's the best in Moscow."

Fine, Falcon thought, *but why is Bistro..."quick"...so appropriate?*

*   *   *

Standing before a full-length mirror, Vasily Kuzmitch tucked his *Malysh* 9mm semiautomatic into his shoulder holster. He then gripped his *Kashtan* submachine gun—the Russian knock-off of the deadly Israeli Uzi—and, holding it in front of him, gazed with satisfaction into the reflecting glass. He had never fired either weapon at a human being before, but in a few hours he may very well get his first chance. Then he would be a *Krovi*—a 'blooded one'—which was the first step toward promotion in the *Rooka*. He just wished that some of Kirilovitch's *Militsiya* would show up so he could blast them. *I wonder what colorful nickname my chums will give me then. It should be something worthy…something that they know is truly reflective of my personality…I've got it! 'Zherebyets'! Yes! That's it…'Stallion'!*

He swung the submachine gun up, pointed it toward the mirror and uttered a rat-a-tat noise. Smiling, he lowered the weapon and glanced at his watch. Zaponki would be picking him up any minute now. He went over the plan in his head. One word had been particularly emphasized by Shramlik…*bistro, bistro*…everything must be done *bistro*.

* * *

Dmitri Kirilovich was uneasy. Although he had increased his forces and placed them on alert at the Metropol, he still felt that more could be done. He could not let slip through his hands this golden opportunity to nail Shramlik and his thugs. After all, it was the first real advance tip that he had ever received concerning a planned criminal activity of the *Rooka*.

Unable to contain himself at his desk at such a moment, he rose, threw on his beaver overcoat and hat and ordered his Zhiguli squad automobile to be brought around. Soon he was being driven across town, past the Bistro Diner, to the Metropol Hotel.

* * *

The Bistro Diner is a small, sidewalk eatery in the old *Kitai-Gorod*— the so-called 'China Town'—that runs northeast from Red Square, just beyond the Lubianka. Brightly lit, with undecorated yellow tile walls and cramped seating, it has remained solvent for years only because the talents of its chef far exceeded the shortcomings of its atmosphere.

Mike Falcon was running fifteen minutes late by the time he arrived at the restaurant.

"Welcome, sir. No, your party has not yet arrived," the maitré d´ said as he led Falcon to the first booth near the street-side window.

Removing his jacket, he sat on the vinyl-covered seat and slid across to the window. He had opened the menu and was looking for the *zhulien*—the house specialty that Medved had recommended when the waiter appeared for his drink order.

"On such a night, something hot…a *Kusmi* tea blend…yes, *Troika* would be fine," he said.

As the waiter left, Falcon gazed absently toward the street. At that moment, two automobiles pulled up—a black Mercedes sedan followed by a gray Zhiguli—and parked directly in front of the Diner, in a no-parking zone. The curb-side doors of the Mercedes opened and two large men squeezed out. Turning so that their backs were to the restaurant they leaned into the auto, obtained some objects which they placed inside their jackets, and then straightened.

An alarm triggered in Falcon's mind. The unusual call from the embassy…the alleged problem with his passport…the unorthodox manner the staffer had chosen to deal with it. He should have known—it would not be the first time an embassy official had been compromised. *Is this to be the unhappy way I finally get confirmation of the Felik's existence?* He rued his careless decision to leave the Glock in his room and suddenly felt very naked. Glancing toward the rear of the restaurant, he rapidly considered his options. Too late. Shramlik and Klopi, who had pulled ski masks over their faces, had already burst through the front door, wielding their stubby *Kashtan* submachine guns. A loud discharge into the air from Klopi's weapon sent the terrified patrons ducking for cover. Shramlik darted forward to the first booth and leveled his *Kashtan* at Falcon's face.

"*Ideetya zamnoi!* Come!" he shouted.

The American stood—too slowly for the *Rooka* boss who seized him roughly by the shoulder and shoved him forward. Falcon stumbled through the doorway, sandwiched between the two mafiosi. As they lurched onto the sidewalk, they crashed into a passer-by. Klopi angrily thrust an arm forward, thinking that this motion would bowl over the irritating pedestrian. Thus, he was quite astonished when his target not only remained standing, but in fact had seized his extended arm and twisted it down and backwards at an unusually disagreeable angle. Both Falcon and Shramlik turned toward Klopi on hearing the latter's yelp of pain. Falcon's eyes were met by those of Sergei Medved.

"Duck, Michael!" the Russian agent blurted. As Falcon dropped to the ground, the befuddled Shramlik hesitated, then raised his gun. His pause, a mere nanosecond of inactivity in a life of squandered years, proved costly. Medved squeezed the trigger of his *Gurza* once and Shramlik's body flew backwards, smashing through the window of the Bistro Diner and tumbling lifeless onto a table, sending several plates of the freshly-baked house specialty clattering to the floor.

Klopi, leaving behind the rifle that Medved had wrested from him, leaped to his feet and bolted for the car. He fell short of his goal, however, as Falcon tackled him. The driver of the Mercedes, Nogi, seeing that the plan had completely unraveled, slammed the gear shift lever into drive and was about to stomp the accelerator when he was startled by the shattering of his side window and a hand grasping him by the neck. It was a grip the likes of which he had never before experienced. His feet flailed wildly, kicking through the windshield as his hands clawed frantically at the steely vise that was dragging him out of the car. It was only a moment before he was yanked completely through the window and thrown to the street, but by then his neck was already broken. Viktor Buzhkin thereupon turned his attention toward the Zhiguli.

Although all of this activity had taken only a few seconds, it was sufficient time for Vasily Kuzmitch to determine that his evening might be better spent elsewhere. He screamed at Zaponki to put the pedal to the floor and get them the hell out of there.

For his part, Zaponki needed no further encouragement. Nogi's body had barely slumped to the pavement when Zaponki stomped on the accelerator and tried to steer around the Mercedes. There was insufficient room for this maneuver, however, and the right headlight and fender of the Zhiguli crumbled as they ground into the rear and left side of the Mercedes.

Sootba, in the passenger seat, thrust his assault rifle through his window and began spraying bullets in the general direction of Medved and Falcon. One of the rounds grazed Falcon's shoulder and another struck Klopi in the chest, leaving a gaping cavity. The projectiles were small—only 5.45 caliber—but were propelled with extremely high velocity. The extra-ordinary speed caused the cartridges to expand and transmit greater energy into the target, thus increasing the shock to the victim's central nervous system and almost guaranteeing the likelihood of fatality or serious incapacitation. They were so lethal that the mujaheddin had dubbed them "the poison bullets." Well acquainted with this peril, Medved hugged the sidewalk and returned fire. Vasily covered his head with his arms, cringing behind the front seat and pleading with Zaponki to get the damned auto moving.

Finally the Zhiguli lurched forward, carrying the rear bumper and left fender of the Mercedes with it. With bullets from Sootba's wild shooting now raining down upon it, the fuel tank of the Mercedes ignited and exploded. As the Zhiguli passed him in a shower of glass and metal, Buzhkin fired the *Gurza*'s entire magazine of eighteen rounds into its windows and doors. The thin sheet-metal of the auto was no match for the steel-cored titanium-piercing cartridges of the *Gurza*. The right side of the Zhiguli virtually disintegrated and Zaponki slumped forward onto the steering wheel. The car ricocheted off a parked vehicle, bounced across the street into a vegetable truck, overturning it, then caromed into a flea market where it crashed into a flower stall.

Miraculously, none of the market patrons were injured. However, all of the occupants of the Zhiguli, now lying beneath the fluttering petals of roses and other blooms from the south, were no more than mangled, bloody corpses. It had been a black day for the Black Hand.

Chapter Twenty-Five

For a moment, *Militsiya* Chief of Police Dmitri Kirilovitch thought he was back in the Afghan War. Metal debris, glass shards, and bullet casings littered the street. A parked auto was smashed in, another was ablaze, a truck was overturned and its contents of cabbages and potatoes were strewn over the road, and a fourth vehicle and its three occupants were completely bullet-riddled and destroyed. Across the way from the shambled, grisly scene in the flea market, there was little improvement. The glass facade of the Bistro Diner had been shattered, much of the restaurant had been reduced to rubble and a corpse lay in a sticky blend of blood and mushroom casserole. Two other victims, both still alive, lay on the sidewalk. And, as if to complete this eerie recall of Dmitri's Afghan experiences, there sat his old commander, Sergei Medved, *Gurza* in one hand, cigarette in the other.

"Ah, Dmitri, where've you been? Sorry 'bout the mess," Medved said casually, drawing on his cigarette. "This one's still alive, but I don't think it'll be for long." He nodded to Klopi, who lay next to him, struggling to breathe on his only functioning lung.

"And this one?" Kirilovitch asked, gesturing to the other wounded man.

"I'm OK...*awchen harasho*...just a little scratch," Falcon responded, still clutching Klopi's assault rifle as he sat up with a grimace.

Kirilovitch instinctively stepped back and reached for his own weapon.

"No, it's all right," Medved said. "He's with me."

The police chief gazed curiously at Falcon.

"Your accent," he said. "American?"

Falcon nodded.

"And this other?" he alluded to the huge man who sat quietly on the hood of the smashed parked car.

"Him?" Medved said, pensively eyeing Viktor Buzhkin. "He's—"

At that moment, the wail of sirens rent the night air and a firetruck followed by an ambulance careened up the street. As they screeched to a halt in front of the Bistro Diner, Dmitri moved closer to Sergei.

"Tell me, were they trying to snatch the American?"

"It would seem so."

"And you and the Yeti over there just happened by?"

"Yes. You might say we bumped into them. Smoke?"

Kirilovitch smiled and plopped himself alongside his former regimental commander.

"It's going to be hard for me to concoct a story for this mess," he said, taking the proffered cigarette. "Especially since you and your friends won't even be mentioned."

The emergency crew had jumped from the ambulance and had begun rapidly administering aid to the heavily rasping gangster.

"It's criminal how these mafiosi manage to shoot each other up," Dmitri shrugged as he observed the feverish work of the paramedics.

"Right," Medved smiled, exhaling a ring of blue haze.

"But look, Major," Dmitri assumed a more serious tone, "there may be more to this. Is there any chance that your American friend is staying at the Metropol?"

Sergei turned and fixed his gaze on Dmitri.

"How did you know that?"

"I think you better come down to the station as soon as you can. Your friend may still be in danger from the *Chornaya Rooka*. I want you to meet someone and to hear the information for yourself."

Medved nodded and they both turned their attention to the paramedics and their efforts. Their patient had gone into shock and then cardiac arrest. For the third time, the two electrodes of a defibrillator were applied to his chest and switched on. For the third time, an electrical impulse of over two thousand volts surged through his ventricular muscle fibers. And, for the third time, the limp body lurched, then fell still.

"Three minutes. Thirty percent," Medved said matter-of-factly.

"How's that?" Dmitri asked.

"I read somewhere that the brain loses ten percent of its functions for every minute the heart is stopped. It's been three minutes."

The urgent tempo of the paramedics began to lessen and they slowly began to gather their equipment.

"Looks like the work of a high-velocity Nikonov," Dmitri said.

"Square in the chest," Sergei replied.

"Not a hit you'll take and expect to see tomorrow," Dmitri added as he watched the paramedics pull a blanket over Klopi's head and lift him into the ambulance. Mike Falcon, too, was assisted into the vehicle as a closer look at his wound warranted a trip to the hospital.

"Ey, Michael, be gentle with the nurses," Medved laughed. "And don't be late tomorrow morning. Remember who we're interviewing first thing."

Falcon, settling next to the blanket-covered corpse, waved acknowledgement as the rear door of the ambulance was closing. The vehicle lurched forward and, with its siren squelched, motored away.

"Could you post protection for him?" Sergei asked.

"Certainly," Dmitri replied. "Consider it done. Well, then, Major, I'll look forward to seeing you soon at the precinct. *Dosvidonya.*"

"Dmitri." Kirilovitch turned back toward his old commander at the call of his name.

"Thanks," Sergei smiled.

"*Nichevo!*" came the response.

∗   ∗   ∗

When Mike Falcon, his wounded arm in a sling, arrived at the Lubianka the following morning, he learned that Medved and Buzhkin had preceded him and were meeting with Aksanov. His presence, too, was requested in the Director's office.

"Ah, here's the winged bird now," Aksanov, delighted with his pun, chuckled as Falcon entered.

"Michael, we were just describing last evening's events to the general," Medved said, as the American took a seat.

"Yes, I'd like to hear about that myself,". "Were they Feliks' hit men? How did you know to be there, Sergei? And you, too, Viktor? And how come—"

"Whoa, let's take it one at a time," Medved interrupted. "No, they were not Feliks. They were Russian mafiosi. I'll know more about their motives after I meet with the Chief of Police this afternoon. As far as me being there…I played a hunch. I became concerned when you told me about your passport problem. The FSB—not the American Embassy—handles such matters for our own 'guests'. Additionally, we're well onto a compromised official within the embassy—this Sam Boresman character. All tallied up, I thought I'd better look after you."

"And you brought some muscle along with you," Falcon said, nodding to Buzhkin.

At Sergei's hesitation, Aksanov spoke. "Not exactly. Because of the Feliks problem to which you have alluded, I assigned Viktor to watch over Sergei. Unhappily, somewhere along the way, Major Medved became distrustful of Viktor and tried to escape his watchful eye at every opportunity. Luckily, Viktor was not thrown off the trail last night—"

"—And if he had not appeared at the Bistro Diner at that propitious moment—"

"We would not all be here enjoying this conversation," Aksanov finished the thought. "But I understand that you have important business to conduct this morning…with a Mister Yusopov, I believe."

"Yes. Strange how he suddenly appeared on our doorstep after we were just discussing him yesterday," Medved said, glancing at Buzhkin.

"Why don't we just skin the chicken instead of wondering why it landed in our coop," Aksanov interjected. "Tell me, Sergei, have you thought about your method of persuasion?"

"I have. And I've decided upon the "Night Sweats.""

"Excellent choice. But remember, this is not the KGB—"

"I have taken that into account. There will be no broken bones or spilled blood."

"Yet, you think this method will still work?"

"Absolutely. The key to its success always was more the psychological impact, anyway."

"*Harasho!* Well then, you have work to do."

The Director stood and the three agents departed.

*　　　*　　　*

"So tell me, Sergei, what this 'Night Sweats' is all about," Falcon said as he, Buzhkin, and Medved descended on the elevator beyond the ground floor.

"You might say it's a motivational tool to induce people to be more cooperative," Medved answered. "I'm afraid that *Gospodeen* Yusopov is in need of such motivation. He believes that if he 'sings', the Feliks will learn of his treachery and then he would be very fortunate just to die swiftly. As for the 'Night Sweats', you are about to witness the procedure. By the way, do you understand where we now are?" the Russian agent said as the doors opened.

"Indeed I do," Falcon chuckled unenthusiastically. The Lubianka Basement."

"Correct. If the KGB had a heart, this would have been the darkest part of it. For years, the very words—Lubianka Basement—struck terror into the souls of our own people and our enemies, alike. Times have changed and the FSB does not employ its predecessor's wide-scale terror tactics. However, we still have means of persuasion for the most dangerous criminals."

As he spoke, the three men walked through a dimly-lit, winding labyrinth.

"You realize, of course," Medved said, reaching for his pack of cigarettes, "you are the first Westerner to see this place...that is, who will also leave under his own power. Ah, we have arrived."

They stopped before a green metal door, which was bolted shut by a two-inch thick green steel bar. Medved tapped on the door and a moment later it swung open. A man, clad totally in black and with grease-blackened hands and face, stepped out. "We'll need three pieces of equipment," Medved said. The man nodded and turned back into the unlit room. When he reappeared, he presented three sets of night vision goggles. "We're bringing him in momentarily," the man said, before disappearing into the black room and closing and bolting the door behind him.

"This way," Medved beckoned, leading Falcon and Buzhkin down a hallway and into a small room that contained several metal folding chairs and was lit by a single red bulb. The upper half of one wall consisted of a thick plate glass window. A panel containing several switches and a microphone were located at the base of the pane. "We don't have much time so you need to put your goggles on right away. They pick up the infrared light that's emitted by all objects and persons and greatly enhance it with photomultipliers. It fits like this."

Falcon, reduced to one good arm, struggled with the equipment. Medved assisted him, then turned off the red bulb. The dousing of the light made virtually no difference as the details of the room and its occupants appeared as if bathed in bright, green-tinted moonlight. "Ah, they're bringing Yusopov in now," he said, glancing through the window into the adjoining room.

Two men, camouflaged completely in black and wearing night vision goggles, led the blind-folded Yusopov to a chair in the center of the room. After securing their prisoner to the seat, they removed his blindfold and stepped back. "He is in total darkness," Medved noted to Falcon. "We can see him, but he can see nothing." He then keyed the microphone.

"Hello, *Gospodeen* Yusopov. I hope you have decided to make this easy on yourself. You are in the Lubianka Basement so you know you will eventually tell us what we want to know. "First, please state your full name...."

For the next ten minutes, Medved led Yusopov through a series of innocuous questions designed to loosen the interviewee's tongue. The two men in the room with Yusopov sat quietly observing, their special abilities not needed as long as the answers

were truthful.

"Good, Gregori," Medved uttered. "You are doing very well. A few more questions and we'll be done. Tell me, what was your position at the Rurik *Korporatsiya*?"

"Director of Transportation," came a distinctly hesitant answer.

"I see. Now think back to last May. As Director of Transportation, did you manage the shipment of half a ton of uranium to the Micratom Company, via St. Petersburg?"

Yusopov shifted in his chair, peering into the blackness but seeing nothing. He knew the game was now beginning in earnest.

"May.... That was a while back. I can't quite remember."

One of the men in the room stood, lifted a bread-box-sized basket and strode toward Yusopov.

"Try to remember. It's important, you see," Medved spoke.

"I'm trying, but I just can't seem to recall," Yusopov replied weakly, unaware of the presence of someone next to him.

"Listen to me carefully, Gregori," his interrogator pronounced solemnly. "With regard to the sensation which you are about to experience, you must remain absolutely still. Any movement on your part will most likely result in your death. Do you understand?"

Yusopov's breathing became yet more difficult. He mumbled indistinctly.

"Was that a yes…you understand?"

"Yes," came a hoarse response.

"Good." Medved nodded to his accomplice who thereupon opened the lid of the basket, pulled the top of Yusopov's overalls away from his body and emptied the contents of the container onto his back.

Yusopov shrieked but steeled himself to remain motionless despite the urge to be free of the creatures crawling on his skin. Whatever they were, the horror had been amplified in his mind by the total darkness.

"That feathery light touch you are feeling is that of the Sydney Funnel Web," Medved said. "Perhaps you would be interested in knowing that it is the deadliest spider in the world, much worse even than a black widow. One bite, and within a few minutes, you will begin convulsing. That discomfort will be short-lived, however, for you will rapidly become paralyzed and unable to breathe. It is an extremely agonizing death. And there are enough on you to kill a very healthy moose. But you're doing well, Gregori. Perhaps you may even survive."

"Get them off me! Get them off!" Yusopov sputtered between snatched breaths. "My death will do you no good. You'll then never learn what I know."

"Whether you live or die makes no difference to me. If you refuse to cooperate, you might as well die here. Of course, we could release you back to your people…."

Owing to the terror-induced heat which he was now emitting, Yusopov's infrared signature was growing brighter. He felt beads of perspiration drip from his nose and from the nape of his neck. It would be just like the FSB to turn him over to the Feliks, he thought. They, and he, fully realized that his 'people' would be certain he had been compromised. And the Feliks had even more unpleasant methods of interviewing.

"I think I remember that contract...I'm not certain, mind you...but, yes, I did direct that shipment," Yusopov stuttered.

"Thank you," Medved replied as he motioned to his accomplice standing near Yusopov. The man began collecting the spiders from the sweat-soaked prisoner.

"We know that twenty kilos of the uranium were diverted from their original destination," Medved resumed. "Please be so good as to tell us exactly where it went."

Yusopov's breathing was now quite labored—a combination of terror and angst over the repercussions of his next answer.

"I honestly don't know where it went. I was instructed only to ship it to St. Petersburg...for loading on the Murmansk...bound for America. I swear."

"I hope that is not your final answer, Gregori. Think again."

Yusopov began fidgeting, weighing his current fate against that which would result from his betrayal of the Feliks.

"I'm trying...I'm trying to recall if I know anything else, but there is nothing more. You must believe me."

"I see. Tell me, Yusopov, are you fond of snakes?"

Medved turned to Falcon. "This is where the 'Night Sweats' really begin. We'll let him think about that for a while. The subject's imagination is truly our most powerful weapon." He leaned back in his chair and lit a cigarette. After a few puffs, he again keyed the microphone.

"Have you reconsidered, Gregori?"

"I swear to you I've told you all I know."

"That's a pity. Again, you'll want to remain very still. Even then, I can't promise you anything this time."

Medved nodded and one of his accomplices in the adjoining room picked up another basket and moved forward. A shrill cry emanated from Yusopov's lips as several snakes slithered through his clothing. Blocked by the knots at the wrists and ankles, their churning became more frantic as they vainly sought a means of escape.

"Those little creatures are Black Mambas...members of the cobra family. I'm sorry to tell you that they are even deadlier than the spiders and cause a yet more painful death."

"The KGB used a more straight-forward method," he noted off-mike to Falcon. "They would simply walk up to the prisoner at irregular time intervals and whack him with a club about the head and shoulders. Those blows coming unpredictably out of the dark took a toll on the psyche and wore down even the strongest of wills. This way is less messy but just as effective. Every person has his own personalized version of hell. We simply have to tap into it. Now for a little more fun."

"Well, Gregori, it's apparent that you don't care for snakes. I'll do you a favor and get rid of them. We have some mongooses that will just do the trick. I'm afraid it will be a bit uncomfortable in your britches, however."

"Enough! Enough! I'll tell you all! Just take them out! But not with the mongooses!"

As the agents in the room began collecting the slithering reptiles, Falcon leaned toward Medved and whispered, "Were they really Funnel Web spiders and Black Mambas?

The Russian lifted his goggles, smiled, and winked.

"Now, once again, what became of that twenty kilos of uranium?" he said into the microphone after the prisoner had been cleared of serpents.

Still shaken, Yusopov cleared his throat, then spoke.

"First...I want to make...a deal," he said haltingly.

"You're hardly in a position...but tell me, what do you have in mind?"

"I'll tell you everything…everything! If you swear you will give me a *legyenda*.

"A legend? A new identity and history?"

Medved grinned at Falcon, then turned back to the prisoner.

"And I suppose you'll be wanting a face-lift, too."

"It would be necessary."

Medved leaned back in his chair, slowly puffing smoke rings. He believed that, with a few more hours of the 'Night Sweats' procedure, he would have Yusopov begging to reveal every secret of his sorry existence. But, there was always that one chance in a million that he would miscalculate a terror threshold and Yusopov would die of a heart attack. No need to take that chance, particularly when he now had no doubt that the prisoner would live up to his side of the bargain.

"All right, Gregori. You caught me in a good mood, today. It's a deal. You have my word on it. But if you're not completely straight with me, I'll arrange it so that your next conversation will be with the Feliks. Do you follow me?"

"Yes." *The word of a FSB agent…what a laugh. Yet, it is worth a crack, for every other option is surely unacceptable.*" Yusopov inhaled deeply, then began to speak.

"We made an arrangement with some people from the Mid-East."

"By 'we', Gregori…do you mean the Rurik *Korporatsiya*?"

"No, not exactly. I mean, the strings were pulled by…my other organization."

"Of course—the Feliks."

Yusopov didn't respond.

"Tell us about the people from the Mid-East," Medved demanded.

"You people in the FSB are well aware of them. Their leader is the one who fancies himself as the 'Mahdi'—Abdul bin Wahhab."

"Yes, we are fully acquainted with this lunatic. The world's most notorious terrorist. And you sought fit to place twenty kilos of U-238 into his hands?"

Yusopov, who had slumped in his chair during this exchange, suddenly raised his head.

"No, that's incorrect," he said with a trace of glee. "It wasn't inactive U-238…it was U-235…highly-enriched uranium."

Medved and Falcon simultaneously pushed back in their chairs as they both realized that their worst fears had come true. Bin Wahhab had the services of some of the world's most brilliant atomic physicists, the foremost of whom was Alexander Marenkov. In addition, he had finagled a significant cache of chain-reactive uranium, and—almost certainly—now was in possession of a nuclear bomb.

Chapter Twenty-Six

It was not the way Preston Higby had hoped to spend his Christmas and he was certain that the President also was not happy about being pulled away from his own family on this special afternoon. But the information he had just received from Mike Falcon was too important to sit on, even for a day. Fortunately, the Commander-in-Chief had decided to spend the Holidays at Camp David so that the logistics of their meeting was simplified. The President decided that the nature of the subject would best be discussed at the White House and that it would be a reasonably simple matter to be helicoptered in and out.

Higby lived across the Potomac in McLean, Virginia, so he could be at Pennsylvania Avenue in twenty minutes provided the weather didn't turn worse. It had been drizzling intermittently, but the temperature had stayed several degrees above freezing, so the roads had not turned to ice. Traffic on the George Washington Parkway on such a holiday and in such weather was virtually non-existent. Higby had been sitting in the Oval Office, briefcase at his side, for nearly an hour by the time his boss arrived.

"Merry Christmas, Preston," the President said as he entered.

"You, too, sir."

"Cigar?" the President said, offering a panatela to Higby as he strode across the Great Seal-embroidered carpet.

"No, sir, I don't indulge," Higby replied, trying mightily to suppress an irrepressible image. Recovering his composure, he said, "Sorry I dragged you away from your family on Christmas day, but I knew you would want to know about this right away."

Lighting his cigar, the President settled in the leather arm-chair behind his desk.

"I'm sure my National Security Advisor wouldn't make such a career-limiting move unless it were quite urgent. Now what's all this about missing Russian physicists and disappearing uranium?".

"This morning," Higby responded, "I received a call from the Director of Russia's Federal Security Service.

"Ah…Yevgeny Aksanov," the President said, blowing a smoke ring. "Tough old bird. Appears that he outfoxed most of his rivals in the fight over the KGB's portfolio. I guess the good news for you is that all those splinter Russian intelligence agencies ensure that your NSA keeps well-funded by Congress," the President chuckled.

"I wish that they were all we had to worry about," Higby replied. "Unfortunately, there are far more serious threats these days. One of them is the reason I asked to meet with you today. You remember this character," Higby said as he drew a black-and-white photograph from his briefcase and handed it to the President.

"Indeed. Abdul bin Wahhab. I believe we put a price of one million dollars on his head—dead or alive. And we haven't been able to pay up, yet."

"Unfortunately, you're correct. We even put a couple of cruise missiles through his bedroom window and still didn't nail him."

"So what's he up to now?" the President asked, returning the photo to Higby. "I hope we're not about to be subjected to another bombing."

"I'm afraid so…only…only…." The NSA Director hesitated, reluctant to actually give voice to the thoughts that had been haunting him for a year. Ever since the recent air attacks on Iraq, which he had opposed, he had feared that the Muslim militants would retaliate with a Holy War against the United States. He also had foreseen the unhappy possibilities of the billionaire bin Wahhab preying upon a devastated Russian economy and seducing some of its uniquely gifted people. He held the President directly responsible for what he must now say. "Only, it will be much worse this time."

"Worse?" How can that be? Weren't there something like four thousand casualties in Kenya and Tanzania? How could it be any worse?"

"Sir, there is good reason to believe that the vanishing of Alexander Marenkov, along with a number of other top-flight Russian physicists and nuclear engineers, the disappearance of a quantity of highly-enriched Russian warhead uranium, and the purposes of bin Wahhab are all related. Mr. President, I fear that bin Wahhab may be in possession of a nuclear bomb."

The Commander-in-Chief sat back, staring at Higby with a mixture of curiosity and disbelief. "How can this possibly be?" he said, wrestling with his anger. "Is this what we have to show for our efforts and money to help the Russians dismantle their nuclear weapons? What have we spent on that?"

"Since 1991," Higby paused as he tumbled the numbers in his head, "around three and a half billion dollars."

"That's just great. And now you're telling me that we've spent that much only to increase the nuclear threat to ourselves."

"I must disagree with your assessment, sir. The overall threat of a nuclear holocaust has been vastly reduced. We are now faced with a terrorist scenario…probably with one bomb."

"Hmph. That splitting of hairs won't matter much to the unfortunate souls at ground zero. And what do we have to show for our grandiose plans of the International Science and Technology Center?" He referred to the joint Russo-American endeavor that had transferred thousands of Russian scientists and engineers from the weapons business to working on medical, nuclear waste disposal, and clean energy projects. The American objective had been to reduce the temptation for these talented people to obtain employment in the wrong places.

"It's still a noble effort," Higby said. "We always knew, with the turbulent state that the Russian economy is in, that we could never hope to completely plug the dam."

The President stood, holding the cigar as an afterthought, and strode to the window looking out over the icy Rose Garden.

"Starting to freeze over," he said. A thought, recurring more frequently to him now that he was nearing the end of his time in office, burrowed into his mind. He began reflecting on his first term and how bright his place in history had seemed. Then it all started to unravel in his second term with that ridiculous peccadillo…all his good works glossed over like those dead, frozen leaves…and now this. Blame would surely be heaped upon him once again by the opposition, by the press, by world opinion…unless…unless….

He turned to face Higby. "What's your source of information?"

"I have a man in Russia. He's been working with the FSB on this. They believe they have more than adequate evidence."

"Where is bin Wahhab operating out of now? And where is the bomb?" the President asked returning to his chair.

"He has two bases of operation. One in Sudan and the other in Afghanistan. He also has been known to hide out in Iraq. However, our best intelligence—from satellite and in-country recon—indicates that he's still in Khowst, in Afghanistan. Our Tomahawks only managed to take out his surface structures. We believe he has a fairly elaborate subterranean complex. And that's where the bomb must be."

"Well, let's loft a few more cruise missiles in there and finish the job."

"That won't work."

"Why? Is the complex too hardened?"

"Ordinarily, it probably wouldn't be a problem for the Tomahawks. However, in this case, we can't get very close to the target before launching. That means putting more fuel in the missiles at the expense of payload and a corresponding reduction in punch. But there's a far more serious problem. The target happens to be enriched, chain-reactive uranium, if you follow my drift."

"I have the picture. That could be quite messy. So, what are our options?"

"The FSB has suggested one. They would parachute in a Spetsnaz force and take the complex from the ground. Their plan would be to capture the uranium, the scientists involved, and perhaps even bin Wahhab, himself."

"Oh, sure. I know how delicately the Spetsnaz runs its operations," the President guffawed. "We'd be lucky if they didn't accidentally nuke half of Afghanistan in the effort. Now listen…there's no way that the Russians are going to run this show. They bad-mouthed us when we hit Iraq last year. They'd love to look like the guys in the white hats over this whole Muslim problem. No way. I've got too much invested in this. I'll personally talk to the Big White Bear and make him an offer he can't refuse. Assuming that's a given, and that it must be a ground operation, what are our best options?"

Having predicted his boss's reaction, Higby reached into his briefcase and produced two untitled, slim black folders. He handed one to the President.

"If you open to the first page, sir, you will see the heading for the U.S. Special Operations Command."

"Yes, I remember the SOC. I visited their command when I first took office. Somewhere down in south Florida, if I recall."

"Tampa, sir. MacDill Air Force Base."

"Right. And I also recall that the Pentagon doesn't publicly acknowledge their existence."

"That hasn't changed, Mr. President. The SOC is still our most covert and elite anti-terrorist organization. If you recall, it consists of the Army's Delta Force and a team of the Naval Special Warfare Development Group, all hand-picked—the best in the land."

"Yes...I do remember...pretty damned rigorous training. Great for attacking those places where conventional military strikes would be unfeasible or impossible."

"Precisely. *And, they are trained to seize or destroy nuclear weapons.*"

When Higby concluded his summary, the President reviewed the materials for several moments in silence.

"There will be trouble here," he said finally, gazing at the NSA Director. "Both the Army and the Navy will be knifing at each other's shorts to get in on this. Who do you think we should go with?"

"They're both equally capable. We should probably do some homework to determine which force might work better with the Russians."

"What? Didn't I just tell you that we're running this show,?" the President said angrily.

"We can run it, but going it alone would not be the wisest course of action, sir. The Russians have an immense store of knowledge concerning that geographical area as well as a thorough understanding of the military tactics we may encounter over there. Also, there are bound to be *ex post facto* reports of the raid. You, and our country, will look much better in the eyes of the world if this is known as a joint Russo-American operation. And the most compelling point is that the Russians will never let us run this alone."

"Well, damn. Since you put it that way...get together all the information you can about the Delta Force and the Navy Special Warfare Group. Get with the CIA and pull all the data that you both can on bin Wahhab and this Khowst complex. And I want to be hooked up with the Bear...day after tomorrow. Of course, I'll want to be thoroughly briefed beforehand."

"Yes, sir," Higby responded, perceiving that the remainder of his quiet Christmas at home with his wife had just vanished.

"Well, if I get moving, I'll be back at Camp David before the turkey's out of the oven," the President said affably. It seemed to Higby that the man was suddenly relishing this looming crisis, perhaps finding in it an ironic redemption. "You'd better get going, too. Looks like the streets are icing up."

With a lurch, the President emerged from behind his desk and approached Higby. "Big game in Miami, tonight," he said, gripping the Director amiably by the arm and escorting him to the door. "Who are you rooting for?"

"I don't follow football that closely," Higby replied.

"Oh," the President said with obvious disappointment. "Well, enjoy the rest of Christmas. See you in my office at eight a.m., day after tomorrow."

"Yes, sir. Merry Christmas."

Preston Higby left the Oval Office, turned right and walked down the corridor to a lone elevator. As he passed the windows, he saw that the President was absolutely correct. The roads had iced up. It made no difference to him, anyway. He had no intention of going home that evening, not with the volume of work that had been just laid on him. The elevator doors opened and he stepped in. He would go underground to the Old Executive Office Building, where he kept his office on the Uranium Oversight Committee. He had a sofa bed there and access to a shower. Before he started work this evening, though, he would first call his wife of forty years. She would be disappointed but it would not be the first time he had made such a sacrifice for his duty. She knew that he could do no other.

*   *   *

It was late in the afternoon, already dark, by the time that Medved arrived at the *Militsiya* station to keep his appointment with the Chief of Police.

"Welcome, welcome, Major," Dmitri Kirilovitch said enthusiastically as he received his former commander in his cramped, faded-yellow office. "Can I get you anything?"

"Perhaps a cup of hot tea," Sergei replied, removing his heavy old army greatcoat and settling into a well-worn leather chair.

"Of course. It's colder than a dead yak out there. Ey, Mitka, bring in the kettle and two cups!" he shouted. "And make sure the cups are clean!" he added as an afterthought. "Well, I must say that for a moment there yesterday I really believed I was back in Kabul. All that was missing were the tanks and helicopters."

"And the Afghans," Sergei rejoined.

"Ha! I don't know which is worse…the mujaheddin or the mafiosi. But I'm quite certain that neither of those groups will be sending you sentimental cards on your namesake day. By the way, I learned from witnesses that your large Yeti friend was responsible for most of the mayhem…."

"Yes. He's a…unique…individual."

"No doubt. Well, running into him certainly was extremely poor timing on the part of the *Chornaya Rooka*. Which brings me to the point of our meeting…but here is my sergeant with our tea."

After placing the copper tea kettle and porcelain cups on a small wooden coffee table, Mitka departed. Dmitri now addressed Sergei in a more serious tone. He related the remarkable story of how a woman—the young, attractive wife of a *Rooka* mobster—had wandered into his precinct station, and how this woman had provided them with information concerning the planned kidnapping of an American at the Metropol. "*Your* American, of that I am certain, Sergei," Dmitri said, stirring his tea. "Only, for some reason, they changed their plans and tried to snatch him at the Bistro. Perhaps they were aware of my reinforcements at the hotel."

"Do you think that the *Rooka* will try again?" Sergei asked.

"That's exactly the issue. After last evening, you would think that the remaining mafiosi would become farmers or sales clerks or something else a little less risky. However, they might actually be stupid enough to make a second attempt. That's why I want you to hear directly from the woman, herself. As you know more about the American than I, perhaps you may pick up a clue from her concerning the *Rooka's* intentions that I am overlooking. Would you be willing to speak with her?"

"By all means." Sergei was equally anxious to learn if there might be a Feliks connection with the mob's attempted kidnapping of Falcon.

"*Harasho!*" Dmitri called for Mitka to bring in the woman. As they were waiting, Sergei reached inside a pocket of his overcoat and produced a palm-sized, stubby handgun.

"You might want to run the ballistics on this against that cartridge I gave you a few months ago," he said, handing the pistol to Dmitri. The weapon had been found upon Yusopov when he was discovered handcuffed to the rear of the Lubianka.

"Aha! A *Malysh*—a silent pistol," Dmitri grinned. "That clears up the mystery."

"How so?"

"You may recall—after my first examination of the bullet you gave me last August, along with that button, pen, and strip of cloth—I thought that we were dealing with a *Stechkin* automatic, but I had some suspicions. The casing just didn't look right. Now, I believe I know why. It wasn't fired from a *Stechkin* at all. It was shot from a *Malysh* such as this. You see, it uses the same 9mm cartridge but a separate charge within the casing drives the propellant gases backward, thus retaining all sound of the gunfire. It is necessary to be fairly close to the victim, and one must be quite accurate, as the effective range is only fifteen meters. It has one purpose only—assassination."

"That fits my theory," Sergei nodded, sipping his tea. "My guess is that this weapon was used to murder a Pasternak-quoting farmer in Peredelkino. I appreciate your running it through ballistics for me."

"Certainly. Well, I see that Mitka has returned with our lady," Dmitri said, rising. "Come in, come in. Don't be anxious, ma'am. Major Medved, this is Yelena Pavlovna Kuzmitch."

Sergei, whose back was toward the door, set his cup on the coffee table, stood, and turned to greet the woman. He was met by the gaze of two large dark sienna eyes set in the graceful contours of a heart-shaped face. High, prominent cheekbones offset a pert nose and angled down to full, sensuous lips—all of which was framed by a thick, shoulder-length shock of auburn hair. Sergei felt that he was dreaming—she was the living image of his Irina.

"The pleasure is mine," Sergei said, clasping her extended hand.

"Major...does that rank mean you're with the Army?" she asked, sitting in another of Dmitri's veteran leather chairs.

"Not exactly," Sergei said and then went on to explain his affiliation. He was pleased that she did not wince upon receiving this news.

"You're with the Federal Security Service?" she said unemotionally. "I heard a rumor in the station-house today that some FSB agents were involved in the death of my husband last evening."

Sergei traded glances with Dmitri.

"I'll be honest with you. I was at the scene. I, personally, did not kill your husband. But I am somewhat responsible for his demise."

The Chief of Police stared at his former commander with incredulity. Here he, Dmitri, had been fabricating an official story that made no mention of FSB participation in the prior evening's mafiosi shoot-out. And then Sergei spills his guts to a mobster's widow. *What the hell's come over him?"*

Yelena looked directly into Sergei's eyes. "For your part in that episode...I want to thank you," she said. "Vasily was a wife-beater, a two-bit thug, a would-be murderer. God forgive me, I would have killed him myself if I had only been stronger."

"He's gone, now," Sergei said, lighting a cigarette. "You don't have to worry about soiling your hands that way. But we still have some concerns that perhaps you may help us with. I need for you to tell me precisely what Kuzmitch said about 'snatching' the American."

Unhurriedly, even serenely, she recounted the rantings of her husband on the night he flung the dinner on the floor and socked her before she cold-cocked him with the brass tea kettle.

"You were very brave—both in the way you defended yourself and in coming to the *Militsiya* station," Sergei said when she had finished.

"I only reacted instinctively," she replied. "I am sure I will pay for that with my life."

"Nonsense. You are completely safe under the protection of Police Chief Kirilovitch. And then you will return to a normal life—the life you had before you met that hooligan."

"She was with the Kirov," Dmitri interjected. "A dancer—just like your little Galena."

The last image he had of his Galya—the sad, doe-eyed expression cast upon him from the back of the retreating FSB Mercedes—flitted across Sergei's mind. "Galena is my daughter," he explained to Yelena. Then, not knowing why, he continued, "Perhaps some day you will meet her."

"I would like that," she answered softly.

An awkward silence descended upon the room and Police Chief Kirilovitch suddenly felt like an eavesdropper in his own office. "Well then," he finally blurted, "thank you for your help *Gospozha* Kuzmitch. I'll have Mitka escort you back to your quarters."

After she had departed, Dmitri turned to Sergei. "Well, didn't I tell you she was remarkable?" he said, a discernible twinkle in his eyes.

Sergei nodded. "Yes. Thank you…for this opportunity to question her."

"Of course. Did you learn anything of value to this case?"

"No. It seems like it was simply a typical mafia hit on a supposed rich tourist. They made a mistake, though. That particular American is not a fat cat."

"And their second mistake was picking on someone who is involved with you and T-Rex," Dmitri laughed.

"Yes, we can take care of ourselves. But I'm concerned about Yelena...*Gospozha* Kuzmitch," he hastily corrected himself. "You know how the mob operates. They'll certainly know that she's been here and they'll suspect that she had a hand in our ambush of them. They never allow snitches to walk away. Tell me, my old friend, what plans do you have for her protection?"

"For now, we'll keep her here. We have fixed up one of the cells pretty nicely and—"

"That will never do, Dmitri. You can't treat that woman like a common criminal. I may be able to arrange something through the FSB."

"Feel free to help us out on this one, Major. We just don't have the facilities that the FSB can boast of." *The old Bear of the Hindu Kush is becoming a cub over this little mink,* Dmitri chuckled inwardly.

*   *   *

At that very moment in the Hindu Kush, a being of a frailer, but no less determined, nature than the bear now struggled toward his goal. Alexander Marenkov had greatly underestimated the distance to—and the difficulty of reaching—the mountain to the north. For two days he had been working his way through the silent forest of cedar, spruce, and fir trees, often being forced to turn in the opposite direction of his objective in order to maintain his concealment. As the sun set on the second day, he had finally reached the foot of the ridge that led into Pakistan. The increasingly steep gradient and rough terrain ruled out continuation of his trek for the night. In the last faint rays of light that flickered through the swaying limbs, he spotted an old tree trunk lying on the forest floor. The bole of the dead pine was the thickness of three large men. *My home for tonight*, he thought, kneeling next to the trunk.

Combating his fatigue, he began scraping and digging the earth beneath the log. After ten minutes, he had carved out a hollow that was just big enough to accommodate his slim frame. Lying on his back, he grasped the underside of the pine and dragged himself into his new home. He completed his engineering effort by extending his arms to either side and gathering twigs, leaves, and soil around the open areas of his abode. Satisfied that he was well hidden, he reached into one of his pockets and extracted a handful of dates and figs. His hands were sticky with sap and his nostrils were filled with the scent of pine, but he couldn't recall having had a more delicious meal. His bed of soft earth and leaves was quite comfortable and sufficiently warm in spite of the below-freezing temperature. It was only a few minutes before he succumbed to the blissful unconsciousness of exhaustion.

He wasn't sure how long he had been out when the noises first reached his ears. In the complete darkness of his hideaway, he brushed his eyes and pinched his face, in disbelief that he was hearing such a thing. But there it came again. And this time, he knew it was real.

Professor Marenkov, give yourself up. Do not die this way.... an amplified voice blurted over a loudspeaker. And then—from another direction—*Alexander Marenkov, show yourself. You will be well-treated.*

The Professor held his breath. *Have they actually followed my trail to this place? If so, then it will be only a matter of minutes before I am discovered.*

Marenkov, do not make us find you. It will only be the worse for you. Give yourself up, a third voice blared in a bull-horn.

Next he heard the natural, unamplified, voices of men calling to each other and, through tiny chinks in the mud sidings of his lodging, glimpsed the erratic dancing of flashlights. They were very near. *I've been found out. Perhaps I should surrender. Maybe they truly will be more lenient.* A twig snapped only a few feet away from his head. It was followed by a rustling of leaves and the heavy tramp of boots. He lay very still. *Let them come. I won't do their work for them. Let them shoot me right here. I could do worse than this forest as my final resting place.*

He felt a weight against the dead pine, then a clank of metal against wood. One of his pursuers had rested his Nikonov assault rifle on the log.

There were at least two Ikhwan, for a quiet, almost inaudible conversation ensued.

I wonder if they are as exhausted and cold as I am, Marenkov mused. *They must be very angry. I expect they will cease talking and poke their heads in here at any moment.*

Again there was a scraping of metal on wood, followed by a shuffling of boots and crackling of underbrush. The sounds began to fade as the Ikhwan moved off. *Perhaps they are trying to trick me.* He remained motionless for five minutes…ten…a full half-hour. The forest was once again completely quiet. It was with some difficulty that he accepted the fact that he had not been discovered. And upon that realization, he again fell into his deep sleep.

Chapter Twenty-Seven

As Alexander Marenkov had been burrowing under a log in the mountains of eastern Afghanistan, the sun was just beginning to rise above similarly snow-dusted ridges on the other side of the world. It was a feeble sun, however, that struggled to peer through a heavy cloud layer above the White Mountains of Maine, and offered little warmth to the creatures below. One such life-form, craggy-faced and gray-eyed, gazed from beneath a black pullover knit cap across the frozen landscape, toward the pastel pink eastern horizon.

Mechanically, he bit down on a chaw of tobacco. It was a habit he had picked up in Vietnam to pass the time and to calm his nerves. In his particular profession, the light and smoke of a cigarette invited trouble. Brushing snow from his forest-camouflaged fatigues, he rose and stretched his tired, frigid limbs. He had pushed them hard the last several days, but it had been necessary. He wasn't about to let those young studs of his command show him up. Besides, the extraordinary effort had paid off. After all, they were still running free—and only half a day to go.

"Time to drop your cocks and grab your socks," he addressed two mounds of snow behind him. The lumps stirred and a pair of sleepy-eyed human heads emerged.

"Oh, hell. Are we still here, Skipper?" one of them said, yawning. "I had the most beautiful dream that I was back in Florida on a beach that allowed only gorgeous naked women and myself."

"Well, Toto," the other wakening man laughed, "this ain't Kansas and we're sure as hell not in South Beach, Miami."

"You got that right," Lieutenant Junior Grade Pete 'Lucky' Ryder responded as he glumly surveyed the snow-covered landscape. "And leave it to the Navy. They spend a ton of money teaching me Arabic and preparing me for desert warfare and then pack me off to survival school in the god-damned north pole. Sure, that makes sense."

"Cut the chit-chat," the Skipper said, spitting brown tobacco juice into the pristine snow. "We've only got 'til noon to make that last checkpoint. I figure it's a good twenty kilometers on the other side of that ridge. If we're going to avoid capture, we'll have to stay high in the mountains and in the roughest terrain. It'll slow us down, but it'll do the same to them, too. We'll eat on the way." He was interrupted by a muffled crack of gunfire and excited yells. "That's less than a klick away. Let's move, ladies." Without further ado, the Skipper set off at a trot.

"Damn, 'Cuda," Ryder cursed. "How'd we get so lucky to be stuck with the Old Man as our 'buddy'? The other guys are probably sitting around having a nice hot breakfast."

"The other guys," 'Cuda—Lieutenant Chris 'Barracuda' Rochelle—responded, "are probably all in the P.O.W. camp by now, and they'd be fortunate to be eating dirt. Trust me, Lieutenant—your nickname is still appropriate—you're 'lucky' to have drawn the Skipper. We better hop to it or we'll never catch him."

Ryder and Rochelle stood, dusted the snow from their parkas, adjusted their packs, shook their legs and lumbered after their Skipper's retreating form. They, and the 'Old Man'—Commander Hardin 'Hardy' O'Brien—had been slogging for nearly four days through snow and the wild terrain of the White Mountain range. The only good thing about being stuck in that outdoor refrigerator was that they were not in the P.O.W. camp.

Lieutenant Rochelle was well aware of the conditions in the camp. He had been through the Navy's SERE—Survival, Evasion, Resistance, and Escape—School once before. He knew how realistically the camp had been set up, complete with barbed-wire, machine gun turrets, psycho guards, and physical and mental torture. It was such a bad experience that the Navy sent only elite combat troops through and deemed that one dose of 'SERE U' was enough for a lifetime. Rochelle was one of the very rare souls to matriculate a second time. He had been accorded this unique 'honor' in order to observe and grade the operations of the camp from a prisoner's perspective and to submit a report to upper brass containing recommendations for improving the realism and the training experience. He chuckled at the thought of what now lay in store for the completely unsuspecting, fun-loving SEAL—Lucky Ryder—who trotted at his side.

After nearly five hours and much slipping in icy slush and tumbling over snow-hidden rocks and logs, the trio finally scaled the ridge to the final checkpoint. Achieving this goal was of no small consequence, as the reward was a sandwich, a hot bowl of soup, and four hours' sleep before entering the camp. An orange parachute canopy hanging from four cedars in a clearing was the marker for this important location. The key was to make it by noon. One second late meant no food, no rest, and a direct ticket to the very unpleasant P.O.W. compound.

"Thar she blows," O'Brien said, pointing to the bright splash of orange nearly a kilometer away. They all simultaneously glanced at their watches. *Seven minutes. An easy jog should do it.*

They left the protection of the forest and began to trot across the open space leading to the parachute canopy. Only three other individuals could be seen at the checkpoint. Assuming O'Brien's group arrived before the deadline—which now seemed certain—that meant that a mere half dozen of their original group of 60 men had successfully evaded capture. They could almost taste the soup and sandwiches as they neared their destination. With a scant hundred meters to go, Lt.(j.g.) Ryder planted a rapidly moving foot on a lump of snow that concealed a narrow crevice. His foot pronated inward and his ankle traveled in the opposite direction. The rest of Lucky continued forward and straight down.

Lieutenant Rochelle had made it to the safety of the canopy and was lying on the ground, catching his breath, when he heard Ryder's yelp. He sat up and gazed back across the field. The Skipper had pulled the j.g. to his feet and was half-dragging, half-carrying the injured man toward the checkpoint. Rochelle glanced at his watch. Two minutes left. "Damn," he hissed, pushing himself up.

"You'll never make it in time," one of the trio in the parachute tent blurted. But Rochelle had already begun racing toward the Old Man and the injured j.g. Overhead, the still, cold air carried the distinctive whump-whump of an approaching helicopter.

"You two just go on," Lucky said as Rochelle grasped him. "The chopper's almost here. No sense both of you missing out on the eats because of my clumsiness."

"Hang on, Lieutenant," Rochelle said as he and the commander lifted Ryder from the ground. "Nobody here is going to miss a thing." A Navy utility helicopter set down a hundred meters away as he spoke. The trio in the parachute canopy waved and shouted encouragement as they dawdled in their boarding of the Sea King.

"*One minute!*" a voice boomed from the helicopter's loudspeaker.

"You ready, Lieutenant?" the Old Man grinned at Rochelle.

"Yes, sir!"

"Then let's move this carcass!"

Clasping their arms so as to take the j.g.'s full weight, they hurtled forward.

"*Thirty seconds…twenty…ten….*" the warning countdown continued.

Now at the Sea King, the two commandos hoisted their package into the open bay. Ryder was grasped by the others and hauled on board. At the *"Zero"* count, and as the doors were closing, O'Brien and Rochelle launched themselves into the bay. The engines spooled up and a few seconds later, the helicopter was airborne. As it motored above the pines, precariously nose down, it picked up speed and began transitioning from vertical to horizontal motion.

"When this is all over and we get back to MacDill," the Skipper wheezed, "you will make sure that our glasses are never empty at happy hour, Lieutenant Junior Grade Ryder."

"Aye, aye, sir,"

"If you should live so long, Pete," Rochelle said, in between gulping his breaths. "Because I may just kill you for this."

The helicopter journey was brief, ending ten minutes later in a small clearing near two mobile homes. Inside the trailers, the six successful evaders received their promised soup and sandwiches and cots with real blankets. It seemed as if their heads had just sunk into the pillows, but it was actually four hours afterwards when they were rudely rousted from their sacks by shouting and the loud bangs of gunfire near their ears. Turban-headed men in long robes seized them and herded them into the back of a waiting troop transport. When the truck stopped a few minutes later, they were at the gate of the P.O.W. camp.

Through the barbed wire and in glaring yellow light, they could see some of their ship-mates being knocked about and others digging holes or filling holes up. Some were running naked in the below-freezing temperatures. Still others were being sprayed with fire hoses. During all this time, mid-eastern music, occasionally interrupted by shrill anti-American propaganda, blared from the loudspeaker system. Machine guns were posted in towers at each corner of the enclosure.

Standing before the entrance, the men of Commander O'Brien's group were slapped, shoved, and punched by their captors. One of the Navy's clear rules for the P.O.W. experience was that prisoners must *never* retaliate or even touch a guard. Breaking this rule would have two unfortunate results. First, the violator would be dropped from the course with an unsatisfactory grade—a blemish on one's record. The second, and more immediate result, was a severe group pummeling by the guards.

"You! Yankee imperialist dog!" a short, be-turbaned guard bellowed at Lt. Rochelle. "Get on your stomach and slide under the gate!"

"I don't think so, sport," Rochelle answered.

The guard struck the officer in the face, knocking him backwards.

"I say again! Under the gate!"

The Lieutenant rubbed his jaw and spat several red drops into the snow before answering, "Kiss my pink butt."

The guard sneered, then swiftly struck Rochelle in the stomach. As the Lieutenant buckled over, his antagonist began to strike him about the head and shoulders. Yet, the blows were unable to drive him to the ground. Frustrated, the guard turned to the rest of the new arrivals.

"Who is the senior officer here?!" he demanded.

O'Brien stepped forward.

"You will order this infidel to slide under the gate or I will beat him under it!"

All eyes in the compound turned to the Skipper. A serious test of his command abilities was now in play. His actions at this moment could have important consequences in the consideration of him for flag rank.

"You heard the man," Hardy O'Brien said laconically. The guard smiled. The Skipper, expectorating his chaw at the guard's feet, continued, "Drop your drawers, 'Cuda, so this dick-head can kiss your ass." The smile had barely disappeared from the guard's face when it was forcefully replaced there by O'Brien's bony-knuckled fist. It was all the direction that the imprisoned men needed. For the first time in the half-century history of the SERE School, and with complete disregard for the cardinal rule of the camp, the inmates rushed their captors. It was to the further misfortune of the guards that this challenge was mounted by the elite forces of the Naval Special Warfare Development Group. It was quickly over. After sustaining an assortment of bloody noses, puffed lips, and bruised egos, the guards were bound and tossed into an unheated bunkroom. The gate was then torn down so that Lt. Chris 'Cuda' Rochelle could enter standing tall.

After a thorough divestment of the compound, a freezer full of steaks and a half dozen sacks of potatoes were discovered along with several boxes of cigars. Sitting in the camp commandant's office with a full stomach and his feet up on the desk, O'Brien was enjoying a smoke in the company of his men. "So much for a brilliant career. Hell, who was I trying to kid anyway. Those ring-knockers would never pin a star on a guy like me," he said in reference to the close-knit fraternity of officers that wore the Naval Academy's ring. The Old Man's rise to command had been via a much tougher road. At that moment, the phone rang and Lucky picked up the receiver.

"No shit...I mean, are you serious?" he blurted.

He handed the telephone to the Commander. "It's the White House, Skipper."

O'Brien gazed at Ryder as if the earlier fall of his junior officer had injured his head more than his ankle. "Commander O'Brien," he spoke into the phone. He said no more until five minutes later and then only, "Aye, aye sir."

He handed the phone back to the j.g. and flicked his cigar ash into the camp commandant's ash-tray. "Listen up. There were two people on the other end of that line," he reported to his eagerly attentive troops. "The Director of the National Security Agency and the Chief of Naval Operations. Gentlemen, the play-acting is over. The President is sending us into combat."

★ ★ ★

"This way, Michael," Sergei said, briskly walking along the spacious, busy corridor. Falcon wished that Medved were not setting such a swift pace, for he wanted to take in every inch of his surroundings. Overhead, gold and crystal chandeliers lit their way. The walls on either side were adorned with numerous oil paintings that depicted centuries of Russian war heroes and the battles that made them famous. The passers-by in the hallway were all in uniform, ranging in color from the raw umber of the Russian Army, to the deep blue of the Navy and the azure of the Air Force.

"Ey, you're making history again, my friend," Sergei smiled. "First, you get to see the Lubianka Basement. Now, just imagine…the War Room of the Russian Ministry of Defense. I never thought I'd see the day when an American sat next to me in there. But now that it's happening, I'm glad it's you. Ah, we've arrived."

The Russian stopped so abruptly that Falcon, who had been inhaling the scenery, bumped into him.

"Listen, My friend," Sergei said, hooking Falcon's arm. "There are some things you should be aware of before we enter. First, do not speak unless you are requested. Second, if you are asked for your comments, never mention the Feliks. It is too sore a subject. Third, do not take any notes. Now, let's go."

At the entrance of the War Room, they were required to pass through another metal detector, the third since they had arrived at the Ministry. They then proceeded through a doorway that was guarded on each side by two impressively tall, spit-polished, rosy-cheeked, young Army corporals who stood with their AN-94s at parade rest.

Falcon was surprised at the size of the room as he entered. The ceiling was several stories high and, if the furniture were cleared out, it would have been possible to set up a full-court basketball game. As it was, a fair amount of furnishings were in place, including an oval table that could provide comfortable seating for fifty persons. The rich, dark wood of the table warmly reflected the soft overhead track lighting. The room was otherwise dark except for a back-lit map of the world that took up three stories of the far wall.

Silently, Medved nudged Falcon, motioning to three chairs at the near end of the great table. Two were empty and the third was occupied by Viktor Buzhkin. As they took their seats, General Aksanov and several uniformed and civilian-clothed men appeared from a side door at the opposite end of the room. Upon seeing his agents and the American, Aksanov smiled approvingly and said something to one of the officers. The man he addressed turned and gazed in the direction Aksanov had indicated. Then he, the FSB Director, and the others in their group approached the American and Russian agents.

"General ," Aksanov said, "I believe you know Sergeant Buzhkin and Major Medved."

"By reputation only," the officer said, shaking hands with the two agents. "It's a pleasure to meet you both."

"And this is the American I've been telling you about. Michael Falcon, please meet General Anatoly Vernadsky, Commander-in-Chief of Russia's Special Assignment Forces—Spetsnaz."

"Ah, yes, *Gospodeen* Falcon," the General smiled. "I've heard a good deal about you. I understand you reduced two of our vaunted MiG-21s into razor blades."

"My apologies," Falcon answered as the General shook his hand. There was a firmness to the grip and a brightness in the eyes that belied the Russian's gray hair and time-worn face.

"No apologies are necessary. That was war and you were simply doing what was required of a warrior. Besides, those were the days that we were enemies, and those days are over. Isn't that right, Yevgeny?" he said, turning back to Aksanov.

"If the world would only be as you wish, Anatoly," the FSB Director replied with a sigh.

"A most agreeable thought," the General laughed. "Well, please be seated, gentlemen, and we shall begin our business."

As the others took their chairs, Vernadsky strode around to the head of the table.

"Gentlemen, you all know the background of the threat now being posed to the world by Abdul bin Wahhab and his gang of terrorists," he began speaking in a clear, commanding voice. "Yesterday, the Russian Federation and the United States of America agreed to join forces to deal with—and eradicate—this threat. I am happy to say that the honor of spearheading this operation has been accorded to our Spetsnaz unit and the American Navy's Special Warfare Group. Soon, a team of the American commandos, under the leadership of Commander Hardin O'Brien will arrive in Moscow to begin training for the mission with their Spetsnaz counterparts. Our Russian commandos will be led by Lieutenant Colonel Alyosha Rodonov, who will speak to you shortly.

"Major Medved…Sergeant Buzhkin…. Because of your vast expertise in the geography of the area and the tactics of the enemy, and also owing to your unique skills, we would like you both to be part of this operation.

"*Gospodeen* Falcon, it is the wish of ourselves and the American Government that you also participate. We would like you to act as interpreter and liaison between both commando groups. However, this is merely a request and, in light of the significant danger and as you are a civilian, you are under no obligation to accept this proposal. Would you like to take a few days to consider your decision?"

The American turned to his two Russian colleagues, both of whom studiously avoided his eyes.

"That won't be necessary, General," Falcon said. "Someone needs to look after these two," he nodded to his companions, "and it may as well be me." Medved grinned broadly and a slight smile even cracked Buzhkin's steely visage.

"*Harasho!*" General Vernadsky said. "Now let me introduce Lt. Col. Rodonov, who will fill you in on more details of this operation, which we've code-named *Macedonian Phalanx*."

As the General sat, a bald, wiry, leather-faced officer of medium height rose near the middle of the table. He pressed a button on the tabletop and instantly a rectangular section of the table slid open and a small desk-size panel of control knobs and switches rose to take its place. Turning one of the knobs, he reduced the ambient lighting so that the participants in the meeting were barely visible. The world map on the far wall, however, was now noticeably brighter and in much sharper focus.

"Thank you, General," Rodonov said as he cradled a light-wand in one hand. "Macedonian Phalanx. So named because we are following in the footsteps of that legendary Macedonian warrior, Alexander the Great, as we strike *here*." He flicked a switch and the global display was completely replaced by a map of Afghanistan. A red dot emanating from his light-wand shone on the town of Khowst. He flicked another switch and the area highlighted filled the wall display.

"This is a satellite photo, provided by the NSA I might add, of the region of interest shortly after it was struck by American cruise missiles. You can see that the buildings are mostly rubble. However, as you will note in this close-up," he said, again adjusting a control lever, "a door has been carved into this mountainside. We now have very reliable information that it leads to an underground complex. Within that complex are bin Wahhab, Professor Alexander Marenkov, and enough enriched uranium to build an atom bomb. It is our hope that we are not too late and that the bomb has not yet been completed.

"We believe that the compound is guarded by as many as five hundred of bin Wahhab's fanatical followers, known as the Ikhwan Brotherhood. With our force consisting of only two commando teams, we will be outnumbered four-to-one. However, we believe that a larger force on our part would ruin the element of surprise and foil our ultimate objective."

"Excuse me, Colonel," Aksanov interrupted. "I see that you and Commander O'Brien are of similar rank. Who will actually be in command of Macedonian Phalanx?"

"Perhaps I may best answer that, Yevgeny," General Vernadsky said. "Our President and the American President discussed and reached agreement on this issue just this morning. Intelligence information from both sides indicates that the Americans appear to be the target of bin Wahhab's scheme. Thus, they have the greatest vested interest in destroying it. In addition, they are willing to finance this entire operation. In exchange for these considerations, we have allowed them to assume the lead role."

"I see," Aksanov replied, nodding. "Go on, Colonel."

"Yes, sir. The American commandos will arrive in three days. They will join our Spetsnaz team for one week of planning and exacting training under conditions that they are expected to encounter. During this period, we will be working closely with both American and Russian intelligence organizations to help us shape our battle strategy. When we feel that we have the appropriate plan and the troops are ready, the teams will be air-dropped into the target area."

"We certainly will hold up our end at the FSB," Aksanov said. "And I am sure that you can count on the NSA and CIA as well," he nodded toward Falcon. "But describe for me, Colonel, the objectives you have established for a successful mission."

"Certainly. The primary objective is to capture all the uranium contained in bin Wahhab's stronghold which, of course, includes any such material that has been fashioned into a nuclear device. Second, we will completely destroy the compound and all its facilities dedicated to the manufacture of weapons of mass destruction. Third, we will eradicate the terrorists. Fourth, we will bring home as many of our own men as humanly possible. But, we are prepared to sacrifice ourselves in order to achieve the higher priority objectives."

"And Professor Marenkov?" Aksanov interposed.

Vernadsky signaled to Rodonov that he would handle this question.

"The greatest effort will be made to extract the Professor," the General said, "and indeed all of the other scientists and engineers in the compound. We are very interested in ascertaining which of these distinguished gentlemen are being held against their wills and which are there for other reasons. But you must understand that the other priorities, as enumerated by Colonel Rodonov, are much greater. It will be quite problematic to save any of the civilians in the stronghold."

The room fell silent and Lt. Col. Rodonov returned to his seat.

"Well, then, that concludes our briefing for today," Vernadsky said, rising. "We will meet here again in four days, with the American commander. Meanwhile, those of you who will be in the front line should consider getting some rest and spending time with your families. That will be all."

The participants filed out quietly, each alone with his thoughts.

Chapter Twenty-Eight

Valentin Tschernin shifted his weight uneasily from one foot to the other. He had never enjoyed being in the presence of the Rasputin-eyed Arab and, at this moment, it was an aversion that was greatly exacerbated. For he now found himself alone with a patently furious Chosen One.

"My patience is at an end!" bin Wahhab fumed. He fixed his abnormally bulbous, radiant eyes on the downcast gaze of the Russian. "No more convoluted physics babble! You will tell me the absolute truth now. Can you or can you not complete this project without the services of Alexander Marenkov!"

To answer in the negative would be the same as asking for a bullet in the head. Fortunately for Tschernin, he had made good use of the several days that Marenkov had been gone. By racking his brain around the clock, he had finally solved the difficult quantum equations posed by the Professor. Indeed, he had arrived at the final solution only hours before bin Wahhab returned from his *hajj*. Now he was able to answer truthfully, "Yes, I swear to you we are now fully capable of finishing the construction of the bomb."

The fiery eyes of the 'Mahdi' burned deeper into their target. "And tell me exactly…not nearly…but *exactly* when the bomb will be ready. And I warn you, think very carefully before you answer."

Tschernin desperately rummaged through his over-taxed brain, trying to compute a humanly possible timeframe against that of a maniac. In his state of fright and exhaustion, the challenge was simply too colossal and his inner computer crashed. For no substantial reason, he blurted, "Three weeks."

Bin Wahhab studied the eyes of his shaken prey, searching for signs of deceit. "Then for the next three weeks," he spoke slowly and softly, "in each of your five daily prayer sessions, pray to Allah that you have spoken the truth to me. You are losing valuable time! Now, go!"

Tschernin needed no further prodding and hastily exited. As soon as he had departed, bin Wahhab called to Talil, who had been waiting just outside the door.

"Now send in the other one!" he shouted angrily.

Reluctantly, but as obedient as always, Talil went off to do his leader's bidding. He had seen this black mood of bin Wahhab too often and the results had never been harmless. *But would he truly visit his wrath upon his faithful servant, Abu Yusuf? Is this not the same Abu who is the wisest of the Mahdi's lieutenants and who has served his master faithfully for ten years?*

A vivid image filled his mind of a campfire just a few months ago. He recalled how they had sat under the full moon in the ruins that had once been their compound before the American cruise missiles demolished it...how bin Wahhab had recounted the saga of his great-grandfather's attack on Riyadh...how this brave ancestor had guided a small band of men over the city walls and then led them to victory over their enemies, the Rashid Clan. *Wasn't it then, as we sat in the bright moonlight, in the rubble of our former home, that the Mahdi had used this story of his great-grandfather to pose the riddle of his own intentions? I was too dense to understand it. But Abu Yusuf immediately realized that the Chosen One meant to carry the Jihad to the home of the infidels. Bin Wahhab could always count on the nimble mind of Yusuf.*

Talil had barely finished this thought when he reached the cell where Abu Yusuf was waiting anxiously. He had been consigned to this space ever since bin Wahhab had returned from the *hajj* and had learned of Marenkov's escape. It had been Abu Yusuf's honor—and great misfortune—to have been left in charge of the compound in his leader's absence. The disappearance of the Professor was a grave blemish on his management record.

"Ah, Talil, my friend," Abu Yusuf spoke with beseeching eyes as he rose from his chair. "Has he softened or is he still angry at his faithful but worthless servant?"

"Who can read the mind of the Chosen One?" Talil answered.

"Indeed, all has been in the mind of Allah and has been since the beginning of time," Abu replied resignedly.

"He awaits," Talil said, escorting his old friend from the cell.

When they arrived at bin Wahhab's quarters, Talil halted at the door and Abu Yusuf proceeded alone. The 'Rightly Guided One' was in the center of the room, his back to the door. From his right hand dangled a long, wide, curving sword. It was an instrument that cut deeply into Abu's memory as well as that of all the Ikhwan who had witnessed the bloody retributions of their leader.

"Mahdi, it is I, your worthless servant, Abu Yusuf," the agonized man said, falling to his knees and bowing his head.

Bin Wahhab slowly turned to face Abu. He raised the sword and rested it across the palm of his left hand.

"Do you recognize this weapon?" he asked.

"Of course, Mahdi. It is the sword that your great-grandfather used to sever the head of the sheikh of the Rashid Clan."

"And that I have continued to wield in the service of Allah," bin Wahhab said.

Abu made no reply but vivid images tumbled through his mind of the many souls who had received the Mahdi's 'service.' The CIA agent that night in the moonlight, in the rubble of their former compound, had only been the most recent.

"Recall the evening when I spoke to you of my great-grandfather's triumph over the Rashids," bin Wahhab said, as if reading Abu's mind. "Do you know why I related this story to you?.

"I do, Mahdi. It was by way of this tale that you first informed us of your intent to carry the Jihad into the heart of our enemy."

"Precisely," bin Wahhab said, drawing his left thumb lightly across the sharp edge of the weapon. "And would we be able to achieve our objectives if we were to manage the Holy War as you have done in my absence?"

"No, Mahdi," Abu said, peering from beneath his lowered brow at his master's caressing of the sword.

"Correct, again. And if the Jihad were to fail because of our ineptitude, would we not have failed the will of Allah? And then would we be no longer worthy to sit with him in Paradise? And therefore would we not be the most pitiful of creatures?"

"Yes, Mahdi," Abu answered weakly. "Yes to all of your questions." The slim hope that he harbored for his well-being now began to ebb and he felt almost faint with a light-headed nausea.

"Then, suppose you tell me, Yusuf, what is to be done with a trusted lieutenant…not a common foot-soldier…but a leader of the Jihad who endangers the entire crusade."

Bin Wahhab now took one more step forward so that he stood directly above Abu Yusuf. He patted the broad sword in his left palm.

Abu Yusuf inhaled deeply before answering. "I do not ask for my life, Mahdi. I pray only that you now be guided by Allah, the Merciful, the Compassionate, the Just." He closed his eyes, not expecting to open them ever again. Thus, he was surprised to hear bin Wahhab telling him to rise. He wrapped his arms around the robed legs of the Chosen One and began to weep—not because he feared for his insignificant life, but because he rejoiced in his leader's forgiveness.

"Stand," bin Wahhab repeated. Abu rose and dragged a sleeve across his eyes. "I promise you I will never again—"

"You need say no more. Go now, and praise Allah for your deliverance."

"Thank you, Mahdi, thank you," Abu said, bowing and backing toward the door. "There is no god but Allah."

"And Muhammed is his prophet," bin Wahhab replied, completing the ritual Muslim credo. "Allah be with you, Yusuf."

Upon his exit, the relieved and ebullient Abu was greeted not by his friend Talil, but by two black-robed Arabs, the likes of whom he had not seen before in the compound. Their headdresses, also black as a moonless Saharan night, were wrapped around their heads and chins, so that only the barest glimpse of their ebony skin and coal-dot eyes were discernible. By prearranged direction from bin Wahhab, one of the men seized Abu's arms and held him tightly. The other raised a pistol and fired it point-blank into the base of the startled man's skull. The bullet severed the spinal cord, carrying splinters of bone with it as it exited at the front of the throat. As to whether or not Abu Yusuf was now with Allah, as bin Wahhab had wished upon him, was anybody's guess.

* * *

Upon returning to the Lubianka after their briefing at the Ministry of Defense, Medved, Buzhkin, and Falcon were immediately summoned to the Director's office.

"We don't have much time. In three days, the American commando team will be here and you will all go into intensive training," Aksanov said as the agents settled into the large, leather-covered chairs that fronted his desk. "Beforehand, it will be necessary to move the Feliks agent, Yusopov, to our safe house. Viktor, I want you to assemble a small transfer team—four of your best and most trusted men. Major Medved, I want you to be part of the team. It will give you an opportunity to see your daughter."

Sergei, who was about to light a cigarette, instantly lowered his burning match and fixed his eyes on the Director. He was speechless only for a second or two…just long enough for the match flame to singe his forefinger. "But how…and where…and—"

"It's all arranged. She's in the same *Dome Byezopasnee* that you'll be taking Yusopov—just outside of Yekaterinburg. Sergeant Buzhkin knows it well. He will guide you there. Viktor, I believe you also have family in Yekaterinburg?"

The big man nodded affirmatively.

"Good, then you will have an opportunity to visit them as well. You can both leave tomorrow, but I want you back here in three days. I'm signing your orders as I speak."

"Yes, of course. Thank you, sir," Medved said, re-lighting his cigarette. "But, I have a further request."

Aksanov glanced up from his paperwork. "Yes, Major?"

"A woman is being held by Chief of Police Dmitri Kirilovitch. She is the widow of one of those weasels that was killed in the fracas the other evening. She tried to warn Kirilovitch of the *Rooka's* planned kidnapping of Michael Falcon. Because of that, she is now in danger of retaliation from the mafiosi. I would like her moved to the FSB facility at Yekaterinburg, also."

"Kirilovitch has an excellent record. What makes you think he can't protect her?"

"I have no doubt that he can. It's just that his facilities…." Medved paused, feeling that his reasons would be too transparent to Aksanov.

"I have two points to make on this subject." Three surprised heads swiveled toward the speaker, Viktor Buzhkin. "Number one, she is in danger because, as it turned out, she tried to help one of our own— *Gospodeen* Falcon. It is our duty to protect such people. Number two, it was we who shot her mafia husband into pieces and thus we are directly responsible for her plight. I would be ashamed to be a member of the FSB if we turn our back on this woman."

Medved's first instinct was to light a match and burn his fingers again. The sensation would reveal whether he was just dreaming or in fact he actually had heard Buzhkin utter these words. Before he was able to act on this impulse, however, the Director spoke.

"Well, what am I to do in the face of such impassioned logic. All right, Sergei, make the arrangements with Kirilovitch to have the woman transferred into our custody. I'll have the papers drawn up. Now, if there are no further requests…"

"I do have one more, General," Buzhkin said. He turned toward the American. "I would like to ask *Gospodeen* Falcon to accompany us to Yekaterinburg."

The Director nodded to Falcon. "That sounds like a wonderful idea," Aksanov said. "But you better dress warmly, Michael. It tends to get a bit chilly on the other side of the Urals at this time of year—you're entering Siberia, you realize. Did you know that, in that land they don't even use cartons to carry their milk? They just tote it around in frozen blocks and let it thaw in pots by their fireplaces."

Falcon laughed but Buzhkin well knew the truth of the statement. "There's no such thing as weather that's too cold," the Siberian said…"Just clothing that's too poor."

"I'll be sure to wear my thermal underwear," Falcon smiled.

"*Harasho!*"Aksanov exclaimed. "I'll have your orders prepared."

Yes, and I wonder just exactly what those orders will read, Medved thought. *How convenient to have Falcon and me isolated on the other side of the Urals with Buzhkin as our guide.* "But is this wise…sending the three of us together so far from Moscow," he said.

"If you'd rather not see your daughter, Major…." Aksanov replied.

"Of course, General. What can there possibly be to worry about?"

"Then all is settled," Aksanov said. "Try not to freeze on me and be back here in my office three mornings from tomorrow. That is all."

* * *

Early the following morning, the green and red *Rossia* passenger train rumbled out of Moscow, headed for the Ural Mountains and eventually Vladivostok on the Pacific Coast. General Aksanov had arranged for private cars for his agents and their two charges, Yelena Kuzmitch and Gregori Yusopov. The trip to Yekaterinburg would take approximately a full day and night, depending upon the amount of snow on the track. Medved preferred the shorter travel time of flying but it was FSB policy to never use air transportation to move people under its protection. It simply presented too big an invitation for an aviation disaster. In addition, control of the rails provided the agency with a number of options in pursuing its own designs.

As Yelena arranged her compartment, Medved, Falcon, and Buzhkin convened around a small pull-out card table. A brass tea kettle and three steaming cups sat on the metal table top.

"Keep your weapons loaded and on you at all times, and stay alert," Sergei said.

"Do you really think that the *Rook*a will try something here?" Falcon asked.

"Not at all," Medved responded. "It's not their style to pick on those that can defend themselves. I'm concerned about a much more dangerous organization. The Feliks will be after Yusopov to silence him or to at least find out what information he has conveyed to us. Viktor, what do you think? Are the Feliks on to us by now?""

"Medved, If you don't know," Buzhkin grunted, "I don't know how you expect me to."

Sergei settled back in his seat and gazed at the flat, snow-blanketed countryside that glided past his window. Lighting a cigarette and inhaling, he then leaned forward and spoke to Buzhkin in a hushed tone.

"Viktor, there is one matter that has been troubling me and I believe you could set my mind to rest."

Buzhkin was busy rummaging through his overnight bag as Medved spoke. "Ah, here it is," he said triumphantly, placing on the table a brown paper wrapped object that was the size of his massive forearm. "I'll be happy to help you if it is in my power," he mumbled, unwrapping his prize. The inner papers were stained with grease and blood.

"You recall our trip to St. Petersburg a little while back," Medved said, watching the large man with fascination.

"Mm-hm," Buzhkin muttered, peeling away the last drenched scrap of paper and extracting a club-sized, freshly cooked goose leg. Although the cuisine on the Trans-Siberian was slightly more palatable than on other Russian railroad lines, it was still common practice for the passengers to bring their home cooking on board.

"The night we were to meet for dinner, we were both late. You were late because you followed me to the piers, am I not right?"

Buzhkin nodded, his full mouth not permitting a verbal response.

"Then you must know that I was shot at that evening and that I wounded my assailant in the leg."

"Yes," Buzhkin said after swallowing a large chunk of the meat and washing it down with half of his cup of tea.

"Viktor, then you also must know how troubled I was to see you dragging your leg the next morning in the hotel lobby."

"Told you. It was my old war wound. It acts up in rainy weather and it was a wash-out that night."

"Ah, yes. The wound incurred while serving with Vaznetsov's 32nd Rifle Brigade, outside of Kabul." *Could it be? Could it be that my first suspicions of him were correct? And here I am locked in a railroad car with him and four of his hand-picked men....*

"I hope you aren't going to quiz me on my military experience again," Buzhkin grumbled, pouring himself another cup of tea. "Look, I wouldn't have been limping at all if you hadn't gotten in the way. I had my *Gurza* trained on that *doo-rok* until you came crashing out of the building and onto the pier. I dove to one side to avoid putting a round into your butt and for my troubles landed in a puddle the size of Lake Baikal—and the same frigid temperature, I might add. By the time I got up, you had both disappeared. I promised the General I would look after you but, *Bozha Moy,* you made the job a lot more difficult. The metal plate in my knee-cap completely froze up. I was lucky to even make it back to the hotel."

"Your metal knee knee-cap froze up," Medved repeated.

Buzhkin frowned at first, then slowly broke into a wide, toothy grin. "All to keep from shooting your tail off."

"Hey, Sergei, here comes your woman," Falcon said, nodding toward the far door.

Medved tamped out his cigarette and rose, his eyes fixed on Yelena Kuzmitch. He didn't notice that the slender, auburn-haired beauty had attracted the attention of every other agent in the railway car as well. He was only aware that, in her flower-embroidered peasant blouse, long suede skirt, and leather boots, she rekindled yet more memories and feelings long thought dead. As she slipped onto a seat next to a window, Sergei strode down the passageway toward her.

"Major Medved," she smiled, motioning him to sit alongside her.

"Are you comfortable in your quarters, *Gospozha* Kuzmitch?" he asked. "Is there anything you need?"

"Thank you, I'm perfectly happy with my accommodations. You…everyone…have been very kind."

Now that he was closer to her, he could see that her eyes did not reflect the feigned joy of her lips.

"You know, where we are taking you is actually very nice," he said. "Much better than the cell you were stuck in back at the *Militsiya* Headquarters. And it will only be for a short time, until…."

"Until the mafiosi are completely destroyed?" she said bitterly. "You know I'll never recover my life, so there's no use in trying to deceive me."

Sergei fell silent, unable to conceive an answer that would not only be reassuring, but truthful as well.

"Forgive me, Major. My outburst was rude."

"No offense was given," Sergei said. "Therefore, none can be taken. It is only natural that all these rapid changes in your life should cause you to feel some apprehension. Here, let me show you something that might help put your mind at ease." Reaching into his back pocket he produced a well-worn brown billfold and from one of its compartments withdrew a faded color photograph of a broadly smiling adolescent girl. Two long blonde braids, each tied at the ends with grand blue ribbons, framed her face. Her bright eyes, the same hue of the bows, shone with the untrammeled vitality and optimism of youth.

"This is my eight-year old daughter…Galena, whom I spoke of when we were in the office of Police Chief Kirilovitch" he beamed, laying the image on the compartment's fold-out metal table. "She prefers Galya…as she thinks that doesn't sound as stuffy."

"She's a beautiful child," Yelena said.

"Yes…that is because her looks are from her mother's side. She is also quite talented—a dancer, like yourself. Her dream is to dance with the Kirov or the Bolshoi."

"You and your wife must be very proud of her."

"We were. I mean, I still am, of course. However, two years ago my wife left this world."

"Oh, I'm so—"

"No, no, please. It's not just because I'm a doting father that I show you this picture," Sergei hastily interjected. "I wanted you to know that my own daughter has been living in the place to which you now travel. I love her more than my own life, so you realize I would have never put her there unless I truly believed it was necessary and acceptable."

"Thank you. You have made me feel better…and somewhat ashamed. I promise I shall try to be every bit as brave as your Galya. I remember now that you said in the *Militsiya* office that you hoped I would meet her. It appears that fate is granting your request. Please, tell me more about her."

"Of course. Why, just this past year, she danced the role of Clara in the Nutcracker...."

Yelena studied Sergei's rugged, yet captivating face as he spoke, observed his rough hands gently cup his daughter's photo, listened to his words of genuine affection for Galya, and wondered if she would ever experience such a pure love.

*   *   *

Encountering no weather delays, the Trans-Siberian was slightly ahead of schedule when it approached Kazan late in the afternoon. A pale yellow sun suffused with the glimmer of pinkish, blue-white snow on the horizon. The train rumbled across a steel trestle bridge that spanned a winding, frozen waterway.

"The Volga," Medved said, approaching Falcon. The two men had not been in contact since Sergei had gone to visit Yelena Kuzmitch that morning.

"Yes, it's beautiful, even when iced over," the American nodded, gazing at the ribbon of white. "The river of song and of the Russian soul."

Medved sat on the bench across from Falcon. "Kazan is next. It's a pity we can't spend some time there. It's quite picturesque and contains much of our history. Ivan the Terrible defeated the Tatars here five hundred years ago. Tolstoy studied law at its university last century."

"And then, of course, there was that other Kazan University law student—Vladimir Ilyitch Ulyanov," Falcon interjected.

"So, you are a student of my country's history," Sergei grinned in surprise. "And do you also know that Ulyanov obtained his surname from his small hometown—Ulyanovsk—located only a few miles south of here? But, of course, he changed his name during the Revolution. The world got to know him better as Lenin."

"Now I don't often say this, but there's one guy who should've just stayed in the practice of law," Falcon quipped.

"Yes, that certainly might have saved many people from much travail," Medved smiled. Then, assuming a more serious tone, he said, "Michael, soon it will be dark. When you decide to retire for the evening, be sure to lock your door. I have asked Viktor to stand watch by Yusopov's room. I will be outside *Gospozha* Kuzmitch's door. As I said earlier, I don't expect any trouble, but it is wise to be on guard. By the way, please join Viktor, Yelena Pavlovna, and myself for dinner this evening. We'll be dining in one hour, just after the train leaves Kazan. Which reminds me…be especially alert when we are stopped at the city station. No telling who will be boarding."

As he spoke, the five-hundred year old towers of the Kazan Kremlin were just coming into view. The train was beginning to slow.

"Well, 'til later this evening," Sergei said as he rose and departed.

A few moments later, the *Rossiya* rumbled to a metal-clattering, steam-hissing halt at the station. Falcon leaned his head against the cold windowpane and observed the movements of the dark, heavily-clad figures on the boarding platform. The swirling snow, the hunched, rigid postures, the scarf-muffled faces and the fog-like breaths combined to aptly convey the reality of the sub-zero temperature.

A family—a man, a woman, and two young children—passed beneath his window, wrestling with their luggage as they boarded. Waiting their turn behind them, two soldiers in gray greatcoats and with duffel bags slung over their shoulders, stamped their feet and blew hot air into their frozen fingers. Soon they were on the steps of the train car and only one other boarding passenger remained behind them. Slowly, this last figure turned, looking up toward Falcon. Only the feline eyes were visible between the fur hat and the face muffler—and then only for an instant—but that was enough to cause Falcon to bolt from his seat. He charged to the door, pushing his way through the congestion of children, parents, soldiers, and luggage, and leaped from the car. There was no sign of life on the platform. Drawing his Glock, he worked his way along the side of the train, glancing beneath, between, and in the windows of the cars.

A shrill whistle pierced the cold air three times, then was followed by the conductor's call for 'all aboard.' Turning back, he tucked his weapon in its holster and trotted back to his car. The *Rossiya* was already beginning to roll when he grasped the stairway handle and swung up to the boarding steps. He cast one final glance toward the platform, then reentered his car.

Chapter Twenty-Nine

After dinner, Falcon and Medved embarked on a second tour of all the cars of the *Rossiya*. Their first inspection had occurred immediately upon Falcon's report of the cat-eyed figure he had spotted on the Kazan railroad station platform. Neither search, however, proved fruitful.

"Perhaps I'm just tired and my imagination has begun playing tricks on me," Falcon said as they returned to their car.

"I wish I could believe that," Sergei replied. "Unfortunately, it seems to me that your mind doesn't work that way. I don't think it was a phantom that you saw and we would be well-advised to increase our vigilance."

As he spoke, they walked past a table where two of the agents were playing cards. The others were on guard at the car entrances.

"Nothing more can be done at this moment, however" Sergei continued. "It's late and you must be weary. We have our top people on board and we're ready for any contingency, so if you'd like to rest...."

"Perhaps in a bit," Falcon responded. "Maybe I'll play a few hands of Queen of Spades."

"Ha! Better guard your American bread from those Russian wolves," Sergei grinned, nodding at his fellow agents.

★ ★ ★

Medved's advice proved all too sound as Falcon decided to cut his losses after three hands.

"We'll be in Yekaterinburg shortly after sunrise," Sergei said. "See you then."

Bidding the Russian good night, Falcon closed the door behind him. His quarters, particularly with the wall berth dropped into place, were extremely cramped. Crawling into the small bed, he was disappointed to discover that he was not quite able to fully extend his legs. This proved to be of little consequence, however, for he quickly fell asleep.

*   *   *

He didn't know what time it was, nor for a brief moment even where he was, when he woke. He knew only that it was still dark and that a thump in the passageway had roused him. He lay still, watching the moonlit white countryside, clutched in long-fingered shadows, glide by his window. And he listened. *There!* The thump was repeated. Silently, he rolled to his right, removed the Glock from its shoulder holster that hung from the guardrail and descended from his berth. Slowly, quietly, he slid the deadbolt open and turned the doorknob. With a slight push, the door pivoted noiselessly on its hinges. The car was cloaked in black except for the soft glow of moonlight that streamed through a window further forward.

In the pale opalescent glimmer, he saw the forms of several FSB agents, still surrounding the table at which they had been playing cards. Falcon stepped cautiously into the passageway and moved toward the figures. It appeared that they had all fallen asleep at the table. Yet, there was a peculiar incongruity between a seemingly restful slumber and their contorted poses. As Falcon drew nearer, the paradox was resolved. Each of the agents had a dime-size dark red hole in the forehead. Their blood had spilled down their chests, over the scattered cards on the table, across the bench seats, and onto the floor. Falcon now felt the sticky liquid squishing beneath his shoes.

His heart began to race as he looked further down the passageway, to where Medved was on guard at the door of Yelena Kuzmitch. In the dim light, he could discern Sergei's frame, sitting with his back against the woman's door. Holding the Glock with both hands and glancing in each direction of the corridor, Falcon began to edge apprehensively toward his colleague. At Falcon's approach, Medved turned his head.

"Michael, is that you?" he whispered.

"Sergei! You're still alive!"

Medved gripped Falcon's arms and held him in his gaze. "You were right, Michael."

"What do you mean? What has happened?!"

"She's on board. It's up to you now to stop her. You must!" In his excited state, Medved's breathing became more labored. Making a conscious effort to regain his composure, he wheezed, "And, Michael, my friend, please look after Yelena, will you? I'm afraid I'll no longer be able."

As he finished speaking, his head rolled forward and he slumped to the floor. It was then that Falcon saw the telltale dark hole in his friend's left temple.

"Sergei! Sergei!" Falcon pleaded to no avail. Gently placing his left forefinger on Medved's carotid artery, he found that the life-giving vessel was completely inert.

Glancing cautiously around him, Falcon rose deliberately and stood before Yelena's door. Holding the Glock at the ready in one hand, he turned the doorknob. At this moment, the *Rossiya* hurtled into a tunnel and, with the moonlight blocked, the car was plunged into total darkness. Seemingly in slow motion, the door pivoted open. The interior was black as a grave and Falcon strained all of his senses to penetrate the gloom. He did not have to wait long, for the train suddenly emerged from the tunnel and the streaming moonlight illuminated the blonde hair, green eyes and grinning face of Svetlana Popova.

The shrill whistle of the train screeched through Falcon's head and he sat bolt upright in bed. A few moments later, the noise of the whistle faded and he could hear sounds from the passageway. There was laughter and light-hearted exclamations. The agents were still playing cards. Most satisfying of all, he could hear an occasional comment from Sergei. He glanced at his watch. A few minutes past two a.m. He decided to get up and put his money at risk in the card game as he didn't expect to fall asleep again this night.

*   *   *

Falcon was still awake when the sun rose. The landscape that now gradually took shape before his eyes was far different from the flat, broad vista through which the train had rumbled the previous day. They were well into the Urals, the range of mountains that divided European Russia and Asia. In only a few more minutes, they would be in Yekaterinburg, a city whose existence was not recognized on tourist maps until recently.

One reason for this secrecy was that a Top Secret missile base was located nearby. In fact, it was missiles launched from this installation that brought down Francis Gary Powers and the American U-2 spy plane during the Eisenhower administration, threatening to turn the cold war hot. But the military significance of the city was not the true reason for its 'non-existence.'

Falcon was all too well acquainted with the angst of the former Communist regime over Yekaterinburg. Two decades earlier, in defiance of the Soviet government's standing edicts, he had slipped into and out of this unique city. He reflected on how young and foolish he had been then...and lucky to have escaped undetected. But he had to see for himself...had to see the place—the Ipatyev House—where Tsar Nicholas II and his family were murdered by the Soviets and the thousand-year rule of the tsars was brought to an end

"Yekaterinburg." Falcon heard the name pronounced almost in a whisper. He turned to see Viktor Buzhkin leaning toward him, gazing through the window to the spires and rooftops of the approaching city. "Yekaterinburg," Buzhkin repeated. "The Ipatyev House is gone. The locals have erected a cross and wooden chapel on the site of the assassination."

"Yes," Falcon nodded, wondering if this enigmatic man could read his mind. "I remember reading years ago that the little known party boss of the town ordered its destruction."

"Boris Yeltsin," Buzhkin grunted. "Gather your baggage. We've almost arrived. And I have a little surprise in store for Major Medved."

∗   ∗   ∗

As he stepped from the Trans-Siberian at the Yekaterinburg train station, Falcon closely scrutinized the passengers disembarking from the other cars. Their number was few enough so that it was possible to examine each face. None, however, fit the description of the apparition that had ruined his night's sleep. Further up the platform, another half dozen FSB agents had been awaiting the arrival of the *Rossiya*. In their midst was the surprise that Buzhkin had mentioned. Medved took no notice at first, as he was concentrating on escorting Gregori Yusopov and Kuzmitch from the train. It was only when he heard the excited cry, "Papa!" that he turned to see the joyful face of his daughter.

"Galyooshka!" he exclaimed, stooping to receive the onrushing child. As he swept her up, she threw her arms around his neck, kissing his cheeks.

"I missed you," she said, clasping him tightly, as though he might disappear if she let go.

"Ey, my little ermine" Sergei laughed, "if you first don't choke me to death, I want to introduce you to my friends."

He lowered her to the ground where she curtsied in turn to Falcon, Buzhkin, and Kuzmitch. Each of these strangers made a distinctly unique and unforgettable impression upon her—Falcon, who fulfilled her lifelong dream to some day meet an American and who further enchanted her with his warm but rascally smile; Yelena, who charmed her with her natural beauty and the fact, as reported by her father, that she had danced with the Kirov; and finally, Buzhkin, who simply frightened her. Owing to this last impression, she was somewhat unnerved when she heard the grizzly-bear sized man invite them to spend the day and night at his house. Even more unsettling was her father's response.

"Thank you, Viktor," Sergei said. "Yes, it would give me a better opportunity to visit with my daughter."

"*Harasho!*" Buzhkin blurted. "And we'll bring along *Gospozha* Kuzmitch, as well. It will be so much the better for everyone." He then turned to the agents from the compound to complete the transfer of Yusopov into their hands.

Settling into one of the FSB sedans, Yusopov glanced perplexedly back at Buzhkin. Even now he was uncertain as to where the Siberian's loyalties lay. But it was a problem that he need no longer worry about. Momentarily, the Zhiguli carrying him rumbled off to the west, flanked fore and aft by two agency escort cars. Shortly afterwards, Buzhkin and his party left the station in another FSB Zhiguli, heading in the opposite direction.

It took nearly an hour to reach the Buzhkin *izba* which was located east of Yekaterinburg, well out in the countryside. The blue cottage would have disappeared against the rich azure of the clear Siberian sky if it had not been brightly accentuated by its white shutters and doors. It was framed on the left by a gnarled old gray oak tree and on the right by a tall, triple-trunked birch. As they pulled into the snow-covered dirt driveway, the front door of the house flung open. A thick-coated brown dog, the size of an adult male wolf, loped out, eyeing the newcomers inquisitively.

"*Ey, Volkodov!*" Buzhkin shouted. 'Wolfdog' paused, perked its ears, then bounded across the snow toward the disembarking group. "Don't be afraid," Buzhkin said to the wide-eyed Galena. "Watch this." He raised his hand and, as if he were wielding a pistol, pointed the index finger at the charging canine. Volkodov was nearly upon him when Buzhkin yelled, "Bang!" The dog sprang into the air and flipped onto his back. He lay motionless in the snow, all four paws pointing toward the wide Siberian sky. At his master's command of "Up!" Volkodov scrambled to his feet and, wagging his tail, approached his master. Galena giggled with delight at the suddenly less fearsome animal.

Two other figures now emerged on the front porch. One was a diminutive, rosy-cheeked *babushka* who was dressed in a shawl, boots, and full-length, flower-print peasant dress. Her plump, weather-lined face radiated a broad, kindly grin at the sight of her son. By her side stood Buzhkin's father, Boltai, a sturdy, bronze-faced man of Mongolian stock who was clad in a sheepskin Cossack jacket, brown, billowing Caucasus trousers, and felt boots. One hand rested on the shoulder of his wife, Masha, while the other held a curving, long-stemmed smoking pipe. It was obvious as they hugged and kissed their son that the elderly couple was jubilant at his arrival and held a genuine affection for him.

"Come in! Come in!" the ebullient Masha said, taking Yelena and Galena by the arms as if they were old friends. "You'll catch your death of cold standing out here."

Falcon peered once more down the road they had just traveled. Again, as the case had been with every such scrutiny the past half-hour, there was no other vehicle in sight. He and Sergei exchanged glances, then followed the others into the house.

In more of a trot than a walk, Masha led her guests into a small foyer, where they doffed their overcoats, *shapkas*, and scarves. The entry was cluttered with iron pots full of dried plants, roots, and herbs. A redolent air of burning cedar mixed with that of a freshly baked sweet potato pie filled their nostrils.

Saying that she must look in on her cooking, Masha hurried off to the kitchen and Boltai escorted the group into the living room. The area was unpretentious with its natural hardwood walls and floor, its one Afghan-adorned sofa, two hand-carved oak chairs, a wooden rocker, and a small birchwood table. Yet, the warm sheen of the wood, the glow, heat and cedar aroma of the crackling fireplace, and the colorful thick Persian rug that covered half of the floor, lent it a cozy atmosphere. Volkodov, still muddy and snowy from playing dead, followed them in and headed directly toward his favorite spot in the household, a rumpled old quilt that lay by the fireplace.

Boltai offered to bring in extra chairs, but Sergei, Galena, and Yelena adamantly refused, insisting that they would be happier on the carpet, sharing the fireplace with the shaggy Wolfdog. Bidding his guests to sit where they pleased and to relax, Boltai took his accustomed position in his rocker and placed the stem of the pipe in his mouth, between the long, drooping ends of his thin, Cossack-style mustache. He began tamping tobacco in the pipe's bowl, which he had skillfully carved to resemble the face of a jaunty old man, curiously resembling himself.

"American, yes?" he smiled, turning to Falcon who had settled into one of the oak chairs. "I like Americans. I met some in '45, just outside of Berlin, or what was left of the Nazi capital then. They were infantry like myself, from a place called Brook Leen. Do you know it?"

"Brooklyn, yes. It's in New York City."

"Oh, have you been to New York?" Galena squealed. She was flush with excitement. This was turning out to be the most important day of her life. Not only was she reunited with her father, if just for one day, but she also felt the electricity between him and this gorgeous woman—a ballerina of the Kirov—whom she could only hope to emulate. And now she had her first opportunity to speak with an American and to find out if the buildings really were as tall as she had read, and if every family had a house and an automobile—some even two cars—which, of course, she knew could not possibly be true.

"*Zakooski. Pirozhki*," Masha laughed, trotting into the room with a large tray of hors d'oeuvres—roasted walnuts, black bread and honey, mushrooms and cream, pickled cabbage, Siberian cranberries, pearl-hued Beluga and golden-yellow Ossetra caviar, Georgian cognac and Buzhkin's favorite brew—*kvass*. She set the tray on the birchwood table, stepped back to admire her creation, and blurted, "Everyone eat! Eat!" Then she pinched her son on the cheek, asked him to help her with the samovar, and bustled back to the kitchen.

As the group began to follow her bidding, Falcon took advantage of the moment to study his environment. Over the stone fireplace hung an antiquated rifle, its well-nicked wooden stock indicative of its many years of service.

"Well, I'll be damned," Falcon muttered. "A Tokarev Forty."

"You know this rifle?" Boltai asked, moving next to Falcon.

"Of course. The Russian infantryman's weapon in World War Two. The rifle that won the Eastern Front. I didn't know any were still in existence."

Boltai emitted a joyful cackle. "More than just in existence, *soodar*. Still in use. This one has served me quite well, thank you very much…first, for five years fighting the Nazis, and the last fifty years in putting food on our plates."

"Remarkable," Falcon marveled, wondering what tales must lie behind the crinkly eyes of the old Cossack.

"Tea, everyone," Buzhkin said, entering with a samovar.

"You must certainly all try this," his father smiled, walking toward the table. "It is my Masha's very own creation, made from berries, leaves, and roots that she has gathered."

"Ah, the iron pots in the foyer…." Falcon noted.

"Yes, enough plants to keep us in tea even through a Siberian winter," Boltai grinned broadly.

They had barely begun to sample the beverages and hors d'oeuvres when his wife scurried in with a tray, full of meats and fish—venison, garlic sausage, smoked sturgeon, and salted herring.

"Perhaps now you understand how my son grew to his size," Boltai grinned.

The succulence—and abundance—of the food, the heat of the fireplace, the warmth of the cognac, and the hospitality of the hosts produced a strong sense of conviviality by the end of dinner. During the meal, Boltai had regaled them with one tale after another about his life in Siberia. Galena was most fascinated by his description of the "bat-sized" mosquitoes that every summer swarmed over travelers in the *taiga*—the dense northern forests.

"Why, I've even seen them carry off a little girl about your size," he said solemnly to the astonished Galena.

"Boltai! Don't frighten the child so!" Masha chided her husband.

"Tfoo! She knows I'm teasing. But I'll make it up to her. Viktor tells me you're a ballerina, little one. If an old Cossack such as myself were to play a tune for you on the balalaika, would you dance for us?"

Galena blushed, shyly refusing the request as she sunk into the security of her father's arms.

"Come," Yelena said, gently resting her hand on the reluctant girl's arm. "We'll dance together."

Galena, flattered by Yelena's attention, nodded assent.

"*Harasho!*" Boltai grinned, swallowing his last piece of sweet potato pie and wiping his mouth with a white cotton napkin. "Viktor, could you please bring me Natasha." He used his pet name for the balalaika that he had crafted fifty years earlier from spruce and birchwood and had colorfully painted with a scene from a Russian folk-tale. "She's in her accustomed place by the bedroom door."

When Buzhkin returned with the balalaika, the group had gathered in a semi-circle in front of the fireplace and the Persian carpet had been rolled out of the way. Settling back into his rocker with his pipe in his mouth, Boltai began to lovingly pluck the strings of the instrument.

Yelena, untying a bright red scarf from around her neck and holding it in one hand, slowly began to move gracefully to the tempo of the balalaika's distinctly Russian sound. Smiling serenely and without interrupting her dance, she fluttered the silken material to Galena. The young girl grasped the end of the scarf and with an excited, joyous face, glided forward. Smoothly, she rose on the toes of her right foot, and with her left leg delicately arced, twirled slowly under the arm of Yelena. The pair moved daintily but confidently, in total concert, admirably interpreting Boltai's airs. They performed as though they had been rehearsing with each other—and with the merry old Siberian—all their lives. When the dance ended, their audience broke into spirited applause, none clapping more enthusiastically than Sergei, whose eyes were glistening with pride.

"Beautifully done, ladies," Boltai chuckled. "Now I will ask my son to uphold the honor of the male gender."

After profusely objecting, Buzhkin finally surrendered to the insistence of the group. Folding his arms across his chest, he leaped onto the hardwood floor, landing in a crouched position. Boltai resumed his playing, but much more zestfully and began singing.

Kalinka, Kalinka, Kalinka Moya! Ey!

In alternating rhythm, Buzhkin kicked his feet out, striking toward the far wall, then rapidly bringing them beneath him once again. It appeared he would surely topple backwards as Boltai increased the tempo on the balalaika, but he continued to maintain his crouched position, his arms folded and his feet flying ever more feverishly. As he performed, he called to Medved and Falcon, beckoning them to join him. Prodded by the women, the two men jumped next to Buzhkin and began kicking and hopping in a Herculean effort at synchronizing their Cossack dance. Medved gazed into Yelena's eyes as Boltai continued his song.

Ah, my beauty, my darling girl,
Fall now in love with me,
Kalinka, Kalinka, Kalinka, my love! Ey!
In the garden…under the pines,
The green boughs above,
Sleep, lie next to me
Kalinka! Kalinka! Kalinka, my love! Ey!

The onlookers clapped and stamped their feet in rhythm and even Volkodov showed his appreciation by howling. Finally, Boltai increased the beat to a level that his Cossacks couldn't match and the three men collapsed to the floor. Galena shrieked with joy as the others applauded and laughed heartily.

"Ey, father, I don't think you got those verses exactly right!" Buzhkin growled.

"I had to adjust so you wouldn't all have heart attacks," Boltai winked.

"Whew, I must stop smoking," Sergei wheezed. "And it's awfully hot in here after all that exercise. I'm going to get some fresh air."

"Can you handle a horse and sleigh?" Buzhkin asked, sitting up.

"It's been a few years…but, yes."

"Fine. I'll hitch up Sophie and you can take your daughter and *Gospozha* Kuzmitch for a little ride. Sophie is a very docile mare. Just let her take the lead and she'll bring you home…slowly but surely."

"Oh please, father, say yes!" Galena blurted, hugging her father.

"You say this Sophie is docile?" Medved, sighing resignedly, asked Buzhkin.

Fifteen minutes later, Sergei, Yelena, and Galena, tucked under several layers of heavy furs, were gliding over the snow in the sleigh drawn by Sophie, a dappled beige 'docile' mare. It was already dark and the three-quarter moon drifted in and out of fluffy, back-lit indigo clouds. Sophie had more spunk than Buzhkin had admitted and set across the white carpet of snow at a brisk clip. Her three passengers, tears streaming from eyes whipped by the frigid breeze, laughed gaily.

Galena had not experienced such a happy moment for two years, when her mother had still been alive. Nestled in the middle of the sleigh, she tucked one arm into that of her father on her left, and the other into Yelena's arm on her right. She squeezed both arms tightly, her bright eyes shining in the reflected moonlight, her face radiant with joy. The image of her father's bold dancing, the tunes of Boltai's balalaika, the icicle-covered trees that flitted by, the sense of security and belonging she felt snuggled between her father and Yelena, invoked in her the impression that she was floating through a fairy tale. Real or fantasy, it was a story that she never wanted to end.

"Oh, papa, I'm so happy," she giggled, kissing first Sergei's cheek, then Yelena's.

An hour later, when Sophie finally stomped to a halt back in front of the *izba*, Galena was fast asleep. Sergei lifted his daughter from the sleigh and carried her into the house. Masha greeted them at the door and led the way to the bed that she had prepared for the youth.

"I'll see that she gets properly tucked in, *soodar*," the cherub-faced *babushka* smiled, taking the sleeping bundle in her strong farmer's arms. Kissing his daughter's forehead, Sergei withdrew and went outside to tend to the mare.

Buzhkin was already on the job when Medved appeared. "I'll take care of her," the Siberian said. "It's a one person task and you would only get in the way." As he spoke, he turned and led the unhitched mare to her stall.

Medved returned to the *izba* shedding his greatcoat, *shapka*, scarf, and heavy, mud-flecked boots in the foyer. The house was now dark except for the faint illumination afforded by the burning cedar logs, once blazing, now reduced to a mellow flame. A solitary figure stood before the fireplace, her hands outstretched above the flickering, warm red tongues. Medved, feeling curiously invigorated in spite of his lack of sleep and his recent physical exertion, stepped toward Yelena, saying, "These Siberians know how to build a house that will keep out the winter."

"Yes," she answered quietly. "There's not a breath of cold air seeping in. Listen...do you hear that?"

He stood motionless next to Yelena, feeling both the warmth of the fire and of her body. The dulcet sound of the balalaika could be heard emanating from another room. "Yes, that Boltai can certainly play. In fact, that's my favorite tune..."*Ochee Chornaya.*"

"Mine as well," Yelena smiled. "'Dark Eyes'...how beautiful."

"Very. Tell me, do you think a Kirov ballerina would risk her toes and dance with an old war-horse?"

She turned, placed one hand gently at the nape of his neck and joined the other in his clasp. Slowly, they glided around the room to the haunting balalaika strains of 'Dark Eyes', feeling the subtle movements and interplay of the muscles of their backs, thighs, and hips.

He felt guilty about the joy he was experiencing but he was not sure why. *Perhaps it is because I hold her up to my memory of Irina. And that is unfair to her.* "Yelena Pavlovna, there is something I must tell you...." he began.

She stopped dancing, placed two fingers gently on his lips and, without a further word passing between them, they fell into a deep embrace. Even at this moment, Medved's eyes were open, gazing through a window toward the barn where he had last seen his inscrutable colleague.

Inside the stable, hidden from Medved's view, Buzhkin was speaking into a telephone. "I told you that it would be too difficult...especially after Falcon saw you board at Kazan...we'll be back in Moscow the day after tomorrow...yes...I understand...the back-up plan will go into effect...."

As he spoke, Mike Falcon pressed his ear against a crack in the wooden stable wall and listened intensively.

Chapter Thirty

Commander Hardin 'Hardy' O'Brien had joined the Navy for two reasons. First, the service offered an opportunity to escape the destitution and despair of his youth in a South Philadelphia slum. Second, his parish priest, Father McGloughlin—who was the young O'Brien's only role model—stoutly maintained that it would give him a chance to combat Communism, *'that atheistic monstrosity that is a greater evil in the world than the gangsters in the neighborhood, my son'*. He was only sixteen when he appeared at the recruiting office at the Naval shipyard on the Philadelphia waterfront, having manipulated his birth certificate to satisfy the military's age requirements. From the first moment, he had found a home. He thrived on the physical challenges and mental mind games of basic training and then SEAL school, that washed out so many others but proved readily conquerable to one from his tough streets.

His greatest moment came early in his career, twenty-five years ago when his unit was deployed to the Republic of Vietnam. The U.S. had thrown in the towel and was retreating from its Embassy rooftop in Saigon. Long after the last helicopter had lifted off and the first North Vietnamese Army tanks had rumbled into the former South Vietnamese capital, O'Brien's SEAL team was still 'in-country'. Their assignment was to mine the harbors and to destroy as much abandoned U.S. Navy equipment as possible.

For two weeks after the fall of Saigon, there were still twenty American fighting men carrying on the war in South Vietnam. The NVA referred to them as phantoms, for they were never seen. Only their work was visible—exploded munitions, sunken ships, blocked harbor channels, and scores of dead sentries. It was during this period that O'Brien had first applied the techniques that he had learned in SEAL school of stealthy disposal of the enemy. Although he found the up-close human element to be decidedly unpleasant work, he continually reminded himself of Father McGloughlin's conviction that he was fighting a Holy War against the Great Satan of the world. For his performance in this operation, he was awarded the Navy Cross and a trip to Officer's Candidate School. He would become, in Navy parlance, a 'Mustang', an enlisted man who has worked his way into the officer's ranks.

In this second phase of his career, it was an easy decision to specialize in Sovietology. He did a tour at the Armed Forces Linguistics School in Monterrey to learn the Russian language and became the Navy's chief expert in Spetsnaz tactics and equipment. When 'the balloon' went up, he would be ready to lead his men against the 'Rooskies'. Ironically, however, his drive to know his enemy had ultimately resulted in the President's decision to select him and his men for a crucial joint military operation with that very same foe. Thus, never in his wildest dreams had he imagined that he would be sitting in the War Room of the Russian Ministry of Defense, having a chat with the Commandant of the Spetsnaz and the Director of the KGB's successor organization while surrounded by a dozen Russian Army officers.

At least, in addition to Lt. Rochelle who sat at his side, there was one other American in the room. *But what the hell was this Mike Falcon's story? He was a spook with the NSA but he seems just as Russian as any comrade in the room. Hell, he even speaks like a native Rooskie. And what did he say...that he had just returned from Yekaterinburg with those other two characters, one of whom looked like the weathered face of a mountain and the other, the mountain itself. These three would bear scrutiny.*

After the introductions, Rodonov began to speak.

"If my American friends are in agreement, we will conduct all our briefings in Russian. If you would like an interpreter—"

"*Nyet*...that won't be necessary," O'Brien said. "Lt. Rochelle and I— *mwee govoreem po-rooski*...we have a reasonably good grasp of your language."

Not fully understanding the American's South Philly accented Russian, Rodonov paused and squinted.

"No interpreters. Please, go on," O'Brien nodded, waving his hand.

"Very well," Rodonov said, "then we'll begin." Dimming the lights, he drew the attention of his audience to the electronic wall map which depicted the town of Khowst and its surrounding mountains.

"Operation Macedonian Phalanx. Spetsnaz and the American Navy Special Warfare Group will train together for approximately ten days in a location that has been designed to replicate this area," he said, using his light-wand to make an indication on the map. The objectives of our training will be to choreograph and thoroughly rehearse our tactics, establish and rehearse contingency plans, fully acquaint ourselves with the capabilities of each other's weapons, and overcome communication barriers. Although, in reality, ten days would not suffice for any one of these objectives, we do not have the luxury of time.

"At the end of this training period, our two teams, led by Commander O'Brien with myself as second-in-command, will be air-dropped into these mountains, just northeast of Khowst. Commander O'Brien has already decided that the Spetsnaz team will cut communications and hold all roads in this sector. The American Navy commandos will attack the enemy's stronghold, here. The NSA has provided us with these satellite close-ups of the target area."

A gasp of amazement escaped the lips of the Russian onlookers. The digital images, taken from miles into space, not only clearly showed the make of the trucks travelling in and out of the target, but their license numbers as well, and not only individual enemy soldiers but their collar insignia, too. The Russians could only imagine the nature of the photos of their own country that lay in the NSA's archives.

"Very impressive," Director Aksanov said, "but does the NSA have any detail of the actual target, itself…that is, inside the compound?"

"Unfortunately, that is our most serious shortcoming," Rodonov answered. "As you, more than anyone else, are aware, it has been almost impossible to infiltrate bin Wahhab's organization. I used the term 'almost' because our GRU Military Intelligence branch has achieved a few minor successes. We also understand that a CIA agent recently penetrated the stronghold at Khowst but was quickly terminated. Unfortunately, none of these efforts have produced significant information concerning the target. We are still hopeful that we will have a breakthrough in the next ten days."

"We can be certain of one thing," Aksanov said. "The security of the compound has been enhanced over the past year…not only because of the lesson learned from the cruise missile strike. We also now know that bin Wahhab has been working closely with the Mukhabarat, the Iraqi intelligence service. This has enabled him to upgrade his secure communications, concealment techniques, and covert operations."

"Obviously, this is not an ideal situation," Hardy O'Brien interjected. "How do I express this in Russian…. Goin' into a target without proper intelligence is like goin' into a whorehouse without a wallet. We'll be completely fucked and then we'll be completely killed."

The Russians exchanged quizzical glances, unable to decipher the American Naval officer's jumble of English idioms and their own thickly accented language. Aksanov turned to Falcon for help.

"The Commander," Falcon said, after a moment's reflection, "is concerned that, without proper intelligence, the mission is in jeopardy."

All of the Russians nodded.

"That's what I said," O'Brien shrugged to Falcon. "O.K., look, my Russian is a little rusty. You translate for me. Tell them we can't wait for the next millennium for one of their GRU comrades to finally slip into bin Wahhab's kitchen. We need to get our butts down there and spook it out. And I mean god-damned NOW."

Falcon turned to the assemblage and said, "The Commander believes it is imperative that we put some of our own men into the target area to begin gathering intelligence immediately."

This suggestion caused a general stir among the Russian officers.

"But Commander," General Vernadsky objected, "there is not a single person in either of our battalions that has the ethnic background or specialized training to infiltrate this particular target."

"It's not necessary that we actually get into the compound," O'Brien said, speaking through Falcon as his interpreter. "We only need to have a chat with someone who's been there."

"Yes, I understand," Vernadsky said, "but even trying to snatch one of the Ikhwan would require some familiarity with the environment and the capability to move stealthily among the Afghans."

"I can satisfy those requirements."

All eyes turned to the speaker, Viktor Buzhkin."

"And I."

They swiveled to Sergei Medved.

"Both of these men served in Spetsnaz units in this area during the Afghan conflict," Aksanov informed the American Commander. "They were quite successful in covert operations there and they both speak the language."

"Perfect!" O'Brien exclaimed. "We'll also need someone familiar with Arabic. I've got just the man in my outfit. We'll bring him along with us."

"You will go?" Vernadsky said with incredulity, finally understanding one of O'Brien's sentences.

"*Konyechno!* Certainly! If I'm going to be top dog in this damn furball, I want to have a personal peek at the other dog's back yard."

Again receiving quizzical looks, he nodded to Falcon.

"The Commander says that, as the leader of this operation, it would be best for him to get a first-hand appraisal of the target. Furthermore, because of the, shall we say…communication issue…he wants me to go along as his interpreter."

"Hey, hold on," O'Brien frowned. "I understood that last part and I never said—". He stopped short, measuring the intense, determined gaze of the NSA agent. "Well, what the hell, if you're that crazy…and I suppose I could use a little communications assistance…."

A flurry of decisions, the speed and confidence of which were typical of both O'Brien and Rodonov, ensued. Lt.(j.g.) Ryder, owing to his Arabic language specialty, was added to the small advance group. The five commandos would board a Russian Air Force Antonov An-12 transport aircraft that afternoon so as to arrive in the target area after dark. They would be extracted exactly forty-eight hours after insertion. During this time, Rodonov and Rochelle would begin the joint training program. The meeting then quickly ended as there was much work to be done, and very little time.

* * *

At first, Yang Lin Su thought she was dreaming. Gradually, however, the persistent beep became more real, rousing her from her sleep. She opened one eye and glanced through the dark of her bedroom to the digital clock on the nightstand. 4:45 a.m. The phone ringing at such an hour was generally not a harbinger of good news. With a touch of anxiety, she rolled to her side and lifted the receiver.

"This is an obscene phone call," a familiar voice came over the line. "Will you accept the charges?"

"Mike," she exclaimed. "Are you all right?"

"I'm good. How are you and the mutt?"

"I'm…never mind about me. Jocko is fine…just a little weird."

"How's that?"

"Well, for one thing, he thinks he's still living on a boat. Every time he sits down, he spreads his hind legs far to each side to be prepared for rocking."

"Yeah, he's been a sea dog since he was a pup."

"He misses you. I'm sure he wonders when you'll be returning....I guess there's nothing you can say about that."

"I'm not sure what I can say to you any more, Suze."

They both fell silent.

"Mike, just promise me you're not taking any unnecessary chances."

"Would I do such a thing?"

"I mean it. Promise me."

"Sure…no unnecessary chances."

"For good fortune, I'll rub Buddha's stomach for you," she said with a hesitant laugh.

"Buddha and Jocko…they have all the luck."

Again the words they sought eluded them.

"Look, Suzie…I've been doing some thinking. When I get back…."

"You're thinking. That's dangerous," she nervously clipped his thought.

"Yeah. You're right. I have to run."

"Wait, Mike…I didn't mean it that way. I'm just afraid.

"Afraid of what?"

"The way we feel about each other. In our line, it's dangerous. But I don't want to give you up. I can't. I love you too much."

"Yes. Me, too. Somehow, though, I feel like we're headed for a cliff. Look. I really have to go. I love you."

Her response was met by the disconnect tone.

"You ready?" Medved asked as Falcon emerged from the phone desk at Marshall Suvorov Air Force Base.

"Yeah. Everything loaded?"

"Yes. The pilots are running the engines up now. Tonight, my friend, we will be in Afghanistan."

The two men quickly trotted toward the revving aircraft.

*   *   *

It was well into night by the time the An-12 reached the Afghan border. The flight had been routine until that point as the only airspace transited had been Russian and the former Soviet Republic of Turkmeniya. Now, however, as they neared Afghanistan, a change in the flight profile was required in order to further foil the possibility of detection. The specially configured An-12 bristled with radar jamming and electronic countermeasure equipment but, in the Russian Air Force, flying beneath enemy radar was not only book procedure, it was a matter of honor.

The pilot reduced power on the four Ivchenko turboprop engines and the lumbering aircraft descended to mountain top level. As the snow-capped peaks loomed in the moonlight, it appeared that the slow-responding transport would never be nimble enough to avoid implanting itself in a mountainside. Hardy O'Brien, sitting just aft of the cockpit, had a front row seat to each impending disaster.

"Jesus, are you sons of bitches totally nuts!?" he would remonstrate to the pilots as the aircraft cleared the jagged hazards by the seeming width of its own shadow.

"Ey, do you want to live forever?" the Captain laughed, enjoying the American 'groundpounder's' anxiety. The Russian pilot was completely comfortable 'pushing the envelope' in his bucket of bolts. On the other hand, he would never dream of parachuting into Afghanistan to do the mission that O'Brien was about to embark upon. Each man was absolutely convinced of the insanity of the other. O'Brien moved to a seat further aft so that he at least wouldn't be subjected to watching his approaching demise in slow motion.

"We're almost at the DZ," he said to his four men, who sat quietly against the bulkheads in nylon mesh seats. They were barely visible in the dim red lighting of the cargo hold. "Recheck your weapons and equipment."

Medved lay his assault rifle across his lap. The weapon was a *Vintorez* "Screw-threader" 9 mm silent sniper rifle, a favorite of the Spetsnaz for covert operations. He made sure that the suppressor was in place, for the rifle was inoperative without this noise inhibitor. As he reviewed the rest of his equipment, he turned to Falcon.

"Michael, just remember what I told you. You'll be hooked up to an anchor cable so your chute will open automatically. Push out from the plane like a swan dive. Then bring your feet together, elbows in, arms over your reserve chute. Count three to four seconds. If the main doesn't deploy by then, pull the reserve D Ring."

"I think three seconds will be long enough," Falcon said drily. He recognized his 'cotton mouth' as one of his body's preparations for danger. As saliva was not needed for the primeval instinct of pending fight or flight, his body had reduced its production. Likewise, he knew that the butterflies in his stomach were the result of blood rushing from now less-essential digestive organs to his survival-critical arms and legs.

Sergei chuckled. "Don't pull that ring sooner than three seconds, though. You don't want to open the reserve too early or it may become entangled with the main. That would be very undesirable…but at least the ground would break your fall," he winked. "Three seconds may seem like a long time, but you'll only have dropped one hundred and fifty feet."

"Yeah, great. I'll still have another three hundred and fifty to play with as I'm accelerating earthward."

"Yes. No problem. "That's at least another second or two. Now, when the chute opens, spread the risers, keep a mild tension in your muscles. Touch down on the balls of your feet and roll to your side and buttocks. Any questions?"

"No, but I must tell you that it's a completely unnatural act for one who's trained as a pilot to jump out of a perfectly running aircraft. Fortunately, this isn't the first time I've had to 'hit the silk.'"

Sergei laughed. "True, but this will be a bit different than ejecting from a burning F-8 fighter jet."

"Yeah. Hopefully, the plane won't be on fire when I leave it this time."

"Well, from that perspective, I guess this won't be too much of an ordeal for you." As he spoke, a warning buzzer sounded and the aircraft's intercom system crackled to life.

"This is the Captain. We are nearing the Drop Zone. In thirty seconds, we will pop up to five hundred feet above ground level. Be alert—the tail door is now opening."

The aircraft pitched upwards and cold air filled the cargo bay as the ramp door lowered.

"Hook 'em up," O'Brien said, as soon as the aircraft leveled off. The men stood and attached their static lines to the steel "idiot's" cable. Several long seconds passed as they stared intently at the red indicator light above the open door. Finally, the 'ready' light was doused and the bright green jump light began to flash.

"Go!" the Commander barked. Lucky Ryder, the most experienced parachutist in the group after the Skipper, was first out. He was followed by Buzhkin, then Medved. Falcon was immediately on Sergei's heels, not trusting himself to hesitate. When O'Brien departed, the An-12 Captain simultaneously cranked his aircraft around to the north and pushed the nose into a dive toward the shelter of the mountains, hoping that his radical maneuvers and electronic equipment had kept them off the Afghan radar scopes.

The five men in the air had a more immediate concern. It was not whether or not their parachutes would open. Each man had done his own packing, so there was no doubt that he would see the successful deployment of his canopy. The question was who else might see it.

* * *

Talil selected a large, flat boulder, dusted off the thin layer of snow, and sat down. His work party of half a dozen men was tossing their picks and shovels into the rear of the canvas-covered troop truck. No one spoke. Talil could not recall the last time he had felt so despondent or had to undertake such a distasteful task. He glanced over at the mound of rocks that marked the spot where they had just buried Abu Yusuf.

I know I am far too simple a man to fathom the words and deeds of The Chosen One. But was this one fault of his faithful servant, Abu Yusuf, deserving of this severest of punishments? Talil raised his eyes toward the sky, in quiet supplication. *Yusuf, may you be resting in peace with Allah in paradise, amid gardens and fountains, in silk and rich robes. May the voluptuous Houri virgins, with their large dark eyes, like shining pearls in their shells, go round you, bringing you fruits and sweet drinks. May....* His prayer vanished from his lips and his mind and he nearly tumbled from his rock at the apparition that now met his upturned eyes.

A large four—engine aircraft roared across the valley, skimming so close to the ground that the Ikhwan soldiers dove for cover. As it disappeared behind a ridge, the men scrambled to their feet, jabbering excitedly and pointing toward the incredible sight. Talil leaped from his rock and raced toward a more advantageous viewing spot.

"There! There!" one of his men exclaimed.

They watched in stunned silence as the plane lurched up, leveled off, and expelled several small floating objects in its wake. It then rapidly descended and was swallowed by the mountains, as if it had never existed. Talil knew he was not dreaming, however, for the drifting white apparitions left behind were still very visible and becoming more real every moment as they spiraled to the ground.

"Get your weapons! To the truck!" he shouted to his men. The Ikhwan soldiers quickly piled into the vehicle which set off in the direction of the descending objects.

* * *

"Bury those 'chutes real good," O'Brien said, relying on Falcon's simultaneous translation to the Russians. "Then pile some rocks and snow over them. We don't want 'em found 'til next spring's thaw. And get a fix on our position, Lieutenant."

"Aye, aye, Skipper," Ryder replied. He removed his hand-size Global Positioning System receiver from his pack along with a map of the local area. In a matter of seconds, the instrument triangulated the three closest GPS satellites and computed the commando team's location within a matter of a few meters.

"The target is ten miles at zero niner zero," he said.

O'Brien gazed toward the east and the series of mountain ridges that rose between them and the Ikhwan compound.

"Roger that," he said, permitting himself a short draught from his canteen. "We don't want to stay in the drop zone any longer than necessary. We'll move to within a few miles of the target and hole up for the night."

The group of five men hastily completed concealing their parachutes, then began working their way east, along the base of a mile-high mountain. Staying in the shadows of the ridge line, they walked parallel to a narrow two-lane byway that wound its way through the passes. The road was quiet, inert, lifeless, like a dead black snake that had been tossed on a pristine field of white. It was a tranquil illusion that was short-lived, however, for ten minutes into their journey, the commandos realized they were not alone.

"Skipper, hear that?" Ryder said, raising his right harm to indicate a halt. "Sounds like a Deuce and a Half."

Each member of the group ceased his movement and listened intently. From the distance drifted the barely audible sound of grinding metal, then the muffled chugging of an engine as a vehicle shifted gears.

O'Brien motioned his team to take cover behind the boulders of the sheltering mountain. Medved readied his *Vintorez* sniper rifle, attaching the night vision optics. Next to him, Viktor Buzhkin propped his heavier weapon on its short-legged bipod. This rifle provided the team's furthest range—two thousand meters—and greatest hitting power. In skilled hands, it could take out an armored vehicle.

It was not an armored vehicle, but a two ton troop truck, that now crept along the road toward them. A bright search light shone from the cab, its beam spilling across the open fields and darting among the crevices of the flanking mountains. The vehicle slowed until just opposite the hiding place of O'Brien's team, less than fifty meters away, then stopped. The canvas flap at the rear of the truck was flung open and five men with rifles leapt out. At the same time, both cab doors swung open and two more armed men alighted.

"Talil, I saw with my own eyes how they came down just on this side of the ridge," one of the men said. "They cannot be far from here."

In the cold, crisp air his words carried easily across the smooth marble-hard snow, where they were received, translated, and whispered into the ear of Commander O'Brien by Lt.(j.g.)Ryder.

Talil turned towards the mountain that hid O'Briens' team. Stroking his chin, he stared directly at the unseen enemy, wondering what Abu Yusuf would have done in such a situation. This tormenting thought was interrupted by the excited shouts of one of his men.

"He's found our footprints in the snow, Skipper," Ryder whispered to his commanding officer.

O'Brien cursed softly. *Two weeks undetected in Communist Vietnam but only ten minutes before we're busted here! That crazy Russian pilot dropped us too damned close to the target. Too late now.*

He motioned specific instructions to each of his men. If possible, they were to take their adversaries alive. Above all, however, none of the enemy could be permitted to escape. Four of the Ikhwan, following the trail in the snow, were now only twenty meters away. Each was personally framed dead in the center of a night optic reticule. Several more steps forward and the lead man would literally bump into the muzzle of Medved's *Vintorez*.

He never got that far, however, for a white mound of snow suddenly appeared to come to life and engulf him. A steel-like vice compressed so tightly on his throat that the startled exclamation that began in his diaphragm never made it to his lips. Ten seconds' total lack of oxygen and the brain slips into unconsciousness; thirty seconds' deprivation can result in death. Hardy O'Brien was well aware of these facts as he dragged his live but insensible prey into the shadows. During this swift attack, the three following Ikhwan raised their rifles. Medved, Ryder, and Falcon squeezed the triggers of their weapons. Neither muzzle flash nor sound was noticeably emitted from their sniper rifles.

Standing at the truck, Talil wondered why four of his men had suddenly decided to lie down. He was about to put this question to the soldier standing next to him when that very same man flew backwards as if kicked in the head by a camel, then pitched face forward into the snow. Instinctively, Talil ducked and as he did a fist-sized piece of the truck exploded behind the spot where his head had just been. Yelping, he dove under the vehicle, rolling to the opposite side. Shielded by the truck from these invisible angels of death, he scrambled to his feet, nearly ripping off the cab door as he opened it, and leapt onto the seat. He was met there by the remaining member of his command who was already starting the motor.

"Go! Go!" Talil screamed.

The truck lurched forward, its gears grinding, and began picking up speed. *In a few seconds, we will be out of their range,* Talil thought. *Then we shall come back with a bigger force to deal with this.* They could hear the ping of the bullets already falling short on the pavement behind them, and they simultaneously broke into the nervous laughter of those who have barely escaped doom.

"We can't let them escape!" O'Brien blurted. As he spoke, Sgt. Buzhkin squinted one more time into his night optic reticule. The rear end of the rapidly retreating truck, illuminated in soft pale green, was in the cross hairs of the scope. He squeezed the trigger.

Chapter Thirty-One

For a heavy, clumsy, vehicle, the Ikhwan 'Deuce and a Half' moved at an impressive rate. By the time the first round emerged from Buzhkin's rifle barrel, Talil and his companion were passing through forty-five miles per hour and accelerating. Unfortunately for them, their steel-cored pursuer was drilling through the air at near the speed of sound. The slug struck the fuel tank, pierced its metal shield as if it were paper, and heated the contained gasoline to its flash point. For a brief moment, the night sky was bright as day as the truck exploded in a huge yellow fireball.

A quick reconnaissance by Lucky Ryder to the burning wreck revealed that there were no survivors. In fact, the sole living remainder of Talil's work party was the Ikhwan soldier that O'Brien had wrestled to the ground. The prisoner was gagged, his wrists were tied behind his back, and a noose with a slip-knot was wrapped around his neck. By this means, he was encouraged to keep pace with the rapidly moving commando team, for sluggishness on his part resulted in the knot compressing his wind-pipe and the stinging pain of suffocation.

The group now proceeded at a steady trot, as O'Brien was anxious to put as much distance as possible between themselves and the flaming truck. The bodies of the other Ikhwan had been thrown into the blaze with the hope that the conflagration would camouflage reality and that the disaster would appear, at least for a short while, as an automobile wreck. They needed to buy only another forty-eight hours.

Gradually, their pace slowed as they worked their way higher into the mountains, where they would reduce their odds of being followed. Just before sunrise they halted and set up camp, less than two miles from the Ikhwan compound. With Ryder taking the first watch, the others stole a few hours sleep.

By sunset, the team was well rested and alert. The same could not be said for the prisoner, who had been forced to remain standing barefoot the full night and day with no more than the thin cotton cloth of his shirt and trousers between himself and the frigid mountain wind. The pistol that Medved held to the miserable man's head was superfluous as the Ikhwan was now quite anxious to cooperate with his captors and receive the promised reward of food, warmth, and sleep.

Skillfully, Ryder picked the brain of the frightened, exhausted soldier. By the end of the interrogation, he was able to construct a rudimentary drawing of the Ikhwan compound. O'Brien had just begun to study the rendering, when he was interrupted by Falcon.

"The door just opened and they're moving pretty smartly," Falcon said as he peered through night vision binoculars at the gaping hole that had been carved in the side of the mountain.

O'Brien set aside the sketch, put a similar set of glasses to his eyes and trained them on the Ikhwan compound. There had been no activity in the area during the daylight hours when, it was believed by the Ikhwan, spy satellites would be more apt to record their every move. Now that night had descended upon their enclave, they felt freer to move about without detection by these eyes in the sky. They, of course, were wrong, as the satellites' effectiveness were not negated by darkness. Neither was O'Brien's' team.

"Looks like they're excited about something," the Commander said, gazing intently through the binoculars.

"Roger that. They're probably wondering why a certain truckful of their people are missing," Falcon noted.

They watched as a dozen Ikhwan climbed into the canvas-covered rear bay of a troop truck, which then lumbered off. O'Brien lowered his binoculars and, switching to his night vision goggles, sat on a rock and again took to studying the prisoner's drawing.

"Looks like there's an entry room for loading and unloading equipment...then quarters for the scientists and engineers and the Ikhwan soldiers...and finally a laboratory. The bomb is here," he said, running his raw-boned index finger across the paper. He looked up at Ryder. "Lieutenant," how far do you think we can trust this sorry son-of-a-bitch?" he growled.

"Who can say for sure, sir. But my professional opinion is that he would've done his best to shit a hard-boiled egg if you told him to."

The Commander glanced at the Ikhwan, who was devouring the dry contents of a mess kit while huddled under an aluminum foil blanket. The thin, hi-tech covering was barely sufficient as an Arctic wind, driving large snow-laden clouds before it, was beginning to sweep through the Hindu Kush. O'Brien drew his pistol from its holster. Like many others in his elite unit, the Old Man preferred the harder hitting Colt Forty-five over the regulation issue Beretta 9mm. "Show him this, Lieutenant. Tell him that we're going to interrogate another one of his buddies. Tell him that if their stories don't agree, I will personally shoot off his dick with this weapon."

Ryder took the revolver, strode to the prisoner, squatted, and began speaking in an Arabic dialect. The Ikhwan listened with rapt attention, his eyes widening as Ryder motioned first to the Commander and then to the Colt. Thereupon, the Arab began jabbering profusely, waving his arms and nodding emphatically. Ryder returned to O'Brien.

"He gets the picture, sir," the j.g. said. "And he's standing by his story."

"Very well, I guess we'll find out if he's lying or not. Tonight, we'll pick up another hostile. Tell him to finish his chow, Lieutenant. Then gag and retie him." O'Brien turned his eyes upward, toward the racing black clouds that were silhouetted in moonlight. "Now that's the kind of weather I like to see," he said. "A good storm is brewing. Soon the moon will be completely blocked and then we'll pay a little visit to those people below."

*   *   *

The massive clouds smothered all light from the night sky and dumped heavy flakes of snow that swirled wildly in the gusting wind. Although severe, the conditions allowed O'Brien's team to move closer than they had hoped possible to the entrance of the Ikhwan stronghold. The doorway, still open in spite of the weather, appeared larger in real life than in the NSA images. Two of the Ikhwan five-ton trucks could easily pass through it simultaneously.

"I doubt if they'll be so accommodating to leave those open when we arrive in force," Falcon whispered to O'Brien as they lay concealed in rocks fifteen yards distant.

"Rog'. Those doors look to be a couple inches thick. Probably plate steel. We've got just the right medicine for that when we hit this place. God, I'd love to get a look inside."

"A few more days and you will," Falcon responded.

"Skipper," Ryder said softly, tapping the Commander's shoulder. "Truck coming."

They looked over their shoulders at the dim yellow lights that were barely visible through the filmy curtain of snow. The vehicle slowly motored up the road, coming almost to a complete halt before downshifting, then lurched forward again. Several minutes later, it rolled to a stop in front of the compound's entrance. The canvas flap at the rear was tossed aside and a dozen agitated Ikhwan soldiers tumbled out. Several men, who had been standing just inside the entrance, stepped outside to greet them, flicking their cigarettes in the snow. An excited exchange of words ensued.

"Lieutenant, can you make out what they're saying?" O'Brien whispered to Ryder.

"It's difficult, Skipper, but something about a disaster...a man named Talil...and all of his group are dead."

As he spoke, the soldiers began removing charred bodies from the truck. A cry erupted from those who had just now learned of the misfortune. Two men ran back into the compound, apparently to report the news to the Mahdi. The others began to carry the corpses, slung in blankets, through the doorway. Almost all had gone inside when one of the soldiers shouted something to his comrades and, his rifle in hand, began trotting toward the rocks some fifteen yards away.

Instinctively, Ryder raised his Colt Commando, a special forces' version of the venerable M-16 assault rifle. O'Brien laid his hand on the Lieutenant's arm and steadied him. The Ikhwan soldier paused in front of the rocks, a few feet from Viktor Buzhkin. He set his weapon against a boulder, unzipped his trousers, rustled out his penis, and began to relieve himself. His hand was still fondly gripping his organ when he crashed to the ground after the stock of a Russian sniper rifle struck him squarely at the base of his skull.

* * *

"Damn, Sergeant, you didn't have to almost knock his head off," O'Brien said as his party retreated to the cover of the mountains.

"He'll live," Buzhkin muttered. "I'm experienced in such matters." The unconscious Ikhwan soldier was draped over the Siberian's broad shoulders.

O'Brien glanced back toward the compound. The falling snow was now so thick that he could no longer distinguish figures, trucks, or even the wide doorway. The storm was also erasing all traces of their tracks. *God, how I love lousy weather,* he reflected.

A negative consequence of the blizzard, however, was its eradication of landmarks leading back to their campsite. This difficulty was overcome by strict reliance on the GPS, and, although their progress was hampered by the weather, they arrived safely an hour later. They were greeted by Medved who, sheltered in a hollow of the mountainside and wrapped in several aluminum foil blankets, had been guarding the first prisoner. O'Brien's unit crouched inside the shallow crevice, seeking any available reprieve from the elements. Buzhkin tilted to one side so that his human burden slid to the ground, next to the other Ikhwan.

The new prisoner moaned, his head rolled in a circle, and he opened his eyes. He recoiled at the sight of the strange creatures with the alien heads that bent over him. Peering through his night vision goggles, O'Brien saw that the man was horrified and confused—a good start for an interrogation. The Commander seized the captive by his jacket and began to shake him.

"Lieutenant," he said to Ryder, "same routine. "Tell this son-of-a-bitch that his only hope of survival is to cooperate with me." Ryder translated his Skipper's message into Arabic. He received only a blank stare.

"Ey, let me try," Buzhkin interjected. He spoke to the Ikhwan in Afghan and got an immediate response.

"As I suspected," the Russian said. "He's Afghan…mujaheddin lineage. "I wouldn't expect to get much out of this one."

O'Brien gazed into the olive-black eyes of the mujaheddin and was now met by an expression of defiance and hate.

"Tell him that he *will* talk and that his story had better match that of his comrade."

Buzhkin translated O'Brien's message to the Afghan. The prisoner scowled, then turned to his fellow Ikhwan and unleashed a torrent of angry words.

"He curses the other one for acting cowardly," Buzhkin said. "He says that this man shall never gaze upon Muhammed's face or Allah's divinity in paradise but will be condemned to everlasting hell."

"Very well, he's about to get his own taste of hell right now," O'Brien grumbled. The interrogation began.

As Buzhkin had predicted, the mujaheddin proved to be of tougher mettle than the first captive. No combination of threats, thrashings, promises of reward or punishment broke his resolve. On the contrary, it appeared that he relished the opportunity to die for his beliefs and to become a star in a distant constellation.

"Let me speak to him for a few minutes alone" Buzhkin said.

The Commander agreed. The Russian drew a broad, nastily serrated knife from a sheath on his waist and, conspicuously brandishing the weapon, led the mujaheddin away. O'Brien turned to Ryder. "Tell this one that this is his last chance. Remind him what'll happen if a different story comes back from his pal."

The Lieutenant relayed the message and the prisoner again reacted excitedly.

"No change," Ryder said.

After another half-hour, Viktor Buzhkin returned, alone.

"No use," he said, matter-of-factly. "It's very rare that one withstands that method of questioning without breaking. He is quite brave." Buzhkin sat on a rock, pulled a mess kit from his pack and began to eat.

"Is he still alive?" O'Brien asked.

"Oh yes. As I said earlier, I am quite experienced in these matters. He's...resting."

"Roger. That's that," O'Brien said. "We can't risk another foray down the mountain. We'll go with what we have. The storm permitting, the choppers will be here tomorrow evening. We'll try to make the extraction zone before dawn. Lieutenant, send a message to that effect."

Ryder removed a hand-size computer from his pack, extended its antenna, and began to key in a command. The coded message, travelling at the speed of light, raced into space where it was received by a Top Secret Milstar communication satellite and routed to a large parabolic receptor dish on Cheyenne Mountain, Colorado. The message slowed for a few seconds as it was processed, then routed to Arlington, Virginia, where it was reviewed and reformatted by Army cryptographers in the Pentagon. Less than half a minute later, it was transmitted to the Russian Ministry of Defense in Moscow. Two minutes later, by the exact reverse process, Ryder received confirmation of his message. The circuitous routing was necessitated by the American military's desire to maintain the integrity of its 'Black World' communication system. Even with the resultant slight delay, it was still the fastest means of protected outside communication for O'Brien's team.

"Message acknowledged, sir," Ryder said.

"All right. Let's move out," the Commander ordered.

The small team hoisted their packs, donned their night vision optics, gathered their prisoners, and set off. The snow was still whipping through the mountains, building deep drifts and hindering footing. The temperature had dipped to well below freezing and the driving wind further chilled the air. Fortunately, one industry in which the Russian people excelled was the manufacture of cold-weather clothing. The Spetsnaz winter uniforms, which all members of the commando unit wore, admirably combated the blustery Arctic blast. Nevertheless, a determined Nature was not to be outdone by any man-made artifice. The powerful, howling wind pressed them against the rock walls, knocked them to their knees, and occasionally completely thwarted their forward movement. Clothing that was impervious to minus forty degrees sporadically succumbed to the tempest, like gauze knifed through by cold steel. Every handhold was a sheet of ice or no hold at all. Solid ground and crevices, concealed by the piling snow, were impossible to differentiate.

Shortly after midnight and approximately half way to their destination, Falcon set his foot on a seemingly firm pack of snow. The white mound gave way and he plummeted through a yawning cleft in the mountainside. Clawing at the jagged rocks from which he caromed, he was unable to gain purchase and continued to tumble several hundred feet. During the fall, he pictured Lin Su at her desk—it would be late afternoon in Washington. It struck him as surreal that she would be calmly going about her business, blissfully unaware that he was plunging into an abyss.

Momentarily, he slammed into a fortuitously placed rock promontory that abruptly halted his downward slide. The snow that had caused his misfortune now worked to his advantage by softening his impact. Badly bruised and reeling from the jolt that had expelled the air from his lungs, he lay motionless. Slowly, cautiously, he began to move his hands, then his arms, feet, and legs. In spite of the pain of the effort, he was relieved that no bones seemed to be broken. That was the good news. The bad news was that he had lost his night vision optics and he had no idea if a step to the right or left would send him flying completely off the mountain. It was then that he heard Medved's voice above him.

"Do not move, Michael. You are right at the edge. I have you in sight and am coming toward you."

Several minutes passed before he spoke again.

"I am sending a rope down to you. Can you grab it?"

Falcon felt the heavy coil land on his legs.

"Tie it securely around yourself and we'll pull you up."

Ignoring the pain in his ribs, back, and chest, Falcon secured the line tightly around his torso. The rope became taut, exacerbating his injuries as it lifted him along the face of the mountain.

"This is no time for sight-seeing, Michael," Medved laughed as he seized Falcon. "Try to stay with the tour group from now on."

*   *   *

All welcomed the brightening eastern horizon the following morning. As if on command from the rising golden sun, the last flake of snow fluttered meekly to the ground, the last swirling breeze dissipated, and the last puffball cloud evaporated. The sky was a rich blue, almost too spectacular to observe in the reflection of the blinding white blanket of fresh snow. Even those involved in such a deadly business could not fail to appreciate the beauty that surrounded them. In all directions, snow-covered mountain ridges undulated off to the horizon like the knobby spines of magnificent white dragons. Overhead, a lone hawk soared in lazy arcs.

"Skipper, we're at the exfiltration point," Ryder said, glancing up from his GPS.

"Roger that," O'Brien responded. "There was a cave entrance about one klick to the west. Must have been covered by the storm. Let's find it."

The Commander's recollection proved to be correct and soon the group arrived at the small natural shelter. Before settling in, they first smoothed over their tracks so that the cave area completely blended with the pristine surroundings. Falcon and Medved took the first watch. The others, their bodies trembling from the exhaustion of having slogged for hours through leg immobilizing packed snow, fell immediately asleep.

Sitting on a rock that just barely accommodated his hindquarters, the Russian stripped the seal from one of his tin mess kits and removed a frozen brown slab of meat. He offered it to Falcon. "I think it's chicken," he said, "but I must admit it's a bit of a mystery."

"I'm just hungry enough to eat some 'mystery meat,'" Falcon laughed. "Here, let me return the favor." He peeled open one of his tins which contained tightly-packed grain.

Staring at the contents for a few moments, Falcon finally said, "I have no idea what the hell this is."

"Ah, we call that delicacy *kasha*," Medved guffawed. "Buckwheat groats."

"Damn. No wonder you Spetsnaz are so tough," Falcon chuckled. "Pass me a hammer and we'll start eating."

The two men began gnawing at the rock hard food.

"I'm curious," Medved said, finally securing a mouth-size chunk of meat, "last night, as you were clinging to the side of a cliff, did the thought ever occur to you—what the hell am I doing in a blizzard, falling off a mountain in Afghanistan, hoping not to get killed by some fanatical terrorists?"

Falcon grinned and shrugged. "Absolutely not. One must never pose such a question to oneself. The answer would be too unsettling."

"Ah, but a wise man—I believe it was Socrates—once said that the unexamined life is not worth living," Medved responded.

"True, although personally, I would change that to say the *unimpassioned* life is not worth living. If one has no passion for what one does in life, for something or someone, then why bother? But I suppose that, since you've raised this issue, you faced this question of 'why' yourself last night."

The Russian nodded. "I must confide something in you, Michael. Something I have never told another soul—no one."

Falcon was honored, yet anxious, that Medved placed this special trust in him.

"For two years now," he continued, "since the death of my wife, I have been doing my best to care for Galena. But what kind of life can I give her. Russia is in chaos. And my own profession puts her in mortal danger. I have a brother who has a fine British wife and a successful business in London. Galya could have a much brighter future there…a more normal life with a 'mother's' touch. I have often thought perhaps it would be best if—"

"Don't even finish that thought, Sergei," Falcon interrupted. "The sun rises and sets on you in Galena's eyes. The rest—Russia, your profession, life in the West—is all superfluous in comparison."

"I have often wrestled with such reasoning without much success…until recently."

"Recently?" Falcon raised one eyebrow, secretly guessing at the cause for a change in his friend's outlook.

"Yes. Very recently, I have begun to feel that perhaps life might become better for Galena."

"Yelena Pavlovna?" Falcon smiled.

"Yes. Yelena Pavlovna," Sergei answered somewhat sheepishly. "Don't you think she would be good for my daughter?"

Falcon chuckled and was about to respond when his attention was diverted by the sonorous drone of an approaching aircraft. Simultaneously, he and Medved peered from the mouth of the cave toward the sound. Less than a mile away, a low-wing, twin-prop aircraft skimmed the nearest ridge line. Intrigued by the sight, they failed to notice the approach of a similar plane that suddenly roared directly above their heads. Both men quickly leaned back into their hideout.

"They're definitely search craft," Falcon said.

"Do you think they spotted our trail in the snow?"

"I guess we'll find out soon enough."

They cautiously peered outside, in time to see one of the aircraft bank to the right and motor back in their direction.

* * *

"Here comes one again," Lucky Ryder said, eyeing the approaching plane. It was nearly sunset and it was the fifth sighting of one of the low-flying craft.

"They're still hunting," CDR O'Brien replied. "It's obvious that they've got an interest in this area. Hopefully, they haven't sent ground troops in this direction yet. What's the ETA on the choppers, Lieutenant?"

Ryder glanced at his watch. "Fifteen-ten Zulu. One hour and forty minutes, sir." As he spoke, two Russian helicopters, an Mi-8 transport and two Mi-24 assault craft were just leaving a snow-covered grass airfield across the border in southern Turkmeniya. Their mission was to extract O'Brien's commando unit. In spite of the time criticality, they were unable to launch any sooner, as the entire flight over Afghanistan was to take place under the cloak of darkness.

"An eternity," the Skipper muttered. "Let's hope they're on time."

"When shall I wake the others?" Ryder asked, glancing at Falcon and Medved who had been sleeping since being relieved of their watch at noon.

"After sunset. Give 'em time to acclimate to the dark before the choppers arrive. All hell may break loose then."

*   *   *

Waking from his sleep of exhaustion, Falcon was not sure where he was when shaken by Ryder.

"Choppers will be here in about twenty minutes," the Lieutenant said.

Falcon rose, packed his blanket, slung his rifle over his shoulder, and joined the rest of the group. The two Russians were standing near the mouth of the cave, peering out at the star-studded night sky.

"It's been an hour since the last fly-by," Medved said to the approaching American.

"Problem is, we don't know if that's good or bad," Buzhkin added. "Wait. What's that?"

The other two followed his line of sight toward the southeast, to a ridge line perhaps a mile away.

"Commander, you better come take a look at this," Falcon called back into the cave.

Instantly hustling to the entrance, O'Brien raised his night vision binoculars to his eyes and focused on the point of interest. There, his gaze was met by hundreds of small, bobbing yellow lights that floated over the blanket of snow in an oddly unseasonal image of fireflies over a white sand beach.

"Looks like they picked up our trail," O'Brien said. "If they have trouble sticking to it, the choppers just might beat them here. If they come directly this way…we're goin' to have ourselves quite a furball. They're about two klicks away, so we have maybe ten minutes."

"And it's ten more minutes 'til the choppers are expected, sir," Ryder added.

"Roger," the Skipper replied. All five men of the commando unit fixed their eyes on the hypnotically beautiful dancing amber beams. Slowly but surely, they were working their way in the general direction of the cave.

"Do you think they're Ikhwan or Afghan Army or both?" Medved asked, to no one in particular.

"Doesn't much matter," O'Brien answered. "You can be damned sure they'll be unfriendly. All right, we can't let ourselves be caught in the cave. Lieutenant, you and Sergeant Buzhkin take the prisoners. We'll crawl out of here toward that ridge to our northwest. Tell the prisoners that if they do not do exactly as told, they will immediately be shot."

One minute later, the commando soldiers were on their bellies, inching their way to the ridge that lay approximately four hundred yards away. By the time they reached their destination, the yellow lights were approaching the cave.

"Damn," Ryder softly cursed, glancing at his watch. "The choppers should've been here by now."

"Very well. Take positions behind these rocks and prepare to meet an attack," the Commander said. "It'll only be a few minutes before they spot our trail leading here."

It took even less time than O'Brien had predicted. One of the enemy soldiers almost immediately stumbled onto the strange swaths that cut through the snow. He called excitedly to his companions and soon over a hundred men, their rifles at the ready, were heading toward the ridge concealing the commando unit.

"Prepare to fire," O'Brien said softly to his command. Just as he finished speaking, their hideaway was lit up by dozens of powerful flashlight beams.

"Fire!" O'Brien barked.

Although there were no muzzle flashes or audible gunshots, a dozen of the advancing troops tumbled in agony into the snow. Their comrades instinctively flattened themselves on the ground, straining their eyes to determine the location of the enemy fire. Many of them began shooting wildly into the rocks two hundred meters directly in front of them. Their officers shouted orders and two companies on each flank began an enfilading movement.

The commando unit maintained a rapid, continuous fire and although they had achieved an initial success, they had no illusions about their longer-term fortunes. Once they were enveloped, there was no possibility that five men could hold off well over a hundred. O'Brien stationed Ryder to the right flank, Falcon to the left and the two Russians to the center. The Old Man roamed among the three positions, adding additional firepower at propitious moments. The bullets ricocheting off their surrounding rocks were increasing in number and proximity. It was obvious that the envelopment was nearly complete and they would all soon be vulnerable to an inescapable crossfire. Nothing could be done other than maintaining their own barrage until their ammunition ran out or they were cut down.

Suddenly, the air was rent by a fast approaching staccato whumping of several engines and rapidly spinning blades.

"Mr. Falcon," O'Brien said unhurriedly, but directly. "Would you please get on the horn and inform our friends of the situation. Tell the choppers that hostiles are two hundred meters west of the LZ."

Falcon quickly relayed the message and watched as the assault helicopters swung overhead, firing rockets, machine guns, bombs, and grenades at the exposed enemy. Right behind them, the Mi-8 transport appeared and set down in the clearing in front of the ridge held by O'Brien's unit. The door slid open and an airman beckoned to the commandos.

"All right, girls. Let's move," O'Brien ordered.

The unit, its prisoners in tow, quickly raced from concealment. Fifty meters away, the missiles and rockets were exploding in yellowish-red bursts of light and flames, halting the enemy advance. Little puffs of snow kicked up at the feet of O'Brien's men, the end results of the Ikhwans' desperate but futile discharge of their weapons. In seconds, the commando team and its captives were aboard the helicopter, which quickly vectored back toward Turkmeniya.

In the midst of congratulating each other for their narrow escape, they failed to maintain a strict watch over their prisoners. The surly one bolted to his feet and dove into Medved, knocking him through the still open doorway. As the Russian flew from the helicopter, he felt a hand seize his jacket. Falcon's action had slowed Sergei's momentum just enough to enable him to grasp the runner of the aircraft. The Ikhwan went hurtling over his head, plunging out of sight in the star-flecked night sky—perhaps attaining his constellational wish. Buzhkin quickly joined Falcon's rescue efforts, hanging from the doorway and seizing Medved by his belt. Together, they jerked their colleague back aboard.

Lying on the deck, Sergei struggled to catch his breath.

"Until the aircraft has landed and come to a complete stop, you really should keep your seat-belt fastened," Falcon said.

Chapter Thirty-Two

A lone, extremely despondent figure stood with bowed head in the richly-decorated room that had been the scene of Abu Yusuf's final meeting with his leader. Bin Wahhab now paced angrily back and forth, slapping the broad blade of his grandfather's sword in his left palm.

"Eighteen killed, you say?" the sheik fumed.

"Yes, Mahdi."

"Nearly three dozen wounded?" bin Wahhab's steps quickened as he spoke and his ire increased.

"Yes, Mahdi."

"Allah!" bin Wahhab cried out, gazing upward, as if importuning his god for a revelation that would clarify the meaning of this latest catastrophe. A commando raid virtually on his own doorstep. Over fifty of his soldiers killed or wounded. Two of his most trusted lieutenants, Abu Yusuf and Talil now dead. He conveniently overlooked the fact that it was he who had ordered the murder of Abu Yusuf. Composing himself, he turned once again to the anxious Fawaz bin Sufya, the sole survivor of his most trusted aids.

"And you were unable to capture any of the enemy, not even a corpse?"

"No, Mahdi."

Bin Wahhab halted his frenetic walking and stood directly before Fawaz. "Yet, you are convinced that the attackers were Russian?"

"Yes, Mahdi. I would never mistake the sound of the Mi-24. It has been with me since the days I joined with the mujaheddin to help them defend their land against the Russian invaders. And we picked up the shells and casings fired by the enemy. They came from Mi-24 machine guns and rockets and Spetsnaz assault rifles. There is one mystery, however."

Fawaz, staring at the Persian carpet beneath his feet, could feel bin Wahhab's glare upon his lowered forehead. Screwing up his courage, he said, "Curiously, we also found spent SS109 cartridges."

"What? They are not Russian," bin Wahhab blurted.

"That is true, Mahdi. These particular shells could only have been fired from an American M-16. My guess is that Spetsnaz is in possession of such weapons, thus accounting for this peculiar discovery."

Bin Wahhab constantly tapped the heavy curved sword in his open hand as Fawaz spoke. He was experiencing a powerful sense of uneasiness. Unquestionably, the loss of fifty men so near to his base of operations was unsettling. But that misfortune paled in comparison to the perplexity and alarm that he felt in wrestling with the meaning of this information. Suddenly, he drove the point of the scimitar into the carpet, startling Fawaz.

"Bring me Valentin Tschernin this instant!" he snapped.

* * *

"Gentlemen, we have no time to lose. The assault will take place in two days."

A general buzz erupted among the Russian brass in the War Room at O'Brien's pronouncement. They had been wondering why, immediately upon his return from Afghanistan, the American Commander had called an emergency meeting of the Macedonian Phalanx strategy team.

By their reaction, it was obvious that they had not expected this turn of events.

"But, Commander O'Brien, we can not possibly complete our training by then," Lt. Col. Rodonov protested. Although he addressed the American, his eyes were focused hopefully on his boss, General Vernadsky.

"Quite true, Colonel," O'Brien responded. "My philosophy, however, is that training is never complete until we go to that big Happy Hour in the Sky. We could always devote more time to play-acting, but at some point you are forced to suck it up and go."

The Russians turned quizzically in the direction of the civilian American. After a moment's reflection, Falcon spoke.

"The Commander said that we are never completely through learning in life, but that eventually circumstances require that we act."

Rodonov, seeming to take a cue from the General, was not so easily convinced. "We have barely begun to familiarize ourselves with each other's tactics and equipment, he said more heatedly. "And we have not even developed our battle plan, let alone rehearse it. Going in ill-prepared will directly translate to loss of lives on our side. I just do not understand the urgency."

The American naval officer fixed his steel gray eyes, like battleships training their guns, on the Russian Colonel.

"I am well aware of the consequences of my proposal. No one in this room is more concerned with protecting the lives of my boys than I. The fact is, much more is at stake here than two commando teams," O'Brien continued. "If we are unsuccessful, hundreds of thousands, perhaps millions could die. If we do not move immediately, the opportunity to accomplish our objective will be lost. We cannot hope that the Ikhwan will now be sitting on their butts, waiting until we are fully prepared to attack them. As far as this new schedule increasing our loss potential, that is a trade-off we must be willing to make. Going into

Macedonian Phalanx, we all knew we might have to make the ultimate sacrifice."

Rodonov would have protested further, but was halted by a wave of the hand from the Spetsnaz Commandant.

"It is with reluctance that I must agree with you, Commander," General Vernadsky said. "Assuming that we now have no choice in the matter, describe for us your plan of battle."

Rodonov boiled silently. It was bad enough he had to play second violin to an American officer of no greater rank. But now he would be forced into the 'Yankee cowboy's' battle plan. And he had to publicly endure his boss siding with an American, and against him.

"Aye, aye, General," O'Brien said. "Mr. Falcon, I'm going to do this in Russian, so make damned sure that they're comprehending as I go along." The Commander dimmed the lights and drew the audience's attention to the bright electronic wall map.

"As I was saying, the attack will take place two days from now, at oh-dark-hundred. That is, in the still black hours of morning when defenses are statistically most lax and we are able to utilize our superior night fighting capabilities. Our people will be airlifted to southern Turkmeniya where they will board six unmarked Mi-8 helo transports. From Turkmeniya, an Antonov An-12 will lead the way into Afghan airspace, using its top secret electronic countermeasure and radar jamming equipment to foil the enemy's air defense systems. The cruising speed of the Mi-8's—250 knots—will dictate our pace. Six Mi-24 Hinds will provide air cover. The flight from Turkmeniya—"

"*Gorbynee*," Rodonov interjected.

"What?"

"Hunchbacks," Falcon interpreted.

"You are applying the NATO code word 'Hind' to the Mi-24," the Colonel added. "In fact, we Russians who invented it call it the *Gorbyn*...the Hunchback."

"I stand corrected," O'Brien said, making a mental note of Rodonov's acid tone. Then resuming, "The flight from Turkmeniya will take one hour and forty minutes. The troops will be flown into the target, to two separate landing areas…here and here."

Using the light wand, he indicated the locations several miles to the north of Khowst. "The Spetsnaz team under Lt. Col. Rodonov will secure and hold this road, which is the only land route to the target. Their main objective is to intercept two hundred fifty Ikhwan soldiers who are bivouacked in Khowst and will certainly attempt to aid their comrades.

"I will lead my team into the compound where we expect to encounter another two hundred and fifty of the enemy. The only access is a steel plate door that is several centimeters thick. Without question, we'll need C-4 for this operation. It's much more powerful than TNT and we won't have to worry about toxic fumes or failure due to sub-freezing temperature.

"Once inside, we will neutralize all enemy activity in the first and second chambers…the loading dock and the living quarters…and then secure the third room…the laboratory. The atomic bomb is located in this area here. Lt. Rochelle will lead his NDDT—Nuclear Device Disposal Team—into this area. They will seize and extract the bomb and all other uranium. When this unit has successfully completed its mission, both teams will re-board the Mi-8 transports. The Hi…er, Hunchbacks…will continue to provide protection as the transports return to Turkmeniya. The whole operation on the ground is expected to take no longer than thirty minutes."

"And your fuel considerations, Commander?" General Aksanov inquired. "Surely you cannot expect to refuel?"

"I am assured that the choppers have the legs," O'Brien responded.

"With auxiliary tanks and a full troop load of twenty-four, the Mi-8 will cover nearly one thousand kilometers," Rodonov noted, turning toward the FSB Director. "The Hunchbacks can go a little further. That is not to say that there is any margin for bad weather or unexpectedly strong headwinds."

Aksanov frowned as he tapped his pipe ashes into a glass ashtray. He was displeased that the Mi-8's would be run up to the edge of their capabilities. "Why not go with the newer, larger, Mi-26? It can carry four times the amount of troops."

"We considered that, General," Rodonov said. "However, we decided against it as two lucky hits would wipe out our entire force. And we must not forget that the Afghans are still in possession of American Stinger missiles which makes such an unpleasant possibility a reality. Besides ensuring greater safety to our men, the specially configured Mi-8's can cruise faster and farther than the 26's. Having sufficient fuel to return to Turkmeniya will still be very problematical, though."

"We would have liked to launch from Tadzhikistan," O'Brien interjected, "which is somewhat closer to the target. But your spooks, General Aksanov, tell me that we'd have to fight our way in and out of there as well."

"Unfortunately true," Aksanov said. "There is too much anti-Russian terrorist activity there to enable us to use it as a staging area. Just recently, the so-called *Muzlokandovs* blew up a Russian troop transport, then gunned down the widows attending the funeral services. Now then, do you plan to return with any of the scientists and engineers?"

"That is a secondary objective. If the opportunity presents itself without endangering the mission, we will certainly take advantage of it."

"How quickly do you think the Afghan Army will be mobilized?" Vernadsky asked.

"The nearest Afghan military base is one hundred miles to the northwest, near Kabul," O'Brien responded. "We believe it would take them at least forty-five minutes to organize and reach the target in force."

"If you are wrong and the army arrives sooner rather than later? Or you are slowed down by stiffer Ikhwan resistance than you expect? Or if for any reason, you are unable to extricate the bomb…?"

"We will have sufficient means to destroy all materials and equipment in the compound. As we don't want to leave behind any prisoners, each of our men will also be carrying cyanide capsules in the event all else fails. If it's any consolation I will say this: not one SEAL has ever been left behind, either dead or as a prisoner."

A gloomy silence settled over the audience. After a dozen seemingly longer seconds, Vernadsky cleared his throat and spoke.

"The plan is not without a great deal of risk, but it cannot be otherwise. It is well-conceived and has my whole-hearted support. General Aksanov?"

The FSB Director lowered his pipe from his lips. "I empathize with Colonel Rodonov that haste in such matters will lead to increased casualties on our side and perhaps jeopardize the entire mission. However, I believe that we have no alternative but to act immediately and," glancing at both the Spetsnaz and SEAL commanders, "we certainly have the best troops in the world for this job."

Vernadsky nodded. "Does anyone else wish to voice an opinion? Colonel Rodonov?"

The Spetsnaz officer knew that any sign of contrariness or even hesitation on his part would result in his removal as leader of the Russian assault unit. He stood, grasped a water glass that sat on the table before him, and turned to O'Brien.

"We were once sworn enemies but now fate has thrown us together for the common good of humanity," he said crisply. "We will succeed only if we suppress our individual interests and truly join together as a team. The Special Assignment Forces—Spetsnaz—is fully prepared to do its part to execute this plan."

He raised the glass, as if in a toast to his American counterpart. All eyes traveled to O'Brien. Wrapping his large, rawhide right hand around his glass, he stood to squarely face Rodonov.

"To our joint team of Seals and Spetsnaz," he heard himself say, amazed that such words could ever possibly pass his lips. And then, with vastly more confidence, "To the success of Macedonian Phalanx."

The others stood, nodding approvingly and clinking glasses with each other.

"Very well. We have two days to prepare," Vernadsky said. "Let's at least make the most of that."

As the assembly began to disband, Sergei tugged Falcon's sleeve. "Michael, come with me," he said good-naturedly. "I'll show you where we are to pick up our cyanide tablets."

Chapter Thirty-Three

Alexander Marenkov was so near, yet so far. Across the rock-strewn fields and valleys that he passed, he could see the chain link fence that haphazardly marked the border between Afghanistan and Pakistan. Unfortunately, his side of the barrier was constantly patrolled by Afghan and Ikhwan soldiers. On two occasions, he had found a seemingly unguarded stretch. Both times, he lay motionless in his hiding place in the mountains, studying the terrain and searching for signs of patrols. Twice, determining that no guards were near, he had emerged from the safety of the hills and ventured across the clearing toward the border. Each time, he noticed the arrival of a patrol just as he neared the fence. He had been fortunate to beat a hasty retreat to his mountain refuge without being discovered.

Gradually, he worked his way northeast, hoping to create greater distance between himself and his pursuers. For twelve days, he had trekked through snow, biting cold, and the rugged terrain of the Hindu Kush…the 'Hindu-Killer', so named for the heavy death-rate of kidnapped Hindu women who were herded through its passes several centuries earlier by Iranian slave traders. For Marenkov, the Kush was continuing to justify its gruesome appellation. The mountains he traversed had become progressively higher and sheerer, which was to be expected as he was on the doorstep of the Himalayas, and his strength was ebbing in direct proportion to the increased height. Ice-cold rivers, colored creamy gray by the rock dust they carried, rushed turbulently beneath him. Passes through the mountains became increasingly rare and then seemed to disappear altogether. He had not seen one since his last attempt to cross the border a week earlier. During that same timespan, he had reduced his rations in half. Even then, he had only enough food for perhaps one or two more days.

The thirteenth morning of his journey emerged bright and clear. Marenkov surprised himself by waking. In his state of exhaustion and in the frigid temperature, he hadn't expected to survive the night. It would be the first of several surprises that day. The small cave that he had discovered and crawled into the previous evening had most certainly been the deciding factor between life and death. Rolling painfully to his left side, he reached inside his last pouch and withdrew two figs and the same amount of dates.

Strangely, for the first time since his escape, he felt no hunger. Knowing he must eat to maintain his strength, he forced himself to swallow one of the fruits. He had no sooner finished than he began to wretch. His dry heaves continued well after the bits of fig had been regurgitated. *So this is how it feels to be in the final stages of starvation.* Wiping the spittle from his mouth, he pushed himself to his hands and knees. *Just once more, I would like to see the beauty of God's work.* That was the second time that morning that he had surprised himself. It had been many years, dating back to his childhood, since he had permitted the concept of 'god' into his appreciation of nature.

With a supreme struggle, he gathered his weary, debilitated muscles and pulled himself up by gripping the sides of the cave. Hobbling the few paces to the entrance, he first glanced to the southwest, the direction from which he came. His eyes were met by snowcapped mountain ranges that undulated off into the distance like frozen white-capped ocean waves. He then turned in the opposite direction and was stunned by what spread before him. It was the most glorious pass between the mountains that he had yet seen. He slumped to his bony backside on the snow-covered ground and gazed at the magnificent sight. The valley was relatively wide and extended for many miles. He estimated that the mountains on either side easily rose to ten thousand feet and that the ranges beyond towered to twice that height. Only one such phenomenon in the world fit that description—the Khyber Pass.

Leaning back against his rock support, he forgot his dire situation in the majesty of the moment. As the sun rose above the peaks, the pearl-white mountains reflected the golden light in glimmering hues of blue, violet, and pink. *Perhaps my own namesake, Alexander, sat here with his Macedonian warriors and witnessed such a sight over two thousand years ago. And how many others had passed this way, this natural invasion route through all Asia, in their efforts to force their will upon others? The Persians...the Mongols...the British...the Russians.... Would the Ikhwan be the next?*

With an effort, he pushed himself to his feet, dusted the snow from his backside, and began to work his way down the mountain. Only a few more hundred meters and he would be in the pass leading to Pakistan and safety. He had not gone far, however, when he encountered yet another surprise—a shout from behind him. Turning in the direction of the noise, he saw several rifle-toting men gesticulating at him. He willed his legs to pick up his heavy feet and began to scramble away from the approaching figures. The next sound he heard was the sharp report of a rifle echoing from the mountainsides. Instinctively, he ducked and clung tightly to a boulder. Glancing back over his shoulder, he saw that his pursuers, now recognizable by their uniforms as Afghan soldiers, were gaining on him. Once more, he summoned his waning strength, pushed himself from the rock, and stumbled on.

"*Sto-ee!*" a voice cried out. The fact that he was being ordered to halt in his own language merely confirmed to Marenkov that his identity was known to these hunters. His legs were now feeling impossibly heavy and a searing pain accompanied every frantic breath for oxygen. Try as he might, he could no longer lift his feet. He sank to his knees and crawled forward a few meters before finally sprawling to his belly. He was still dragging himself over the ground when the soldiers grasped him by his collar.

✶ ✶ ✶

Marenkov opened his eyes, trying to make sense of his blurred surroundings. In spite of the indistinct features, there was a vague familiarity about the place in which he now found himself. The plush carpeting upon which he sat, the elegant wall tapestries, the low table and large, colorful pillows in the center of the room gradually stirred his weary memory. He sensed motion—yes, a figure all in white seemed to float unceasingly to and fro before him. Rubbing his eyes, he focused more intensely on the snowy apparition. The imposing image of bin Wahhab immediately took form. The sheikh was pacing back and forth, patting a broad, curved scimitar in his left palm.

"Only two weeks ago, I was in this room discussing physics with a very reasonable expostulator of that subject," bin Wahhab said softly. "Tell me, Professor, what became of that reasonable man? At what point did he lose his reason and attempt to betray me?"

"There was no attempt at betrayal, sheikh," Marenkov said. "That would imply a trust between us that never existed."

Bin Wahhab halted his pacing and, lowering the sword to his side, strode toward Marenkov.

"This weapon served my great-grandfather well three-quarters of a century ago. He used it to relieve some infidels of the burden of carrying their misguided heads. I have since used it to the same effect. I have long harbored hope that I could reach inside your soul and that we would not come to this conclusion. But it appears that my optimism was in vain. Fortunately, I have been somewhat more successful with your compatriots. It is with pleasure that I tell you that your friends,

Valentin Tschernin and Stephan Perov, have completed assembling the bomb. The writing is now clear, as are our fates. This moment, you will descend into hell, and I will go on to wield the sword of Allah upon those who deny his word. Allahu Akhbar!"

At these last words, the tapestry behind Marenkov rustled and in stalked two men, appearing like monstrous ravens in their midnight robes and inky chin-covering headdresses. One of them held a pistol.

"I will do this myself," bin Wahhab said. "The Professor deserves to die at the hands of the Chosen One. Hold him."

The two men roughly seized Marenkov, twisted his arms behind his back, and shoved his head down and forward. The nape of his neck was fully exposed. Bin Wahhab, his eyes fixed on the vulnerable spot, stepped forward.

Marenkov had no misgivings about the rash course he had taken with the sheikh. In fact, the tactic had been employed to achieve such an end. He had done all he could and had no strength left to carry on. Images of his devoted wife, Marianna, and of his two sons floated behind his closed eyelids. And then…there was his smiling old friend, Seryozha, sitting on the bench at the University, feeding the pigeons and wrens.

Hovering above Alexander, bin Wahhab raised his great-grandfather's scimitar. The other two Arabs leaned away.

At the top of the arc, the sword nearly flew out of the sheikh's hand as the entire room shook violently. The quaking motion was accompanied by a loud blast. Bin Wahhab lowered the weapon and exchanged quizzical glances with the two fluttering blackbirds.

Wild shouting and gunfire could be heard beyond the confines of the room. Suddenly, the door was flung open and a hysterical Ikhwan soldier dashed in, crying, "Mahdi! Mahdi! We are being attacked!" It was yet another wonderment in Marenkov's surprise-filled day.

* * *

Surprise—Hardy O'Brien's first objective—had been almost completely achieved. The only warning the Ikhwan had of the impending attack was the clattering engines and whirring blades of a half dozen weapon-bristling helicopters suddenly appearing at their gate. A score of the Ikhwan raced from their stronghold, opening fire upon the mysterious, completely black aircraft. They had just begun to squeeze the triggers of their rifles, however, when a barrage of heavy caliber cannon fire from the low-flying Hunchbacks decimated their numbers. The few that survived and were still mobile tried desperately to reenter the compound before the door closed. As the thick plate steel barrier began to shut, the side door of the nearest helicopter was just opening. And the first person to leap out was the old Mustang.

O'Brien sprayed the area in front of him with his weapon as he dashed forward. He was immediately followed by twenty of his SEALs and Mike Falcon. Behind them, forty more commandos spilled from two other helicopters. The handful of the enemy that had survived the withering fire of the Hunchback were quickly dispatched and lay in a pile before the now closed steel door.

"C-4!" O'Brien barked. The order had barely escaped his lips when Lucky Ryder and a Chief Petty Officer ran to the barrier and slipped off their backpacks. Carefully, they removed small packages of the white, putty-like explosive and their detonators. As they worked, deliberately but smartly, O'Brien motioned to his men to take positions on either side of the door. Rochelle led his platoon to the side opposite O'Brien's unit. Falcon stayed with the Commander in order to be available for communications with the Spetsnaz team.

That unit had landed at the same time as the Americans, but a little over a mile away. Their objective was to defend the sole road leading from Khowst to the Ikhwan stronghold. At least half of the enemy were bivouacked in the town and would soon be mounting an attack to relieve their comrades. Rodonov positioned one platoon near the compound to intercept any Ikhwan that slipped through his first line of defense. That line consisted of two platoons placed on either side of a narrow mountain pass so that any troops entering the defile would be subjected to a deadly crossfire. A significant portion of this barrage would come from the machine gun manned by Sergeant Viktor Buzhkin, who lay prone in the snow, peering along the barrel of his tripod-supported weapon. A few paces behind him, Sergei Medved and the Spetsnaz Colonel were attempting to contact their American counterparts.

"Yes...the Spartans are at Thermopylae," Medved said, using the prearranged code to inform Falcon of the Russians' position. He skillfully balanced a dangling cigarette from his mouth as he spoke. "No sign of our hosts. Over."

"Roger. The Macedonians are at the Granicus." As Falcon spoke, an explosion shook the ground and reverberated from the mountainsides. "We're in hot."

The steel door had been blown off its hinges and tossed several yards into the entrance of the compound, where it landed on the stone floor with a resounding clang. Rochelle took advantage of the smoke and confusion to promptly spearhead the attack. He and his men lay down their own sheet of metal in the form of steel cartridges that burst from their Colt Commandos as they penetrated the compound. Their fire effectively pinned down the dazed and disorganized Ikhwan, allowing O'Brien to lead his platoon in from the opposite side of the entrance.

Surveying the situation from behind an unopened box of machinery, Fawaz bin Sufya realized that his people were too befuddled and too panicked to make a good show in the loading area. He ordered the men behind him to retreat to the bunkroom where they could reorganize and provide the Mahdi the precious time necessary to complete his hasty arrangements. And, with any luck, the Afghan Army would quickly respond to their call for help. Unfortunately, the few dozen followers that were trapped in the entryway would have to be sacrificed.

In his twenty-eight years of service with the Navy's Special Warfare Group, Hardy O'Brien had made his share of mistakes. But he had never failed to learn from them and he never forgot a lesson learned in the crucible of battle. He knew that the element of surprise was one of the very greatest weapons in a battle. Another was swift, relentless pressing of an attack against a stunned, flustered adversary. In the interests of keeping their casualties to a minimum, he could have his troops maintain their positions and with their superior fighting and armament capabilities, gradually decimate the enemy. But that would not be doing what was necessary to achieve the objective.

"Hand me the squawk box," he said to Ryder, who was replacing a hot, spent magazine in his assault rifle. The j.g. complied and O'Brien held the phone to his ear.

"Macedonian Two. One, here. Attack! I say again…Attack!"

Rochelle immediately ordered his men to toss grenades in the direction of the enemy. The explosions were earth-shaking and deafening. Before the Ikhwan dared to raise their heads from their shelters, the SEALs were on top of them. At the same time, O'Brien led his men behind Macedonian Two, across the hundred-foot debris-riddled expanse of the loading area to the bolted door leading to the bunkroom. Exactly one minute had transpired from the time the steel plate door at the compound's entrance had been blown off its hinges.

It quickly became apparent that a similar treatment would be required for the barracks door as the rifle bullets directed on it ricocheted harmlessly away. Once again, Ryder and his Chief Gunners Mate gingerly moved forward with their package of C-4 and a detonator. Only a handful of the enemy in the loading room were still combative and they were mostly glued to the floor by a hail of fire from both SEAL platoons. Ryder and the Gunney went swiftly about their business, molding the explosive into a two-inch thick rectangle and attaching the blasting cap. Unfortunately, they didn't move fast enough. One of the Ikhwan, who was relatively secure behind a stack of lead plates, had an unobstructed line of sight to the men working at the door. He raised his rifle to his shoulder, aimed, and squeezed the trigger. Instantly the Gunney hurtled backwards, slamming into and knocking over Ryder.

The j.g.'s nickname was justified on two counts, as he was lucky not to be wounded from the gunfire and even luckier that the detonator he held in his hand had not been hit. The Ikhwan, however, was not through and continued to direct his fire toward the two vulnerable SEALs. The Gunney, who was more exposed to the gunfire, took several more hits as Ryder struggled to drag him to shelter. Exasperated that one of his intended victims might survive, the Ikhwan shifted his position so that he had a good look at Ryder. Before he was able to squeeze the trigger, however, he sensed the presence of someone behind him. Instantly turning rearward, he found himself staring into the barrel of Mike Falcon's Glock. It was the last thing he ever saw.

Losing no time, Ryder scrambled to his feet, set the detonator and connecting 'leg' wires and dragged the Gunney and himself behind a large piece of tube-laden machinery. When the C-4 blew away the door, O'Brien's men lobbed a few dozen grenades through the gaping hole left behind. Shouts, cries, and rifle fire were mixed with the din of numerous explosions in the second chamber. Again pressing the attack, O'Brien charged into the smoke and dust-choked room at the head of his men.

In spite of the mayhem caused by the grenades, there still remained over two hundred Ikhwan soldiers in fighting form. Well-trained and wielding their Russian assault rifles they presented a formidable obstacle. The extent of the challenge was immediately apparent to O'Brien when the fire laid down by the Ikhwan ripped into his men as they transited the doorway. Their Kevlar jackets helped somewhat; their toughness and training helped even more. Because this second room consisted of the compound's barracks, there was no wide-open area as in the loading dock. Instead, the space was filled with dozens of sleeping quarters which proved to be a mixed blessing for the SEALs. It was an advantage in that the enemy was unable to bring its greater numbers to bear at any particular location. The disadvantage was that it would take additional time to secure each bunkroom. And time was their enemy. It would not be long before the Afghan Army would arrive in overwhelming force.

Methodically, the SEALs worked their way down the hallways, clearing the way with grenades and other explosives, isolating small pockets of the enemy, then wiping them out. It was becoming obvious to Fawaz bin Sufya that his men could not stop the juggernaut approach of this strange army of death. But he was buying time. He needed only another ten minutes…perhaps even less…then he could die smiling, knowing that he had preserved the Jihad and would thus be transported directly to Paradise. Meanwhile, on the road leading to the compound, other Ikhwan were being transported to a much less pleasant locale.

*   *   *

"How many?" Medved asked as he watched the first canvas-covered trucks rumble into the pass.

"Ten," Rodonov replied without lowering the night vision binoculars from his eyes. "Probably two dozen men per truck. We'll wait until the first vehicle is at the head of the defile."

That would take only a few more seconds, Medved surmised as the five-ton trucks were moving at top speed in spite of the dangerously snow-slicked roads.

"Prepare to fire," Rodonov said quietly but firmly.

"Steady…steady…."

Each Russian Commando peered in anticipation through his night vision reticule at a green image of a truck. Each had been given an assignment, by squad, as to which of the vehicles to target.

"Fire!"

As loud as the command was, it was still muffled by the explosion of several rocket-propelled grenade launchers, a couple of anti-armor missile systems, and three dozen assault rifles triggering simultaneously. The first truck swerved, crashed into the far mountain wall, then became airborne. Flipping upside down, it hurtled earthward, landing squarely on the following vehicle. Both trucks erupted into a burst of brilliant orange, red, and yellow flames. Behind this fireball, the other trucks stopped and their occupants spilled onto the road, desperately seeking cover in the shelter of the mountains. It was a short trip but a deadly one as the accurate barrage from the Spetsnaz rifles continued to take its toll.

Rodonov, however, could not afford to gloat over the success of the ambush. He was still outnumbered five to one, and Afghan Army reinforcements were almost certainly on their way. He glanced at his watch. 'T plus ten'. In eight more minutes, he would lead his men back to the landing zone to be picked up by the helicopters. With them or without them, the transports would be lifting off at 'T plus Thirty'.

"Major, see if you can raise the Americans," he said, turning to Medved.

Setting his overheating rifle aside, Sergei lifted the phone and made the connection.

"The Macedonians are at Issus," the report came from Mike Falcon.

"Shit!" Rodonov sputtered, employing one of the only English words in his repertoire. He had hoped that the Americans would be at Arbela, the laboratory, by now.

"The schedule doesn't call for Arbela until 'T plus fifteen'," Medved reminded the Spetsnaz commander.

Rodonov glanced again at his watch. The second hand had moved only thirty seconds since his last inquiry. "For their sakes, I hope they make it by then. Check back exactly one minute from now."

As he spoke, a squad from Rochelle's platoon was just arriving at the door leading into the laboratory. Once again, C-4 was positioned around the frame and detonated. The door boomed away and, although the bunkrooms were still being hotly contested, O'Brien ordered Rochelle to lead his squad into the main target.

No advance screen of grenades was employed in this attack, owing to the assumed presence of highly enriched uranium. Darting through the shattered doorway, Rochelle and his eight men rapidly sought shelter behind wooden benches, machine lathes, dresser-sized computers and metal containers with electrical wires that dangled spaghetti-like. The pungent odor of charred flesh mixed with defecation filled their nostrils. Although his squad had not fired a shot in this room, dozens of bodies, almost all clad in blood-drenched white smocks, stiff in their awkward poses of sudden, violent death, covered the floor. There were no living beings in sight.

Using hand motions, Rochelle directed his men to investigate every corner of the room. Crouching, and keeping his head on a swivel, he inched toward the glass-paned enclosure located in the center of the laboratory. The door leading into it was wide open. Cautiously, and with his rifle barrel extended before him, he stepped through the opening. The floor of the lab was littered with papers, wiring, tools, and computer equipment. It carried the earmarks of some very hasty activity. He gazed across the room to the far wall, to the work-bench where, according to the Ikhwan captured on the previous raid, the two hat-box size sections of the bomb were to be found. The wooden platform was empty.

"Damn," he muttered, fearful that the operation had been in vain. Grasping his phone, he was about to report the bad news to the Skipper when his attention was diverted by a faint scraping noise emanating from behind a stack of lead plates. He shoved the phone back into his vest, raised his rifle, and stepped toward the sound. Peering around the pile of metal, he came eyeball-to-eyeball with a trembling, ruddy-complected, cherubic-faced man who sat mumbling incoherently. Clad in the same attire—a white smock—as those who lay slaughtered around him, he clutched his drawn-up knees with all the strength of his arms.

"Hey 'Cuda," one of the SEALs shouted, "Over here."

Hoisting the petrified man from the floor and into a fireman's carry, Rochelle exited the central lab and, careful to avoid the strewn corpses, hustled to the call. As he moved, he was startled to see the beckoning SEAL and other men in his squad disappear into a wall.

"It's some sort of secret passageway, Lieutenant."

Lowering his human burden to the floor, Rochelle ordered one of his men to "get on the horn to the Skipper. Tell him we're going to be a little late, but we have to check out this corridor." Without further pause, Rochelle and three of his men headed single-file through the dark, narrow tunnel. Aided by their night vision optics, they were able to maintain a respectable trot and in just under a minute and a half reached the end of the quarter mile long corridor. There they were confronted by another door, but this time, instead of an explosive charge, only a slight nudge was needed to swing the barrier away. Rochelle and his men then stepped out into the cold night air. From where they stood, a one-lane dirt road snaked down the mountain toward the distant town of Khowst. And on the road, a lone vehicle was rapidly negotiating the winding course.

"That's it!" Rochelle cried. Immediately, he was on the phone to O'Brien.

"Mac One, the package is in a fleeing vehicle. We have it in sight. We could vector a Hunchback to take it out. Over."

O'Brien weighed the options of allowing the bomb to slip through his fingers versus destroying it and risking the low percentage but real possibility of touching off a nuclear explosion. It took only a few seconds for him to respond.

"Negative, Mac Two. Return to the nest double time. I say again, return double time. Out."

As he re-pocketed his phone, O'Brien glanced at his watch. 'T plus twenty' and they were still in the compound. Worse, he couldn't even begin the extraction until Rochelle's squad regrouped with him. "Get me Rodonov," he growled to Ryder. "Stand by, Mr. Falcon."

* * *

Beyond the pass held by the Russians, above the dark, jagged peaks far to the northwest, numerous tiny red lights were beginning to dot the night sky.

"The Afghan Army will be here in less than ten minutes," Rodonov muttered to Medved. "Call the American Commander again. He must know that it will soon be impossible to hold our line."

"O'Brien is already calling us," Sergei responded, flicking his cigarette to the snow and handing the phone to Rodonov.

The Spetsnaz Colonel quickly grasped the receiver and held it to his ear. Even in the dark, Medved could see that his commander was not happy as he listened to the report.

"You are asking for the impossible, Commander," Rodonov said coolly. "If any soldiers can do the impossible, it is my men. However, even we cannot hold off an entire army."

He handed the phone back to Medved.

"The American is delaying extraction for seven more minutes. Tell the men to continue to hold their positions."

Sergei glanced at the growing red lights, then at his watch. *Seven minutes would be a very fine slicing of this salmon.*

Meanwhile, the Ikhwan in the pass had recovered from their initial shock and had begun to establish a fairly effective counterattack. After several minutes, they even felt bold enough to attempt a breakout. With half of their comrades laying down a heavy covering fire, nearly a hundred of the Ikhwan dashed to the vehicles. The lead truck had barely inched beyond the wreckage of its predecessor in the pass when it too was ripped apart by an infrared tracking missile and the convoy was halted. This time, however, sensing their numerical superiority and possessing fanatic recklessness, they charged from their vehicles directly toward the Russian commandos. Although their losses were fearful, their impetus carried them through the Spetsnaz lines and a desperate hand-to-hand struggle ensued.

Medved, his face grimy with sweat, oil, and gunpowder, and with bullets shrilly singing off the rocks near his head, swung his machine gun to meet this new assault. With his left hand helping to guide the ammunition belt through the red-hot weapon, he squeezed the trigger with his right. The shock of cartridges spraying at ten rounds per second checked the attack. But only momentarily, for he was knocked from his weapon by a force which felt like a heavy sack of potatoes. Pushing clear, he saw that the tumbling weight was, in fact, the lifeless form of Lt. Col. Rodonov. He looked up to see Viktor Buzhkin, standing three meters away, with his rifle now aimed toward him.

Medved swung his own weapon around just as Buzhkin fired. A hurtling body landed behind Sergei. He turned to see the lifeless form of an Ikhwan soldier.

"Ey, that beggar just did in Rodonov," Buzhkin said, surprisingly calmly. "Lucky for you I came along in time, Medved. Now crank up your weapon again or we shall soon become owners of this prime Afghan real estate."

*   *   *

As the battle in the pass hung in the balance, Rochelle and his squad exited the lab, leaving some well-placed C-4 calling cards in their wake. Over his right shoulder, the Lieutenant himself carried the lone survivor of the Ikhwan laboratory massacre. Joining their shipmates in the barracks, the disposal squad detonated the charges and the laboratory disintegrated in several rib-rattling explosions. The American commandos then began to fight their way out of the barracks and back into the loading docks. Fawaz bin Sufya, gathering his troops for one last glorious charge into Paradise, shouted "Allahu Akhbar!" With this rallying cry bursting from their lips and with their assault rifles blazing from their hands, they attacked.

It was then that fate turned on Rochelle. A bullet drilled through his left biceps shattering the humerus and slamming him into a bulkhead. Falcon, who was alongside, caught the wounded SEAL as he dropped his human cargo and slumped to the floor. Rochelle was hemorrhaging but the absence of spurting blood encouraged Falcon that no major artery had been severed. Quickly tearing a sleeve of his shirt, Falcon pressed the cotton material against the wound. Before he could do more, Rochelle and his human prize were lifted by two passing SEALs and carried away.

Falcon seized his Glock and turned again toward the rampaging enemy. One of the Ikhwan was nearly on top of him. Although he had only a split second to react, he felt as though time had suddenly slowed to a near standstill and that his powers of observation had vastly increased. The Ikhwan wore a red and white checkered headdress that drifted slowly around his ebony face. His long white robe hung loosely over a wiry frame. He was gradually turning his assault rifle toward Falcon. As if in a dream, Falcon slowly raised his Glock and squeezed the trigger. He blinked in slow motion, the gun lazily recoiled, and Fawaz bin Sufya melted away.

A hand slapping his shoulder returned Falcon to the full-speed world.

"Good shot, Mr. Falcon," the Skipper said. "But don't be caught sitting here counting your money."

As Falcon looked up, he was disturbed to see blood flowing from O'Brien's head and arm. The two men—the last Americans to leave the compound—backed toward the exit. Upon emerging, O'Brien gave the order for the helicopters to begin spooling up. Each of the transports carried twelve stretchers and an unfortunate number of them would now be needed to accommodate the American wounded.

"Are you certain that all are present and accounted for?" O'Brien demanded sternly of Ryder, as the relatively laborious task of loading the wounded proceeded. The j.g. knew that the Old Man would personally never leave if one man remained behind. This was one answer in his 'happy-go-lucky' life that he had to have right.

"Affirmative, sir."

"Very well. Tell the Hunchbacks to cover us."

"Aye, aye. Here are the Russians."

O'Brien and Falcon turned to see the Spetsnaz commandos approaching on the double. Although they moved in good order, it was obvious that they, too, had experienced heavy fighting.

Falcon anxiously trotted to the Spetsnaz unit, trying to distinguish features among the dark visages of the soldiers who brushed by him.

"Ey, Michael, I see you cheated death again," a familiar voice called out. Falcon turned to see Medved's broad grin just before the Russian hugged him and kissed him on both cheeks. He then felt an even stronger grip as Viktor Buzhkin seized him in a bear hug.

"We keep turning up like two bad kopecks," Sergei laughed. "Now, go. Your taxi is about to depart."

Falcon raced back in time to clamber onto the revving helicopter. As it lifted from the ground, Ikhwan soldiers began pouring from the compound, shooting at the transports. Two Hunchbacks rolled toward them, achieved photo-electric locks and launched their laser-guided rockets. The initial two explosions were followed by two more, then three, four and five from within the compound as stored munitions and gasoline erupted. The pyrotechnics were awesome, humbling, hypnotic, and when they ended a full minute later, there was only rubble to mark the sight of the former Ikhwan stronghold. The Russian helicopters accelerated to maximum speed and soon began to outdistance the more antiquated aircraft of their pursuers.

As the transports sped across northern Afghanistan, hugging the spiny mountain peaks, O'Brien visited his wounded troops. His right arm was in a sling and his head was wrapped in a white bandage that began just above his eyes. The last stretcher in his circuit held Chris Rochelle. Two bottles of fluids were attached through plastic tubes to the Lieutenant's arms. One contained an intravenous saline solution and the other was providing some badly needed plasma.

"Hell of a good job, 'Cuda," O'Brien said, squatting next to the stretcher. It was the first time he had ever referred to his Lieutenant by his nickname.

"Ahh, I let you down, Skipper," Rochelle rasped, wincing. "We didn't get the package."

"Not a damned thing more anyone could've done, son. Now hear this. You get better post-haste. Don't forget…Lt.(j.g.) Ryder will be paying all our happy hour bills at MacDill from here on out."

Rochelle managed a half-smile through the pain. O'Brien stood, crossed to the far side of the helicopter bay and plopped himself down next to Mike Falcon.

"Hell of a furball, Skipper," Falcon said softly, his head leaning back against the cabin's forward bulkhead.

"You didn't do badly, Mr. Falcon," O'Brien grunted. "For an 'airdale', that is." It was the best compliment the grizzled Commander could bestow upon a non-SEAL, particularly an 'airdale'—a jet-jockey—who, in his air-conditioned cockpit, rarely got up close and personal with the mayhem of war.

"The performance of you and your men…" Falcon answered. "Well, it was damned incredible."

"My men…yes," O'Brien shrugged. "They went above and beyond. The Russians, too. Hell of a shame about Rodonov. And damned rotten we didn't achieve our objective."

Falcon was about to remind O'Brien that some good had come of the mission, including the destruction of bin Wahhab's main base of operations and the elimination of his elite bodyguard. But he realized that they were scant consolations compared to the loss of the primary goal.

Now, as O'Brien and Falcon gazed about them and their eyes fell not upon a steel case of uranium or a captured nuclear bomb, but upon wounded and, in too many cases, dying troops, it was hard to characterize the mission as a success. The one ray of hope was the dazed, frightened man in the white smock that trembled at the foot of Lt. Rochelle's stretcher.

Chapter Thirty-Four

The mood in the War Room of the Russian Ministry of Defense matched its setting: black. Even when the soft overhead lighting and the three-story backlit map were turned on, there was no lightening of the souls of the dozen people who quietly sat before the fifty-chair, dark cherrywood oval table. Mike Falcon, wedged between Sergei Medved and Viktor Buzhkin, stared blankly at the wall unit as an unseen hand changed its image of the world to a close-up of the Khowst area. To his left, Sergei once more inhaled the smoke of his cigarette, then crushed the dwindling stub into a glass ashtray. The butt joined three other of its fellow dead soldiers there, testimony to the long wait of those gathered at the table. Falcon glanced to his right where Buzhkin also was intently eyeing the map. The Siberian's stoic demeanor, however, thwarted any attempt by Falcon to fathom his thoughts.

Directly across the table, Yevgeny Aksanov and his musings were veiled in a lazy swirl of bluish-white smoke that rose from the pipe he held absently to his lips. Next to him, Hardy O'Brien sat ramrod straight, his always alert dancing gray eyes belying his calm demeanor title.

Momentarily, the door on the far right wall opened. The small assembly stood as five Russian officers, led by General Vernadsky, filed into the room.

Pausing at the head of the table, Vernadsky said, "Please be seated. Do we have the hook-up to Washington?"

An army general hopped from his chair and switched on a lunch-box size speaker in front of the General.

"Hello, *Gospodeen* Higby. Are you hearing me?" Vernadsky asked. After a few seconds pause—caused not so much by the round-trip satellite travel as by the sophisticated encryption and decryption procedures—a voice was heard in the speaker.

"Loud and clear, Colonel," the President's Security Advisor answered. "I have with me the Deputy Assistant Secretary of State—Harold Pettigrew; Larry Dahlgren of the CIA; and Warren Fredericks from the FBI. Please proceed."

After informing the Americans of the names of the participants at his end, Vernadsky began the briefing.

"First, I want to commend all who took part in this operation. Much was accomplished. Bin Wahhab no longer has a base of operations in Afghanistan from which he can launch his terrorist attacks. The elite core of his military was wiped out. Not one American or Russian soldier was left behind. However, as you all are well aware, the enriched uranium and the nuclear bomb, if indeed one does exist, were not captured. I will now ask Commander O'Brien to brief you in greater detail."

The SEAL Skipper, his head still bandaged and his right arm in a sling, rose and began speaking in a gravelly voice. "Mr. Falcon, I'd appreciate your interpreting skills," he said, reaching for a glass of water with his free hand. Swallowing two long draughts, he coughed, set the glass down, and growled, "Thanks to some very skillful flying by your pilots, General, we infiltrated undetected and on-time to the target."

After describing the battle in clinical detail, O'Brien drew their attention to the point of main interest. "In the lab, numerous freshly slain personnel were discovered. We now know that these people were the scientists and engineers who were constructing the nuclear device. Bin Wahhab must have ordered their murder just before he fled with the bomb and a few select disciples. Fortunately, one of the intended victims escaped the killing and was recovered by our team."

"The man you recovered," Higby asked anxiously, "was it Professor Alexander Marenkov?"

"No, sir. The scientist's name is Valentin Tschernin, another Russian nuclear physics expert who had been missing for nearly a year."

"And was Marenkov among the dead?"

"We must assume so, although we may never be certain…."

"Please continue, Commander," Higby said.

"The other unfortunate discovery made by Rochelle's squad in the lab was that the uranium was gone."

"Gone, you say?" another voice blurted over the speaker. "This is Warren Fredericks, Director of the FBI. I thought NSA assured us that its spy satellites would have detected any movement of the uranium from the compound. No such activity was seen. How could it have disappeared in the midst of your troops?"

"We had a bit of a surprise inside the compound," O'Brien responded. "My men discovered a secret passageway that had been cut through the rock, exiting the east side of the mountain a quarter of a mile away.

"But how is it that the American satellites never detected this secondary access?" Aksanov asked. "Did it not occur to the NSA to look for such a possibility?"

"Perhaps, as Director of the NSA, I can best answer that," the voice of Preston Higby crackled through the speaker. "The answer is, yes, we did look for alternative accesses to bin Wahhab's stronghold, in anticipation that he would try to flee with the bomb during the attack. We scoured every foot of the mountain. Our focused surveillance, however, produced negative results."

"And I can explain that," O'Brien interjected. "The doorway to this rear escape was set slightly inside the mouth of a shallow cave. There it was completely hidden from aerial surveillance."

"Quite unfortunate. But go on, Commander," Aksanov said.

"Lieutenant Rochelle led his men on the double through this corridor," O'Brien continued, "and emerged just in time to see a truck motoring in the distance toward Khowst. We believe that the uranium, and the bomb, were in that vehicle."

"Then why, for god's sake," Fredericks sputtered, "didn't you order one of the assault helos to destroy it?"

"I made a judgement call not to chance nuking half of eastern Afghanistan," O'Brien said crisply and firmly.

"But now we're back to square one, or worse," Fredericks persisted. "At least at one point we knew where the bomb was. Now it's disappeared into the night and could pop up, or better put, explode, anywhere."

"It was the correct call—militarily, politically, and ethically," Higby interceded. "Let's hear the rest of the Commander's report."

O'Brien went on to describe how the SEALs held off the charge of Fawaz bin Sufya and his men in the compound's barracks while at the same time the Spetsnaz were defending their mountain pass against another Ikhwan counterattack. "We estimate enemy losses at four hundred. The elite guard of bin Wahhab is no more. Our combined casualties were thirty-seven dead and over a hundred wounded. We left the target only moments prior to the arrival of approximately two thousand enemy troops. Four of our Mi-8's made it all the way back to our base in Turkmeniya. The other two made it safely across the border before running out of fuel and making emergency landings. Those personnel were recovered safely. That completes my report and I'll stand by to answer any questions you may have."

"Commander, this is Larry Dalhgren of the CIA," a voice came through the speaker. "Were you able to pick up any clues as to where bin Wahhab—and the bomb—may be heading?"

"No sir. If I were him—and I admit that it's a stretch to believe that I might think like bin Wahhab—but if I were him, I'd be out of Afghanistan by now. His base of operations there has been demolished.

Also, he must certainly realize that we'll quickly bring every available surveillance resource to bear on that country. By tomorrow, if he's still in Afghanistan and goes to take a piss, we'll know it."

"The Commander's absolutely correct," Higby said. "My guess is, he's already left the country and is headed for territory friendly to him…a country that sponsors terrorism…Iraq, Libya, or Sudan. We'll enhance our vigilance in those countries as well. And of course, you were able to bring back a prisoner who may be able to give us some leads. Have you been able to glean any information from Tschernin?"

"Not yet, sir, but the interrogations are ongoing as we speak."

"Thank you, Commander," Higby said. "General Vernadsky, I suggest that we keep our channels of communication open twenty-four hours a day so that we may be prepared to act as necessary on a moment's notice."

"Agreed," Vernadsky replied. "Then if there is nothing further…."

The meeting adjourned and Falcon, Medved, and Buzhkin were headed for the exit when they were intercepted by Aksanov.

"Major Medved," he called, quickly crossing the room. "Take this with you."

He extended his right hand, in which was clasped a white, business letter-sized envelope. As Sergei took the envelope, Aksanov said, "It's from our President. He thinks you might find it helpful in your questioning of Tschernin."

Medved hastily stuffed the envelope into his pocket and Aksanov departed, ambling back down the hall. Emerging from the Ministry of Defense building, Falcon stepped into falling snow.

"Damn," he muttered. "When I bought my ketch a few years back, I swore I'd sail to the tropics and never be cold or in snow again."

"So what the hell are you doing in places like Russia and Afghanistan?" the Russian chided.

"Good question."

"Ey, look at the bright side, Falcon," Buzhkin quipped. "It's warm in some part of the world."

"So it is," the American said, turning up his collar against a cold-knifed wind and reflecting momentarily upon his days of cruising the warm Caribbean. "I just need to be there."

* * *

As Falcon spoke, a woman stood on the bowsprit of a fifty-six foot schooner anchored at Flamingo Bay off the little island of Rum Cay in the Caribbean. Her blonde hair, a golden shimmer in the early morning sun, fell lightly about her cream-colored shoulders and halfway down her back. Further down, a few centimeters of a thong bathing suit provided her only concession to modesty. The exposed portion of her body, which was virtually all of it, was strong, graceful, and beautifully proportioned, a seaman's dream.

In fact the woman was the fantasy of the schooner's skipper, Guy DeMaté, as well as every other poor male sap on board. DeMaté now lounged on the helmsman's seat, sinking his teeth into a soft juicy papaya, and leaned against the port jib winch where he found the best view of this virtually naked sea nymph. The other men who had been cruising on the *Night Hawk* were not permitted such a luxury. The two crewmembers were required by DeMaté to keep their noses to their splicing. The three men who had paid five thousand dollars each for a two-week luxury cruise aboard the yacht were kept in line by their wives, all of whom hated that 'French hussy.' None of the married women had actually experienced any unpleasantry with the 'hussy'. In fact, they had individually found her to be quite gracious and charming. It was only when they caught their husbands ogling the woman—an unfortunately common occurrence—or when they were conferring together that their negative opinion surfaced.

DeMaté watched the blonde ease her arms backwards and dip into a crouch. With the back of his right hand, he wiped the dripping papaya from his short brown Vandyke beard. Unconsciously, his eyes squeezed to narrow slits, like a camera lens focusing, as he drank in the sight of her taut rump and leg muscles, coiled in preparation to spring. The next moment her arms swept forward, her lithe form extended, and she soared off the bowsprit into the jade-green Caribbean.

"*Merde*," he muttered. He'd like to either screw or kill that cock-tease. Unfortunately, there was one small problem in achieving either of these aspirations. The first, and only, time he tried to force himself on her was a year earlier when she had hired him in St. Kitts to assume captaincy of the *Night Hawk*. They had taken the shiny new schooner out for a one-day sea trial and she had flaunted her sleek, bare body at him like a red cape before a bull. *Hell, I'm a red-blooded Frenchman…what did she expect?* At his first advance, he was burned by her rejection, as if she were made of dry ice. *But of course, 'no' means 'yes', n'est-ce pas?* It was his persistence that proved to be his undoing.

As he had cornered her in the aft stateroom and tried to sandwich her between his one-hundred sixty pound frame and the cabin's berth, he suddenly found himself on his knees and in excruciating pain. All the air had been exploded from his lungs as though he had been struck squarely in the solar plexus with the ship's anchor. But, struggling to breathe as he looked up at her, he realized she could not have possibly concealed any such device on her nearly naked body. She now stood over him, legs spread, fists on her hips, a smile on her face. Slowly she leaned towards him, cupped his face in one hand, puckered his lips between her thumb and forefinger and said, "Thank you in advance for never touching me again." She then casually stepped over him and went topside.

After such a humiliation, he would have quit then and there if not for the very generous terms of their contract. She had offered to pay him fifty percent more than the going rate for a skipper of such a vessel, with the proviso that he keep *Night Hawk* in seagoing condition (at her expense) at all times. He wondered by what means was she able to own, outfit, and charter a million dollar yachting operation. She had not even visited the ship for a full year, yet the checks drawn on the *Credit Lyonnaise* and made payable to him continued to arrive like clockwork. If he had wanted to, he could have cheated her blind. But of course he had thought twice about that. He sensed that somehow she knew all the details of the charter operations and exactly how seaworthy the ship was at any given moment.

And now why had she suddenly appeared, as if she had dropped from the sky, when he sailed into St. Thomas? And why did she insist on joining the cruise back to the Bahamas? And where...and why...had she learned her deadly skills?

Then there was the mystery of *Night Hawk*, herself. First, there was the puzzle of the enormous inboard diesel engine...three times more powerful than was necessary to adequately motor the ship. Furthermore, his thirty years of sailing, twenty of which had been as a charter captain in the Bahamas on literally hundreds of sailboats, told him that something more fundamental was amiss with this vessel. He couldn't quite put his finger on it...a strange imbalance when tacking or heeling beyond fifteen degrees. It was as though the lead pigs in the keel were shifting...but of course, that was impossible...they were fused into place by molten lead. Still, he was looking forward to the first annual overhaul in Nassau so that he could get a look at the ballast.

Nassau....The thought occurred to him that in the two days remaining in their sail, Mademoiselle Tigere's eyes might be finally opened to his attributes. Meanwhile, perhaps it might be wise to learn a little more about this *femme fatale.*

Swallowing the last chunk of the fruit's sweet meat, he tossed the skin of the papaya into the sea, wiped his sleeve across his mouth and beard, and rose. A quick glance over the starboard bow confirmed that the French woman was a few hundred meters away and swimming further off toward a coral reef that protected the bay. No one else was on board, as the wives had dragged their husbands to a snorkeling area that was conveniently far from the 'hussy' and the crew was ashore purchasing fresh bread, fruit, and other supplies.

Sliding around the teak wheel, he grasped the deckhouse lip and swung through the open hatchway. Passing the navigation table, he stole a quick look at the latest weather fax…high pressure front, northeast trades at fifteen to twenty knots, no precipitation. With the usual following sea of this area, they would have an easy go of it in their northwest run to Nassau. He moved on, through the main salon that gleamed in highly burnished mahogany and polished brass, past a hand-carved teak door, and into the crew's quarters. Although as elegant as the rest of the yacht, this space was quite simple, consisting of two-tiered bunks port and starboard and four sets of mahogany drawers. It was here that Tigere had insisted on bunking and had stowed her duffel bag, which was hardly larger than a knap-sack.

Laying his hands on this prize, DeMaté sat on the edge of a lower bunk, slipped open the nylon binding cord, spread the mouth, and flipped it upside down. A passport, purse, cosmetics case, several changes of bikinis, tank-tops, and shorts spilled onto the bunk, along with a lacquered, rectangular wooden box that was slightly larger than his hand. Finding it to be locked, he set the box aside and seized the purse. Its contents, too, were summarily dumped out. Ten thousand dollars in Travelers Cheques and several thousand more in francs and American dollars, plus pens, lipstick, paper clips, tampax, a comb, and a rubber band tumbled out…but no key that might unlock the intriguing little box.

He shifted his attention back to the other objects on the bunk and his eyes immediately fell on the French passport. Scanning through it, he read that Cherisse Tigere was born in Lyon twenty-nine years ago, was blonde, green-eyed, 5'7", and 120 pounds. Most of these facts he had already deduced from his own thorough and highly personal scrutiny.

The more he thought about it, the more he convinced himself that the key to unraveling her mystery lay in the lacquer box. Perhaps he could pick the lock. He glanced anxiously through the starboard porthole. The woman had just reached the reef a quarter of a mile away. At the very least, he would have five or six minutes to act. But if he screwed up the lock....

As DeMaté wrestled with his decision, Svetlana Popova pulled herself from the sea onto the reef. Running her hands through her wet hair, she gazed back at the yacht and smiled sardonically.

Chapter Thirty-Five

Bin Wahhab was constantly searching for signs, for affirmation of his anointment by Allah as the Chosen One. Such confirmation was never more important in light of the calamity that had befallen him and his household guard less than twenty-four hours earlier. Now, as his private Airbus A-340 touched down at Khartoum International Airport four kilometers southeast of the Sudanese capital, he was gripped by the significance of this very moment, as though he were seized by the hand of The Prophet, himself. The custom-made aircraft cleared the runway, its four high-pitched jet turbines winding down, and rolled to a halt on the taxiway, far from the main terminal. Bin Wahhab rose and proceeded aft, through the high-tech communications room and into the main cabin. He was accompanied by two black-robed, ebony-faced men who now were constantly at his side, AN-94's slung over their shoulders.

Although there were seats for two hundred people, only twenty-five men—those who had fled with him from Afghanistan—were there to greet him. They were clad in an assortment of robes and the brown and green Ikhwan uniforms, the motley combination providing physical evidence of their hasty escape. Their downcast eyes and slumped postures were testament to their mental disposition. Alone among them, bin Wahhab burned with zeal.

"Let us pray, brothers," he said, extending and raising his arms, his palms turned upward. Slowly, mechanically, his handful of followers knelt in the aisles and bowed their heads toward Mecca, which lay across the Red Sea to the northeast.

"One hundred and twenty years ago, another arose here in this land," Bin Wahhab said softly, his eyes lifted toward the overhead bulkhead. "His name was Muhammed Ahmed and he called himself the Mahdi. He sounded the trumpet of the Jihad against the satanic forces of the world. The ten thousand man army of British and Egyptian infidels that was sent against him was wiped out by Allah's hand. The British garrison here in Khartoum, along with its supposedly invincible general, Chinese Gordon, were put to the sword.

"But ultimately Ahmed failed to defeat the armies of the non-believers. This is because he was not, in fact, the Mahdi. It was foretold that the true Mahdi will bear the name Abdul, will have descended directly from the line of the Prophet, will appear from the imprint of Abraham's foot in the Grand Mosque at Mecca in a time of troubles, and will be attacked by armies from the north. Only I, Abdul bin Wahhab, fit this description and now it is fitting that Allah has called me to Khartoum to begin his work anew. Let us go forth and do his bidding."

The men, still subdued at the thought of their abandoned and dead comrades, quietly rose, shouldered their assault rifles and proceeded to the exit. Their leader did not immediately join them, however. Instead, he continued forward through the fuselage to his private cabin, which comprised nearly half the passenger quarters of the aircraft. The side bulkheads of this section were finished in Italian marble and the deck was covered by a rich, intricately designed Persian carpet. Two mahogany tables, each surrounded by four plush, leather covered armchairs were affixed to the deck in the center of the cabin. Fully enclosed sleeping quarters were located further forward. A stairway led down to showers, a spa, and a private prayer room.

Upon his entrance, several more of his followers, rifles in hand, rose to their feet.

"*Al laikum el sallam*," bin Wahhab responded to their bowed greeting. "And how are our guests?"

"They are just now waking," one of the soldiers answered.

"Good. Move them along. But make sure no harm comes to them!"

With a swirl of his robe, bin Wahhab turned and, in his characteristic long strides, stepped through the open hatchway and onto the service stairway. The sun had just set and only a taxiway light afforded a faint blue glow to illuminate the disembarkation. Waiting on the tarmac were a Humvee, six five-ton trucks, a container loader, and two dozen men wearing desert camouflage uniforms and toting AK-47's. As bin Wahhab descended the stairs, one of the greeting party stepped forward and snapped a stiffened right hand smartly to his brow.

"It is an honor to welcome you to Sudan, sheikh," the tall, broad-shouldered man said ceremoniously. Like the others in his group, a red and white checkered bandana covered his face from just under his eyes down to his neck. "I am Colonel Asman Hamed, here to escort you to your new home. Shall I have my men load your equipment into the trucks?"

Nodding perfunctorily in return to the Colonel's salute, bin Wahhab responded, "No, my men will attend to our equipment. Just point them to the proper vehicles."

As they spoke, a hydraulic pump hummed and the starboard cargo bay doors at the rear of the Airbus slowly parted. The two men, followed by their entourage of bodyguards, began walking toward the opening.

"Tell me, Colonel, have the Sudanese rebuilt the Shifa pharmaceutical building in Khartoum?" he asked, referring to the chemical weapons plant that had been destroyed by American cruise missiles.

"No. It was decided to relocate that effort. You shall see it during your visit."

Bin Wahhab nodded. They now had reached the opening in the rear of the aircraft. Red lights in the hold revealed eight shiny, steamer-trunk sized aluminum containers and, set apart from them, three somewhat larger rectangular black boxes. Bin Wahhab's soldiers quickly ran beneath the aircraft fuselage, taking up positions directly below the open cargo hold, their fingers on their rifle triggers.

Hamed issued an order and the cargo loader and one of the five-tons were immediately positioned before the open bay of the Airbus. With a resounding clang, the truck's iron gate was swung open and backed close to the loader. Aided by a computer, the loader's steel scissor-like mechanism adjusted its platform to accommodate the height disparity between the aircraft and the vehicle. The Ikhwan then leaped into the bay, using the truck's rear bumper as a stepping stone. There, they began to jockey the aluminum containers onto the loader platform.

"You were lucky to escape with so much equipment, sheikh," Hamed said.

"No luck was involved," bin Wahhab replied, watching the activity of men and machines. "My aircraft was always kept fully fueled and fully stocked, ready to depart at a moment's notice. I bring you Nikonov assault rifles, *Bizon* submachine guns, grenade launchers, Stinger missiles, and many other modern weapons."

Hamed's eyes, his only visible facial feature, crinkled into a smile. "We shall put them to good use."

"How much time do we have?" bin Wahhab asked.

The Colonel consulted his watch, grimaced under the burden of a mental taxation, then answered. "The next fly-over will occur in fifty-seven minutes, sheikh. Your aircraft and all of our vehicles must be under cover by then."

Bin Wahhab frowned. "But is not the base still in the *Sahra*—the 'Desert'—of Nubia?"

"Yes, between the fourth and fifth cataracts of the Nile."

"But that is at least two hundred miles away—and over some very bad or non-existent roads. It will take over five hours."

"More like seven. But since you last graced us with your presence, sheikh, we have constructed hiding places along the way. We must stop and take cover every hour and fifteen minutes. Although we will be slowed somewhat, our movement will not be detected by the satellites."

"Can you be certain?"

"Yes, your generous contributions to the cause has enabled us to purchase some very interesting data from sympathetic parties in the United States."

The ends of bin Wahhab's lips curled into a crooked smile. It would be interesting to know what the going price was for 'sympathy'. He was diverted from this thought by the revving of a diesel engine. Turning toward the aircraft, he watched as a five-ton pulled away from the cargo bay, its iron gate slamming shut. Its place was quickly taken by another truck. Now, however, all the aluminum containers had been off-loaded and one of the black boxes was being carefully eased toward the open hatch. The work slowed as it was obvious that the men had a healthy respect, or fear, of the contents.

"Put only one to a truck!" bin Wahhab ordered.

Slowly the heavy steel container slid onto the cargo loader, coaxed every inch of the way by straining, sweating, jabbering men. Thirty-five minutes later, all three boxes had been loaded and the convoy was ready to proceed.

"Good," Hamed said, glancing at his watch. "We are on schedule. Now if you would join me in the Humvee, we'll be on our way."

"Certainly, Colonel," bin Wahhab responded. "Tell me, how many passengers does this vehicle accommodate?"

"Besides the driver, five easily, sheikh."

"In that case, I have two very special guests that I would like to join us."

As they walked toward the Humvee, bin Wahhab turned to one of his bodyguards and said, "Have the two Russians brought to me."

* * *

Although he was not in the infamous basement, just being inside the walls of the Lubianka was sufficient to terrify Valentin Tschernin. He had been born in 1922, the same year that Josef Dzhugashvili became General Secretary of the Communist Party. It was Dzhugashvili who was most responsible for burning the spectre of the KGB horror palace into the national psyche. And it was the *starozheels*—the old-timers—such as Tschernin who, having lived through this era, were most scarred by this legacy of Dzhugashvili…better known by his alias of Stalin. Thus, sitting across the table from his three inquisitors, Tschernin was far from convinced by the rumors of the newer, gentler Lubianka.

The small, windowless room was brightly lit to an unpleasant glare and was heated to an uncomfortable stuffiness. *Of course, the Intelligence Service still has plenty of rubles to pay its electric bills*, Tschernin mused. With a white handkerchief drawn from his pants pocket, he mopped his perspiring brow and wondered what unpleasantries were in store for him.

"Please, drink some water," Sergei Medved spoke, sliding a clear glass full of the liquid toward the anxious scientist. He waited until Tschernin had completed his long gulp and had replaced the glass on the table.

"Personally, Valentin, we do not care one whit about how you fell in with the mad sheikh, "Medved said in the most reassuring tone he could muster. "We are interested in one thing, and one thing only. We need to know where the bomb is."

"I…I…what assurances do I have that I will not be harmed once I tell you what I know?"

"I was hoping you'd ask," Medved replied, reaching into his shirt pocket and producing the envelope that Aksanov had given him. He opened it and extracted a letter which he placed on the table before the scientist.

"This letter pardons you from any and all crimes you may have committed, including treason, in connection with your activities with bin Wahhab. It is contingent, however, on your full and honest cooperation.

Any deceit on your part or failure to fully divulge your pertinent knowledge will negate this pardon. As you will note, it is signed by the President of the Russian Federation, himself."

Tschernin quietly read, then reread the document.

"If you doubt the authenticity, we will bring in the President's Chief of Staff as a witness."

"No, that won't be necessary," Tschernin sighed, resignedly. He knew, in fact, that he really had no choice. One way or another, these men would obtain the information they sought from him.

"I heard some talk, as they were frantically preparing to leave. They thought we were all dead. I still cannot believe how he butchered us…after all…." He caught himself.

"After all you did for him?" Medved completed the thought. "But never mind all that. You were saying that they thought you were dead?"

"Yes. I managed to hide behind a stack of lead plates as they began shooting. There were so many bodies and the Ikhwan were so rabid that they did not notice I had crawled away. The screams of those that were shot…the blood everywhere…I shall have nightmares the rest of my life."

The color left his face and he appeared on the verge of fainting. Medved poured another glass of water and held it before Tschernin's lips. The scientist cupped the glass and, looking gratefully at Sergei, drank several gulps.

"Thank you," he said weakly. "As I said, I heard them talking. It was clear that they mean to detonate the bomb in the United States. Exactly where, I do not know, but there was much talk about America being the 'Great Satan'. However, there was also some indication that they could not immediately carry out their plans. Something about the U.S. air defense system that would prevent their flying the bomb into that country."

Sergei turned to Falcon. "Michael, you're a former American fighter pilot. Does that make sense to you? Can your air defense system prevent this? After all, it was unable to keep one of our pilots from flying a MiG-21 fighter from Cuba to Miami."

Falcon allowed himself a slight smile before responding. "If I recall, my friend, your people had a little problem with a German teenager flying a simple pleasure craft through your territory and landing in Red Square. But to answer your question, our system was vastly improved after that MiG episode and, of course, our level of alertness will now be at a peak. Trying to fly the bomb in, especially if it's in his private Airbus A-340, would not be his wisest move. I think he'll try some other way."

"But how?" Sergei blurted.

"If we come up with that answer, we should definitely put in for a bonus," Falcon answered. Then, turning to Tschernin, he asked, "Has the bomb been completed?"

The scientist, who had buried his head in his hands, looked up. "I regret to say that it is fully operational."

"What is its projected yield?"

"One-half megaton."

Falcon sat back in his chair, eyeing Tschernin as if he were looking at the dead walking the earth. "My god, that's ten times bigger than we thought," he said.

"The sheikh has been stealing enriched uranium for some time," Tschernin sighed.

"Excuse me," Buzhkin intervened. "I am not a scientist. Could you please explain the significance of this half megaton for me?"

Tschernin inhaled deeply, then began speaking in a mechanical, flat tone. "After ignition, the temperature of the bomb accelerates to millions of degrees…hotter than the center of the sun…almost as hot as the Big Bang that created the universe. All in less than a tenth of a second. Then the fireball bursts in a searing flash. If one could look upon it, it would appear as if the sun had swelled to fill the sky from horizon to horizon. But of course, one cannot look upon it without being instantly blinded. It will then completely incinerate everything within two miles. Buildings will seem to self-combust. Peoples' skin will be stripped from their bodies before their skeletons fall to the ground. The burst will then appear as a boiling, malignant red eye glaring down on its destruction. The blast wave will travel outward for another five miles at over three hundred miles per hour—four times the speed of an average hurricane—powerful and hot enough to level almost every building and melt virtually all life. Radiant heat will be so intense that at twelve miles anyone in the open fortunate enough to escape falling buildings and flying debris will still be fatally burnt. Even up to fifteen miles, the firestorm will inflict human skin with second-degree burns. For twice that distance beyond, just looking at the blast will cause total blindness.

"Then of course, it would all be followed by radioactive fallout. In a week, with an average wind, a lethal dose of radiation could fall over a downwind area that is roughly ten thousand square miles. Subatomic matter like alpha and beta particles will cause internal damage if consumed by eating, drinking, or even breathing. But the greatest danger is the gamma rays. They are pure energy and will penetrate just about anything short of lead. They will burn or destroy internal organs, resulting in nausea, vomiting, then death. In sum, a populated area such as Europe, Moscow, or the eastern United States could expect well over a million casualties, ranging from radiation sickness, blast injuries and live cremation to virtual vaporization."

A pall descended upon the room. After a few moments, Falcon cleared his throat and spoke. "One more thing…how is the device to be triggered?"

"It is a very simple yet elegant design. It consists of several layers of concentric spheres. The outermost is a chemical high-explosive known as HMX. It surrounds a band of U-238 uranium. Beneath that is a compound of lithium deuteride. And at the core is the trigger of beryllium, polonium, and highly enriched uranium."

"Damn," Falcon hissed. "A *Sloika* thermonuclear bomb."

Tschernin, in obvious surprise, peered above his wire glasses at Falcon. "You are familiar with such a device? But, you're American… then how…?"

"*Gospodeen* Falcon studied astrophysics at Moscow University," Medved interjected, "under some of our most renown physics professors."

Perov studied the American, then said, "You were a student of Alexander Marenkov's?"

Falcon nodded. "Yes, and I hope to renew our acquaintance when this is all over. But please go on."

Perov collected his thoughts, then began again. "As I indicated, there is a sphere of high explosives surrounding the nuclear materials. When this is detonated, the bomb implodes. The core is compressed until it becomes so dense that its nuclei split, a chain reaction occurs, and the energy of a forty kiloton nuclear bomb, enough to destroy a small city by itself, is released.

"But it won't stop there, will it," Falcon interjected.

Tschernin wiped his spectacles and resumed. "No. The shock wave from the core will compress a surrounding layer of highly enriched uranium which will then ignite. In a few nanoseconds, the temperature will be ten thousand times higher than the sun's surface. The nuclei of this layer will then fuse together with triple the fury of the initial core explosion. All this energy is then blown into the final layer of U-238, which in turn fissions, then delivers the real punch of the device. You know the rest."

A grim hush ensued. After several frigid moments, Medved cracked the ice. "I'm curious. We know how bin Wahhab was able to obtain the uranium through the Rurik-Micratom scam. But how on earth were these other exotic materials acquired that were necessary for the bomb's construction?"

"That was not so difficult," Tschernin shrugged. "The HMX, as a main component of Russian nuclear warheads, was also obtained through the Rurik-Micratom connection. The lithium was purchased from Chile. And then of course, the polonium…. There are so many hospitals in the world that use radon for radiation treatment of cancer. Some of these hospitals are more than happy to sell their used radon capsules, and...."

"And the daughter product of radon is polonium," Falcon completed the thought."

"Precisely."

Medved was simmering. Fighting a nearly overwhelming urge to leap across the table and strangle the cherub-faced scientist, he said, "We appreciate your cooperation. Does anyone else have a question to ask of *Gospodeen* Tschernin before we adjourn for now?"

Buzhkin glared at Perov with a baleful intensity that caused the little physicist to visibly tremble. He then turned away without speaking.

"Well, I do have one more question," Falcon said. "Do you know what became of Professor Marenkov?"

"Alexander was quite something," Tschernin answered, relieved at a diversion from the focus of the man-grizzly. He suddenly became animated. "The Professor resisted their attempts to compromise him, even though he was horribly tortured. He actually escaped at one point. Unfortunately, he was captured and returned to the compound just before you attacked. I saw him momentarily in the laboratory as we scientists were all rounded up. Then of course, the butchery began. I do not know what then became of him."

Silence again prevailed.

"Well, then, you will have to remain as our guest here just a bit longer," Medved said. "I'm sure you understand."

The scientist nodded. He would have been surprised at any other outcome.

With a scrape of the wooden legs of their chairs on the well-scuffed linoleum floor, Falcon, Medved, and Buzhkin stood. As his interrogators began to file through the door, Tschernin suddenly straightened in his chair and, with a distant look in his eyes, said one word. At the utterance, Mike Falcon stopped in his tracks.

"Excuse me...I'm not sure I heard you correctly. Could you repeat what you just said?"

Tschernin turned toward Falcon and, with no change in his detached expression, said, "Salvador."

Falcon quickly reentered the room and sat directly across from Tschernin. "Tell me exactly what you mean by that," he demanded, leaning forward so that his forehead nearly touched the Russian's.

Tschernin raised his eyes to meet Falcon's. He squinted, then shook his head, struggling with his memory. "There was talk...about a place or a person named Salvador. But I cannot remember what was said."

"Think! Think!" Falcon blurted, partially fulfilling Medved's wish as he grasped Tschernin by his lapels and began to shake him. The scientist instinctively recoiled, raising his arms in front of his face to ward off the expected blows. Buzhkin and Medved instantly grasped Falcon and pulled him from the terrified man.

"I can't remember! I can't remember!" Tschernin sobbed.

Falcon stood and as his muscles relaxed, his partners released their grips.

"Come, he's too frightened, tired, and confused now," Sergei said. "We'll let him rest and then start again. Meanwhile, we must report our findings to Aksanov and Higby."

Falcon knew that his friend was right. But at the same time, he was racking his brain...what had he missed in the 'Salvador' clues contained in the Slater CD-ROM? The fate of millions might be riding on his successfully resolving this question.

Chapter Thirty-Six

Night Hawk, with a warm easterly breeze of twenty knots hard off the starboard beam, had been gliding effortlessly west of the Exumas, heeling far over so that her port rail skimmed the jade green Caribbean. In mid-afternoon of the second day, Nassau hove into view. DeMaté ordered the crew to begin dousing the sail, as they would now turn into the wind and let the diesel engine power them the rest of the way.

It was with some trepidation that he steered the craft northeast into the Nassau channel. By law, he was flying the yellow "Q" flag to indicate that the schooner had not yet cleared customs in Bahamian waters. That meant that Bahamian officials would pay him a visit when he docked. Ordinarily, he would not be concerned. His paying customers were always forewarned to dump their 'recreational painkillers' well before arriving in Nassau. But this Tigere woman was an unknown…a wild card.

He had been unsuccessful in his attempts to open the little black box that she kept in her bag. If it contained drugs or a weapon, and was discovered by the customs agents, he would lose his captain's license and be jailed. He wrestled again with the thought of confronting her, but how could he tactfully approach the issue without revealing that he had rifled her belongings?

The decision was rapidly being taken from his hands as he swung the helm over and *Night Hawk's* bow turned toward the Hurricane Hole Marina on Paradise Island. Pastel pink, lime green and plaster white colonial-style buildings, surrounded by stately, lightly-swaying palm trees, coasted by as the vessel eased toward an empty slip. When the docking was completed, the three couples on the cruise brought their bags topside and, with the crew's help, began to disembark.

The 'French' woman, clad in a skimpy bikini, sat on the deck housing. Munching a mango, she waved good-naturedly to the departing passengers who were boarding fringe-topped golf carts. One of the plump, middle-aged men began to sheepishly return her gesture when he was hauled off by his frowning wife into the waiting vehicle. They were soon whisked away to the coral-pink colonial building that overlooked the marina and then on to customs.

"They were fun," Svetlana laughed in her throaty tone, turning to DeMaté. "And now we can expect a visit from customs officials?"

DeMaté, who was busy on the pier securing a springline, felt as though she had been reading his mind. "Not for a few hours," he answered, tugging the line tightly around a wooden piling that was twice as thick as his frame. "They like to play a little game here in Nassau. The agents make sure they don't come down to arriving ships until after official business hours. That way, they get to charge you overtime."

"Neat little scam," she chuckled.

"Everybody's got one," DeMaté grunted, casting a knowing glance at her. Making fast his bowline knot, he re-boarded the schooner. "So we have a couple of hours if there's anything you want to declare or 'offload'," he said in his most casual manner.

"Why what on earth do you mean by that? Are you implying that I'm concealing contraband? Perhaps you'd like to search me yourself."

She stood, spreading her arms and turning slowly. The two crewmen, their twenty year old hormones now on full throttle, forgot about furling the sails and gawked.

"Hey, I'm not paying you to sit on your *derrieres!*" DeMaté shouted to the youths. Surprised at the unusual rage of his tone, they quickly dropped their eyes and returned to their work.

DeMaté was in fact furious. He knew that she was toying with him, intending to make a fool of him. But he would not be trifled with. He would turn the tables on her.

"I will take you at your word, Mademoiselle Tigere," he said cavalierly. "Perhaps you might be good enough, however, to inform me of your plans for the *Night Hawk* and her crew."

"*Certainment, mon capitan,*" she replied gaily, grasping the main boom and swinging from the deck housing into the cockpit. She settled onto the cushioned seat on the starboard side of the helm, lying back so that her long, graceful legs were fully extended, her toes touching DeMaté's right hip.

"The ship is due for its annual haul-out and inspection, *n'est-ce pas?*"

"Yes…right here in Nassau."

"No…not Nassau. There has been a slight change in plans. We will leave here at dawn tomorrow and head for a little island a few days' sail to the south. I've made arrangements to have the boat hauled out there."

DeMaté stroked his beard pensively. "Hmm. And would you mind telling me the name of this island?"

"Not at all. Indeed, you have a right to know as you are the captain," she winked. "Tomorrow you will follow in the wake of *Monsieur* Christopher Columbus. Chart your course for…San Salvador."

✶   ✶   ✶

It was in the last hour before dawn that Colonel Hamed's convoy arrived at the camp in the *Sahra Nubiyah*. The trucks were driven into stalls that were covered with desert-camouflaged awnings; brown and beige curtains were drawn, and the vehicle tracks were whisked away. By the time a pinkish glow began to illuminate the eastern horizon, it was impossible to tell that anything but sand was home to this part of the desert.

The sonorous, haunting wail of a muezzin calling the faithful to worship wafted from an unseen minaret. Bin Wahhab laid his prayer mat before him so that it was directed to the northeast, to Mecca. Kneeling, he bent forward and touched his forehead to the ground. He remained in this position for a number of minutes, his mind racing with thoughts of the future, that once amorphous blob that now was taking shape due to his 'genius', like clay molded by the potter. When he finally rocked back on his heels and straightened his torso, the orange sun was peeping above the horizon, painting the low-lying hills and desert to his east with tinctures of gold, vermilion, and crimson. He stood, feeling very self-satisfied.

"You must be exhausted, sheikh," Hamed said, rising along side the Arab. "If you'd like, I'll have one of my men show you to your quarters."

"There will be time enough for sleep, Colonel," bin Wahhab replied, with no trace of weariness in his voice. "First, I wish to see more of the operation."

Hamed's eyes brightened. And now, his smile was also evident in the crooking of his thick, fleshy lips. For, in the safety of his camp, he no longer felt the need to conceal his face. "It will be my pleasure and honor to escort you, sheikh. Every morning, after sunrise prayers and in-between satellite fly-overs, we conduct a training session. Please come with me."

The two men, followed closely by their half-dozen personal bodyguards, began walking through a maze of weapons, vehicles, and bustling soldiers. All were shielded from overhead eyes by the ubiquitous desert-camouflaged canopy. As bin Wahhab and Hamed advanced, every man in their path gave way with a bow or salute.

"To the left are former members of Hamas," the Sudanese said. "They are now dedicated to the Ikhwan cause. Those to your right came from

Hizballah and those beyond from the Algerian Armed Islamic Group and the Iranian Mujaheddin. All now recognize you as their leader. Ah, but here is the morning report."

A short man clad in a brown and beige uniform and blue-checkered headdress, an AK-47 slung over his left shoulder, saluted and handed Hamed a single piece of paper.

The Colonel quickly scanned the document, then grinned. "You are in luck, sheikh. The first satellite will not be overhead for another hour. You will have an opportunity to see your men in action."

Issuing an order to his aide, Hamed escorted his leader from beneath the protective awnings and into the open desert. Yet it was not a completely arid land into which they stepped, for less than a mile to the west a narrow strip of vegetation wound toward the horizon like a carelessly flung green ribbon. It was the mark of the world's longest river, the Nile, winding its way north to Luxor, the Valley of the Kings, and the Pyramids, before trickling exhausted into the Mediterranean. Two thousand miles before the its subtle death, however, it provided its gift of life to a small band of inhabitants of the Nubian Desert.

"Our water purification building is on your left, sheikh," Hamed said as they walked. "We can now convert enough of the Nile daily to support fifteen hundred men."

"How many soldiers are in the camp now?" bin Wahhab asked.

"We have approximately a thousand at any given time, sheikh," the Colonel replied, positioning a pair of sunglasses on his nose. "They generally stay here for several months, then return to their own countries to train others. There are a few, however, who have nowhere to go. They stay here as instructors."

As he spoke, a group of twenty soldiers trotted by in lock step, their AK-47's held at 'carry arms'. A series of commands was heard and, in unison, they first halted in line, then lay prone, and finally raised the wooden stocks of the rifles to their shoulders.

"Set single shot!" an officer barked. A metallic clicking sound indicated that the weapons were being switched from automatic to selective fire. A hundred meters away, twenty bulls-eye targets were set into place.

"Prepare!"

Twenty eyeballs sighted through the Kalashnikov's rear notch, lining it up with the foresight blade and the black center of the target.

"Fire!"

With a resounding bang, the rifles erupted as one. The soldiers then continued to shoot at will as their instructor, a bronze-faced, ramrod straight officer, excoriated their technique. When Hamed and bin Wahhab approached, the martinet ceased his drilling and drew himself into a rigid salute.

"Excellent work, major," Hamed said, returning the formality. "Carry on."

As the officer turned to his troops, Hamed noted to bin Wahhab, "Major Zidah is a former Iranian Mujaheddin commander and one of our very best officers. When the Holy War begins, he will be at the forefront of our cause."

Bin Wahhab nodded. "I have recently lost all of my top people," he said, gazing at Zidah. "If the Iranian major is all that you say, I could use such a man for the most important task of the Jihad."

"Certainly, sheikh. The arrangements shall immediately be made to transfer him directly to your service."

"Excellent."

"Now, if you will accompany me, we will watch a Stinger missile system training session. Soon these skills will be applied to downing passenger-carrying jumbo jets."

The two leaders and their entourage moved on, leaving the Iranian's group to their target practice. Uncharacteristically, Major Zidah ignored his troops as he intently eyed the slowly departing form of bin Wahhab. His gaze then shifted to the two trucks that were surrounded by the sheikh's elite troops. This was the pivotal moment of his life, the culmination of four years' sacrifice and extreme personal danger. Like bin Wahhab, he, too, was developing a plan...an end game...for the contents of the two heavily guarded trucks. His plan would have to be inspired; the execution flawless. And by all that was sacred, it *must* work.

✶　　　✶　　　✶

Preston Higby sat on a leather-covered couch, his hands neatly folded on his knees. The only other person present in the Oval Office was the Commander-in-Chief, himself, who, hands clasped behind him, was anxiously pacing the floor. Stopping in front of his National Security Advisor, he jammed his fists against his hips and said, "Are they certain that the target is the U.S.?"

"Yes, Mr. President. According to the scientist they recovered from the raid."

"What precautions have we taken?"

"By your approval, the military has moved to Threatcon Charlie, the penultimate of four terrorist alert conditions."

"So now we're red-flagging that a terrorist action is imminent. And what the hell am I suppose to tell the press when they start demanding to know why we're at this heightened level?"

"For now, Mr. President, I think it would be best to simply indicate that bin Wahhab may retaliate for the destruction of his stronghold. Going into further detail at this time...until we know more...would simply cause unnecessary panic."

The President plopped his well-fed frame into a Louis Quinze chair opposite Higby. "Hell. Seems to me I've been down this path once before and it didn't turn out so hot."

"Sir?"

"Half-truths, Preston. Half-truths. Nibbling the corners. Blowing sunshine up peoples' skirts. Whatever the hell you want to call it."

Higby felt like saying, 'Interesting metaphors. And now you're paying the piper at the worst possible moment'. Instead, he intoned, "You would not be telling a half-truth, sir. You would be telling the facts as we know them. In a joint operation with the Russians, we have destroyed the Afghan terrorist base of bin Wahhab. Unfortunately, he has escaped to parts unknown. We do not know what his next move will be but we are taking all precautions both to effect his capture and to defend against his terrorist activities."

The shade of a smile crossed the President's face. "Sounds convincing, Preston. Maybe I'll just let you give this little speech."

"You're much smoother than I, sir," Higby answered, meaning it, but not necessarily as a compliment.

The President gazed inquisitively into his advisor's eyes, then frowned. "They'll still bury me on this issue of the raid on the Arab's stronghold," he grunted. "What the hell was that all about, they'll want to know, and why the hell were the Russians involved?"

"That's an easy answer. We have evidence of bin Wahhab's financing of the bombings of the World Trade Center, the Khobar Towers and the U.S. embassies in Tanzania and Kenya. Thousands of lives, including those of many Americans, were lost in those atrocities. It is also well known that, ever since our strikes against Iraq, bin Wahhab has vowed to conduct a Jihad against the U.S. Just recently, thanks to satellite monitoring of his communications, we have thwarted his plans to attack six more of our embassies from Albania to Uruguay. In addition, we've foiled his plots to assault a U.S. managed electric power plant in Pakistan and the Prince Sultan Air Base in Saudi Arabia.

"With regard to the Russians," he continued after a slight pause to collect his thoughts, "we have been saying for some time now that the presence of bin Wahhab so close to their border, and the hostility that he generates among extremist Muslims toward their former rulers, poses a serious danger to Russia's security. It was only natural that they joined with us to eradicate this threat. Again, that is the truth."

"But not the whole truth," his boss interjected.

"As far as we know—"

The President cut off Higby with a wave of his hand, saying, "All right. We'll try to slide by with that. Now, tell me what your plans are for dealing with this crisis."

The elderly statesman ran his right hand through his still thick shock of silver-gray hair and inhaled deeply, as if this full breath might summon the strength needed to prevent the looming catastrophe. "We have a three-pronged plan. The primary approach is aggressive...on the theory that the best defense is a good offense. We'll find out where the bomb is socked away overseas and then go in and destroy it."

"I thought we just tried that."

"And we missed by a gnat's hair."

"So we go again."

"Yes, sir."

"All right. And the second prong of your plan?"

"If our offense fails, we go to defense. All land, sea, and air routes into the U.S. are already receiving increased scrutiny. Satellites are being reprogrammed to cover traffic ingressing our sea and airspace. Customs agents, rangers and border patrol personnel are all on alert. An ad hoc organization of the Defense Intelligence Agency, the CIA, FBI, and the NSA has been established to exchange information and establish a dragnet.

"All leave has been cancelled for the Coast Guard and every available coastal gunboat is being put into action. The Navy has three carrier task forces on the east coast and two on the west that have put to sea, looking for any suspicious vessels. The Air Force and Air National Guard have been fully activated. Their F-15 Eagles, with their big radars and long-range missiles, were built for just this sort of operation. One of their original roles was to intercept the Soviet long-range Bear and

Badger bombers before they penetrated close enough to inflict damage with their nuclear payloads. Well off the coastline, at the ADIZ—the Air Defense Identification Zone, every incoming aircraft will be electronically interrogated through an IFF—an 'Identify Friend or Foe'—transponder."

"And your third prong?"

"That will be coordinated through the Federal Emergency Management Agency."

"Oh, great. FEMA. You mean after the bomb has been detonated."

Higby made no reply.

The President gazed absently across the room toward the white-curtained window behind his desk. "You know, that's something else they'll blame me for."

"Sir?"

"That damn Strategic Defense Initiative…'Star Wars'…a missile defense shield. They'll pillory me for not pouring more billions into it. In fact, the Congress just approved deployment of such a system over my threatened veto. Hell, the Senate vote was 99-0 in favor. And that comes right in the middle of our START II ballistic missile negotiations with the Russians."

Higby smiled, shaking his head. "The Russians won't like that."

"Preston, you're a master of the understatement. The Russian Prime Minister has already publicly declared that our development of a missile shield will trigger a new arms race. Their Duma is even refusing to ratify START II unless we drop our anti-ballistic missile plans. It's like we're kicking a hibernating bear."

"I remember when SDI was all the rage at the height of the Cold War," Higby interjected. "Then, after a few billion was spent, it was calculated that the very best we could do would be to knock down ninety percent of the Soviet Union's missiles. The ten percent that leaked through, unfortunately, would pretty much annihilate the American people."

"Yes, but now we aren't facing thousands of Soviet warheads. Just the lobbing of one by a terrorist. SDI would've taken care of that, they'll say."

"Sure. If the terrorists were dumb enough to play by our rules. It's a safe bet that they'll try to bring it in covertly, rather than via a missile capable of being intercepted."

A sharp buzzing sound emanating from a box on the desk interrupted their conversation. The President wearily stood, crossed the room, and keyed a button on the intercom. "Yes?"

"Sorry to interrupt, sir," a female voice said, "but Director Reilly is on secure line one. I told him you were indisposed but he said it's a matter of national emergency."

"Put him through."

The conversation lasted less than two minutes, with the President saying only, "Are you certain?" and "Thank you" to his CIA Director. When he hung up, he keyed the intercom and said, "Lottie, get me the Secretary of State and then Admiral Moore." Opening a gilt-edged box on his desk, he selected a cigar before returning to his chair and his anxiously waiting Security Advisor.

"Bin Wahhab and the bomb are in Sudan," he said, lighting the panatela.

"How did the CIA find out?"

"Ever hear of an operative code-named Darius?"

Although he did not immediately reply, the expression in Higby's eyes were answer enough.

"Well hell, that's a fine thing," the President fumed. "Both my CIA Director and National Security Advisor decided to keep their Commander-in-Chief in the dark," he said angrily. "Would you care to explain?"

Higby was never one to be intimidated, especially when he knew his actions were well-founded. "Sir, we have a number of operatives who are in 'deep cover'. The less they are discussed, the better their chances of survival and completion of their objectives. If you'd like, however, we could sit down and review the twenty or so files."

Frowning, his boss emitted a puff of cigar smoke.

"I'll keep that in mind," the President said. "For now, just fill me in on this Darius character."

"When it comes to cover, he's at the deepest end of the pool. He is posing as a member of the MEK…the terrorist Iranian Mujaheddin Group…but in reality he works for the Iranian government in cooperation with us."

"You just lost me. He works *for* the Iranians as well as *against* them?"

"As you well know, sir, things are not always as they seem."

Although somewhat suspicious at the innuendo, the President nodded.

"The real policy of many Islamic countries, while outwardly hostile toward America, is actually much more rational and pragmatic. A perfect example is the Iranian attitude toward the MEK. While devoutly anti-American, that group's first objective is to overthrow the current Iranian regime and replace it with the Ikhwan Brotherhood. Obviously, the present Iranian government is not particularly pleased with the MEK's primary goal."

"So they plant this so-called Darius inside the MEK and he winds up in Sudan, right smack in Ali Baba's den of thieves. But how does he communicate to us?"

"He has one of our highest-tech transmitters. That allows him to send micro-bursts of information to our Milstar satellite net."

"Damn. That son-of-a-bitch must have balls of steel."

"Yes, sir. If he ever got caught…."

"No more balls at all."

"Right."

"OK, Preston, tell me…this camp…how far away is it from the nearest populated area?"

Higby reflected for a moment, then replied, "If memory serves, around two hundred miles from the twin cities of Khartoum and Omdurman."

"And smack dab in the middle of a desert?"

"With the exception of the little strip of the Nile, yes sir." Higby, with a sinking feeling, was beginning to guess the meaning of the questions.

The intercom buzzed again and Lottie announced that the Secretary of State was on the line.

"Put her on the speaker," the President said, tapping cigar residue into a glass ash tray that was engraved with the blue and gold Seal of the United States.

"Hi, Maggie, how was your mid-east trip?"

"Exhausting, but productive," the hoarse but feminine voice answered. "Glad to be back."

"I want to hear all about it. As it turns out, the goodwill you built on that swing is very timely. We have ourselves a little mid-eastern issue here."

"I heard something about it, sir."

The President tossed a knowing glance toward Higby. They both wondered how much was already known 'out there'.

"Listen, Maggie. You're well aware of the Ikhwan terrorist enclave in the Nubian Desert. We need to go in and clean it out...in fairly rapid order. What are the chances of getting some ex post facto Arab support of such an operation?"

The other end of the line was silent for several long moments.

Finally, the Secretary of State cleared her throat and spoke. "It'd be better if the approval were in advance."

"Sorry. No time. Anyway, I said 'after the fact support', not 'approval'."

"I think, with the proper massaging, we could get the Saudis and the Egyptians on board. I take it that you don't even plan to consult with the Sudanese?"

"Waste of time. We'd just be tipping our hand. The first two countries that you mentioned are the most important for what I have in mind."

"I see. Let me put together a strategy and get back to you…in say, fifteen minutes."

"Make it ten. Thanks, Maggie."

As he hung up, the intercom buzzed, "Admiral Moore on line two."

"Brett, let's get right to it," the President said to his Chairman of the Joint Chiefs of Staff. Bin Wahhab and his fireworks are at the Nubian Desert site. The last time we went after him, we were sensitive to possible collateral damage to the local populace. I'm not screwing around this time. What do we have on location that can take it out right now?"

"The Sixth Fleet is in the Mediterranean, fifty miles north of Libya. We also have an F-15 Fighter Wing at Prince Sultan Air Base in Saudi Arabia."

"I don't want to use aircraft. Can you do the job with cruise missiles?"

"Yes, sir. But that would mean over-flying Egypt."

"That'll be my worry, Admiral. Stand by for further orders. I'll call you back in fifteen minutes."

Hanging up the phone, the President shoved his cigar back into his mouth and clamped down, like a horse chomping on its bit.

"And Congress…?" Higby asked.

"Fu…." The President caught himself. "Look, Preston, my opponents have had my lunch over the past two years. But I'm going to look at this situation as objectively as possible and not let politics muddy it up. This is just too damned important. I would hope that at least you would see that. At any rate, I'm pressing on. Let Congress and the rest of the world judge away. But they can do it with the goddamn historians…after the fact. What I'm doing is the right thing and I won't be deterred.

"Now I have a task for you. I want you to get me the best scientific opinion on the odds of detonating that bomb if a Tomahawk makes a direct hit on it. Then I want to know what the prevailing winds are and what the fall-out—literally—would be. I'd like those answers in the next ten minutes, please."

Higby continued to sit, seemingly bereft of both the ability to move and to speak.

"Look, Preston," the President said in a more conciliatory tone, "We've got two hundred miles of sand as a buffer. Worst case, perhaps, is that we convert a few miles of desert into glass. Meanwhile, maybe we save millions of lives. Get me the info so I can make an informed decision."

Higby rose as if in a trance. He was torn between turning in his resignation and staying as close as possible to the center of the storm, so that he could…could do what? He experienced a profound sense of disappointment in himself. All those years of hard study at the nation's best universities followed by his impeccable forty year career of statesmanship…all that education and experience…and at this most epic moment, he had nothing in his arsenal to call upon. Vaguely aware that someone was talking to him, he turned.

"It's for you," the President said, handing him the phone with a bemused look. "It's your man…Mike Falcon…."

Chapter Thirty-Seven

"Mr. Higby, are we on a secure line?"

"Yes."

"I'm sorry to interrupt your meeting with the President," Falcon spoke hurriedly, "but I wanted to immediately relay a clue concerning the possible whereabouts of bin Wahhab and the bomb—"

"We already know where they are," Higby interrupted.

"That's great…or is it?"

"Reliable intelligence places them at the *Sahra Nubiyah* terrorist encampment," Higby answered, studiously avoiding Falcon's question.

Falcon paused for the briefest moment, rapidly working the math of this equation. The plus was that the location of the bomb was now known. The minus was that the device was still in hostile territory.

"I guess that's basically good news. Is the President negotiating with the Sudanese?"

"Not exactly."

"What, then…another Special Forces operation?"

Higby sighed, replying wearily, "No Mike."

Falcon again fell momentarily silent before saying, "God, you don't mean—"

"Mike, I'm a bit under the gun here. Things are moving pretty fast."

"But if I understand you correctly," Falcon persisted, "this could result in a holocaust."

"Nothing has been definitely decided yet. Look, Mike. There's nothing more you can do over there. Why don't you grab the next plane home. I can use you back here. Besides, we're having a winter heat wave here in Washington. Must be sixty degrees outside and I know how much you, in particular, must hate that Moscow winter. Look, I've got to go."

"Sir—" The phone clicked and a disconnect tone followed.

Falcon removed the encrypting device from the receiver and stepped from the *Taksophon* booth. As he walked along the snow and ice-encrusted sidewalk toward the Lubianka, his thoughts became increasingly troubled. Assuming the intelligence reports were correct, then the bombing of the terrorist enclave in the Nubian Desert could lead to a nuclear detonation. Even if the blast occurred in a basically empty desert, the international repercussions would not be pretty. And then there was that other disturbing business. Although inexplicable even to himself, Falcon was absolutely convinced that the key to bin Wahhab's intentions lay not in the Nubian Desert, but in Tschernin's single utterance…Salvador.

* * *

San Salvador—Holy Savior—was the name given by Christopher Columbus to the first land that his flotilla had reached after sailing for thirty-five days from the Canary Islands. The day of that landfall, October 11, 1492, would be revered and celebrated in history, for it marked the discovery of…a small island in the Bahamas. The intrepid mariner would die fourteen years later, never having actually seen that vast continent to the northwest whose people would eventually proclaim a national holiday in honor of his 'discovery'. In fact, discovery was a relative term, for it was not a deserted island upon which he landed, but one already populated, in Columbus' words, by "tall, friendly, bronze-skinned natives".

Half a millennium later, this population had burgeoned to five hundred souls, most of whom were descendants of the slave trade of the 18th and early 19th centuries. The past five hundred years did not catch the island sleeping. Houses, restaurants, churches, a marina, a lighthouse, a jail, and an island-circuiting two-lane asphalt road connecting all of these structures were built. Electricity and plumbing were installed. The jail was boarded up for lack of use. And then came a runway, capable of accommodating large commercial jets. Most of the passengers were scuba divers who had learned that San Salvador's reef was one of the best-kept diving secrets in the world.

The entry through this reef into the marina was not to be taken lightly. The prevailing southeasterly current created a powerful surge through the narrow opening, occasionally shredding wind-tossed or carelessly handled ships on the razor sharp coral skeletons. Larger vessels, such as the *Night Hawk* which now motored through the cut, required a skillful hand at the helm. And it was precisely for his seamanship abilities that Guy DeMaté had been hired.

The sun was low on the western horizon, sinking into a bed of long gray clouds, as the Frenchman piloted the schooner through the reef passage. The rolling surge was at his back, causing the ship to heave up from the stern where, on the crest of a wave, it would gyrate nose down in a figure eight. *Night Hawk* then bucked alternately port and starboard, anything but straight ahead, like a thoroughbred resisting being coaxed into a barn. Sitting on the bowsprit, clutching the security of the coiled-steel forestay, Svetlana Popova laughed into the splashing salt spray.

Adroitly, with strong and confident turning of the teak wheel, DeMaté outfoxed the recalcitrant vessel and kept her bow aimed steadily at the safety of the cut. Finally, they took their last roller, riding its impetus clear of the reef and into the shelter of a tiny marina. A substantial, well-placed concrete jetty broke the force of the surge and

Night Hawk glided onto waters so glassy and calm, it seemed as if the wind and ocean had been turned off.

DeMaté swung the helm to port and the schooner eased toward the marina's quay. Three men, black silhouettes against the darkening sky, stood silently on the wharf. Lines were tossed to them by the ship's crew and *Night Hawk* was quickly moored. The captain watched curiously as his sole passenger nimbly leaped ashore and formally hugged each of the men. Turning to the Frenchman, the woman said, "I'll be off the ship tonight. We'll haul *Night Hawk* at dawn." She and the three men, clustered in secretive whispering, walked away, their retreating forms followed by DeMaté's mystified gaze.

* * *

"Excellent," the President beamed, leaning back in his roomy desk chair as he reviewed the report that his National Security Advisor had just handed him. "One in a thousand. I'd say those are pretty damned good odds."

The only other person in the Oval Office, Preston Higby, sat uneasily on the other side of the desk. "There's still a chance that a direct hit could cause the uranium to implode and then go supercritical," he frowned.

"Yes. One in a thousand. And what are the odds of a direct hit? The Navy could even target those Tomahawks so that they strike the periphery of the camp. That would essentially wipe out the risk while still resolving our problem. On top of that, the winds are in our favor. What'd they say...here it is..." the President remarked, thumbing through the pages. "This time of year, winds are out of the northwest. Couldn't be better. Even if there were a detonation, which is almost mathematically impossible, The wind would blow any fall-out over three hundred miles of uninhabited desert."

"Not totally uninhabited," Higby protested.

"God damn it, Preston. It's a hell of a sight more uninhabited than the eastern seaboard of the United States! No, the course of action is clear."

"Mr. President, I strongly urge you to reconsider, to at least consult with your cabinet and key members of congress before undertaking this action."

"Preston, I've already consulted with those who count. The Secretary of Defense, the Chairman of the Joint Chiefs, the National Security Council, and the Secretary of State are all on board. Hell, Maggie even got permission for a fly-over from the Egyptians."

"They gave that permission without any knowledge that a nuclear detonation was a possible outcome."

"Now listen to me…I want to tell you," the President's voice hardened as he balled his right hand into a fist and directed his thumb at his advisor. "My mind is made up and this conversation is now over." Keying his intercom, he said, "Lottie, get me Admiral Moore."

✶   ✶   ✶

Oblivious to the freezing temperature, Mike Falcon ambled along the left bank of the icy white Moskva River. He had decided to take a long detour around the Kremlin before returning to the Lubianka in the hope that the clear cold air would freshen his mind and help him solve the riddle of Tschernin's one word utterance…'Salvador'. Was it a person, a place, or a code for something else? He felt that he had the answer but he was frustratingly unable to pull it from his brain cell files.

Now it seemed that his walk was only serving to torment him further, for the Russian version of Salvador—*Spaseetyel*—was continually leaping out at him. First it was the *Spaseetyel*—'Salvador'—Cathedral, a modern monument to the Russian victory over Napoleon, located near the river. Then the Upper 'Savior' Cathedral jutting above the Kremlin enclosure, followed by the Renaissance-style *Spaseetyel's* Tower, in the red brick wall, itself. *Spaseetyel*, Savior, Salvador…the words haunted him.

As he rounded a corner, Saint Basil's Cathedral burst into view, its multi-colored cupolas radiating brilliantly in the clear azure sky, giving the impression of a castle transported straight from the 'Arabian Nights'. It was a sight that always surprised him by its massive, coarsely powerful structure mingled with graceful oriental beauty…that paradox that distinguishes Russia from Europe and Asia…simultaneously revealing and confounding…a blend of west and east…both, yet neither.

He wiped a thin layer of snow from an empty wooden bench and sat down. Perhaps St. Basil's could provide the inspiration he was seeking as he wrestled with his own puzzle. His thoughts had already gone beyond the terrorist encampment in the Nubian Desert. He was certain that bin Wahhab would not tarry there…would not allow himself to be trapped or targeted in so obvious a place.

No, he would move quickly. But he would not try to fly the bomb into the States. Covertly penetrating the ADIZ would be far too problematic. Sea transportation would be more promising. But where would the transfer from aircraft to ship take place? Somewhere short of the ADIZ but probably close to the U.S. Perhaps in the Lesser Antilles, the Virgin Islands, the Caicos, or maybe even the Bahamas. But what island would permit him to enter inconspicuously and still be able to accommodate his sizeable Airbus jet?

As he contemplated these issues, his gaze shifted absently from Saint Basil's to the Savior's Tower, then back again. From Saint…'San'… Basil's to the Tower of the *Spaseetyel*…the 'Salvador'. Then it hit him. It all suddenly fit together. "Bingo," he blurted, quickly turning and hastening across Red Square to the nearest *Taksophon*. Now he only hoped that he would be in time.

*   *   *

As Falcon trotted toward a phone booth on snow-covered Red Square, the aircraft carrier U.S.S. Eisenhower, located nearly two thousand miles to the southwest in the sun-splashed Mediterranean, had just completed its turn to the west, into the wind. Jet engines were whining on the flight deck and yellow-shirted plane directors were guiding the warplanes up to the catapult tracks. Radar-domed E-2C Hawkeyes and EA-6B Prowler jets, with their electronic detection and jamming equipment, were already launching from both the bow and waist catapults. They were soon followed by swing-wing F-14B Super Tomcats capable of achieving twice the speed of sound and armed with Phoenix missiles that could knock out enemy aircraft over one hundred miles away. The launch of Ike's fighters was a precautionary measure, aimed at preventing any interference of the pending mission from Moammar Qadhafi.

The Libyan dictator would be very nervous upon learning that a number of cruise missiles were nearing his imaginary 'Line of Death'. He would have no immediate way of knowing that the weapons were headed further east, across neighboring Egypt, and then south for a target in the Nubian Desert. He might even snap and launch his air force of Soviet-built Sukhoi-17 fighter jets to try to shoot down the perceived threat.

He had faced a situation once before where he thought that the U.S. Navy should feel his sting and had ordered four of his Su-17's against a pair of F-14's. Two of the Libyan fighter jets had been quickly 'splashed' by the Tomcats and the surviving Sukhois had beaten a hasty retreat back across the 'Line of Death'. Now, hunkered down in his concrete bunker beneath his palace, Qhadaffi would be easily convinced by his advisors that aggression against the twenty Super Tomcats now in the air would be injudicious.

Once the F-14's were on station, the guided missile cruiser Gettysburg rolled into the Eisenhower's wake and onto its course. At the same time, the lids of the vertical missile tubes between the forward gun turret and the bridge opened. In the Combat Information Center, just below the bridge, brown-uniformed officers and blue-clad sailors inputted data into their IBM computers. At the speed of light, the electronic information was relayed below decks to the missiles and their crews. Armament sailors, distinguished by their white fire-retardant head coverings, ensured that the Sea Launched Cruise Missiles, fondly known as 'Slikkums', were armed. Final adjustments were made and a 'go for launch' was reported back to the CIC. Thereupon, the crew quickly exited the launch area.

The men in CIC double-checked their data and switches, then relayed the 'go' signal to the bridge. Peering from his aerie, the captain scanned the fore and after decks, the surrounding sea and sky and the bridge's radar screen. Satisfied that all was in order, he issued the command to his executive officer to 'launch the birds'. With a resounding boom, the first Slikkum ignited and popped skyward at an awkward angle. As its inertial guidance system and air-breathing turbofan engine took control, it quickly straightened out and locked onto course, giving the eerie impression of an organic predator that has suddenly smelled blood. In seconds, only a dissipating trail of white smoke was visible by the naked eye. The scene was repeated three more times and then all attention onboard turned to the scopes displaying the satellite tracking of the streaking weapons.

* * *

At the encampment at *Sahra Nubiya*, several hundred Ikhwan soldiers were sitting in numerous groups, trying to make sense of the multiple steps required to launch a Stinger missile. The tedious learning process was sustained by the joyful image of a fully loaded jumbo jet being ripped apart in mid-air, causing mayhem, grief and consternation among their avowed enemies. Only a few meters away, other groups were being tutored in the intricacies of C-4 explosives that were earmarked for the New York Stock Exchange.

None of them saw the black speck low on the northern horizon that was hurtling toward them at 550 miles per hour, leaving all sound of its approach in its wake. Like a science-fiction creature whose approach can not be deterred, the cruise missile eyeballed the camp, its computers correlating the optical view with its digitized target maps. Final minute course corrections were made and the fate of the camp was sealed. Even if those on the ground had seen the Tomahawk, they would have had only a precious few seconds in which to dive for cover. As it was, the first notice of its arrival was nearly simultaneous with its massive explosion in the center of the camp.

Those who were further to the south, near the water purification plant were well clear of the impact. If they did not look away, they saw a mountainous orange and black fireball that hurled trucks, metal wreckage, and human carcasses high into the air. Their witnessing of the spectacle was short-lived, however, for the following cruise missile struck almost immediately in their midst. By the time the third and fourth Tomahawks impacted, there was little left to churn but ashes and sand.

* * *

"We did it!" the President said, striving mightily to control his ebullience and appear presidential before his staff. "That damned terrorist camp is out of business. Bin Wahhab is history. No big bang! We did it, Preston!"

Higby managed a wan smile, fully realizing that the real fury, in the form of outraged world opinion, was about to hit. Ever since the decision had been made to initiate the strike, the Oval Office had been abuzz, like a mosquito-laden pond. Staffers, speech writers, spin-doctors, and make-up artists hummed about their boss. The speeches that had declared a Pyhrric victory, albeit at the expense of an unfortunate nuclear 'incident', were destroyed. The spiels announcing a major victory over international terrorism were now being reviewed by the President. As he read, the white make-up bib under his chin giving him the appearance of a Thanksgiving Day pilgrim, an elderly woman coifed his hair so that not one strand fell out of place.

"Ten minutes, sir," his Chief of Staff said, referring to the time left before his television address directly to the nation and indirectly to the world.

"I like this one," the President smiled, slapping the paper with the back of his hand. "It uses a lot of your ideas, Preston!"

Ironically, these were the precise words that Higby did not want to hear. "Well, then," he responded wearily as he rose, "I guess you don't need me any more today. I'll be on my way."

"Hey, stick around," the President grinned, examining his own visage in a hand-held mirror. "This is the icing on the cake. Enjoy your just desserts."

Higby was searching for a credible protest when the intercom buzzed and Lottie said, "Call for the National Security Advisor. Secure line two."

"Thank you. I'll need some privacy," Higby said, casting a meaningful glance at the buzzing swarm, "so if you don't mind, Mr. President…."

"Sure. Use the anteroom. If anybody's in there, kick them out."

Thankful for an excuse to escape the Oval Office, Higby grasped his briefcase and quickly entered the small, adjoining room. Making himself comfortable in a roomy green leather chair, he waited for the call to be channeled into the anteroom's secure phone.

"You can pick up now, sir," Lottie said. "It's Mr. Falcon."

"Mike, I thought you'd be packing once you heard we're having some warm weather here," Higby half-heartedly joked.

"I've been too busy roaming through the snow in Moscow…trying to figure out how bin Wahhab plans to smuggle the bomb into the U.S."

"Well, you can stop wrenching your brain. Do you get CNN over there?"

"I know that they can pick it up at the Lubianka."

"You might want to high-tail it over there. The President's addressing the nation in ten minutes."

"Did we do it?"

"Yes."

"And I'll bet there was no mushroom cloud, right?"

"Right. But why were you so confident in saying that?"

"Because the bomb's not there."

"More likely the odds just played out in our favor and the raid didn't touch it off."

"No, I have a hunch the bomb is in the Bahamas…on a little island called San Salvador. Can you have the President direct the Navy or Coast Guard over there to check it out? We probably don't have much time."

"Mike, the President will never do that now that he's declaring this victory over the Ikhwan operation in the Nubian Desert. And he certainly won't move out on a mere hunch."

Neither party spoke for several moments.

Finally, Falcon said, "In that case, I think I'll take my vacation on the way home."

"Let me guess. The Bahamas?"

"Yes, sir. You're right. I could use a little warm weather for a change."

"All right. You deserve it. See you back in the office a week from Monday."

"Thanks. I'll be well-rested with a nice tan when you next see me."

★   ★   ★

The President, although not tanned, projected a healthy glow, a sense of serenity and triumph as he sat before his desk, awaiting his on-camera cue. His staff, and even his critics, remarked that he had not looked this good for nearly two years, since the beginning of the 'nasty business'. Now his old charm and confidence were returning as he sensed that his prayers had been answered and he would now leave office on a high note. A red light flashed on the camera dolly directly facing him and, with a warm, sincere smile, he began to speak.

"My fellow Americans. Today the United States struck a blow against one of the gravest threats now facing not only America, but the entire civilized world...international terrorism. In the past several years, we have seen a pattern of activity among terrorist organizations which are intent on holding the world hostage for their own personal gain. Many of these organizations hide their murderous acts under the guise of one or another religious doctrine. But we know better. We know that no religion condones the murder of diplomats and their embassy staff, or the haphazard destruction of a crowded commercial aircraft, or puts a price on the head of innocent women and children. Nor does any religion support the infliction of chemical, biological, or nuclear weapons upon a peaceful nation.

"One terrorist organization that is guilty of executing or planning to execute all of these criminal acts is the so-called Ikhwan Brotherhood, led by the terrorist financier, Abdul bin Wahhab."

As the President spoke, an Airbus A-340, flying Air France markings, touched down on the lone runway on the Bahamian island of San Salvador. Applying its brakes and full reverse thrust, it rapidly slowed, then turned onto the taxiway. At the far end, on a side ramp, several persons standing before two Land Rovers and a red mobile stairway awaited the approach of the aircraft. As the four jet turbine engines wound down, the A-340 rolled to a stop in front of its greeting party. The stairwell was quickly trundled up to the cabin door, which was just beginning to open. The three men and one woman ascended the stairs and passed through the entrance as the door closed behind them.

"It has long been known that bin Wahhab has financed numerous terrorist activities around the world, causing thousands of deaths of innocent people," the President continued. "Now we also have incontrovertible proof that this international outlaw has formed an organization known as the Ikhwan Brotherhood, with the avowed objective of waging a war of violence and terror against peaceful nations, including the United States of America. We can not…must not…and will not let that happen."

A squad of heavily armed soldiers met the three men and one woman as they entered the aircraft. By the sheikh's orders, the newcomers were not searched. Escorted by the Ikhwan troops, they walked into the forward cabin with the woman in the lead. She halted at the side of the sheikh who, flanked by his two black-robed bodyguards, sat a few feet away from a large television screen. She neither bowed nor showed any sign of deference. The Ikhwan soldiers were shocked and offended by her insolence and each hoped that he might have the honor of dispatching her from this world. Thus they were chagrined when the Chosen One smiled upon seeing her and motioned her to sit near him. Without speaking, bin Wahhab put a finger to his lips, demanding silence, then nodded toward the TV screen. Svetlana Popova followed his gaze and her eyes came to rest on the image of the President of the United States.

"Recently, it has come to my attention that Abdul has stolen a significant amount of highly enriched uranium," the President said in a raspy voice. "It was his intention to fashion this material into a nuclear device to further his maniacal intentions. Obviously, it was necessary to act immediately. Working with our Russian allies, we destroyed the Ikhwan stronghold in eastern Afghanistan. I, as your Commander-in-Chief, then ordered an additional preemptive strike, with the cooperation of our Arab allies, on Abdul's base of operations in the Nubian Desert in Sudan. I am happy to report to you that the two operations were extremely successful. Both bases, as well as the nuclear capability were destroyed. Following my talk, the Chairman of the Joint Chiefs of Staff, Admiral Moore, will provide more details from the Pentagon.

"However, before closing, I do want to say a word about the legality of our actions since there are some who will question our right to take military action in a foreign country. In July of 1996, a meeting of concerned nations was held in Paris to adopt measures to counteract international terrorism. One of these measures was to treat terrorists as criminals and pursue them aggressively. This tenet will not be foiled simply because some nations unwisely extend sanctuary to these menaces to all mankind. It would be unethical and in violation of all common sense and the very foundations of international law to allow criminals to hold the world hostage.

"We will never surrender to terror. America will never tolerate terrorism. America will never abide terrorists. Wherever they come from, *wherever they go*, we will go after them. We will not rest until we have brought them all to justice or eradicated them from the face of the earth. Thank you."

The scene shifted to a CNN news desk where a commentator indicated that the Pentagon briefing would begin in ten minutes. The sheikh aimed his remote at the TV and turned down the sound.

"He purposely insults you, Mahdi," a man sitting next to the sheikh said.

"Of course, Major Zidah," bin Wahhab responded softly and assuredly. "He believes I am dead and can no longer hurt him. Rejoice in the knowledge that we will prove him wrong."

Kahlil Zidah smiled wryly. He knew that bin Wahhab was actually seething over the President's speech. Perhaps it might veil his thinking and cause him to make a mistake. But Zidah could not count upon such good fortune. It was enough that he had caught the sheikh's eye at the desert encampment and had been included among those who departed in the Airbus. The rest, with Allah's guidance, would be up to him.

Bin Wahhab turned to the Russian woman and said, "*Sallam al laikum.*"

"*Al laikum el sallam.* I am pleased to see that you arrived safely," she continued in Arabic.

"By God's grace. We left none too soon. And how are you progressing here?"

"The *Night Hawk* is out of the water. The keel will be taken off tonight."

"Excellent. Then we should be able to make the transfer tonight?"

"Yes. And we will set sail tomorrow morning. Are we fortunate to still have technical expertise?"

Bin Wahhab turned to one of his 'ravens' who, as always, hovered nearby. "Bring our guests here," he said. The man bowed, then quickly descended the stairwell.

A few moments later, he returned with two gray-haired, decidedly haggard men, clad in ill-fitting brown and green camouflage uniforms.

"These are your compatriots. This is Stephan Perov, a most able nuclear engineer," the sheikh said, referring to the shorter of the two. Perov, who bore a striking resemblance to the former Soviet premier, Nikita Khruschev, awkwardly shook the woman's outstretched hand.

"And I'm certain that you know—" bin Wahhab said, turning his attention to the other man, whose gaunt face revealed much suffering.

"Yes. Of course," Svetlana Popova interjected. "Hello, Professor Marenkov."

Chapter Thirty-Eight

"But the Americans have declared that the threat has been eliminated," Aksanov said, leaning back in the brown leather-covered armchair behind his desk.

"And what if they are mistaken," Medved countered, crushing a cigarette butt in a styrofoam cup. He and the FSB Director had been chasing each other's tails for half an hour on this issue, with neither side gaining on the other. The only other person in the Director's office, Viktor Buzhkin, had held his counsel while intently watching and listening.

"Suppose that Falcon is right, though," Medved argued. "Suppose just for a moment that bin Wahhab defied the odds and escaped with the bomb. The situation would be significantly more dangerous than ever before, because now our guard will be down. He will be able to move much more freely."

"But this whole business of that Caribbean Island…based on no more than a hunch," Aksanov demurred. "I cannot justify committing two of my people to such a wild goose chase. Forget that it might cost me my job. You know me well enough, Sergei, that if I believed that it was the proper thing to do, I'd do it regardless of the consequences."

Medved fell silent.

Aksanov turned to Buzhkin, who stared absently toward the window that looked out toward Red Square. "You have said nothing, Viktor. Tell me your thoughts."

The big man slowly inhaled, then began to speak in his heavy, gruff tone. "I was thinking that all my life, I have lived in Siberia, Moscow, and Afghanistan. I have never been to a tropical climate. I don't even own a bathing suit. Perhaps it's time I bought one."

Both Aksanov and Medved fixed their gazes on Buzhkin, awaiting further elucidation of his remarks. The Siberian, however, appeared quite content with his soliloquy as it stood. The awkward silence was broken by a buzz of the intercom on Aksanov's desk and the announcement that Mr. Falcon had arrived. "Send him in," Aksanov responded into the device.

When the door opened, the three men in the office rose to greet Falcon.

"So, you've come to say *Proshai*," Aksanov said, warmly clasping the American's hand.

"Farewell is too final," Falcon smiled, glancing at Medved and Buzhkin. Shall we just say, '*po-ka*'...."

"I agree...'for a little while'...that's much better," Aksanov chuckled. "Please sit. Can you spend a few minutes with us?"

"Only a few," Falcon answered, settling into an Afghan-covered sofa. "I have a flight to London that is leaving soon."

"And from there?"

"Miami."

"And then...?"

"The Bahamas for a little R and R...a vacation."

"I see. May I offer you some Kousmichoff tea? It's a delicious brew from Ceylon and it may be your last from a samovar for some time."

As the Director filled a white ceramic cup with the aromatic, steaming brown liquid, Falcon took note of Buzhkin and Medved, who were unusually subdued.

"So you call this a vacation," Aksanov said, handing the cup to the American. "Going to this place...what's it called...San Salvador? Going there on a hunch that you might track down bin Wahhab and the bomb."

"I hope I'm wrong," Falcon said stirring the tea. "I hope the Tomahawks in the Nubian Desert took care of it, but I don't think so. There's this matter of an irritating loose end that keeps popping up...first in the files of a dead man. Then again, thousands of miles away, on the lips of a Russian nuclear physicist who has spent this past year working on the sheikh's bomb. There's something to it, and I can't let it slip by."

Aksanov carefully studied Falcon as the latter spoke. He thought briefly about his own long, decorated career with the army, then his equally distinguished years of service with the FSB. Especially vivid in his mind were the risks that he took, the enemies he had made, the deathtraps he had escaped in forging his career in very dangerous times. And now, could he really gamble it all on an American's intuition? His opponents were already beginning to convince the Russian President that the joint raid on Khowst was a political blunder that would come back to haunt their country. And if they were to learn that two FSB agents had been dispatched to the Bahamas, after the apparent resolution of the matter in Sudan, and based on no more than an American agent's guess.... He transferred his attention to Sergei and said, "Major Medved, do you think that swim trunks large enough to fit a Siberian moose could be found on San Salvador?"

*   *   *

Resting on wooden blocks, *Night Hawk*, once so sleek in the water, now revealed her portly underside. A dozen men swarmed around her, like drones attending their queen bee. Several powerful lamps provided light for their work on this otherwise dark, moonless night. Some of the men were bending arm-sized wrenches onto the heads of heavy bolts at the top of *Night Hawk's* keel. Others were positioning and tightening steel jacks against her hull. Still others roamed the perimeter of the work area, warding off curious townspeople.

One of those who stood on the periphery, in the shadows, was Svetlana Popova. It was her habit to remain in concealment, to watch and listen and learn. She had just returned from a bungalow a few hundred yards away on the beach where she had left Guy DeMaté sprawled on a bumpy bed. The sedative she had given him had knocked him out as he was half way out of his pants. He would not engage in any activity with either Svetlana or *Night Hawk* that night.

The two Land Rovers that had been parked near the A-340 now rumbled into the dry dock area. Almost as one, the drones ceased their work and gazed silently, and somewhat anxiously, at the vehicles. Someone barked an order and they returned to their labors. At the same moment, the Russian woman turned to casually survey the inland side of the dock. The few unlit buildings…a dive shop, a bath house, and a marine repair facility…were eerie silhouettes on the fringe of the lights aimed at the schooner. Oddly, however, one shadow among them moved, flitting from the dive shop to the bath house. Careful to maintain her secrecy, Popova glided noiselessly toward the phantom.

Crouching in the shadows of the bath house, Major Zidah drew a deep breath and listened. Satisfied that no one else was in the vicinity, he peeked around the corner, then quickly dashed toward a dilapidated wooden cabin cruiser that sat rotting on its blocks. From there, he could peer through the worm-eaten hull and directly into the activity surrounding the *Night Hawk*.

Amid some excited voices and scurrying, the keel of the ship was beginning to move. Slowly, the massive lead ballast was lowered onto supporting blocks and jacks. When it was firmly secured, the workers began to rapidly remove hundreds of brick-sized lead bars from its interior. The scheme was now evident to Zidah. Soon the keel would be no more than a lead shell. The contents of the two Land Rovers would then be loaded into the shell, the keel would be reattached, and the schooner would set sail. Even if stopped and boarded, there would be no way of detecting the ship's deadly cargo.

Zidah rolled to his side and pulled a device from his jacket pocket that resembled a large cellular phone. He extended the foot long antenna and keyed the 'on' switch. A panel containing numbers, letters, and other symbology was illuminated by a soft green light. Zidah inputted a command, then sat back and waited. A series of numbers raced through a screen that was not much larger than his thumb. After several moments, a tiny red light appeared, indicating that the device had achieved a lock on a black world communication satellite. Quickly, he began typing a coded message. It would not be lengthy…just enough to alert the American military of bin Wahhab's scheme…a quick data burst and all would be revealed.

Just as he was about to key the 'send' switch, however, he sensed the presence of another being, almost as if his own electromagnetic field were being invaded. Turning, he saw a leg swing toward him and felt a boot crash into his face. The transmitter flew from his hand. Bleeding from the mouth and reeling from pain, he instinctively reached inside his jacket for his Beretta automatic pistol. His fingers had no sooner wrapped around the plastic grip when another kick knocked the weapon away. Pushing himself from the ground, he lunged at his antagonist who, sidestepping the charge, leaped and spun in the air.

In all his years of commando training and real-life experience, he had never seen such quickness and cat-like agility. A boot struck the base of his skull with the force of a sledge hammer. He buckled and fell unconscious to the ground. Leaning over his inert form, Svetlana Popova picked up the transmitter and smashed it against a rock.

* * *

It was late in the afternoon when a chartered Beechcraft King Air, carrying three jet-lagged passengers, touched down at San Salvador. As the aircraft, with its twin turbo-props winding down, taxied clear of the runway, it passed an Air France A-340 sitting alone on a side ramp.

"Are you thinking what I'm thinking?" Falcon said, turning to Medved.

"Perhaps we are in luck," the Russian answered. "We won't be sure, though, until we find the boat that you believe is the link."

"Right. When we get off this bug-smasher, I'll pay a visit to the marina. Maybe you and Viktor could find out a little more about that French Airbus."

As he spoke, the King Air rumbled to a halt in front of the terminal, which was not much larger than a three-bedroom house. The pilot cut off the engines while the co-pilot pushed open the exit hatch and extended an accordion stairway.

"Welcome to San Salvador," beamed a handsome young black man at the foot of the stairs. "My name is Reynaldo. I've been sent by the hotel to pick up you gentlemen."

"Very good, Reynaldo," Falcon answered, eyeing the Land Rover behind this solitary greeting party. "Before going to the hotel, however, we'd first like to visit the marina."

"Ah, just can't wait to get into the diving, yes?" Reynaldo laughed, flashing two perfect rows of ivory-hued teeth.

The three 'divers' grasped their bags and piled into the vehicle. With a grinding of gears and squeal of spinning tires, the Land Rover headed across the tarmac.

"Tell me, Reynaldo," Falcon shouted above the combined din of engine and Calypso tunes that blared from the radio, "do you know when that French airliner landed?"

"Oh, yes. Such a beautiful plane. It's the first of its kind that we've seen here."

"Yes. But when did it arrive?"

"Let me think." Reynaldo turned down the pulsating island music just enough to permit him to at least hear his own thoughts. "It was two days ago…in the late morning, if I recall. It's odd, though. There was no passenger off-loading to speak of. It just pulled over to the ramp and parked."

"Yes, that is strange," Falcon said, exchanging glances with Medved and Buzhkin. "Wouldn't the passengers be sweltering in this heat?"

"Oh, no. A generator has been hooked up to run the air-conditioning and the rest of the electricity."

"I see…or perhaps there were no passengers on board. Maybe the crew is just ferrying the plane somewhere."

"I don't think so," Reynaldo said, bouncing in his seat as the Land Rover ricocheted from a water-filled pothole. "A few persons did exit the plane. As a matter of fact, they went exactly where we are going…to the marina, to work on a large sailing vessel."

"You seem like a man who knows what's going on around here," Falcon smiled.

"Ah, San Salvador is a very small island. Not many secrets."

"That must be hard on romance."

Reynaldo looked askance at Falcon, then broke into a hearty laugh. "Quite true," he said.

"About that ship you mentioned," Falcon resumed, continuing his casual air. "Did you happen to see her name?"

"Oh, no. The owners wouldn't let anyone near her. But here we are at the marina. Perhaps you shall see her for yourself."

Reynaldo slowed and turned the vehicle onto an unpaved road.

"You can let me off right here," Falcon said. Before the vehicle had fully stopped, Falcon hopped out.

"Enjoy your sightseeing," Medved winked. Then, in a cloud of dust, the Land Rover sped away.

Falcon began walking along the dirt path that led to the marina a few hundred feet away. Directly in front of him was a small, U-shaped harbor that was nearly saturated by the presence of half a dozen weathered old fishing trawlers. The pungent odor of rotting fish mixed with grease and brine filled his nostrils. To his left were a dive shop, a bath house, and a marine repair facility. Beyond the buildings, several wooden vessels, their paint peeling and their hulls decaying, rested on their supports of jacks and blocks. There was no vessel, either in the harbor or in dry dock, that was a candidate for the work required by bin Wahhab.

The marina was devoid of life except for two men clad in faded blue overalls who were sweating over an engine in one of the trawlers. Falcon, his eyes continually searching his surroundings, strolled toward the laboring men.

"Hard work on such a hot day," he said, drawing near.

One of the men, a tall, broad shouldered Negro, wiped a greasy hand across his indigo forehead and stood.

"I'm afraid it's the transmission, chief. We'll probably have to pull the boat," he answered, gazing wearily at the stranger.

"Tough luck," Falcon said. "Say, have any other boats been dry-docked recently?"

"Five or six days ago," the fisherman said, reaching into a white ice cooler near his feet and retrieving a bottle of water. "She was in the back yard." He nodded toward the dry dock. "But not for long." Taking a swig, he then offered the bottle to Falcon. "She left a couple days ago."

"I think you need that more than I do right now," Falcon smiled. "But thanks for the offer and the info."

Leaving the fishermen to their engine repair, Falcon walked around the wooden wharf to the dry dock which, with its dead and decaying ships, seemed more like a cemetery than a 'back yard'. One area, however, showed evidence of fairly recent activity. The weeds were trampled, the soil was fresh underfoot, and hundreds of unrusted bits of metal of various shapes and sizes lay about. Falcon leaned down and picked up one of the cast-offs. He recognized it as a lead 'pig', the type of ballast used in the keel of a sailboat. Holding the brick-sized bar of lead in his hands, he gazed toward the northwest, where he imagined the ship had gone, and added another piece to the puzzle.

*   *   *

Medved had decided that the best way to learn any secrets the French Airbus might hold was to get inside the aircraft and examine it, himself. There were only two people, a radio operator and a mechanic, on duty in the airport. It was a simple matter to bind, gag, and hide them away. The uniform of the mechanic turned out to be a reasonably close fit to his frame. Once the power to the generator supplying the A-340 with its electricity and cooling air was shut off, it was just a matter of waiting.

"Here they come, now," Buzhkin said, peering through a window at two approaching figures.

"Didn't take them long in this heat," his companion grinned, tightening a tool belt around his waist. "How do I look?"

"Like you missed your calling," Buzhkin nodded approvingly.

"All right, I'll take that as a compliment. Now look, if I'm not back in half an hour, shoot their tires out…whatever you have to do. Just make sure that plane doesn't leave."

He rose, opened a screen door, and went outside to greet the visitors. Buzhkin watched discreetly from the window as Medved, after a short discussion, accompanied the two men back to the aircraft.

Sergei was pleased to see that the generator, in order that it be kept from boiling in the sunlight, was located under the belly of the plane. It thus was not visible to anyone inside the passenger cabin. The electrical lead from the power box ran through the slightly open, aft cargo door and into the hold. The Russian walked around the generator, mumbling some nonsense. "Your problem is the multi-flexing rheostat." Lying on his side, he cried out, "One of you give me a hand here, please."

One of the soldiers stepped behind the generator and knelt next to the 'mechanic'. He was totally unprepared for the steely grip that suddenly fastened on his throat, pinching his Adam's apple so that no sound could be emitted. Medved pulled him closer, then struck the bulging-eyed head with a wrench. The other Ikhwan, dulled by the heat and bored with this assignment, was absently gazing at the blue sea just beyond the end of the runway. He too was quickly dispatched by use of the same weapon.

Medved dragged both of the men under the belly of the aircraft, where he bound and gagged them with duct tape from his tool belt. He then stood on the generator, eased open the cargo door and hoisted himself into the hold. Sliding the door nearly shut, he began to make his way through the aircraft's bowels. His progress was greatly enhanced by the sunlight that knifed through the partially cracked open door. The pencil-like shaft was just sufficient to give form to dozens of fully stuffed canvas bags, rectangular wooden boxes and upright aluminum containers. None of these items, however, appeared reasonably capable of housing highly enriched uranium.

The heat in the enclosed bay was thick and oppressive. Medved sat on one of the canvas bags, and using the sleeve of his shirt, wiped the perspiration from his brow and eyelids. The respite allowed his eyes to become more accustomed to the near total darkness and he began to scrutinize his surroundings. As he gazed around, his attention was arrested by a door leading to the forward section of the aircraft. Rising, he reached behind his back, under his tool belt, and wrapped his fingers around the polymer grip of his *Gurza*. With the weapon held before him, he cautiously approached the door.

To his relief, the doorknob turned easily and the barrier swung open. The sight that met his eyes was completely unexpected. Instead of more bags, boxes, and containers, the area resembled a miniature Arabian palace. The bulkheads of the rooms on either side of the passageway were adorned with filigree arabesques of delicately intertwined gold, sky blue, and silver. The first alcove to the left was decorated with richly woven Persian carpets and brightly colored, tasseled pillows. To the right, a fully filled hot tub sat in a marble enclosure.

A moaning sound coming from just beyond the spa caused Medved to stop and raise his pistol with both hands. Cautiously taking a step forward, he peered around the hot tub enclosure, where he found himself looking into a shower stall. A pipe ran from the showerhead to the deck, where, lying in a pool of blood, a handcuffed figure lay. The Russian knelt alongside the groaning man, whose beaten red, purple, and green face resembled week-old ground meat. The man was still conscious. Sergei slowly reached up, turned on a faucet, and cupped a handful of water. Cradling the swollen, battered head in one arm, he held the cool liquid to the suffering man's mouth. The water was eagerly gulped.

With the one eye that was not completely swollen shut, the man gazed at this savior in mechanic's overalls. Painfully moving his puffy lips, he rasped a question in Farsi, the language of Iran.

Hoping to find a common communication ground, Medved whispered, "Do you speak English?"

The man nodded and, switching to that language, said softly, "You're no mechanic. Who are you?"

"A friend. Why have they done this to you?"

"Slight political disagreement."

"It appears more than slight."

The man winced in pain as he tried to sit up. "I must...do something very important. Will you help me to get out of here?"

Medved glanced at the metal handcuffs that were shackled to the pipe, then followed the water shaft upwards to the shower head. Rising, he tucked the *Gurza* in his waistband behind his back and grasped two wrenches from his tool belt. Applying one to the pipe and the other to the shower head, he put his muscles to the task. The corroded fixture gradually began to turn and then finally sprung free. Quickly, he slid the tubing from the handcuffs and was beginning to raise the injured man from the shower floor when he was startled by a shout from behind him.

Medved slowly turned to see an assault rifle aimed squarely at his chest. His mind was rapidly calculating the options available to him when several other armed Ikhwan soldiers appeared. It was obvious that resistance in this situation would be futile or worse. He raised his hands, hoping to soon have a more favorable opportunity. The Ikhwan who had shouted poked his new captive in the stomach with his rifle and motioned toward a stairway. Medved ascended the stairs and, amid excited jabbering, crowding, and pushing, stepped into the aircraft's luxurious forward cabin. Struck in the back by rifle butts, he was shoved forward, through a throng of angry, weapon-wielding soldiers. A word was said and the mob parted, bringing him face-to-face with Abdul bin Wahhab.

Chapter Thirty-Nine

Falcon was continuing to poke around the ship-yard when his portable transceiver beeped.

"Michael, I think you better join me," Buzhkin said, his normal understated tone now tinted with a sense of urgency. "I've sent Reynaldo around to pick you up."

Falcon tossed aside the lead bar he had been holding and trotted along the wharf and down the dirt road leading to the street. The Land Rover, beating out its percussive calypso airs, was just screeching to a halt in a whirl of dust.

"From the airport to the marina…for half an hour…then right back to the airport," Reynaldo grinned. "What kind of tourist are you, anyway?"

"I'm actually not a tourist, Reynaldo. I'm a government inspector of island transportation."

"Oh, I see," Reynaldo laughed, grinding into first gear, whirling the vehicle into a sliding U-turn, and careening away. "How's my driving?"

"A little crazier and you're New York cabbie potential. Now step on it."

It took only five minutes to reach the airport. Falcon was met by Buzhkin at the front door of the nearly empty terminal.

"Sergei is in there," the Russian said, nodding toward the Airbus. "It's been over half an hour now and I don't like it."

Falcon gazed toward the aircraft that was now only a gray silhouette in the dying sunlight. "How'd he get in?"

"We shut off the generator and he posed as a mechanic. He went up into the rear bay."

As Buzhkin spoke, Falcon's eyes followed the electrical lead of the generator through the partially open cargo hold doorway.

"Time is absolutely critical," Falcon said. "It'll be night in a couple of minutes…unlike your homeland, there's not much twilight in the tropics."

"With their power out, they'll soon be pretty much in the dark," Buzhkin added.

"Yes." Falcon slowly scrutinized the Siberian hulk. "We'll go in about five minutes."

*   *   *

A thousand miles to the northwest, *Night Hawk* swung to port and left the Atlantic Ocean in her wake. A stocky man, clad in a blue peacoat, jeans, and a black knit cap stood on the bow alongside a similarly dressed blonde-haired woman.

"Beautiful," DeMaté said, his smile barely discernible in the waning light. "See there…crab pots."

Popova gazed at the numerous rows of yellow and orange globes that bobbed as far as the eye could see.

"And why do you find that so enchanting?" she asked.

DeMaté laughed. "Don't you see? It means we are in the Chesapeake Bay…almost to our destination."

"Yes, we've made excellent time," Popova replied.

"Thanks to the Gulf Stream current and, of course, that magnificent engine that you had installed," the Frenchman grinned. "I always knew that you had an ultimate reason for such horsepower."

As he spoke, a large figure carrying two mugs emerged from the cabin.

"I thought you could use some hot coffee," the rough-hewn, unshaven man said, handing a cup each to Popova and DeMaté.

"Yes, thank you, Vorontsov," Popova smiled. Without responding, the man returned below.

"Friendly fellow," DeMaté said. "Much like those other two you brought on board at San salvador."

"Don't worry about them," she replied. "They're not your concern...yet."

DeMaté, who had just begun to sip the hot beverage, looked up at her. He had long ago suspected that this entire chartering operation was a scam for an illicit business...almost assuredly drug running. Ever since the 'French' woman had come aboard in St. Thomas, his suspicions had been confirmed a number of times. And equally validated was his nautical acumen that the *Night Hawk* just did not sail properly. Now, after much brain-bending speculation, he was sure he knew why. *The drugs were hidden in a false keel. And that was what caused the schooner to be imbalanced when heeling over.*

DeMaté began to wonder how he might convince the woman to cut him into the operation. Obviously, he had played a major role thus far and yet he was working for a pittance. If they wanted to continue running this route, it would make sense to keep him on rather than trying to find another captain as skilled and dependable...one who knew how to keep his mouth shut. Then, too, he had other qualities—of a more romantic nature—that this minx would surely come to appreciate. In his overzealous thought processes, however, he had missed a most obvious consideration...

One, that, ironically, was being mulled at that very moment, by Svetlana Popova.

I wonder how I shall kill him, she thought, smiling at the Frenchman. Taking her pleasant expression as a positive sign, DeMaté grinned affably back.

*   *   *

"A *Gurza*. Not the sort of thing that a Bahamian mechanic normally carries in his tool belt," bin Wahhab said in English as he examined the weapon that was taken from his latest prisoner. "It would seem more appropriate for a Russian intelligence agent. Perhaps you would care to explain…or would you rather be persuaded in the manner of your friend—Major Zidah?"

Medved stood a few feet from the Arab, his wrists clasped before him in handcuffs. "Have you seen the size of the flies down here?" he said. "And how they sting! I asked for a bigger gun to shoot them down but this was the best they could do.…"

An Ikhwan soldier swung his rifle butt into Medved's stomach. As the Russian doubled over, the soldier raised his weapon as if to strike again. He was halted by a word from his leader.

"I hope we will have no further need for that. Now tell me how many others are with you."

"I'm here with an entire brigade of Russian Special Forces and a division of U.S. Marines," Medved wheezed as he straightened up. "It's useless for you. You really should give up."

Bin Wahhab tapped the fingers of his right hand on the table top before him.

"You realize, of course, that I am not stupid. I also accord you the same benefit of the doubt. And if you are not stupid, then you know that eventually you will tell me what I wish to know. Please do not cause us all a lot of unnecessary time and trouble. Now, if you'll excuse me, I'm late for my sunset prayers. My men will take you below."

Medved was seized and roughly shoved toward the stairway.

"And someone go to the terminal and find a real mechanic," bin Wahhab called after his men. "I want that external power restored. I don't want to drain our batteries. We may need them to start the auxiliary power unit."

Medved was half-pushed, half-thrown down the steps. Landing awkwardly on the lower deck, he was grasped and dragged into the shower stall. Major Zidah was where he had first found him, although the Ikhwan had not gone to the trouble of re-securing him to the dismantled water pipe. While four soldiers prepared to interrogate the Russian, two others continued on to the aft cargo door exit.

Now that the sun had set, taking with it the thin sliver of light that had snaked through the cracked doorway, the cargo hold had become pitch black. The two men walked cautiously, feeling the starboard bulkhead for reference and security. One of the soldiers lit a match in an effort to better guide them. It was a fatal mistake. The brief light only managed to destroy the little amount of dark adaptation thus far achieved by their retinas. When the flame died, the hold was even blacker to them than before. Two other pairs of eyes, however, had averted the destructive illumination and, having been in complete darkness for ten minutes, were now vastly more adapted to the gloom.

The Ikhwan were completely unaware that two men were standing directly behind them...until they felt hands on their foreheads and arms jammed at the base of their skulls. A quick backward snap of the necks over these forearm fulcrums and their stark but brief terror was permanently ended.

Lowering their victims silently to the deck, Falcon and Buzhkin stole forward, toward the sounds of blows and laughter emanating from near the nose of the aircraft. There, too, the Ikhwan were careless of the dark, having set two glaring flashlights on a chair. The yellowish-white beams of the lights were focused on Medved who, still handcuffed, was being held by one man and struck by another. Two other soldiers looked on, laughing and awaiting their turn. Another man, apparently unconscious, lay at Medved's feet. Falcon tapped Buzhkin on the shoulder, motioning to the husky soldier who was meting out the punishment.

It must have been somewhat surreal for the other three Ikhwan to see their beefy comrade suddenly rise in the air, toss his head back and disappear onto the shadows. Perplexed by this odd event, one of them stepped into the dark, his curious head perilously stretching his exposed neck. He, too, quickly vanished. The remaining two Ikhwan, now jolted from their paralytic fear, seized their weapons. At that same instant, Falcon squeezed the trigger of his noise-suppressed Glock once, then twice. The only sound heard was akin to two sacks of flour plopping to the floor.

In the next moment, Buzhkin had slung Major Zidah over his shoulder and Falcon supported the still ambulatory Medved. As they began to run back through the cargo bay, they heard voices and footsteps at the stairway. Falcon was the first to leap from the cargo doorway onto the generator. As he helped Medved descend, he heard the excited shouts of the Ikhwan who were just now discovering the bodies of their comrades. Major Zidah was lowered down to him and Buzhkin immediately followed.

"They're coming into the hold now," the Siberian said. "I'll hold them off while you take these two to the terminal."

Falcon hesitated, but Buzhkin turned forcefully to him and barked, "Go!"

Sliding from the generator, Falcon loaded Zidah on his back and threw an arm around Medved. Although he still felt uncomfortable in exposing his back to Buzhkin, he turned and, supporting his human burdens, broke into a staggering trot. Behind him, he heard the rattle of automatic fire. Setting his jaw against his chest, he pressed forward.

Once inside the terminal, Falcon retrieved the rifles that had been left behind and handed one to Medved.

"Are you well enough to use this?" he put to his friend as they settled near a window facing the aircraft.

Medved managed a smile. "Even now," he replied, "old Sergei can still outshoot you, Michael."

"I hope you're right, because you're sure as hell going to have a chance to prove it."

"Look!" Medved blurted, "Viktor is making a run for it!"

Falcon peered through the window just in time to see Buzhkin zigzagging toward their position. Half a dozen soldiers were leaping out of the cargo hold, some already beginning to shoot at the fleeing figure. Falcon and Medved instantly brought their rifles into play, sweeping the area beyond Buzhkin with a deadly fire. Several of the Ikhwan spun around or flipped backwards to the ground. The others took cover behind the generator and the giant wheels of the aircraft.

"Perfect," Medved grunted as he aimed his weapon toward the tires. "Even if I miss those hooligans, I'll still get the wheels. This plane won't be leaving soon."

"Look out!" Falcon shouted, lurching forward. "Viktor's been hit."

Buzhkin lay sprawled on the tarmac, with tiny plumes of asphalt, driven by ricocheting bullets, erupting around him.

"I'm going after him," Falcon said, sprinting for the door before Medved could object.

As Falcon weaved his way toward Buzhkin, ten more Ikhwan leaped from the aircraft and added their firepower to the fray. It seemed impossible that their bullets would not cut down both of the exposed men. Medved rapidly swung his rifle from side-to-side, maintaining a slim hope that he could suppress the enemy fire if only for a few more moments. His intensity was such that he did not hear the rustling of a body next to him, the clank of a rifle barrel, and the click of a cartridge bolt, until a shot was fired almost next to his ear. He turned in surprise to see Major Zidah shouldering a rifle and aiming toward the enemy.

"I still have one good eye," the Iranian said, squeezing the trigger.

As Zidah's weapon fired, Medved took advantage of the moment to change the magazine of his own rifle. When he rejoined the fight, the combined firepower of the two men was sufficient to temporarily suppress the Ikhwans' zeal.

With Buzhkin's log-like arm draped across his shoulders, Falcon began dragging the wounded man toward the terminal. He suddenly felt a burning sensation in his right cheek, as though someone had slashed him with a hot knife. Although he knew no Ikhwan could possibly be that close, he instinctively glanced to his right. A warm liquid was now beginning to trickle over his jaw and into his mouth.

"*Bistro! Bistro!*" Medved shouted.

Drawing from an unknown reserve, Falcon hoisted Buzhkin to his back and ran to the terminal. The Ikhwan, recovering from their initial retreat and now disregarding their own safety, stood and fired at the dark, fleeing form. The high-pitched whine of ricocheting bullets filled the air and jagged splinters of the wooden terminal flew in all directions. The door of the building burst open and Falcon and Buzhkin tumbled to the floor.

The Ikhwan soldiers on the ground were surprised to hear the four jet engines begin to spool up, one after the other. The amazement intensified when they turned to reenter through the aft cargo hold and found that the door had been closed. It was then that they realized they had been sacrificed to the Jihad. As their shelter began to taxi away, a few of them raced toward the sides of the runway. Most, however, ran straight at the terminal, their rifles blazing and their mouths screaming. In such an exposed manner, they were quickly erased by the fire laid down by Medved and Zidah.

The throttles of the A-340 were already being shoved to full power when the aircraft turned onto the runway. Although several tires had been shot out, the Airbus was still able to accelerate to take-off speed. As it roared past his position, Medved darted from the terminal and emptied an entire magazine of forty-five rounds in the aircraft's direction.

The plane hurtled away, reached the end of the runway and lifted into the air. The Russian watched helplessly as it rose higher, then began to bank away. Oddly, however, the roll became increasingly steep and the A-340 began to nose down toward the water. It seemed as if no attempt were being made to right the plane and prevent its plunge. Medved had no way of knowing that much was being done in the cockpit to correct the situation. But the sophisticated fly-by-wire, quintuple redundant computer flight system was no longer of any use, as the hydraulic lines feeding the port ailerons had been completely shot away. All the efforts of the panicked pilots merely served to compound the problem and the aircraft continued its death spiral.

It took only a few seconds for the Airbus to strike the water in a nose-down, nearly inverted attitude. It cartwheeled once, the force of which ripped off the port wing and peeled away the port bulkhead as if it were a fresh food tin. Live bodies, seats, and seats containing live bodies were hurled from the aircraft. Electrical shorts in the wing tanks now ignited the jet fuel and before the A-340 could cartwheel again, it exploded in a brilliant orange, yellow, and red ball of fire. It then disappeared into the indigo sea.

Chapter Forty

"Ah, there you are," DeMaté said as he peered through the inky night toward a blinking green beacon. "Flashing every five seconds."

"What does it mean?" Popova asked.

Careful to point the bow to the starboard side of the warning buoy, DeMaté grinned, "*Ma cherie*…we are now in the Potomac River."

Popova experienced a rush of adrenalin at the announcement. A rush she would have liked to satisfy physically if the Frenchman had been half way appealing. As he was not, she simply replied, "How much longer before reach Washington?"

"Well, we won't be able to travel quite as fast now, but we'll be there in a day or so."

* * *

"I'm sorry, sir," the operator said officiously, "but you'll have to obtain an AT&T credit card if you wish to place a call."

"But, operator," Mike Falcon simmered, courageously controlling his temper, "as I've been trying to tell you, this is a matter of national emergency."

"And as I said to you, sir, long distance service on the island is only done through AT&T."

Falcon moved the phone away from his ear and took a deep breath.

From the floor of the terminal, where he sat tying a tourniquet to Buzhkin's wounded leg, Medved watched and listened to Falcon's plight.

Raising the phone back to his ear, Falcon gritted his teeth and spoke slowly. "All right then, I'd like to make a collect call to Washington, D.C. To the White House."

"Sorry, sir. That's not possible without an AT&T calling card number."

"Now listen to me. Millions of lives are at stake. It's imperative that you put this call through. Do you understand me?"

"Perfectly, sir. And I hope you understand that you must have an AT&T card number. Since you do not, there is no use in continuing this conversation. Have a nice day."

"No, don't hang—", before he could finish, the phone clicked and a disconnect tone followed.

With an incredulous look, Falcon replaced the receiver on its hook and knelt next to Medved. "How is he?" he nodded toward Buzhkin.

"He's lost a good deal of blood, but no bones were broken," Sergei said. "He'll be fine if we can get half a case of kvass and perhaps a roast pig into him. Do you think maybe we've pegged him wrong all along?"

Falcon shrugged. "If he's with the other side, he's sure killing off his comrades at an alarming rate."

Medved nodded, saying, "How's your cheek?"

Falcon felt the tender welt on his face. "It should make for a very nice scar."

"Yes, it will do you good to look a little tougher. Like Major Zidah, here. He's got a nice head start on the 'tough' look."

The Iranian, sitting cross-legged with his rifle in his lap, broke into a painful smile.

A flash of headlights and squeal of tires interrupted their conversation. Falcon rose, crunched across the shattered glass and splintered wood strewn throughout the room, and peered through a window. A lone uniformed black man, rifle in hand, was anxiously descending from a jeep. He constituted the island's entire police force. Upon seeing Falcon, he stopped and raised his weapon.

"Easy does it, sheriff," Falcon said. "We're the good guys in here."

"So you say, mon—but how do I know dat?" the policeman replied, glancing around at the carnage on the tarmac.

"Believe me. If we wanted you dead, that already would've happened. The important thing now is that we contact the U.S. military."

"You tink I'm crazy to come here witout back-up? A detachment of United States Marines is flying in as we speak, mon."

The sheriff was not bluffing. A battle group, led by the aircraft carrier Abraham Lincoln, was situated one hundred miles to the east. At the request of the Bahamian government for U.S. military assistance in quelling what appeared to be a raging drug war, the Lincoln was authorized to dispatch its contingent of sixty Marines to the trouble spot. Their helicopters began landing only a few minutes after the sheriff's arrival at the terminal. It took Falcon considerably longer, however, to convince the Marines' commanding officer that they were on the same side. Finally, a call was put through to Washington and, to the Marine captain's surprise, the White House eagerly accepted.

"Mike, are you O.K.?" the voice of Preston Higby echoed. It was clear that he was on a speaker phone.

"Yes. Just a little nick. Who is on at that end?"

"Only the President's Chief of Staff besides myself. Looks like your hunch was right. As soon as we received word from the Bahamian government about the gun battle on San Salvador, we knew you were onto something. The President immediately authorized the intervention of the Marines. Did you have complete success?"

"I'm afraid not. We got here a little too late. But we did learn that the package is on a twin-masted schooner, approximately fifty or sixty feet in length. It left here five or six days ago. It could be anywhere from here to the Outer Banks by now. You've got to ensure that all inlets to the southeast coast are tightly controlled. Anything fitting the description of that vessel should be intercepted and held offshore."

The Chief of Staff immediately reached for another phone. "We're on it right now. What else?"

"Have the Navy give me a hop to MacDill ASAP…something large enough to carry a dozen people. Contact Commander O'Brien there and tell him we need to borrow his nuclear disposal team again."

"Where do you think the package is headed?"

"I believe there's no doubt, now. While in the Airbus at San Salvador, Major Zidah overheard bin Wahhab discussing the target with a woman."

"Popova?"

"Probably, from the description Zidah gave me. At any rate, the nation's capital is in the cross hairs."

"I was afraid you'd say that. All right. Sit tight. A COD from the Lincoln will pick you up in half an hour."

"Roger, sir. Thanks."

Falcon handed the phone back to the marine corporal radio operator, then turned to the officer. "Captain, there are a few bad guys still left out there somewhere. You'll want to stay heads up tonight."

The captain surveyed the dozen bodies that had been lain in a neat row inside the terminal. "Damn, I'd just like to know what the hell is going on."

"So would I," Falcon muttered. "So would I."

* * *

It was near midnight when the Lincoln's C-2A COD—'Carrier Onboard Delivery'—aircraft touched down at MacDill Air Force Base in Tampa, Florida. A lone man in the khaki uniform of a Navy officer, his left arm in a cast, stood waiting before the arrival shack. The plane taxied up to the sidewalk leading to the red brick building, pivoted on one wheel and came to a stop. As the twin turboprops wound down, the hatch opened, a stairway unfolded, and Mike Falcon emerged.

"Chris," Falcon grinned, descending the steps. "What the hell do you think you're doing?"

Lt. Rochelle strode forward and clasped Falcon's outstretched hand.

"I'm going with you, Mike. As soon as the COD's refueled, and my people have arrived, we'll load her up. Sorry my guys aren't here already, but they all were on some well-deserved leave. I had to recall them."

"But your arm…you're in no shape…."

"No way I'm going to sit this one out, Mike."

As they spoke, Buzhkin, supported by Medved and an airman, descended the steps. They were followed by the still wobbly Iranian Major.

Rochelle shook his head and softly whistled. "Jeezus. What happened back there?" he asked, gazing at the wounded men.

"Tell you on the way," Falcon answered. "Will Commander O'Brien be joining us?"

"The Old Man's jetting back from the West Coast. He'll meet us in D.C. Hey, I like that nasty gash on your cheek. Makes you look tougher."

"Yeah, so I've heard."

*　　　　　*　　　　　*

"What do we have," the President said, swiftly entering the Oval Office at 8:00 a.m. and settling into the chair behind his desk. The room was filled with his top people from the Pentagon, Coast Guard, FBI, intelligence agencies, and his own staff.

"All vessels fitting the description provided us are being denied entry into the U.S.," the Chief of Staff answered.

"Why are we so certain that this is the right type of ship?"

"The information comes from one of our agents—Mike Falcon. He obtained it from an Iranian intelligence officer, code-named Darius... you're familiar with Darius?"

The President shot a bullet glance across the room at his National Security Advisor.

"I am now. How did Darius get his info?"

"Apparently, he was with bin Wahhab during the flight from Sudan. He saw the bomb being loaded into the schooner's keel at San Salvador. Unfortunately, he was unable to transmit the information to us before he was compromised."

"Is he dead?"

"No. There was a gun battle involving our man, two Russian intelligence agents, and the Ikhwan terrorists. The sheikh's private Airbus was totally destroyed and we're fairly certain that bin Wahhab perished as a result. Darius, however was recovered."

The President tilted back in his chair, gazing at the ceiling as he assimilated the information. "All right, what safety precautions do we take with regard to the public?"

After a resounding silence, Higby finally ventured forth. "I think it would be unwise and irresponsible to make a general announcement at this point. We would merely cause a panic and a general disruption of communication and transportation capabilities that could be crucial to saving lives. We should wait at least a few more hours until, hopefully, the schooner is found or we at least have a better handle on the situation."

"I disagree," the Chief of Staff interjected. "You're going to look very bad, Mr. President, if an atomic bomb explodes and it's learned that you had advance notice of the threat, yet issued no warning. At least if you make an announcement, many people will be able to evacuate. Those who stay behind will have been forewarned and no one can then point a finger at 1600 Pennsylvania Avenue."

The President stood, turned, and strode to the window overlooking the Rose Garden. Although all the snow had melted with the recent warm spell, it was still far too early for the first buds to make their appearance.

With his hands clasped behind him, he gazed at the wet, bare tree branches and glistening grass that had been soaked by the melting snow. "I agree with Preston that speculation on this matter would lead to mass hysteria and would therefore be counterproductive. Until we have further information, we'll hold off making any announcements."

As his aides began to file from the office, the President resumed gazing through the window, but this time his sights were focused beyond the Rose Garden, far to the south.

*   *   *

From that southerly direction, *Night Hawk* was making its way up the Potomac River. In the main cabin, Svetlana Popova knelt next to a gaunt, sickly figure.

"Well, how are we feeling this morning?" she asked, not completely insincerely.

The elderly man gazed upwards, peering as if through a thick filter.

"What have you done to me?" he rasped.

"It's nothing serious," she replied. "You'll be fine in another hour or so."

Marenkov tried to pull himself up to a sitting position, but suddenly experiencing a wave of nausea, he slumped down.

"Wha…what do you intend to do with me?"

"Why, Alexander, I think I detect a note of hostility. You should be thanking me. You're going to get a chance to reap the fruits of your work…up close and personal."

"I had nothing to do with the construction of this device," Marenkov objected. "In fact, I tried my best to prevent it."

"Indeed you did—with regard to this one. Look upon this as more of a lifetime achievement award."

Marenkov frowned and looked away.

"I'm not going to try to defend what I thought to be necessary actions during the Cold War," he said drily without looking at her. "But those days are gone. Why are you doing this now? For the mad Arab's Jihad? Surely you don't believe…."

"Of course not," Popova laughed icily. "Bin Wahhab thought he was pulling the strings, when in fact he was merely being used. His money, people, and facilities all played into our hands. He has no idea of the extent and dedication of the power to which I answer."

"But, if it's not bin Wahhab, then what…."

"I'm sure you've heard rumors of our organization. We have been wielding more control every day in Russia."

"Can it really be true," Marenkov whispered, turning to her. "Do the Feliks really exist?"

"Considering the situation, perhaps you can now answer that question yourself."

"What do you hope to achieve?"

"You of all people should know, Professor. My cause is yours…our former self-respect, our rightful status in the world. When the West was being crushed by the Third Reich, they were only too happy to see us throw ourselves by the millions into graves to halt the Nazis. And now, when we need a helping hand, we are just the penniless, crippled, forgotten old soldier. But we will not quietly die. We will reestablish the ideal communist state and once again Russia will be a power to be reckoned with."

"And so, in the final analysis," Marenkov fumed, "you are no different than the very man you use with such contempt."

"Oh? And just how would that be, Professor?"

Although his pain caused him to speak with difficulty, Marenkov's mind was now alert and fully engaged. "Like bin Wahhab, you too have your own religion and your own Jihad. And to achieve your goal, you are willing to sacrifice millions of people."

"Yes, but our religion is not a dream of salvation in the hereafter but the salvation of our country in the here and now," Popova smirked. "From the chaos of our enemies, our nation and people will emerge stronger and more formidable."

"I beg you. It's not too late to stop. Think of the good you would be doing if you ended this…."

Popova stared thoughtfully at the emaciated man, then said, "I suggest you keep such thoughts to yourself. Otherwise, I'll have no choice but to give you another injection."

She stood, took a step toward the open hatchway, then paused. "We'll be in Washington soon," she smiled, reassuming her customary lighthearted demeanor. "Enjoy the trip, Professor. It will be your last."

CHAPTER FORTY-ONE

"That's it, sir," a blue-uniformed Air Force Master Sergeant said to his passenger in the Humvee.

"Can you pull up alongside her when she stops?" Rick Jensen asked as he stroked his mustache.

"Yes, sir. I just need to get clearance from ground control."

As the aircraft taxied toward the Navy's auxiliary hangar at Andrews Air Force Base, the sergeant placed the call. Receiving clearance, he re-hooked the transmitter, engaged the Humvee's transmission, and stepped on the accelerator. Two other Humvees followed.

The passenger aircraft from the Lincoln had halted and its wheels were being chocked when the trio of vehicles pulled up. As Mike Falcon was descending the mobile stairs, he heard a familiar voice.

"Welcome home, boss," Jensen said.

"Rick," Falcon grinned. "I heard you were getting some warm weather, so I thought I'd come back."

Jensen wasn't fooled by Falcon's cavalier remark. He sensed the tension in his boss's voice and saw it in his face, where the distress seemed etched by the black and blue gash on Falcon's right cheek. After being introduced to Medved, Buzhkin, Zidah, and Rochelle, Jensen announced that he had orders to bring them all into the Old Executive Office Building.

"We're setting up our command post there," he remarked as the equipment was piled into the vehicles.

"Oh?" Falcon's eyebrows raised. "What happened to the FBI's role in the President's counterterrorism policy?" He referred to the recent Presidential Decision Directive that designated the FBI Headquarters as the focal point for all counterterrorist activity. "I'll wager that Fredericks isn't too happy about that."

"No, sir. But, the Commander-in-Chief didn't want this operation run from down the street. He wants to be right on top of it."

"I think he's about to get his wish," Falcon responded as he and Jensen climbed into a Humvee.

"In more ways than one, if your report was correct about D.C. being the target."

"It's right, unfortunately."

"Yeah, well, some smart people did a calculation based on the info you gave us about the bomb's construction and yield. The explosion would leave nothing but a crater from Capitol Hill to the Potomac. The entire city would be incinerated. At least a million casualties in the blast and fireball. A lot more through radiation. I gotta warn you…the folks in the command post are a bit on edge about all of that."

"I can imagine."

Falcon peered pensively toward the southern horizon as the Humvee convoy passed through the sentry gate.

"By the way," Jensen remarked, steering the vehicle onto Suitland Parkway which was lined on either side by grayish-brown, bare-limbed trees, "I spoke to Lin Su just this morning. I didn't tell her you were coming back today, but she seemed to sense something was going on. She told me that she dreamt you were coming home this week. If you want to call her, you can use the car phone."

Falcon did want to talk to her…to tell her to get the hell out of Washington as fast as she could. What would be the harm in saving at least one person? After turning the thought over for several moments, he said, "Not yet."

*   *   *

A few miles away, in the Washington Channel, at the Capitol Marina, *Night Hawk* swayed slowly at her mooring. Below, in the main salon, her deck boards had been removed and three men and one woman were huddled around a dark, barely visible metallic object. One of the men wiped his perspiring forehead with his sleeve, pushed his glasses back over the slippery bridge of his nose, and made a final adjustment with a screwdriver on an electrical switch.

"There, that does it," he wheezed. "It's now armed."

His trio of onlookers instinctively moved back.

"Don't worry," Perov said, reassuringly. "It cannot possibly detonate unless this electrical connection is made. Once the circuit is closed, however, the countdown will begin. In two hours, a powerful current will run from the battery bank along these platinum wires. The surge will vaporize the wires, initiating this primary lead azide explosive. Krytron switches, which can handle the surge, will trigger the four main circuits. The secondary charge will then detonate, the device will implode, and the nuclear reaction will ensue. Once the counter reaches zero, the whole process from ignition to thermonuclear reaction will take about one second. Are there any questions?"

The others stared silently at the black, steel-enshrouded device and the small chrome switch that would begin the sequence leading to its other-worldly power.

Finally, Popova asked, "How easy would it be to stop the timer?"

"Ah, that's my proudest achievement," Perov smiled. It's encased in titanium, several centimeters thick. It would take another atomic bomb to open it."

"Then if I were to do this…." Popova said, leaning toward the bomb and, to the astonishment of the others, flicking the chrome switch from SAFE to ON. "Seal the titanium case, *Gospodeen* Perov. We now have two hours."

The ruby neon counter, portraying the passage of each tenth of a second, cast a hypnotic effect on its observers as it began to rapidly digitize downward.

"Well, then, I suppose we shouldn't tarry," Popova said. "Vorontsov, bring me the Professor and the Frenchman."

A few moments later, Marenkov and DeMaté, both still wobbly from drugs injected into their bodies, were herded to the main salon.

"I guess I just got bored with you," she smiled at the Frenchman. "Toying with you offered no promise of excitement or even amusement. So, I'll permit you to just die quickly."

DeMaté looked about in a daze. The words made no sense to him. *Weren't we about to discuss our business relationship?*

He became even more confused when he was handcuffed to the black object in the bilge. Popova leaned over and pressed her lips against the Frenchman's. She kissed him long and deeply. "A kiss for all eternity," she said, backing away. "Oh, and that little case of mine that you were so curious about…." She reached inside the right hand pocket of her peacoat and produced a box, the opening of which revealed several hypodermic needles and vials. "You may now have it." She tossed the case into the bilge. *"Au voir."*

Vorontsov quickly taped shut DeMaté's wide-open mouth.

"Well, Professor," she said, turning to Marenkov. "I'm afraid that this is where we part ways. Ironic, don't you think, how the career—and life—of Russia's greatest nuclear scientist will end."

Popova smiled acidly, then turned to Vorontsov. "Andrei, please help the Professor to get comfortable."

Vorontsov and another man bound and gagged Marenkov, then cuffed him to the bomb alongside DeMaté. Popova turned to Perov.

"We are greatly indebted to you," she said. "Without Professor Marenkov's assistance, and having lost Valentin Tschernin in Afghanistan, you have played a vital role in bringing our plan to fruition."

Perov smiled weakly as he patted his moist, rubicund face with a white handkerchief. "Thank you, thank you," he muttered, his head bobbing in jerky bows.

Popova continued, "That's why it pains me somewhat…but not much, mind you…to also bid farewell to you."

The kowtowing ceased and Perov froze as if he had just been doused with ice-cold water.

"You…you can't possibly mean…."

At a glance from Popova, Vorontsov and his comrades seized the terrified, sputtering man. Soon he was muzzled and chained next to Marenkov.

Popova turned to Vorontsov. "So, *tovarisch*, your destiny is clear. The fate of our new world order is in your hands. I know you will not disappoint."

She kissed him on both cheeks, then quickly left.

*   *   *

Upon entering the National Security Advisor's conference room in the Old Executive office Building, Falcon and his team encountered three dozen people—military officers, White House staff, uniformed D.C. police, and plain-clothes FBI agents. Milling about, purposefully, yet aimlessly, some were involved in intense phone conversations, while others were huddled in small, nervous klatches. The President's Chief of Staff was on a direct line to his boss every five or ten minutes. From his strained expression, it was obvious that the discussions were not going well.

"Ah, Mike," Preston Higby smiled, looking up from a map of the eastern seaboard. "Pull up a chair. Warren here was just giving me his theory on the terrorists' next move." He nodded toward the FBI Director.

"Welcome home, Falcon," Fredericks said, barely suppressing a frown. "I see you almost made it back unscathed."

Falcon ignored the reference to his facial wound and eased into a leather-covered swivel chair at the conference table.

"I was just telling your boss that a guppie couldn't slip through the net the Navy and Coast Guard have cast from Florida to Norfolk. I don't think we'll find them out at sea, though."

"Oh? And why is that?" Falcon asked.

"Because they know that, with their slow speed they'd never make it far enough north before we caught them," Fredericks smiled smugly. "If they're smart, they'll have headed straight for Florida. Probably Port Everglades. There they could load the bomb into a truck or even a private airplane. But even that won't work because we've got every road, track, and airfield in Florida locked up tighter than a drum."

As Fredericks spoke, Falcon doodled some numbers on a yellow pad. "That's magnificent," he said, peering up from his scribblings. "But what if they're not so accommodating?"

"And what's that supposed to mean?" Fredericks asked in a distinctly unfriendly tone."

"May I?" Falcon asked as he reached for the map that rested under the Director's elbow.

"I once knew a schooner captain that just despised being becalmed," Falcon said as Fredericks reluctantly moved his arm from the map. "So, he outfitted his vessel with an engine that had twice the normal horsepower. It was so fast, you could ski behind it."

Falcon glanced at his numbers on the yellow pad and then back at the map. "Just for the sake of argument," he continued, "let's say you install an engine with two or three times the normal horsepower on a schooner with a waterline of around fifty feet. Making an educated guess at the displacement and keel design, I figure it could double it's rated speed under power. In that case, and with the favorable current of the Gulf Stream, our suspect vessel could be.......here."

The index finger of his right hand came to rest on the map at a snaking blue line that read, "Potomac River."

"That's not possible," Fredericks objected. "The Navy or Coast Guard would've spotted her long before that."

"Not if she was moving so fast that she was already north of the interception net. I think we'd be well advised to broaden our search to include the Chesapeake Bay, the Potomac River and all the marinas on both of those bodies of water."

"We're already spread thin from North Carolina to Florida," Fredericks fumed. "We don't have the manpower, resources, or time to waste on such a wild goose chase."

Leaning back in his chair, Falcon turned to Jensen and sighed, "He may be wrong but he's never in doubt."

"What—!" Fredericks snapped.

"Let's all settle down," Higby intervened, "We're all just a little edgy right now. I'll have the Virginia and Maryland Marine Patrols alerted to scour the Bay and the Potomac."

"That may still not be enough," Falcon said, rising. "Mind if I take some people and do a little snooping of my own?"

"What do you have in mind, Mike?" Higby asked.

"Just a hunch. If they've made it up the Potomac, they could be right under our noses as we speak."

"In Washington? That's goddamned crazy!" Fredericks exclaimed.

"This is one time I hope you're right, Warren," Higby said. "At any rate, Mike, take the people you need and follow your hunch."

Several minutes later, Falcon, Medved, Buzhkin, Zidah, and the SEAL unit were in a Humvee headed down Maine Avenue for the Washington Channel.

Chapter Forty-Two

Stepping from the Humvee at a parking lot on the Washington Channel waterfront, Falcon was immediately greeted by the pungent odor of dead fish and rotting crabs. Business was continuing as usual at the water's edge, with professional fishermen and crabbers hawking their fresh catch directly from their boats. Thanks to the atypically warm weather of this late winter day, the docks were filled with patrons, mostly office workers from 'Downtown'—the Executive Branch—and Capitol Hill. Their dark suits and business attire presented a stark contrast to the blood and offal stained clothing, gear, and boats of the merchants.

So as not to create a stir, Falcon decided to leave the automatic weapons in the vehicle, with Lieutenant Rochelle and his unit standing guard. Medved, Buzhkin, and Zidah would accompany him in his search of the marina; all three might be needed for their language skills and, of course, Zidah was the only one who had actually seen the deadly vessel.

As Falcon and his trio moved toward the mooring piers, Andrei Vorontsov glanced at the ruby counter that flickered from the black object in the hold. The number 450 had just given way to 449 and the sequence continued its rapid, inexorable plunge downward.

Less than eight minutes, now, he mused. *Then my atoms will mingle with those of the universe. The cause is just...but was it necessary that I* sacrifice myself this way? Even if the bomb is discovered, the counter could never be stopped in time. But Svetlana wanted additional assurances that the mission would succeed and....

"Andrei, come quickly," a voice from the cockpit interrupted his ruminations.

"What is it Nicholas?" he grunted resignedly as he climbed up the ladder leading to the main deck. *And why the urgency? Wasn't Nicholas' fate fixed, just as his and Fyodor's—the other Feliks on board?*

"There," Nicholas whispered pointing toward the end of the pier nearest the marina. Vorontsov's gaze followed the direction of the outstretched arm, coming to rest on four approaching men.

"Well, perhaps Svetlana's prudence is about to be justified," he said softly.

"What do you mean?"

"Nothing. Tell Fyodor to prepare for action. I'm going below for my weapon."

*   *   *

"Are you certain?" Falcon asked, turning to Zidah.

"Absolutely," the Iranian replied. "The image of that ship is burned in my brain."

Falcon fixed his attention once again upon *Night Hawk*, just in time to see Vorontsov hastily depart from the cockpit. "Well, so much for the element of surprise," he intoned. Switching on his portable transceiver, he directed Lieutenant Rochelle to join him "pretty damned quick" with their weapons.

*   *   *

Seizing his *Kashtan* submachine gun, Vorontsov glanced yet again at the swiftly ticking red counter before he ascended the ladder. The numbers blinked back at him...400...399...398.... His gaze shifted to the three men bound to the thermonuclear device. Perov was paralyzed and nearly unconscious with fear. DeMaté struggled maniacally, desperately trying to scream through the tape that bound his mouth. Marenkov sat quietly, staring back at Vorontsov.

"So, Professor, it appears that we'll have a little excitement before we mix our atoms together. But it doesn't matter. Nothing can stop the counter in time now. *Proshai!*" He turned and hurried up the ladder.

That word again, thought Marenkov...*farewell*. Not while he still had a breath of life in him. He set once more to working his bony wrists in the handcuffs. Blood from the chafed area ran down his forearms and dripped onto the black metal sphere. His hands were so close to slipping free...only a few more millimeters of flesh to tear away. But then, of what use was freedom now?

*   *   *

"Kahlil, do you know if it's on a timer or is it a manual detonator?" Falcon asked, not relishing either answer.

"That, I'm sorry, I do not know," the Iranian answered.

Falcon peered from behind a piling toward the schooner. "Well, there's no time to waste. I'm going forward."

"I'll go with you," Medved said.

"No," Falcon objected. "I'll probably only take two steps before I get shot."

"Then you'll need someone to drag you away," the Russian grinned. "Besides, if we do get closer, you'll need my language expertise...perhaps in Arabic as much as Russian."

Falcon took a few seconds to mull over Medved's words, then nodded.

"As they say in my country," Sergei smiled, "if you're going to drink poison, you might as well lick the bowl."

"Cover us, Chris," Falcon said as he and Medved began to walk forward.

"Here they come," Vorontsov called to the two other Feliks. "We need to hold them off for only a few minutes. Open fire!"

Like the sound of dozens of cars backfiring, the submachine guns burst to life, spraying the pier, pilings, and moored boats. Both Falcon and Medved reeled backwards, struck down by the first volley. Well behind them, fishermen and their clients dove for cover or scattered in panic. The gunfire from *Night Hawk* was immediately, and overwhelmingly returned by the SEAL team. Splinters from the wooden wharf exploded into the air, bullets ricocheted with a metallic ping from masts and spars, the glass portholes of the schooner shattered. Neither Falcon nor Medved moved.

* * *

In *Night Hawk's* hold, Alexander Marenkov gritted his teeth and, ignoring the grinding pain in his wrist, jerked his right hand free. Frantically, he cast about for a tool—anything—that might be used to jimmy the counter box. A long-handled screwdriver lay near the door of the engine room, well out of his reach. DeMaté was somewhat closer to the tool, however, and if he could only get a grip on himself, perhaps he could kick it over. Marenkov ripped the tape from his mouth and seized the Frenchman.

"*Bistro!* Quickly!" he exclaimed, motioning to the screwdriver.

At first his plea was met with wild-eyed terror. After some more insistent prodding, however, the concept sunk into his brain and he began to extend his body and work his feet toward the tool. As DeMaté fumbled, Marenkov glanced at the counter. It continued its maddening plunge, descending now through 250.

Finally, the Frenchman eased the screwdriver within Marenkov's reach. Grasping the plastic yellow handle, the Professor began to feverishly strike and pry at the counter housing. For all his effort, he might as well have been using a noodle. The titanium box was completely impervious to the assault. Overhead, bullets continued to fly.

✶ ✶ ✶

"Michael, are you OK?" Medved asked, hugging the pier and wishing he were thinner.

Several moments passed before the response came.

"Yeah, I think so. I've got a couple of pretty good bruises under this kevlar jacket, though, and a crease on the other side of my face. How 'bout you?"

"Yes, my jacket stopped a few slugs as well. And at least now, your face will look balanced."

Falcon grunted as he rolled to his stomach and began inching forward, closer to *Night Hawk*.

"*Dyrak*. Lunatic,"Medved muttered as he drew his *Gurza* and followed Falcon's lead.

After the first barrage of gunfire from the SEAL unit, there were no further signs of life on board the schooner.

"Perhaps they're all dead," Medved said hopefully.

Without responding, Falcon slipped behind *Night Hawk*'s stern and sat upright. Taking a deep breath, he abruptly stood and aimed his Glock into the cockpit. To his chagrin, he found that the enemy was still very much alive. A *Kashtan* swung in his direction and its trigger was squeezed at the same moment that the Glock was fired. It was with no small sense of amazement that Falcon realized that he was unscathed. His lifeless assailant lay slumped over *Night Hawk*'s wheel.

Falcon quickly pulled himself onto the afterdeck. A hail of bullets chewed up the planking around his feet, inspiring him to dive into the cockpit. The new attacker crouched behind the foremast and realigned his aim toward the helm, where Falcon sought cover. A shot rang out, the *Kashtan* flew up into the air and its owner tumbled into the drink.

Falcon turned to see Medved, holding his just fired *Gurza*, climbing onto the stern. *Now down into the hold and the moment of truth*, Falcon reflected as he approached the cabin ladder.

*   *   *

Bleeding profusely, Vorontsov propped himself against the port bulkhead and aimed his submachine gun toward the ladder. A figure appeared in the hatchway and Vorontsov was about to squeeze the *Kashtan's* trigger when he was suddenly seized by the throat and jerked backwards. With his one free arm, Marenkov hung on for all his worth as Vorontsov fought to escape. In the struggle, the weapon fired and both DeMaté and Perov reeled under the impact of the bullets. Swinging from the ladder into the hold, Falcon lunged forward and struck Vorontsov's head with the butt of the Glock. The Feliks terrorist slumped unconscious next to the counter. There, Falcon spied the flickering ruby numbers that were now tumbling through 200.

"Does that mean—" Falcon blurted.

"Yes!" Marenkov retorted.

"Can we smash it open?"

"Impossible! But there may be one other approach—get a pair of wire cutters from that toolbox by the engine room door! Quickly!"

Falcon dashed in the direction indicated by the Professor, rooted through the bin and quickly returned with a small pair of wire snippers.

Grasping the tool, Marenkov bent over, his perspiration dripping from his forehead onto the dull surface of the thermonuclear device. The world was starting to fade into a gray dream and his hand felt limp around the wire cutters. Marenkov was not a young man and over the past few months he had been tortured, starved, and exhausted to near death. It was now that his weakened condition exacted its toll. He slumped over the bomb, his hand opened and the tool clanged into the bilge.

"Professor!" Falcon blurted as he seized the elderly man by the shoulders and eased him gently onto the deck.

"This is not good, this is distinctly not good," he muttered, gazing first at the unconscious Marenkov, then at the counter. Only a minute and a half left. Quickly turning, he shoved his hand beneath the bomb and into the oily bilge. Unfortunately, he had no idea what he intended to do even if he could find the wire cutters. Desperately, his fingers clawed through the greasy sludge.

"It's a spherical shape...a *Sloika*," Marenkov suddenly moaned, striving to fight through his fatigue.

"Yes! I remember now! A Sloika!" Falcon repeated almost joyfully, finally understanding what the Professor had intended with those damned wire cutters. If only he could find them. Forcing his arm under the bomb and into the bilge, until his shoulder felt that it would pull from its socket, his fingers finally grasped the elusive object.

Retrieving the tool, he reached beneath the thermonuclear device and felt a number of wires dangling spaghetti-like. Without hesitation, he began cutting one after another. "So you see, I did do my homework, Professor, and I did read all of your books, no matter how arcane," Falcon grunted as he worked. He had thoroughly enjoyed studying astrophysics under Marenkov those many years ago. And while it had been stimulating and intriguing, there was virtually no practical value in learning the secrets of quasars and black holes. What had now turned out to be of significant use, however, was his perusal of Marenkov's accounts of his design of the *Sloika*. He knew that, in order for the nuclear reaction to occur, each lead from the surrounding chemical charge must be triggered at precisely the same time.

"If I can effectively...change the...shape...of the implosion...."

With one last snip, Falcon pulled his arm and shoulder from beneath the bomb. "That should do it, Professor," he said, "but there's still going to be quite a bang. Time to go!"

"I'm afraid I'm still fettered here," Marenkov replied.

"Lean away!" Falcon exclaimed, aiming his Glock at the handcuff chain.

As a squinting Marenkov stretched the chain to its full two-inch length, Falcon fired. The chain exploded and Marenkov pushed himself to his hands and knees. He took one step and began to fall. Falcon caught him and in one smooth movement lifted the emaciated man onto his shoulder. On the way up the ladder, a last glance at the counter revealed to Falcon that the seconds were running down from 15. He was amazed at how light the Professor felt and how quickly he was able to scamper over the taffrail and onto the pier with him.

On board *Night Hawk*, the ruby numbers of the counter ticked down to zero. A powerful current surged through the platinum wires surrounding the upper three fourths of the spherical bomb. The wires vaporized, initiating the lead azide explosive which in turn triggered krytron switches leading to the main circuits. The secondary charge of the powerful HMX chemical was then detonated. Normally, the device would now have imploded and the *Sloika*'s massive thermonuclear reaction would have occurred, obliterating Washington and a good portion of Virginia and Maryland. However, owing to the fact that its underside platinum wires had been cut, implosion was not achieved. Instead, the force of the chemical explosion on its upper portions blasted the uranium core from the lead keel of the schooner, through ten feet of water, and deep into the muddy bottom of the Washington Channel. The thirty-ton *Night Hawk* was tossed several feet into the air. Before returning to the Potomac, she had virtually disintegrated.

Epilogue

A rousing rendition of the "Stars and Stripes Forever", played by the Navy Band filled the cavernous main hangar at MacDill Air Force base. Several hundred people, some in civilian clothes, the majority in Air Force, Army, Navy, and Marine dress uniforms, sat in rows of metal folding chairs. Photographers crowded around a wooden platform that was draped with red, white, and blue bunting. On the dais were a podium with a microphone, a three-star Air Force general, a three star admiral, and a Navy captain. At the culmination of the Sousa march, the captain—newly-promoted Hardin O'Brien—stepped to the microphone.

"Thank you for the kind words, admiral and general," he said, nodding to the two senior officers.

"And now, ladies and gentlemen, it is my very great honor and privilege to present the following citations. Lieutenant Commander Christopher Rochelle and Lieutenant Peter Ryder, front and center."

The two men, also both recently promoted, left their seats in the front row, approached the podium, and saluted O'Brien. The Old Man's face cracked into the biggest grin they had ever seen as he returned the salute.

Regaining his typically severe countenance, O'Brien said, "Lieutenant Commander Rochelle, Lieutenant Ryder, by order of the Congress of the United States of America, I am hereby authorized to award each of you the Congressional Medal of Honor for conspicuous gallantry above and beyond the call of duty. While serving with the Naval Special Warfare Group, Team Six, in Afghanistan, on the night of...."

As O'Brien read the citations, images of the battle at Khowst flitted through Rochelle's mind. It all seemed so far away, so unreal and yet it had changed his life forever. As his thoughts drifted, his eyes gazed upwards at the spacious, steel-girded ceiling of the hangar. For once, he was not listening to a word the Skipper said.

*   *   *

Lowering his eyes from the vaulted ceiling and overhead wooden beams, Lev Aksanov, standing on the ground floor of a gutted warehouse, looked through a shattered window to the Moskva River. Although it had thawed some weeks ago under the strengthening spring sun, the waterway still carried large chunks of ice on its winding course through the city.

"My men are ready," a voice came from behind the General.

Aksanov turned to face Chief of Police Dmitri Kirilovitch.

"Hmm? Oh, yes, good. Come with me," Aksanov said, setting out so quickly that Kirilovitch had to scurry to catch up.

The two men crossed the floor to the front door. Twenty black-clad, black-masked men carrying *Kashtan* submachine guns followed them. Some were *Militsiya*, others were FSB agents. In their current garb, however, it was impossible to distinguish them. Aksanov peered through the glass window of the door, across the street to a tall brick building. Over the doorway of the structure was a sign that read: *Rurik Korporatsia.*

"All right then," the General said turning to his troops. "You all know what to do. Bring in the ringleaders alive, if possible. By all means, prevent them from destroying documents. Remember, today you are striking a blow for the freedom the Russian people have never before enjoyed. Now, go!"

The twenty men filed through the doorway and raced across the street. They were quickly inside the Rurik building. *Militsiya* Fiats and black FSB Zhugulis screeched around the corners of the warehouse and converged on the building. Any of the Rurik officials or Feliks agents fortunate enough to sneak by the first wave of troops would be rapidly apprehended by the back-up team.

Dmitri Kirilovitch shook his head as he watched the successful unfolding of the plan. "And to think there were those who were calling for your resignation, General," he chuckled. "I can tell you that the Feliks wish you would go off and draw your pension."

"Believe me, Dmitri, I would like nothing better. But Russia is at such a critical juncture in its history. I've fought too hard and too long to allow the thugs to take our country back. Little by little, we will break the power of the Feliks...and then I will go fishing in the taiga."

∗   ∗   ∗

Spring comes late to the dense woodlands of Siberia known as the taiga. With the thawing of the snow-pack comes a torrent of clear, ice-cold water and an awakening of life on and over the land. In April, brown bears emerge from their dens to begin foraging through the endless forests of green-needled spruce, pine, fir, and larch. Caribou, red foxes, wolves, hares, mink, and sable, shaking snow from their fur as they issue by the thousands from their winter sanctuaries, embark in a mass northern migration in search of nature's fresh bounty. In another month, their numbers would vastly increase with the advent of new life springing from the female loins of the various species. Overhead, the skies blacken with honking geese, green-necked mallard ducks, crested-headed waxwings, long-billed herons, hawks, pheasants, ravens, and numerous other winged foragers and predators.

It was the place and the time of year that Viktor Buzhkin loved most. Now, in the company of his bandy-legged father and his wolf-like dog, he trudged through the mud and rivulets of the taiga's melting snow.

"Ey, I'm getting a little tired," Boltai said as he sat on a boulder that glistened from the transformation of ice to water. He was not, in fact, being truthful. Even though an octogenarian, he still had the stamina of a gray-backed wolf and could easily walk another three or four more hours. However, he sensed that his son, who had been limping behind him, was struggling to keep up.

"*Harasho*," Viktor said, resting on a boulder opposite his father. Volkodov, his fur matted with mud, twigs, leaves and tiny icicles trotted to Viktor's feet and lay down.

"How is your leg?" Boltai asked as he unslung his rifle and propped it against the boulder. He carried the weapon on this excursion only by habit. If he were alone, he would have employed it, and the result would have been goose, pheasant, or perhaps hare for Masha's culinary talents. When he was accompanied by Viktor, however, he might as well have used the rifle for a walking stick as his son opposed shooting the creatures of the taiga.

"Ah, *nichevo*...it's fine," Viktor replied, rubbing the healing wound that, instead of a tan or bathing trunks, was the only memento of his visit to the Bahamas.

A cool breeze rustled through the forest, shaking loose clumps of snow from the pines and firs. Water dripping from the evergreen needles sparkled in the sunlight like diamond necklaces. The wail of a bull moose resonated among the trees and the high-lifted tail of a red fox flitted among the shadows.

"This is where I belong," Viktor said.

"Yes, my son," Boltai nodded as he tamped his long-stemmed pipe. "You always felt close to the taiga."

"True, father...but now it's more than that. I mean I'm not going back."

Boltai lit his pipe and puffed several times to get the flame going. When the smoke began to curl with some consistency, he said, "Perhaps you are just feeling weary because of your wound."

"No, sir. I have been thinking about this for many years…as far back as when I was a soldier in Afghanistan—over a decade ago. It all just seemed to finally come together as we walked through the taiga. I feel this connection to all life…even my enemies. I'm through with deception…playing the double dealer. Sometimes I forget who I am. Most of all, I'm through with the killing."

Boltai puffed on the pipe and gazed at Volkodov who lay contentedly at his son's feet. The scent of the smoke was that of fresh cedar. Lowering the pipe from his lips, he said, "But even though you were required to take lives, you saved many, many more. The sum total was that you did much good."

"Perhaps. But I'll let others fight these battles now."

"Well, then, what will you do?"

"I don't know. The Feliks don't take double-agents lightly. I'm sure they'll come looking for me. But perhaps…just perhaps…if I built a cabin out here…."

"Ah, yes. And get yourself a bride so you can give me many grandchildren," Boltai cackled. "But not one of those soft Muscovite 'princesses', mind you. No, you must search east of the Urals, in Siberia, to find a strong, hardy woman like your mother. Someone who can chop wood and reach up into a mare's loins to pull out its new-born colt."

Viktor grinned, thinking of his coarse, broad-shouldered, loving mother. "I don't think I'll be taking a bride," he said matter-of-factly. "I'm far too ugly."

"Nonsense! Just take your friend, Sergei Medved, for instance. Why even with his grizzly bear face, he was still able to win the hand of the beautiful Yelena Pavlovna."

"How true," Viktor laughed. "Perhaps there is hope for me."

"When is their wedding?"

"In three weeks."

As he spoke, Viktor gazed toward the treetops which now hid the setting sun. His thoughts were of Sergei, of their initial distrust of each other when they traveled to St. Petersburg looking for Professor Marenkov...the scuffle with the *Chornaya Rooka*...the Cossack dance at his father's home...the battle at Khowst where he saved Sergei's life...the melee at San Salvador.....

"That little girl of Medved's," Boltai said, exhaling a pale blue smoke ring, "what was her name?"

"Galena."

"Yes. A remarkable youngster. She has a natural feel for the soul of Russian music."

"Unquestionably. She will be a great ballerina someday," Viktor nodded.

"Well, the sun is getting low," Boltai said, tapping the bowl of his pipe lightly against a boulder. "Perhaps we should make our camp here this evening."

Without further words, Boltai began rigging the tent as Viktor and Volkodov went in search of firewood.

*   *   *

"She dances marvelously," Yelena said as she rested her head on Sergei's shoulder.

"Yes," Medved beamed. "I always told Galya that she was made for the part of the mischievous Odile."

As they spoke, they strolled with the other theater patrons through the open doors to the balcony and fresh springtime air. It was intermission of *Swan Lake*, performed entirely by the youths of Galena's elementary school.

"I am going to love being a mother to her," Yelena said, lightly kissing Sergei's cheek.

"Ha! You may regret those words soon enough," he laughed. "Maybe even just three weeks from now!"

She smiled and wrapped her arms around his waist. "It's like a dream, isn't...that we'll be married then. I can't wait."

"You just reminded me...speaking of our wedding...I just received a letter from Mike Falcon...."

"Wonderful," she said, glancing up into Sergei's eyes. "Will he be your best man?"

"Oh yes. In fact, he's quit his job at the NSA. Guess that last episode was enough excitement for him."

"What does he plan to do?"

As she spoke, the lights in the theater hall began to blink, signaling the theater-goers that the ballet was about to resume.

"He mentioned something about chartering his sailboat in the South Pacific."

"I guess he's not totally tired of adventure. And...that Chinese woman...will he take her with him? From what you've told me, they seem very much in love."

"True," Sergei laughed. "Now someone just needs to tell them. But come. The last act is starting."

They walked arm-in-arm back into the theater.

* * *

Nearly six thousand miles away, over the Chesapeake Bay, the sky was a royal blue, the wind was a warm steady fifteen knots out of the southeast, and the smooth sea sparkled like liquid sapphire in the brilliant sunlight. It was not until late afternoon that white puffball clouds gathered their strength and began to douse the returning day-sailors with their obligatory April showers.

Mike Falcon, after sailing for the better part of the day, almost beat the downpour back to the Annapolis docks. But before he had finished docking *Stardust*, he was thoroughly drenched. With the mooring lines secure, he ducked below into the aft cabin. Doffing his wet clothes, he wiped his hair with a bath towel, then wrapped the towel around his waist. He put a CD—*Madame Butterfly*—in the disk player. As night was falling, he removed the glass chimney from a brass lamp and lit the kerosene wick. He then lay back on the queen-sized berth, closed his eyes, and folded his hands behind his head.

Once again, the same thoughts began tumbling through his mind. He had hoped that it would be getting easier by now…that images of Lin Su and of the intense love they once shared would finally begin to fade. After all, it had been half a year since that awkward moment at her apartment as he was leaving for Russia. They hadn't seen each other and, except for his short phone call before the commando raid into Afghanistan, had not even communicated in all that time. As the thoughts began to pile up, he forced himself to concentrate on something else. He considered feeding Jocko, then preparing his own meal. It was best to keep busy. Before he began to move, and with his eyes still shut, he heard footsteps on the dock, just outside the ketch.

"Mike, may I come aboard?" the familiar female voice said.

At first he thought he was dreaming.

"It's me. Suzie."

A few moments later, they were once again looking into each other's eyes. As the soothing patter of rain on the upper deck mingled with the gentle tapping of halyards against spars, they searched each other's souls. The kerosene wick slowly burned down. Through the galleon style port holes in the stern, red and green lights of distant buoys danced on the dark, rippling water.

"It had nothing to do with my job," she said. "I loved you. I still do…as much as ever. Do you…?"

He hesitated, then nodded. "We've made a pretty good mess of it, haven't we?"

She sighed, gazing through the porthole.

"Suzie, I quit my job."

She turned back to him, the surprise evident on her face. "What will you do?"

"I'm getting *Stardust* ship-shape for a voyage to the South Pacific."

She made no response.

"Come with me," he said.

She breathed in deeply before whispering, "Mike…I don't know…I don't think they'll ever let go of me."

"The hell with them all. Just walk away. Think of the beautiful future we'd have sailing the South Seas…together. Come with me."

He stroked her long black hair in the ensuing silence. She nestled inside his arms. The drops of her tears moistened his cheek.

"Suzie, what's wrong?"

She wiped her eyes. "Nothing…it's just this part in the opera…where Butterfly's been waiting for so long for her lover's return….One fine day, she sings, she'll see his boat on the distant horizon, and then it will enter the harbor…and when he comes to her, he will call her his sweet-scented flower and the pet names he had for her. Ah, but it's all so hopeless."

Neither found the words to speak and, after half an hour of silence, they fell asleep in each other's arms.

* * *

Two hours later, the kerosene lamp had died and the aft cabin was cloaked in shadows. Sliding as noiselessly as possible to the deck, Lin Su slipped into her clothes. The ship's nautical clock chimed six bells.

Falcon stirred and pushed himself up on one elbow. "Ah, eleven o'clock," he yawned. Then, realizing that Lin Su was dressing, he said, "So you're one of those love 'em and leave 'em types,".

"I don't want to go, but I must. I have to work tomorrow and I have no good clothes here."

She leaned over the bed, feeling in the dark for Falcon's face. "Ah, there you are," she murmured. Cupping his head, she kissed his lips and ran her fingertips along his cheek, neck, and chest. She turned to go but Falcon held her tightly against him. .

"Think about what I said," Falcon whipered.

"I will. Perhaps…just perhaps…we could make it happen."

As she walked toward the ladder that led topside, she called back, "Jocko wants to go out. Shall I let him?"

"Why not?" Falcon said in mock disgust. "Seems like everybody is bailing out on me."

"Poor baby. I'll see you tomorrow," she answered as she departed.

*   *   *

Falcon had barely resumed sleeping when he once again felt a light touch of fingernails running along his chest and up his neck.

"So, you decided to stay after all," he said, opening his eyes and peering into the near total darkness.

The only response he received was that of warm bare skin, soft breasts, and supple muscles flush against his body and the tickling of long hair brushing across his face. Moist, full lips, slightly parted, then pressed against his own. The kiss was long, deep, and demanding. Falcon started to push up from the bed, but the arms around his shoulders and neck, and the legs intertwined with his own, tightened. It was not Lin Su's touch.

Instantly, he was fully awake. Before he could react, however, a hand grasped his right wrist and clamped a steel band around it. Two strong thighs squeezed his rib cage as another hand seized his left wrist. Yanking his arm away, he pitched to one side and immediately received a blow to his neck, just behind the right ear on the temporal bone of his skull. An electric current of pain raced through his brain and he nearly passed out. The pressure against his lungs was also becoming unbearable and he knew that he had only a few seconds before he became unconscious from oxygen starvation.

Balling his right hand into a fist and summoning his remaining strength, he swung his right arm up and across his body. The welcome crunch of his knuckles against flesh-covered bone and the release of the tension on his rib cage were his notice that his counterattack had met with some success. Leaping from the bed, he lunged at his attacker, hoping to capitalize on this advantage. He grasped only thin air, however, and suddenly felt two arms around his head. The next moment, he was somersaulting through the air, into the galley.

"Ah, *lyoobeemets*, this is enjoyable, but I had hoped you would spend your last few minutes alive making love to me," the female voice of the attacker laughed.

"I thought *this* was your idea of making love, Svetlana," Falcon retorted as he stood and wiped a trickle of blood from his lower lip.

She was already in mid-air as he spoke, her left leg fully extended and her heel driving into his solar plexus.

The force of the blow knocked Falcon backward into the main salon. There he slammed into a teak coffee table, smashing the two wine glasses it supported, and tumbled to the deck.

Svetlana Popova's lissome form now became visible as she slinked into the dim moonlight peering through the open forward hatch. "I've been watching your demure little friend," she said, "and I must say I do not understand why you prefer her when you could have me."

Carefully extracting shards of glass from his bare flesh, Falcon slowly rose and muttered, "Maybe it's because I couldn't afford the medical bills with you."

"Yes…well, I've already decided to remove her from the picture… permanently. Then you and I can go to the South Pacific and start a charter company."

"I've seen enough of your charter operations," Falcon said as he crouched and prepared to attack the woman.

As he charged forward, she grasped the lip of the cabin hatch, swung up and clamped her legs around his neck. Quickly, Falcon gripped her arms and ripped her fingers from the hatch. Laughing, she raked her fingernails across Falcon's face, tearing open the fresh wound on his cheek. He felt warm blood flow over his jaw and trickle onto his lips.

As she intensified the steely vice of her thighs, Falcon swung her around, knocking her against the electronic gear hanging over the chart table. She moaned but managed to maintain and even intensify her grip. Gasping for oxygen and buckling under the Anaconda-like squeeze, Falcon slammed her back against the engine room door. Accompanied by a grunt, air evacuated her lungs and her body shuddered.

Falcon thrust his arm upwards, clutched her hair and jerked down. Her skull banged into the forward bulkhead, ripping the ship's nautical clock from its screws. The timepiece, its chimes ringing, clattered to the deck. Emitting a cry of shock and distress, Popova fell backward, landing with Falcon's weight on her as her head bounced on the hard teak. Her thighs relaxed and she lost consciousness.

He knelt over her inert body, lightly rubbing his bruised throat and catching his breath. Placing his forefinger next to her jugular vein, he was relieved to feel a pulse. Although bruised and bleeding, he was buoyed by the thought that he now had, alive in his hands, the Feliks' top operative. Collecting himself, he staggered back into the galley. Rifling through a drawer beneath the sink, he extracted a roll of masking tape. *This should hold her*, he mused as he returned to the main salon. When he arrived at the hatchway, however, Svetlana Popova was nowhere to be seen.

Stepping quietly toward the navigation station, he lifted the lid of the chart table. He didn't need any light to know exactly where the Glock lay among the dozens of charts. Seizing the weapon, he slowly ascended the ladder to the cockpit. The clouds had scudded away and the still wet topside decks glistened in the light of a three-quarter moon. Surveying a full three hundred-sixty degrees, he was unable to detect any sign of

Popova. A curious sight resembling a sail bag at the base of the main mast, however, captured his attention. With the Glock held at the ready, he glided stealthily forward to the spar.

As he neared his goal, he realized that the puzzling object was not a sail bag, but a human being bound to the mast. "Suzie," he breathed, rushing forward. Kneeling next to her, he rapidly removed her gag and untied her restraints. "Mike," she whispered weakly as they held each other and stood. "I was afraid you might be dead. She attacked me as I left the boat."

Hearing a rustling above him, Falcon turned at the same moment that Popova sprang from the top of the main boom onto his back. Upon the impact, she swung a heavy teak belaying pin, cudgeling the back of his head. He fell forward, unconscious, at Lin Su's feet. The Glock flew from his hand, across the rain-slicked deck toward the bow.

"I hate to use weapons," Popova said, dropping the club, "but he was making this so difficult."

The two antagonists, neither moving, glanced at the pistol. Suddenly, Lin Su dashed toward the bow. Catlike, Popova leaped to intercept her. Reeling under the force of Popova's arms slapping around her legs, Lin Su pitched forward and tumbled to the deck. Popova rose and stepped between Lin Su and the pistol.

"Now, *you*, I will enjoy killing with my bare hands," Popova said.

As she stepped forward, a black form hurtled through the air and crashed into her head and shoulders. Returning from his late-night ousting of cats from the marina, Jocko had smelled the blood and sensed the danger and fear onboard *Stardust*. Instinctively recognizing the source of the threat, he attacked. As his jaws sank into her left arm, Popova emitted an involuntary cry and crumpled to the deck under the furious attack.

Frantically grasping the animal's fur, she was unable to prevent its teeth from sinking further into her flesh, tearing tissue and sinew. In desperation and agony, she rolled over and groped for the pistol. Finally, the fingers of her free hand wrapped around the metal barrel. Seizing the pistol and swinging with all her might, she pounded the grip against Jocko's skull. The dog released his bite and fell away.

Popova, bleeding profusely from the punctures in her shoulder, rolled to her knees. With a wince, she forced herself to stand. Her face then transformed into an icy smile as Lin Su again became her focus. "Now we'll finish this," she said, advancing.

Lying on her side, Lin Su's eyes fell on a blue nylon cord that ran from a brass bolt in the deck to a trunk-sized white canister. She grasped the cord and yanked. The lanyard triggered a CO_2 cartridge inside the canister and a life raft as large as a king-sized bed boomed out as it inflated. Popova, struck in the face by the sudden burst, reeled backward. Seizing the moment, Lin Su rolled to the forward pulpit, rose, and snatched the thirty-pound auxiliary anchor. When Popova pushed the raft aside, Lin Su was already swinging the high-tensile steel hook.

With her feline reflexes, Popova was able to thrust her right arm up in time to ward off the major impact of the blow. Then, in a motion that was no more than a blur, her right knee snapped upward, the leg whipped from under it and the foot drove into her victim's solar plexus. The anchor flew from Lin Su's grasp, landing point up against the starboard rail, and she slumped to the deck in agony. Unable to breath or move a muscle and barely conscious, she gazed up. Popova, resuming her frigid smile, knelt above her.

"If you would peacefully accept the inevitable like the good Buddhist bitch that you are," she said, brushing a few strands of hair from Lin Su's face, "this won't take so long."

She wrapped her fingers almost tenderly around her foe's throat. "Look upon it as your karma," she laughed as her fingers began to tighten. In her mind, Lin Su desperately commanded her arms to move, her hands to fight off her attacker, but her limbs failed to respond. Popova's voice was now becoming distant and her image was fading at the same time as the pain was becoming overwhelming.

Mike Falcon had been jolted back into consciousness by the sound of the CO2 cartridge exploding. Rolling onto his stomach, he gazed toward the bow. With his head still ringing from the nasty blow it had suffered, he tried to make sense of the two dark forms, one lying, the other kneeling, that met his eyes. Slowly, he pushed himself up and lunged toward the images.

Hearing the deck planking creak behind her, Popova seized the Glock and whipped around. She squeezed the trigger just as Falcon barreled into her. Her movement was a nanosecond too late, however, and the bullet whistled over Falcon's head as she spilled backwards toward the business end of the auxiliary anchor. The pointed fluke drove through her thick blonde hair and split her head at the left temple.

Gazing with vacant eyes at Falcon, she emitted a long exhalation, her bleeding head rolled to the side, and she ceased breathing.

Falcon knelt next to Lin Su, cradling her head in his arms. Jocko, whimpering, crawled over the deck and lay next to them. Lin Su opened her eyes, started to sit up, then fell back into his lap.

"No, just rest, Suzie," he whispered. "I anchored her."

*   *   *

Alexander Pavlevitch Marenkov removed his spectacles and wiped his brow as he stepped outside into the mid-day sun. It was an unusually balmy spring day in Moscow and the warm air had a rejuvenating effect on his weary bones.

Resetting the eyeglasses on the bridge of his nose with a tap of his forefinger, he sauntered across the street, feeling a bit younger as he approached his goal. He carried with him a liter of milk, the nose of a loaf of black bread, and two cucumbers. All of these goods had been purchased at the local *lafka* after the usual exchange of pleasantries with the babushka who owned and managed the grocery.

Entering the park that bordered the university, his eyes brightened and the corners of his lips turned upward. Here was his long-time friend, as always, sitting on the same bench, sprinkling sunflower seeds to an eager assemblage of wrens and pigeons.

"Ah, Professor," Seryozha said, doffing his trucker's cap and exposing his pink, balding scalp.

"*Dyadyooshka*," Alexander smiled, placing the food on the bench between the robust old veteran and himself.

"And were you able to make any progress with your *cherpakas* today?" Seryozha asked as he began to carve the bread.

"I think I saw some hope with this batch of turtles," Alexander snickered. He filled two plastic cups with milk and handed one to his companion.

"Ah, let me toast you, Professor," Seryozha said raising his cup. "To a fellow soldier and hero of the Russian Federation. *Na Zdorovya!*"

Somewhat embarrassed, but honored by the respect of such a great man, Alexander tapped his cup against that of his friend. They each swallowed a small amount of the milk.

"Now then," Seryozha said, wiping his mouth and setting his cup on the bench, "tell me that tale again."

"Again? But so many times, already, *tovarisch*...."

"I never tire of this story."

"Well, then...which part? When I was captured...or perhaps when I was tortured...or when I escaped."

"No, no...tell me about when you were in the boat, in Washington."

"Oh, yes. That was quite exciting. Well, there I was...gagged and handcuffed to a nuclear bomb. The situation seemed impossible, but I never gave up hope. I was determined to prevail, for you see, I too was waging a Holy War...."

THE END